ALL OUR DARKEST SECRETS

ALSO BY MARTYN FORD

Every Missing Thing

ALL OUR DARKEST SECRETS

MARTYN FORD

Published by Thomas & Mercer, Seattle

www.apub.com

ISBN-13: 9781542027557
ISBN-10: 1542027551

Cover design by @blacksheep-uk.com

Printed in the United States of America

ALL OUR DARKEST SECRETS

Prologue

Two children standing side by side, alone together in the snow. They look up through the branches of a tree to the highest twigs, the sky's veins, bare enough to seem black against the low clouds.

I feel closer to them than I really am—close enough to see them shake falling flakes away—because I say I'm not myself when I remember these things. Like when you dream in third person, or speak in second, and suddenly realize you've been someone else all along.

But I am one of these children. I'm the little boy. And I'm unsure about the world, as scared of it as any child paying attention should be.

To my left, Rosie. She's the girl. As sure and brave as ever. Now, she must be ten. So I am eight, turning nine, and already certain I love her.

We're staring up at a fluorescent green frisbee hooked perfectly on one of those twigs, bouncing and turning in the high breeze.

These two children are both dressed head to toe in thick winter clothes and, for Rosie especially, they are very much of the early nineties. Pale denim, highlight-pink fingerless gloves poking from her puffer sleeves, and a pair of Sony Walkman headphones hissing around her neck. I can see her lip gloss, smell her cherry bubblegum in the cold, empty air.

There is not another soul in sight. We contemplate the daunting height, just me and her. Small. Alone.

A plastic *clunk* as Rosie pauses the cassette tape, eyes locked on the green disc above.

"Just do it," she says.

"But . . ." I'm not sure. "David and Mary . . . they told you—"

"They also told us not to come as far as the lake, and yet here we are." Rosie shrugs and says, "Fuck 'em."

Fair hair tied in a ponytail, knotted on the very top of her head with a thick pink scrunchie. She's taller than her years. Her teenage makeup is at odds with her child's frame. And yet she seems the same. Like the present-day software update has installed automatically, overriding any truth left in these memories. She looks like she's always looked—just like she looks now. Whenever now might be.

But me? I'm always the little boy.

"Let's just go back and . . . and tell them we lost it," I whisper.

"Tell them *you* lost it. Listen, I'm too heavy." Rosie looks down at me and splays her fingers. "Plus, if I went up and got stuck, you wouldn't be strong enough to come and rescue me."

She tilts her head. Eyebrow up, pulling rank. It's checkmate, and I should know it. And I do. She's right. This is my job. I have to get the frisbee. Me. But . . .

"What about Matthew?" I add quickly. "He can climb. He can—"

Rosie's heard enough and gently pushes me forward. When I take my first step, my boot rests for a moment on the packed ice, then crunches down through to the rocks beneath. And I trudge away as she lifts the headphones onto her ears again.

A few paces and I stop at the tree, hesitate, look back with puppy eyes, wondering if maybe we can do something else, only to have Rosie nod me on in time with the music she can hear. As I go, am I nervously humming the tune? Do I walk like an Egyptian?

No, I just sigh and turn and tilt my neck, look up through that network of black sticks and back down to the snow stones at my feet.

OK. Here we go. My gloved hands take hold of the first branch, my boot in a knot as I get a grip. And I yank myself up to the low nook. Close to the trunk. Once here, the remaining limbs almost form a ladder. Some are snapped, so just a few inches of wood protrudes, like pegs for my feet, grips for my hands. And I climb.

I climb and climb, but halfway up—*snap*—my boot slides off and I slam my torso into the trunk and hug it and feel the gray, cold, damp bark on my cheek, hard on my chest. My heart pounds out deep, head-rush pulses in my ears. The left side of the tree is frozen, ice-blast frost where moss might have been in the summer. But my face is hot as I pant every aching breath. Hold on here for a while. Calm down. It's going to be OK.

Below, I see Rosie. She turns and moves to the rhythm. I watch her from above, turning and turning, the powder kicking up from her feet. Shoulders, hips, arms—dancing like she's alone in her bedroom. She turns. All she's missing is a hairbrush microphone. And she turns.

But it's cold and quiet for me now. The only sound is the slight breeze or the lake at her side that shifts, cracking in the moving weather with that expansive sci-fi echo of deep, frozen water. All of it muffled in the fog of winter and memory and snow.

"Oh, I'm nearly there," I yell down. But she's not listening. Rosie can't hear me.

And I'm with myself all the way to the frisbee. Only when it's in reach do I truly appreciate this deadly height. This new silence.

All the shrouded judgment of recollection and size set aside, I estimate it is forty feet to the ground. Forty fast feet to the rocky earth beneath the ice.

The frisbee, green and bright and plastic against the black wood, hangs vertically from a twig, tilting and twisting but stuck. To reach it I must lean out from the trunk.

Eyes wide and white as I try to secure my feet. My left boot pressed hard against the tree, my right shifting heel, toe, heel, toe, up and up the branch. Out and out over every bit of nothing below.

And still, there is pride. He's almost done it; this little boy has almost won Rosie's approval. Just think of her smile. She'll hug you. She'll kiss your cold cheek with her warm, cherry lips.

Reaching out. Leaning. A little further. It's at his fingertips—my hand stretched, my gloves reaching and touching and tapping the edge of the frisbee, and it's just there and—

Crack. He's gone.

It's so peaceful up here now with the black sticks. The soft whistle. No birds or children, just gently falling snow. And if I follow any flake, through the white ice that swirls in fresh silence, all the way down to the ground, I see that below, he's there.

Below, spread out, arms at his sides, the little boy I always am is on his back and still. Both his legs clearly broken, snapped near the knee, his pelvis well off center. Like a puppet you might have dropped.

Before I pass out, I think I am awake enough to see her from the ground. Rosie, turning, passing across the backdrop of sky, turning, headphones on, turning, music hissing. The fluorescent green frisbee—a steering wheel now—clasped in her hands. She's dancing. My God. I *swear* she's still dancing.

PART ONE—
LIFE

Chapter One

There's an old homeless guy sitting on the sidewalk—his cardboard sign says he's a veteran. Says he lost a foot in the desert and now needs any change you can spare. He's got four plastic buckets, a watercooler bottle, and a trash can lid, and he's drumming with his bare hands.

Someone drops a coin into his ragged, upturned wool hat, and he says, "God bless you" as he drums out his thanks.

Me and Nell are parked just across the street. I roll down the window, the quiet car's hot air sucked out into the city's scream—the horns, the trains, the sirens we can only hear.

"Well, this is it," she says, checking her watch. "Remember, less is more."

"Sure." Nodding, I climb out of the car and close the door behind me. *Thud*. Few seconds before the traffic clears and then I go. Across the road, down the sidewalk, past the drums—he's speeding up now, like he knows—and out onto the huge paved expanse in front of the building.

Round the ground light beaming up the side of the Leyland & Lang sculpture—two *Ls*, each letter a ten-foot block of shiny marble. There are low, trimmed hedgerows and a fountain to my side—a tube of water rising and flitting left or right in glowing neon gold.

I stop and check my phone. It's 4:26 p.m., and I turn full circle, looking up at these glass towers that blot out the sky at every point of the compass. They seem to exist in a parallel world. Across the street, at ground level, every storefront I can see has boards on doors, graffitied shutters, real estate posters. Rent this, buy that. Everywhere is empty. Down here, the city's closed.

But up there? Business is booming.

I'm in a really good mood as I stride inside, slowing to a stroll within the revolving glass door. Suited men and women step past with purpose—they're on phones, they're holding takeout coffees. They're so fucking busy. They can't sell this shit fast enough.

Weaving through the suits, I walk to the wide front desk.

"Good afternoon." The receptionist glances up from her keyboard, moves a couple of envelopes. She eyes my chest, my belt. No ID. "Can I help you, sir?"

"I'm here to see Edward Lang."

"Oh, yes, you're his four thirty."

She snatches up her phone and presses a button as I turn, look around the grand, modern lobby. Could be anywhere, any corporate monolith selling anything to anyone.

"Mr. Lang is on the sixth floor," she says. "Elevator's just over there. Someone will meet you."

I thank her, check my phone again—4:29 p.m.—and head toward the silver doors. My hand's shaking as I press the button. I take a breath, make a fist, but it won't stop.

As I rise up through the spine of this building, a TV in the elevator wall shows me a silent Leyland & Lang commercial. White Hollywood smiles and a wholesome family of beautiful people. The blonde mom is drinking iced tea and watching her kids play in the yard in the evening sun. She seems happy. She seems like she's jacked to the eyeballs on whatever fucking pill they're pushing this year. You forget the names. But you never forget that smile. Yes, please, Doc. I want to feel like that. Name your price.

The elevator slows smooth and gentle to the sixth floor.

And when the doors beep open, he's there.

For the first time—the first time in our lives—Edward Lang and I make eye contact. And it feels momentous. It seems like something we'll both remember. This is where the drums should be.

"Hello," he says.

"Hi."

We stare so long the elevator doors start to close. I lift my trembling hand to stop them.

"Sorry," I say. "I, uh, I'm James Casper. I called your assistant yesterday."

"I know who you are," he says as he grabs my hand and shakes it.

"Yeah?"

"You drive the silver Chevy."

I tilt my head. "Fan of cars?"

He releases his grip, steps back, and gestures down the corridor. Edward is a big guy. Broad shoulders, thick neck. Heavy beard. Tall. He's wearing suit pants, a white shirt, and a dark red button-down vest. Looks like he's in the wrong place. Or the wrong time.

"Please," he says.

I follow him down the hallway toward his huge corner office. It's obvious which one is his. Glass walls, slat blinds, a wide pine door with his name printed across the wood. He holds it open and makes me duck under his arm. Then he looks back at a nearby woman carrying folders and gestures for a drink.

"You want anything?" he asks. "Coffee? Soda? We have some ice cubes. You like ice cubes?"

"I'm fine."

"Sally, grab some ice cubes for James," he shouts. "The big ones. The round ones for the scotch." He looks back at me. "We've got all different shapes and sizes."

"Ice . . . ice is good," I say, distracted.

Half of his desk is covered in paper—maybe five or six sheets. Printouts of . . . I peer closer.

"Squares and triangles and cubes and—Yeah," he says, arriving at my side. "I've been drawing cats."

I see now that they're not printouts. They're pen sketches. They're pretty good. Shit. They're *really* good.

"You want one?" He slips out a small sheet. "Here."

He hands it to me. It's a photorealistic drawing of a tiger's face. Dense foliage in the background, hardly any white left. And it trembles slightly in my fingers.

"This is . . ." I shake my head. "No."

"Hey, it's cool." Edward pats my shoulder. "You keep it." Holds my shoulder. "Give it to your wife. How is she?"

I wonder if he's seen my ring. "She's fine."

"Rosie, isn't it?"

There's a really long pause before I nod. "Yeah, it's Rosie."

While this is no doubt a good opener, if it's going to be a contest of who knows the most about the other, I suspect I'm going to win.

He finally lets go and steps around his desk—and the way he moves is strange. Like his upper body is rigid, arms don't sway like they should. He slides his swivel chair out, turns and sits, then drags himself to the desk with his heels. Elbows on the wood, he holds his hands together as though he's praying and points to a chair opposite.

"Sit down," he says.

I pull the seat back.

"No, not especially," he says. "I have a few, but I rarely drive myself nowadays."

"Excuse me?" I sit.

"Cars. I'm not a fan of cars. Not really. But I tend to notice vehicles parked outside my office. Word gets around."

"And I thought we were being subtle."

He's adjusting his cufflinks, his expressive face flexing too much. Staring hard now at the material on his shirt. "Agents on a stakeout," he says, suddenly looking up, lifting his eyebrows. "Didn't realize you guys did that anymore."

"Good to get away from the office."

"Oh, I agree." His new posture keeps his head high. He places both palms on his desk. "And did you learn anything of value?"

Yes. "No," I say. "It's a formality. Complicated investigation, lots of boxes to tick."

"Ice."

The door opens and a woman, his assistant, walks in holding a tray of drinks—clinking glasses like a waitress on her first day. There's a tall bottle of scotch in the center. I read the label. It's older than me.

"Here you go," she says as she carefully hands me a tumbler of whiskey. Then she places the tray on his desk.

Edward lifts the remaining glass. "Sally has the most incredible singing voice. This is just a day job for her. She's singing in a play. *Cats*. Hence . . ." He waves his hand over the drawings. "Imagine if cats really could sing. The sheer horror of it."

Sally ignores him as she takes a pair of silver tongs from a silver bucket and drops a perfect sphere of ice into each of our drinks. Like a glass golf ball.

"Enjoy," she says as she leaves the room.

"Cheers." Edward raises and sips his whiskey. "The investigation." He strokes his thick beard. I see a few gray hairs. He's like an old bear. "How can I help?"

"I have a question," I say. "It's been playing on my mind for a while."

"Go ahead, please." He carefully places his drink on a coaster, pushes his fingers together to listen.

"Leyland & Lang is a big corporation."

"That is not a question."

"You don't strike me as a . . . suit-and-tie kind of guy."

"James, I'm afraid that too was a statement. Are you confused?"

"Why are you here?"

"Well, this is where I work. I'm the boss. I'm in charge."

"Coming up on ten years now." I point toward a framed copy of *Forbes* magazine on the wall behind him, Edward on the cover, standing, arms folded, dressed like a lumberjack. "And what a decade it's been."

He turns slowly to look over his shoulder. Nods. "Yeah."

The headline on the magazine is "Breaking the Mold." I've read that interview. I read it again this morning. It has a long profile on Edward's father, Thomas Lang. Talks about how he founded the business in the seventies—started out selling vitamins. The company has since gone on to become one of the largest suppliers of pharmaceuticals in the world. And in the last decade, it has made billions upon billions selling opioids to the lost and hopeless souls of America.

People not close to the figures underestimate the extent of the opioid epidemic. Epidemic is too soft a word. These drugs, if we play the numbers game, kill more American citizens than guns. Fucking *guns*.

When old Thomas died, he left the empire to his only son. This was a surprise given that he had disowned his only son many years prior.

In his late teens and early twenties, Edward served time for possession and a string of similarly low-level crimes. His father's subsequent disapproval meant he was no longer a front-runner for the sizable inheritance that would have otherwise been waiting for him. Instead, he was left poor—virtually destitute. Cast from the silver-spoon comfort he so brazenly took for granted.

But he soon found his own success, rising up from the gutter to launch a chain of gyms.

This, I suspect, was a front for something else.

Since these historic misdemeanors, Edward has gone straight—at least on paper. He hasn't had a single run-in with the law for twenty-five years now. And this, it seems, was enough to slide back into his father's will.

Or perhaps Thomas just couldn't bear to give it away. Maybe his own blood was better than a soulless board of strangers.

So here we have Edward Lang. Riches to rags to riches again. It's the American dream, with a splash of redemption for color.

And it has left me wondering . . .

"Why so hands-on?" I ask. "You don't need to be here. Why not take the money and run?"

"Opportunities multiply as they are seized," he says. "You know who said that?"

"You?"

Edward laughs.

"It's just," I say. "I mean, what do you know about the pharmaceutical industry?"

"I'd recommend you google my net worth."

"I have."

"Well, then you know. And what else, James, do you know?"

I know that, before this year is done, Edward will be in jail. The mighty look so small when dressed in orange. It's going to suit him well.

Raising my drink, I say, "Clearly not as much as you."

"Look at us." He leans back in his chair; it creaks. "Sitting here, sipping scotch. Exchanging pleasantries. You people . . . it's just talk. All bark and no bite. All jerk, no jizz."

I smile.

"Let's play a game," he says. "I'll be totally honest with you and you be totally honest with me."

"Seems fair."

"Why is the DEA investigating my staff?"

"Does the name Ryan Payne ring any bells?"

"This is about Ryan Payne?" He frowns. "We employ something like thirty thousand people, they won't all be saints. I don't even know what he did. Did he even get charged?"

"Yes, and he'd be serving time for supplying heroin. If he was alive."

Edward pretends to be surprised. "Tell me more."

"He crashed his truck out on the highway. Whole thing went up in flames. He had something like two pounds, wrapped in neat little bricks. Hidden among Leyland & Lang products."

"I'm pleased you caught him." He rests his glass on his stomach, leaning even further back. "But two pounds? Forgive me, but I read about the city's new taskforce in the newspaper. I thought you were looking for the big players?"

"Ryan was a very small cog in a *very* large machine. He worked out of this warehouse across town. We found guns, explosives, maps, extremely advanced surveillance equipment. Even more sophisticated than the Carrillo cartel."

Edward yawns. "Wow."

"Did you . . . did you know him?"

He looks around the room—overly dramatic, as though he's trying to remember the first food he ever tasted. "Ryan Payne . . . Ryan Payne . . ." He clicks his tongue, taps the table with his knuckle. "Nah, nothing."

This is, in fact, a lie.

"So, right now, in simple terms, we're looking for the guy he was working for," I say. "That would be our big player."

He sits up straight again. "And you think this individual is connected to Leyland & Lang?"

"Does sound crazy, doesn't it?" I sigh. "What if we started at the beginning. Heroin comes from a poppy field, right? Fentanyl? Made in a lab. Who has access to the largest poppy fields and most sophisticated labs on earth? Who has thousands of international shipments every year? Boats, planes, trucks."

"Medicine and illegal drugs are two very different products."

"Ask half the junkies in this city where they started and they'll tell you it was painkillers. Meds. The prescription always dries up eventually, but the demand goes nowhere."

"So . . . ?"

"So they cross the line of the law and head to the streets." From their doctor's office to some sweatpant wannabe with gold teeth, neck tattoos, a pocket full of folded fifties, and a bag full of empty hope.

"To be crystal clear, you think someone at Leyland & Lang is trafficking illicit drugs?"

"Yes. Huge quantities too. Under the cover of legality. Hiding in plain sight."

The company is laying the tracks for American citizens to swallow pills, inhale smoke, or even feel that glorious rush of optimism flow from the cold end of a cold needle.

The model is flawless. And they're making a killing.

"So this guy," Edward says, finishing his whiskey. "A drug trafficker . . . and . . . wait a second. Hang on one damn second. What if this person arranged to have Ryan Payne killed? Keep him quiet, you know?"

I give him some fake shock. "Oh shit, good point."

We're both acting now—I'm really enjoying myself.

"Well, then, we're talking about a dangerous criminal."

"Very."

He drops the half-melted ball of ice into his mouth, crunches it between his teeth, and mumbles, "Probably handsome too?"

I smile. "Could be."

Edward swallows, takes a breath, and sighs. "I trust it goes without saying."

"Perhaps you should say it anyway, just for my peace of mind."

"It's not me."

There he goes again. Another lie.

But it doesn't matter. He could confess right now and he'd spend the rest of his life behind bars. Or he could drag this out for a couple of months and, well, then spend the rest of his life behind bars.

"Relax," I say. "I wouldn't be telling you this if you were a serious suspect." See, I can lie too. "We just want your help. You have ears and eyes where we just can't be. Anything, anything unusual, financially or otherwise, you just call."

We stand up at precisely the same time. I slide the tiger drawing into one pocket and remove my card from the other.

Edward glances at my hand as he takes it.

"Special agent James Casper," he reads. "You seem a confident young man. But your hand is shaking. It's always shaking, isn't it?"

Clasping my fingers together, I hold them as still as I can.

"Do you know why?" he asks.

"Go on."

Edward stares with wide, mad, open eyes. "It's doubt," he says. "You're anxious because you're afflicted by *doubt*."

I dip my eyes and nod my goodbye. "Speak soon, Edward," I say.

And I leave.

Outside, I breathe in the cool, dark air and cross the street. The heavy clouds above are low, gray, and ready to fall.

Along the sidewalk, I drop all the change I have in the homeless veteran's hat.

"Oh, God bless you, sir," he says, and I notice the right leg of his pants is tied in a knot at his knee.

And he drums me all the way back down the street, *thud-thud-thud-thud*, the final *thud* as I pull the car door closed behind me and exhale.

Nell stares ahead, eyes on the Leyland & Lang building.

"Fun?" she asks.

"Extremely."

"Is it him?"

"It's him," I say.

"And you think it worked—was it worth the risk?"

"Yep. He's definitely rattled."

I pull my seatbelt on, start the engine, and we drive out of the city. We talk about how far we've come, how close we are to finishing this. It's raining now, but not enough to dampen our spirits.

We wait in traffic where there seem to be a hundred red lights, signs glittering on the sides of buildings, long and shimmering in the asphalt mirror below. Piles of trash on the sidewalk. Garbage bags glisten every color of a neon rainbow next to my car.

Under the nearby bridge, I see a burning barrel with three silhouettes hunched over it—their shadows long, flickering on the gravel, their hooded faces hidden.

These people, sitting in doorways, camping out on corners, in the dirt and weeds of any unclaimed land—torn tents tucked away deep within the brambles. The hundreds you see, the thousands you don't. Some have shopping carts, some have dogs. But they all have that glazed deathbed distance in their eyes. People who simply have nothing left to do.

The traffic edges forward and I spot another. A woman.

She's sitting on the sidewalk, back pressed against the glass wall of a convenience store—bright blue and white glowing bold behind her. Bent over, her head between her knees. There's a slack belt hanging from her elbow, and I count three needles on the ground.

The woman lifts her head. She looks like a skeleton. Dead. She stares into my eyes with a desperate loss, a desperate lust, a desperate need to escape the world.

And when she smiles and blows me a kiss, I see she has no teeth left.

"God," Nell says as the light changes and we pull away. "This city."

"Yeah," I whisper. "This city."

Chapter Two

Rosie wipes her hair away with the back of her hand as she lowers the electric mixer into the bright-green bowl. A white puff of flour as it jolts into life. Suddenly loud, it turns and turns in on itself.

I'm sitting on a stool at the kitchen bar, in my right hand a cup of black coffee, which Rosie ground fresh this morning. In my left hand, a newspaper supplement from last week. It contains an article about Leyland & Lang's timely lobbying for tighter restrictions on opioids in the US.

There's even a quote from Edward himself: "These substances are vital when used properly and lethal when abused. We welcome any legislation that keeps people safe."

This bold, counterintuitive move—apparently putting public health before profit—is seen as evidence of, at best, a good heart and, at worst, a cynical PR move.

It is, in fact, neither of those things. This is simply Edward strengthening the other arm of his operation. Why would the director of a pharmaceutical firm enthusiastically support stricter restrictions on its most profitable product? Unless, of course, he was also providing the illegal alternative. Edward Lang is a genius. And I'm going to arrest him.

So what, I wonder, does that make me?

The last paragraph of the article should have been the first. It simply reads: "The CDC estimates 70,000 people died from drug overdoses last year, making it the leading cause of injury-related death in the United States. Around 68 percent of these deaths involved a prescription or illicit opioid."

Imagine what 70,000 human bodies would look like. It'd get pretty dark in the shadow of that pile.

The mixer finishes.

Silence.

"Fuck," Rosie says.

I look up. She's crouched on our kitchen's chessboard tiles searching a cupboard below the toaster.

"Powdered . . . fucking"—she moves items aside—"sugar. I'm sure we had some."

Rosie slams the cupboard door, stands, and, hands on hips, sighs.

I fold the paper, set it on the breakfast bar. "I'll get more tonight."

She doesn't respond. She just pats some flour from her apron and carries on baking. I watch as she uses a spatula to scoop the cookie mix into a piping bag. Rosie seems small today. Stressed. Her dark-brown eyes stay focused on the nozzle as she leans over the worktop and makes circles on the baking tray. Danish butter cookies that she'll dip in melted chocolate.

Climbing off the stool, I step around the bar and lean my back against it, sipping the last of my coffee, now facing Rosie.

She looks over her shoulder. "I'm fine," she says, before I even ask.

"Not a peep."

"It's . . ." She places the piping bag on the counter and turns to face me. "Frank emailed about a new portfolio. He's going to drop it off this evening."

"It's your day off."

"I know, but he wanted . . . well, I want to get a head start on it."

"Are you OK with that?"

She hesitates. "He's insisting." I see a tray of cupcakes behind her—the sponge rising, browning in the oven. Smells great. Warm, sweet.

"You'll have time to finish this?" I tilt my cup toward the cluttered countertop.

"For a conference tomorrow. Delivering them in the morning."

"You're gonna do some extras, right?"

"He keeps . . . he keeps adding more and more." Rosie rubs her eye. We're still on Frank, it seems.

"Just stand up to him."

She pauses for a moment, considering this. "I don't think that's the best idea. I've been trying really hard to keep my head down."

Rosie has been the gray man at work for a while now—blending in, avoiding conflict. I agree, it's probably a good idea, but it does mean she brings a lot of this tension home with her.

"Tell him that—"

"There's literally nothing I can say that will change how he treats me. I've tried. It's just the way it is. And it's normal. You're meant to hate your boss."

"Not this much. Maybe explain that—"

"James. James. We don't always have to solve problems. Sometimes I just need to complain and you need to listen." Rosie curls wisps of hair over her ear. "Believe me. There isn't a solution here."

"I suppose you could always kill him?"

Her eyes brighten for a moment—dark jokes usually cheer her up. "Yeah." She nods. "That might work."

"There we go . . . a smile." I put my cup down and step away from the breakfast bar. "I know the last week has been rough.

With . . ." I don't say it. It doesn't need to be said. "But remember who I am. Remember that you can always, always ask me for help."

Rosie comes forward, across the black-and-white tiles, and puts her hands in mine.

"Just me and you," she whispers, blinking slowly.

"Me and you."

We stare. Sometimes I see the strain in her eyes—she looks so lost on mornings like this. It's as if she's shrinking. Monday was tough for both of us, although it fell off the calendar without anyone mentioning Matthew. We never talk about him.

Take care of Rosie.

And her face suddenly warms again. "Brownies," she says as she turns and crosses the kitchen. She grabs a bag of cocoa and gets to work.

"Make sure you have some day off on your day off," I say, picking up my wallet and keys.

I kiss her on the cheek; she tilts her head, makes the noise, and drops a cup of brown powder into the bowl. The sweet dust fills the air as I collect my phone and head for the door. In the hallway I turn back and wait.

The ground floor of our house is bigger than most on the street, because the previous owners had half built an extra section at the back. It's why we got the place so cheap. That was the catch—they'd left an external wall that now forms a partition between the old living room and the new kitchen. At first we planned to knock it down but, as time went on, decided it gave the house some much-needed character. So we removed the door but left the bricks just as they were.

And there is a window, just like in an external wall, complete with a basket of flowers underneath. It's like you're looking outside, but instead of a yard you see the kitchen.

We have this ritual. When one of us leaves, the other stands at the window and waves. Sometimes Rosie holds her coffee cup to the glass and draws a heart in the tear of steam. Sometimes she blows a kiss. Sometimes she simply smiles.

I look at her through the glass and wait. But today Rosie just keeps baking. So I wave to her back and leave.

Another reason the property was cheap is because it's in Singers. Suburbia. Right at the edge of the city. The kind of neighborhood that would have looked nice in the fifties when it was all white wood, mailboxes, picket fences. Now it's chain link and rust, it's junkies, dirt lawns, and howling sirens that give it more of an apocalyptic feel. Every night you'll hear something smash. But during the day, residents just carry on as normal. Civil society ignoring the imminent decay all around them. Like a low-budget zombie movie. They don't even realize the world is ending.

We need to get out. Sooner rather than later.

I climb into my car and drive around and down the hill; the city is bold in the sunlight across the horizon. When I turn and head south, the glistening glass offices become gold blocks in my rearview mirror. Sweeping past, I see the pitted basketball courts, some bust in progress on the corner, my car's reflection flashing, warped in the surviving store windows. A homeless man stepping out of his tent to tell the sky that we're all sinners now.

Remember, you are all she has left. Take care of Rosie.

I think about Rosie's boss. Thing is, Frank seems like a nice guy. Every time I've met him, he's been friendly to me—asks questions about work, praises Rosie. It's phatic, empty stuff. Charmless, harmless.

But she hates him. She hates him with her uniquely passionate brand of fury and spite. You don't know venom until you've seen one of Rosie's red days.

Couple of weeks back, she came home angry that Frank had landed her with a load of work—again, on her day off. Time she had allocated to decorate a birthday cake for an extremely wealthy client. She said she hoped Frank got cancer in his bone marrow and took months to die. Clocking the disapproval on my face, she apologized and qualified with, "Sorry, years."

I think that's what upsets her—he's like a constant reminder that baking is a hobby and not a career. The day job literally crawling into our domestic life and rooting itself where it doesn't belong. They say that, don't they—you should never bring your work home with you.

I pull up outside Nell's place, and she's already coming down the path in the low morning sun. She climbs in and pushes her thermos of coffee into the cup holder.

"You smell like chocolate," she says, holding her neck.

"Thanks."

Nell winces, rolls her head.

"New pillow?" I ask.

"Old body."

I notice she's had a haircut. Number three-guard job, all over, every time. She does it herself.

We drive further away from the city, toward the Taylor–Samson building site.

"You seem better today," Nell says, looking out the window. "Brighter."

"Than what?"

"Than the rest of the week."

I frown and check my blind spot as I signal out onto the freeway. "I'm fine."

"James, I know what Monday was." She turns back into the car. Sympathetic. "Trust me. I've buried two husbands. Anniversaries.

You always forget the ones you want to remember. And always remember the ones you want to forget."

I drive silently for a few seconds, then say, "I do worry about Rosie. She's . . . I don't know. She never mentions him."

"That's how some people cope. You don't know what's going on in her head. She might think about him as much as you. Maybe more."

I think about Matthew's suicide every single fucking day. I recite his note, in silence, again and again, each night before I go to sleep. On Monday, the five-year anniversary, I repeated the letter sixty-seven times in my mind before the words became a dream. And in the morning, as always, they were real again.

There really is a divide—BC and AD, my life before his death and my life after. On this timeline, I'm five years old. I'm just a little boy.

Maybe Rosie does think about him more than I do. After all, I only lost a friend. She lost her brother.

But still. "I seriously doubt that," I whisper.

We arrive at the building site. I park on the dirt track at the top of a ramp. We climb out, zip up our blue DEA jackets, and head down the hill, shoes crunching on gravel. There are deep foundation trenches at our side—a digger dragging out huge buckets of heavy mud. Ahead, I see "Taylor–Samson Construction" written on the side of a white trailer.

The foreman is standing on the metal steps, wearing a high-vis jacket and a yellow hard hat. He takes it off to welcome us.

"Morning," he says.

We follow him into his office.

"Busy today?" I ask, looking out the small window.

"Yeah," he says, hanging his hat up on the wall. "Preparing. Monday's a big day. Got a hell of a pour. See all these trenches on the south side?" He stands next to me, leans down to point through the glass. "A lot of concrete. A lot of trucks."

"It's looking like it'll be quite big for a school?" I say.

"Hey, I just build what I'm told to build."

"We wanted to talk to you about some of your workforce," Nell explains.

His eyes widen slightly as he looks between us. "I . . . Listen, we hire them through the agency. Some of these guys have young kids. They're hardworking."

"Relax," Nell says. "We don't care where they've come from. It's about money. You pay them in cash?"

"Some, sure. But, as I say, it's the agency that handles it. I give them the time sheets for the men, and they do the rest."

"How many on site?" I ask.

"Now?"

"Average day."

"Maybe forty. Fifty when we're pressed for time."

"What's the most you've ever had?" Nell says.

"Never more than sixty."

Nell and I make eye contact.

"Is that a problem?" he asks. "I got the register." He pushes some paper off a pile and lifts a leather folder from his desk.

"No, no, it's fine." I show him a hand. "You got a contact for that agency?"

He passes me a business card—Willow Recruitment. I smile.

He tells us some more about how it all works, and we listen politely.

"Thanks for your time," I say when he's finished.

The trailer door swings open and I step down the steel stairs and back onto the mud and gravel.

We watch the men, the trucks, the diggers hard at work. Summer sun cutting sharp shadows on the dirt. Nearby a drill pounds through big rocks in the mud, filling the air with dust that collects in my nose. Feels like pollen. Like I might sneeze.

"So that's three now, right?" Nell says. "Each doubling the workforce on the books, paying in cash."

This is how Edward Lang is cleaning his money. Selling labor. Taking a real cut of imaginary wages.

Profiting from people who do not exist, I think, as I look across the building site, down into the deep, empty foundation trenches.

◆ ◆ ◆

A few years ago, our field division office granted pilot funds for a local taskforce. It was Nell's idea—a new model. Trying to get to the bottom of the city's crisis. In the past decade, property crime, robbery, violence, and homelessness have been rising. The line is going the wrong way. There are countless explanations circulating. But they all have one common theme. Lots and lots of heroin is making its way onto the streets. The task is simple—find out how and who.

They gave us our own tiny office not far from the trainyard. This means that when freight engines pass, which is often, they thunder along slow and loud on arrival. And the whole building trembles.

Today, deputy special agent in charge, Rob Sanders, is here. This is the first time he'll hear the details of my and Nell's investigation. I'm nervous. We need his support for next week. The final piece of the puzzle.

Our meeting room has a long wooden table, varnished and covered in paperwork, photos, a few glasses of water. He sits at the end, his chair turned around, facing the screen on the wall.

Foster and a few of the other agents are also sitting around the table behind him, but they're mostly silent observers. Really, this entire presentation is for Rob Sanders.

Still, Foster throws in snide, jokey comments from time to time. He just can't resist. Like a disruptive teenager in an otherwise peaceful classroom.

Me and Nell stand at the head of the table, on either side of the projector. Even though she's in charge of the taskforce, I take the lead.

"The vast majority of heroin that reaches US shores historically came from Asia," I say. I'm speaking fast, establishing the basics. Behind me there's a glowing image of a map on the wall. "It's imported to South America, then travels up across the border. Estimates on percentages vary, but much of the product pulled off the streets, in the Pacific Northwest at least, is connected to the Carrillo cartel. But in the past decade the dynamic has changed significantly. We believe a domestic operation, based here in the city, is now commanding an increasing share of the market."

I click to the next slide—a photo of the Leyland & Lang building, the big marble sculpture, and the fountain out the front, beamed up for Rob to see.

"Leyland & Lang," I say. "That's where it's coming from."

Beyond the glare of the bulb, Rob clears his throat, scratches his bald, liver-spotted head, then raises his hand. "You're suggesting an international pharmaceutical corporation is acting as a front for importing illicit substances?"

I take a step sideways, moving out of the projector light. "Yes. The supply chain is vast, complicated. Hundreds of movements. Thousands."

With his pale, redhead complexion, it looks as though Rob doesn't even have eyebrows. But the left side of his face, where one would be if he did, still rises. It's obvious he needs more or, by the look of things, he'll start laughing.

"The operation, we believe, is very slick," I explain, clicking to the next slide—the collage of photos. Thick, black, plastic containers, lined with gray foam, all spread out on a desk, tagged up with evidence markers. "Military-grade surveillance equipment—cameras, bugs for phones, listening devices, they have it all. We found this at one of their warehouses—following leads from a . . . an employee, Ryan Payne. Who was murdered just last month."

"How would it work?" he asks, turning and slouching in his chair, arm flat on the table. "How could these traffickers get away with it, right under the company's nose?"

"Well," I say, swinging back to the projection. "Someone high up in the firm would need to be not just aware of what was happening, but ultimately in control. Someone out of place. Someone with a rap sheet as long as your arm." *Click*. The next slide appears. "Edward Lang," I announce, standing by the same lumberjack photo used in *Forbes*. Big beard, folded arms, red checkered shirt. "Businessman, philanthropist, and, we believe, an extremely active importer of enormous quantities of heroin and fentanyl. Today we secured further evidence that Willow Recruitment, owned by a subsidiary of Leyland & Lang, is using municipal contracts to launder eye-watering sums of cash."

I see Rob Sanders's posture change again—even in the shade, I can tell a slight smile is creeping up his face.

Lifting a cautious hand, I acknowledge this is all outlandish. "There's a cargo ship, the *Hamburg*. It's arriving next week." *Click*. New slide. A photograph of a shipping container. *Click*. Another image. A pallet of wrapped pharmaceuticals—the logo plastered across the side. "There is one point five tons of heroin hidden among Leyland & Lang produce. It's in that container at this very moment. We seize that, we'll have everything we need."

"These photos are from Interpol?" Rob asks.

"Yes."

"And they're just going to let it sail all the way here?"

"If what we think is true, seizing it on American soil will be the cleanest way," Nell says. "All we have to do is wait."

"You say you met Edward yesterday?" Rob asks, looking at me.

"Uh, yeah."

"And?"

"Oh, he's crazy. Batshit. Surprisingly good at drawing, though." I remember the tiger—I've even put it up on our fridge.

"So he knows we're onto him? Seems a risk?"

"We have all the cards," I say. "It doesn't really matter what he does. If he does nothing, the ship arrives, we seize the drugs. Everything comes out in the wash."

"What if he stops the ship?"

"Can't just stop a cargo ship."

"Or has someone dump it in the sea?"

"Edward doesn't know that we're tracking this container. The *Hamburg* is in transit. It strikes me as unlikely that they would dump such a quantity. But, as you say, not impossible. So . . ." I lean into the laptop and find the video feed. It beams up onto the big screen. A wonky frame. Piles of boxes. It's dark, but lit black and white in the tunneled night vision. All the tells of a hidden camera.

"What are we looking at?" Rob lifts some glasses to his face.

"This is a live feed from inside the container," I say. "We'll know if someone tampers with it. I believe Edward will expose himself further. Even though the operation is professional and ambitious, I don't think we're talking about hundreds of people. A select few. Yesterday I spooked him. Over the coming days, he's going to be very busy. We'll be keeping a close eye on who he talks to. And what he does."

"If that container gets opened before next Thursday?"

"Then Interpol will be on it within minutes," I say. "Or, more likely, it'll stay closed and they'll hand it over once it's in our waters."

"Well, seems to me we can't lose?"

"No." I shake my head. "We can't."

"OK," Rob says, visibly satisfied. "What do you need?"

"A sizable special response team for Thursday," Nell says. "*Hamburg* arrives early morning."

"You want to raid a cargo ship in broad daylight?"

"That's right," Nell says.

He pats his legs and stands with a concluding groan. "Then it's all yours," he says. "Let's hit them hard."

"Thank you, sir," I say.

Me and Nell smile at each other.

When we've finished, the room clears. Only Nell and I are left. We sit side by side at the front, all the lights off apart from the projection on the wall.

Edward Lang, big and bright, looks down at us with his folded arms. His proud, magazine-cover stance. His shirt painting the room red, the shadows black.

"Exciting, isn't it?" she says, opening a beer. "Being so close."

I nod, taking the bottle.

"You worry that this will just pave the way for the cartel?" Nell opens a second bottle for herself. I hear it hiss. "They've been making moves for a while. Someone will fill his shoes."

"So what if they do?"

I think about the city. The politics. The news. The free needles, the clinics, the compassion. Maybe we've gone soft. Or maybe it works. It doesn't matter. I'm not in the business of helping victims.

You learn early on in this game that they lie about the goal. The very point of my job is, on paper, to stop the supply of illegal drugs. But this is impossible.

No, my job is not to prevent perpetrators. My job is to punish them. To hurt anyone who profits from this shit.

"Matthew used to make these T-shirts, when he was a teenager," I say. We clink. "Cheers. They had these dark, nihilistic slogans on them. Some were crazy, but some were good. I remember one, white text on dead black. It said: 'What do you do when you fall into a bottomless snake pit?'"

"I don't know," Nell says. "What do you do?"

"On the back, in bold letters, it said: 'You start killing snakes.'" I lift my beer. "To killing snakes," I add.

But Nell shakes her head. "To Matthew," she says.

So we toast him instead.

"Things like that, puts it all into perspective." Nell sighs. "You just realize . . . when you lose someone. None of it matters. Nothing. Not work. Not money. Nothing. Nothing matters more than family."

◆ ◆ ◆

You see those old posters from the fifties, when Singers looked nice, where the wife has blonde curls. She's wearing an apron over a polka-dot dress. Perfect. It's all so perfect. Like the commercial in the elevator. She's dressed for a five-star dinner. And the husband has a suit and a briefcase. Hair slick and black. Clark Kent's glasses. The kids play marbles. The little boy with a striped T-shirt, face full of freckles, the girl just like her mother. In the yard there's a barbecue. You laugh and roll your eyes because, sure, who wants that? The suburban house, the stable job, that wholesome vanilla life.

Society's moved on. Didn't you hear? Happiness is just another chemical. It comes in a pill now. You don't need anything as insipid as attachment to other people. Just go to school, get a job, live in a box, and then fuck off and die.

But they were right. Nell is right. Doesn't matter what color, what shape, whether the bond is blood or promise, it really is all about family.

Sometimes these old ideas are just true.

Rosie is the only family I have. And I'm all she's got too.

The divide between home and work is important. I do try to keep them separate. But today, all day, she keeps appearing in my mind. She's at the glass. Waving. Smiling. Blowing me a kiss. She could be on one of those perfect posters. Rosie in the window.

On the way home, after I've picked up some powdered sugar, some bread and eggs, I stop off at Rainbows' Florists to buy Rosie some flowers. A nice big bunch from a bucket near the counter.

When I arrive in Singers, I slow down, watch the houses drift past—a barking dog, a set of swings, fences, fences, fences, cones of faint evening fog beneath every streetlight—and finally I swing the car into the driveway.

In the rearview mirror I notice Frank's shiny four-by-four parked on the side of the road. He's still here. I look at the clock—it's 7:32 p.m..

Walking up the path, I hold the groceries at my side as I wrestle my keys from my jacket pocket. My car's locks clunk and flash yellow behind me. Beneath the porch bulb, the bouquet's plastic crinkles by my face. And I smell the flowers as I push the door open with my hip.

The honey-I'm-home moment is gone before it arrives.

Something is wrong. I know instantly.

The atmosphere. Like that ambient tone in the air, the invisible throb you only sense with a sense that has no name. The way you just know when no one is home—the empty hiss of an empty house.

"Rosie?" I say.

Down the hall, past the coats, I pause at the glass, squinting into the gloomy kitchen. I see the tiles through our waving window. There's running water and paper on—

She appears. "Hey."

"*Fuck*. Jesus. Fucking heart attack, Rosie." I step into the kitchen. "You scared the shit out of me."

"Don't be mad." She has a look in her eyes I've seen before, when she crashed my car last year. An expression that says she's done something terrible and she's sorry and she's scared. All the while with her gentle smile—the don't-be-mad-smile—hidden from everyone but me.

"What have you . . . ?"

Rosie steps aside, and I see it all at once. Blood. Something black on the floor, behind the breakfast bar. A pair of legs? More blood. So much blood running between the chessboard tiles. Even now, the red grid grows.

Some kind of joke or trick or . . . God . . . I go further into the kitchen, drop the bag on the countertop; groceries roll out as I lean around and oh—

Fucking hell.

"What is this?" I mumble, my hand clamped over my mouth.

"Listen, I—"

"Is that Frank?" I pass her the flowers. She smiles and smells them. "Rosie, what the fuck?"

Swooping toward him, I crouch but stop. He's clearly dead—spread-eagle on his back. There's a puncture in the center of his throat, neat and black, like a slot for a coin.

"I was gonna clean up," she says, "but I . . . I don't know how to get rid of it."

Grabbing my head, I stand, turn to her, and open my mouth to speak. But it's like a bad dream. No words come out.

"Help me," she whispers, "please . . . you know what to do."

I look at the body. I look at the phone. Body. Phone. My fingers slide all the way down my face, stopping at my chin.

"No, Rosie," I finally say. "Really . . . I don't."

Chapter Three

My eyes are shut. I'm standing in the kitchen with my eyes shut tight. I breathe through my nose. Fuck. This is bad. This is really, really bad.

"Rosie, this is so bad."

My hands are trembling. My heart—Jesus Christ—it might explode.

"We can fix it," she says.

Returning my attention to the room, I look down to see the blood drawing squares around the tiles has reached my feet. So I step back.

A display of cakes on the worktop has been half-crushed, spots of red across the sponge and soaked crumbs.

"We have to call 911," I say.

"No." She grabs my arm. "James, stop."

I'm lost. I stare at the wall and . . .

"Look at me."

I look. Fuck. I look at her.

"Listen." Rosie holds my shaking hands. "I need you now," she whispers. "Solutions . . ." She nods. Eye contact and nodding. "*Solutions.*"

"What are you asking me to do?"

"Help me get rid of the body."

"No, Rosie. I . . . I can't. You . . ." I search the room, turn, step away, turn back. "You take the car." I reach for the keys. "Money. Take my credit card. Just . . . just go."

"Go? Go where?"

"I don't know. You'll have a head start. You could get . . . get out of the country. We can buy you time."

"And then what?"

"Or . . . I mean . . . mitigating circumstances, self-defense."

"Self-defense? Come on, that's not going to happen."

"You don't know that. They . . ."

"I stabbed him."

"It could be—"

"With a knife."

"There's a chance—"

"In the throat. This is a murder charge unless you help me."

Staring now at the corpse, I feel my heart rate steadily drop back down to reality. My body's just on the safe side of a panic attack. But my chest is aching for it.

This descent into rationality is a double-edged sword. At least the nightmare dread felt incredulous. Now it feels real.

Now Frank really is dead on the tiles. He really is wearing a gray suit with a white shirt. There is just so much blood down his front. It almost looks fake. And the expression on his face—that shock and outrage you only find in the wide eyes of the fresh dead.

The blood. Oh my God, *the blood.*

The blood's squirted—pumped out in splash ribbons across the worktop, across the wall, as though he spun and spun and flailed to the floor.

On the white tiles, it's stark and red. But on the black, all this blood could pass for water.

I whisper, "Why?" Or maybe I just think that and Rosie reads my mind.

"You pretty much told me to do it," she says.

"*What?*" I turn to her.

"You know all about forensics."

Shaking my head, I shrug. "W-wha . . . ?"

"You said I should remember who you are. If there was anything you could help me with. You. *You.*"

"I meant *as your husband.* Jesus." I take a breath. "Just . . . tell me exactly what happened."

Rosie hesitates. "Well, OK," she says. "So Frank came around, dropped off some paperwork." She passes her hand near the folders on the breakfast bar. "I was just getting the cakes ready—to ice them. Did you buy—"

I glare.

"Not important," she says. "Then . . . then we were talking and he came into my personal space. Maybe he was trying something, I don't know. And I saw the knife. Uh . . . He said something and then I just . . ."

"What? You just what?"

"I just, you know." She gestures a stabbing motion.

"Then?"

"Well, then I leaped backward because . . . well . . . look."

The blood.

"What did he say?" I ask.

"He . . . he was being threatening. I can't remember the exact words—"

"What did he say?" I yell.

"Would it matter?" Rosie squints at me—turning her palm to the ceiling. "Is there anything he could have said that would justify this? Please, James." She steps closer. "Just help me." She tilts her head. "We lost Matthew. We can't lose each other."

"Please, don't."

This world.

"Take care of Rosie," she whispers. And she swallows, blinking. "He told you to take care of me."

"Tell me why . . . why did you do it?"

"I realized what Frank was."

"What do you mean?"

And Rosie looks at me with a face I've seen before. As though I should already know the answer. Surely, it's obvious?

"He was a bully," she says.

I stare at her for a lifetime. Planets spin. Clouds sweep the stars.

Neither of us says a word.

Then I cover my eyes with my hand and I think.

OK. There are now two courses of action.

Scenario A. I call the cops. Rosie goes to jail for . . . maybe ten, twenty years? She might get lucky. Pay for a good lawyer. Women fare better in these situations. Maybe she's released early. But no matter what, we go our separate ways.

"*James.*"

"Shut up, Rosie. I'm thinking."

Scenario B. I help her. We dispose of the body. We clean it up. We seed enough doubt. We get away with murder. A run-away. Frank ran away. He bought a train ticket. He's gone. Where though, where did he go?

I look across the scene. The blood. I think about Frank's car parked on the street outside. All the people who might have seen him. No. They've definitely seen him. Someone would have seen. He's here. He's been here tonight. That is a fact. But could he have gone somewhere else after?

Is it possible? No point trying unless it's possible.

It could be.

And what about morality? She was right. No matter how you cut it up, this is murder.

But what's done is done. What good would come of reporting her? Is she dangerous? This small girl. This small, grieving girl. There's probably less risk if she's with me. If I take care of her.

Take care of Rosie.

Fuck.

I think about Matthew. His suicide note. Those words written five years ago. Written to the world. Written to me.

Goodbye, James.

Take care of Rosie.

Then I see a glimmer of light, for a flash, just for a moment, I see hope. I see the life we daydream about. By the ocean. With some kids. Some dogs. The smile they try to sell.

We could have it all for free. We could be a family.

Matthew told me I had to take care of his sister.

And there, on the kitchen's chessboard tiles, I make my decision.

I'm going to do what any good person would. I'm going to do *the right thing*.

Slowly, I open my eyes again and take a big, deep breath. "Listen to me, Rosie. From now on, you must do absolutely everything I say."

"OK." She nods.

"Where is his phone?"

"On the coffee table. In the living room. Should we turn it off?"

"No," I say. "Leave it on. Now, we need garbage bags, the plastic sheets, all the cleaning stuff. Those trash cans in the shed. The big ones. With all the wood in them. Bring it all into the kitchen."

"You mean the barrels?"

"Yes. The barrels."

As it stands, our percentage chance of success is close to zero. But I know all the things we need to do to bring it up into the nineties.

And I watch myself as I go into autopilot. To the garage. I press the button. The door shudders, slides up and open. The driveway. I reverse my car inside. The big gray shutters buzz and close slowly, the last of the streetlights coming across the concrete floor, a shrinking square, a line, and then *clunk.* It's shut. I pause in the dark. And then I pull the cord for the garage bulb. A bright white workshop hiss.

Back into the house. To the living room, where I grab Frank's phone.

I look over at the kitchen, through the glass.

Rosie at the waving window. She's perfectly framed. I watch as she ties her hair into a ponytail, then leans down to pick up a pair of yellow washing-up gloves.

And she's ready.

"What now?" she asks as I step back onto the checkered tiles.

All the blood is still. The scene has settled. It's as messy as it'll get. I shake out a pair of latex gloves and watch as my fingers crawl into them.

"Now," I say, "we clean."

Two hours of hard work and the kitchen looks . . . well . . . still like a murder's just happened, but it's getting better. The body is wrapped up in plastic. Tight. Sealed. All visible blood is gone, apart from a few spots on the last few wads of tissue paper. Couple of smears on our clothes. All the bleach is making my nose run. It's stinging my eyes. Reminds me of a swimming pool.

Rosie is still on her knees, scrubbing between the tiles. She looks up at me, wipes her hair away with her wrist. "You can still . . . they can still detect blood, right, even when you can't see any? We need stronger chemicals?"

"You can't get rid of it."

"But—"

"Do your best," I say, rolling out another plastic sheet. "It just has to look normal."

"I thought they have lights and . . . and machines?"

"No matter what you do, if forensics come, they *will* find evidence. We could burn the house to the ground and they'd still find something. It is as simple as that."

Rosie looks terrified.

"The idea now is to ensure they never come here," I explain. "That is the objective. Do you understand?"

She nods.

You get numb, I find, at times. Maybe numb isn't the right word. It's more that you feel nothing at all. Like in memories. It's not really you. Not in any meaningful sense. It's only you when it's now. But now is fed to the past every second of the day. Fed to history, like wood to a fire—the real story's in the flames, the smoke, the ash.

What really happened is only seen in the things we leave behind.

Two pairs of gloved hands slide Frank's corpse into the plastic barrel and fold his legs inside. I feel his kneecap. The way his skin moves over his shin. There's a dent in the bone. He must have bumped it. I think about my own knees—the metal, the scars.

My panic comes in waves—a surge now, hollow, aching, desperate anxiety in my chest and stomach and I breathe and my heart, fuck, my heart. There's nowhere to go—no escape and there's no hope and . . . and the flames simmer.

"You good?" Rosie whispers.

Breathing, I nod as numb rationality makes a welcome return. I've made my decision. We've already done too much to turn back now.

It's time to move.

And we move.

We move to the garage, turning the plastic barrel, left side, right side, shimmying it along the floor. Rosie's thick yellow gloves gripping tight. Her breath heavy, her fair brown hair blown aside as she leans over, panting. We're going fast now.

I fold my car's backseats down, throw away the dividing shelf.

"OK, ready?"

And with a *one*, *two*, *three*, we lift it and roll it into the trunk. The suspension sinks.

"First things first." I remove my gloves and put them in the second barrel—with all the trash. "We need to rewrite the narrative." I kick off my shoes. "I am going to drive Frank's car to your office." I'm unbuttoning my shirt. "Where are the cameras? At work. Where are they? This is important."

"Uh, there's one out front." Rosie closes her eyes—moves a finger as she navigates her memories. "Above the door."

"Good." Socks off. "And the parking lot?" Pants down. "Have you seen any there?"

"Maybe. I . . . Yes. There's one on the wall."

"Is it high?" I unclasp my watch. "First floor? Second floor?"

"Yeah, it's on the edge of the roof."

"Great. Take your clothes off."

Rosie strips. We stand naked on the concrete floor, in the garage light, morgue white. All the clothes, the tissue, the gloves are in the second barrel.

She spots something on her wrist, then, without hesitation, licks it off.

"Chocolate," she says.

I just stare.

Upstairs we shower. Scrub nails. Ears. We wash each other's backs.

Dry, we dress.

I put on a new outfit made of old clothes. Rosie picks up a green top, then a blue top. Holding the hangers, she places each one over her chest. I pick my least favorite.

"Blue."

She puts it on.

These, like those we cleaned in, are clothes we will later burn.

Back in the garage, I wipe myself with a wet towel, then wrap my head in bandages, covering my hair. In the small mirror by the garage door, I tape the gaps. Then Vaseline for my eyebrows. "Were there any cakes already finished?"

"Sure," Rosie says, her damp hair hanging in clumps by her cheeks. "Some in the fridge."

"Get a small container, Tupperware, put a couple in there."

We pack some cakes and I pick up the tub with my bare hands. "I'll take these with me."

"Who are they for?" Rosie asks.

"They're not for anyone . . . they're for the police . . . I'm going to drive Frank's car. All these precautions will help, but it's possible I will leave some of myself inside. An eyelash. Flake of skin. The cakes can explain why."

Rosie looks at me with slight alarm. "You know everything."

The anxiety is as low as it'll go, so I'm able to ignore her and move on with the plan.

"I want you to call Frank's office at eleven thirty. OK?"

"Leanne will answer, she'll still be there, she's always there late on Fridays. I told you, she even sleeps at work sometimes."

"I know. This is good. You will ask her if she's seen Frank. She will say no. Ask if his car is in the parking lot. She will look out the window and say yes. She will see his car as I drive away. She will believe he's inside. Tell her that he was acting strange."

"In what way?"

"No. No. Those exact words. He was acting strange. Say it."

"He was acting strange."

"Good."

"Then *I* will call you on *Frank's* phone. You will answer."

"What shall I say?"

"Nothing . . . it doesn't matter. It'll be me. We just hold the line open for thirty seconds."

"Why?"

"He's been here tonight." I put on Frank's jacket. "That is now established. We need to put him somewhere else after."

"OK."

"Then you come and pick me up in *my car*. I will be down the street from your office, at the amusement park, in the alley near the old pizza place."

"Mario's?"

"No, not fucking Mario's. Sorry, no. The one near your work. Near the old bowling alley. The one that's closed down."

"Oh. This . . . seems elaborate."

I look down at my hands as I put on a new pair of latex gloves. Then I reach into Frank's pocket and remove his car keys.

"That's because it is," I say. "It has to be. This is how you get away with it."

I put on a wool hat and button up Frank's jacket.

"We," Rosie whispers.

"What?"

"How *we* get away with it."

"Eleven thirty," I say as I open the garage door and walk out into the night.

Chapter Four

I drive Frank's car out to Hawk's business park—dark at this time of night. A few windows glow in the office blocks, but only one seems active in the Limehouse building. There is a single car in the lot. It belongs to Leanne, Frank's assistant. I expect the yellow light in the second-story window does too. I'm parked against the fence, with the office behind me.

My phone is back at home, so the wait feels lonely. Radio silence making me uncomfortable—detached, stranded, I bite my thumbnail as I watch the front of the building through the rearview mirror.

Looks sterile, boring—an insurance broker on its left side and a paper merchant on its right. Limehouse is an advertising agency, and the disappearance of its general manager will be the topic of every watercooler conversation in this business park next week.

When eleven thirty arrives, I stare at the second-story window until, fifty seconds later, a female silhouette appears. Leaning closer to the mirror, I recognize the shape of her hair from the Christmas party. It's Leanne, looking down at the car. Maybe she can see the side of my face, the popped collar of Frank's gray, double-breasted jacket, as I reverse back into the lot, then drive away. At this distance, I am her boss—and these are his car's red lights disappearing down the long, straight street.

And just like that, Limehouse PA Leanne Willis is the last person to see Frank alive.

I take his car all the way to the edge of Hawk's, past the water tower, along the river, and toward the old amusement park.

There's an abandoned bowling alley—its tall sign out front leans slightly to the left, and spots of rust have made holes in the giant metal pins. This place would have been buzzing years ago, crowds of families, dating teenagers strolling with cotton candy and their whole lives ahead of them. Maybe they'd ride the old Ferris wheel by the water, before all its swinging seats rusted in place—now every bolt cries long brown tears.

Me and Rosie caught the bus here when we were young. One night, I spent almost all my money trying to win her a giant teddy bear by throwing rubber balls at tin can targets. With my last dollar, I took out all three, and she carried that big bear in a headlock for the rest of the date.

Back then the ground flickered with pink and yellow light from the singing arcade machines and hotdog stalls. Now it's full of potholes and apocalypse grass, and not even junkies waste their evenings here.

Crucially, there are no cameras—this whole place is offline. But there are countless routes Frank could have walked on foot from this point onward. This will be where his journey goes cold. The rest of his evening movements are now conjecture. We'll pick up the thread tomorrow.

Frank's car fits nicely between a pair of empty dumpsters behind Party Paul's Pizza. The restaurant's faded wooden banner hangs vertically from a single screw—the fat Italian cartoon chef kissing the air on his side. I cut the engine, remove Frank's phone, and, ignoring six notifications, scroll down to Rosie. He's saved a rose emoji next to her name.

A quick flash of Frank on the tiles. I had to hold his phone above him, tilting it until facial recognition unlocked it for me. Then I was able to change the pin number. I didn't know if it'd work. I suppose, as long as his eyes are open and his features have retained enough of their form, the camera has no concept of life or death.

It's just matter. Shapes. Reflections.

Rosie answers on the first ring.

"Did she see?" I ask.

"She saw."

We wait in silence for a while, just getting this all-important call logged onto a server somewhere. Putting some miles between us and Frank.

I listen to Rosie's quiet breaths, then tell her to leave her phone at the house—and to make sure it's charging next to mine.

"Both phones have to stay at home," I add. "Then come and get me. Do not stop. Drive at exactly the speed limit."

Having turned Frank's phone off, I stash it under one of the dumpsters, lean around the building, and am reassured by the distant hum of traffic. No witnesses.

I wait against the brick wall at the side of Party Paul's until I hear an engine approaching. It's not until the headlights cut long, sweeping shadows through the weeds in front of me that I'm certain the car is mine.

"Shuffle over, I'll drive," I say, opening the door.

Rosie clambers to the passenger seat. Climbing in, I take off my gloves and my hat and wipe myself clean.

The barrel has rolled against the side of the trunk, half of it resting on the folded-down back seats. And the lid has popped off. Luckily the opening is pressed against the very back of the trunk so, from here, you can't see Frank's corpse wrapped up inside.

It seems to be stuck in place now. With luck, it won't bounce around too much.

Still, I drive carefully.

About a mile from the river now, on the wide, empty freeway. We're heading south, away from the tall city glitter stealing the stars.

"Thank you, James, really," Rosie says.

"It's fine." I'm distracted.

"I know this . . . well . . . This might be a strain on the limits of loyalty. I just want you to know that I appreciate it."

"Sure." I can't take my eyes off the mirror.

"For better or worse."

"Yeah." There's a car behind us.

"We'll be OK." Rosie puts her hand on my thigh. "Just me and you."

A long pause while she waits for me to say it back to her. "Just me and—"

Blue lights.

"Oh fuck," I say. "Oh, fucking hell, God, no."

Blue lights flicker across the back of my car. Blue lights strobing on the dashboard. Blue lights dazzling my eyes from the mirror.

"Shit." Rosie sinks in her chair.

"Calm. Be calm."

I signal, pull over, and take deep breaths. My shaking hands squeeze the wheel as a shape in the side mirror walks up through dimmed headlights, then becomes legs and a belt and he's close enough for me to see the cuffs, and I press the window button.

Wincing in the flashlight, I try not to act terrified as I turn to face him.

"Good evening," the officer says. "I was just—*well, would you look at that*."

Oh no.

"It's the DEA," he adds.

Relieved, I realize he's seen my badge on the dash.

I squint. "Yep, that's, um . . ."

"Special agent . . ."

"Uh, James . . . James Casper."

"Donnie Rhodes," he responds. "How's it going, bud?"

"Yeah . . . pretty good," I say. "Pretty good, pretty good."

"Too many," Rosie whispers.

"I've been pulling strangers over all night. Great to see a friendly face." Donnie leans lower, hand on the door. "And is this Mrs. Casper? Oh, at this time of night, I do hope it is."

Charmed, Rosie waves and smiles. She is totally cool. Totally normal. "It's me. Ball and chain. Guilty as charged."

"Have we . . . have we met?" I frown. "You go to the police awards last year?" This is a stab in the dark, but a reasonably safe one.

"Yeah, I did . . . Some of your guys were there. Ellie, Eleanor?"

"Oh, Nell."

"That's right, head of that new taskforce. I won't shake your hand," he says, sniffing, looking back down the quiet freeway. "I've been scraping roadkill off the barrier. These truckers hit a deer and carry on as if it's some kind of bug. It's like a butcher box up there—the amount of *blood* I've seen tonight, you wouldn't believe." He laughs.

I kind of half laugh along with him. "Yeah."

"Pair of antlers, wide as I am tall, sticking out the front of a grille, head smashed to bits and I—shit. Sorry. It's late. Where you guys heading?"

"Uh, just . . ." I point ahead through the windshield.

"We've been at a party," Rosie says across me. "Old school friend. She's going away on Monday—working in Poland. Fancy spa. We might be in for some free tickets." She holds up crossed fingers. "Just heading home now."

Fucking specific lies. But I nod.

"A party, hey? Designated driver. Good boy. Anyway, you folks have a nice night now." He pats the roof. "You send Eleanor my best."

"Thanks, Donnie." I put my hand on the key.

"Oh, shit," he says, leaning down again. "You got a tail light out. You wanna get that changed, OK?"

"Sure thing."

"Now you get yourselves home to bed and get—" Donnie looks at the back seat. Looks right at the barrel. There's a terrible pause, and I'm falling and sinking and I can't breathe and—"Say . . . what's that?" he asks.

No one speaks. No one moves. He's seen it. He's fucking seen it. I search for an answer but—

"A dead body," Rosie says.

Slowly, I turn to face her. The deadpan expression of a tasteless joke glinting in her creased eyes. No more. No less.

And when I look back to Donnie, he laughs.

"Well, get it buried before sunrise," he says, checking his watch.

"Will do." Rosie gives him a thumbs-up.

Finally, Donnie leaves.

We sit in total silence, and I don't even need to say anything. Rosie reads my mind.

"It worked, didn't it?" she says, and I can tell from her voice that she's smiling.

The engine rumbles alive as Donnie drives past, giving us a parting wave and a short *wahhrp-wahhrp* from his patrol car's siren.

Fifteen minutes later, we arrive at the Taylor–Samson building site. It's dark. No security. No overlooking windows. Ideal. Through the fence, I can see the long brown shadows. The deep, empty foundation trenches. They've got a big day on Monday. They're going to fill those holes with tons and tons of concrete.

We get out and move a fence panel aside.

Quickly, carrying the barrel, both half-crouched, we shuffle through the gap. I'm stepping backward, checking over my shoulder. We get a rhythm going, cut across the gravel, and arrive at the trench.

I sit on the edge, turn, slide down into the ground, clumps of mud coming with me. Rosie passes me the spade and I dig and scrape the earth aside.

When I'm finished, I sigh, out of breath, my shoulder against the trench wall.

"Is that deep enough?" she asks from above.

"It's fine," I huff. "Do it."

Rosie pulls the lid off the plastic barrel and tilts, tilts, and it slips from her grasp, turning upside down at the edge. I leap backward as the wrapped body falls headfirst and thuds, folding and slumping flat. The dead weight of heavy meat.

Grabbing it by the feet, I drag it into the shallow grave.

Once it's well covered, we retreat. I use a broom to scuff the dirt and gravel, walking backward, scrubbing our footprints away like an ice curler.

We lift and slide the fence panel back into place.

It's as though we were never here.

Then it's back to the car and back to Party Paul's, where we collect Frank's phone. A long stretch of road, the freeway, the tall city lights that pretend to be stars, and we're back home.

We don't say a word as we go inside. Showers. Side by side at the sinks. Toothbrushes. Eye contact in the mirror. Silence.

And to bed, where I listen to Rosie's breaths grow longer and longer. On my side, a couple of strands of her hair tickle my face. So I roll to my back.

She's sound asleep now. Peaceful. Like a weight's been lifted.

Me, I just stare at the ceiling. Because every time I close my eyes, I see those black-and-white tiles and the expanding grid of blood.

◆ ◆ ◆

She's done it before. Nothing this bad, but Rosie has solved problems with violence in the past. And she even used that concise explanation. In exactly the same tone too. As though her actions were not only justified, but maybe even necessary.

We grew up in Treaston Mills, a small town about thirty miles outside the city. Right on the edge of wilderness, at the foot of the hills. It had a trailer park, a couple of schools, the renowned Treaston Gallery, and a population of about twenty thousand residents.

Everyone knew everyone else. You'd see the faces, hear the names, and pity those who'd given up trying to escape.

There was this kid called Austin. A real nasty piece of shit. His dad was a marine and his mom was a notorious alcoholic. The town drunk. Turbulent household. You know the kind. He had this curly black hair and a snarled-up little face. Always looked like he had mud on his cheeks, but I think it was just the wear and tear of that junkyard hellhole he called home.

Either way, Austin and his friends used to pick on me. It started small. They'd throw a comment or two down the hall, slam me against the lockers, hide my clothes during gym—that kind of thing.

But, as violence invariably does, it began to escalate.

I can see myself. I'm walking to school.

This child, this eleven-year-old boy, with his backpack over both hunched shoulders, cautious eyes, his timid way of moving—I can see him. God, he looks so much like me.

It is me. It's me and Matthew walking side by side. Two best friends. Eleven years old. We cut through the park, just like we do every day. It's huge. Wide, open green fields and asphalt paths.

As always, Austin and his cronies are waiting up the hill near the old elm tree. A popular hangout for teenagers. The gang are all sitting on their BMX bikes. Maybe eight of them. A few cycle in circles, like sharks.

We have to walk right past. My heart races, though I make an effort not to appear scared.

They ignore us. They say nothing, letting us pass. I look back over my shoulder, and it seems like we've got away with it. So we carry on.

But then I feel a sharp, hard thud on the back of my head. I turn and hear laughter. A full can of soda has landed a few feet away; the bottom edge, the hardest part, is dented.

This little boy touches the back of his head and sees that he's bleeding. Austin shouts out, asking if I'm gonna cry.

But I won't cry. Not in front of them. Not in front of Matthew.

I pretend like it doesn't even hurt.

The nurse at school tapes a bandage into my hair. I tell her I fell off my bike.

"And landed on the back of your head?" she asks.

I nod.

It aches so much for the rest of the day. And when the bell rings, I can't wait to go home. I feel sick. The little boy looks pale. He's got concussion. Is that why these timeless memories seem dark? Like the blinds are drawn? Like it's overcast, even when it's midsummer?

Matthew has choir practice tonight. So I have to walk home alone. Back through the park fields. Back past the old elm tree. And it's the same. Austin is there with his friends.

"Why didn't you cry?" he asks.

And I understand now. I get why he's been doing all this.

He wants tears.

And he's coming for them.

Suddenly he's dropped his bike and he's on me, he's here, he's swinging, and I'm ducking and protecting my eyes. I see flashes of his face, the anger, the primal rage in his snarled, hate-filled face—he looks like he's trying to kill me. Maybe the little, pale boy pleads for him to stop as he falls to the grass and curls up. A boot to the back, to the head, the head, the head. And one final punt to the center of my face and they depart, laughing but indifferent. Austin doesn't seem to have even enjoyed himself that much. But he got what he wanted.

I am crying.

I'm shaking, shivering, breathing fast as I shuffle out of the park. When I touch my face, I feel strange shapes, new lumps, wet and sore. All the fingers on my right hand throb and turn red because he stamped on it. Why did he stamp on it?

I'm desperate and hugging myself now on the sidewalk near my house.

Rosie and Matthew live opposite. And, to my horror, I see her on the driveway. Thirteen years old and a clear foot taller than me, wearing a tied shirt and denim shorts—Daisy Dukes.

She frowns. I stand there, shaking, hands out, asking for help without saying a word.

But I hate that she sees me crying. I wish I looked strong. My best friend's big sister. I'm so embarrassed it doubles the pain.

In their bathroom Rosie has put me on the toilet seat. She's at my scarred knees, thumbing cold cream onto my eyebrow. Why can't I calm down? I'm never going to stop panicking, no matter what she says. But eventually I do.

And everything aches. Everything dries.

"Can you move your fingers?" she asks.

I can. They hurt, but I can move them. Rosie tells me that means they probably aren't broken. She's only two years older than I am, but she seems like an adult to me. Especially now, administering first aid. Steadily the toilet paper in my nose stops the blood.

She knows who did this. Everyone knows about Austin and his friends. Now all the first aid is finished, Rosie kneels down in front of me, gently places her soft hand on my chin, and lifts my face. Direct eye contact. No pity. No anger. Just one simple question.

"James," she whispers. "Do you want it to stop?"

My knee jitters as I nod. "Yes."

Friday night, and me and Matthew are heading back through the fields again.

This time, the clearing by the old elm tree is like a party. Two pickup trucks parked, their headlights beaming out, crisscrossing across the grass. Music is playing. People are drinking. The dusk sky grows dark. There has got to be almost a hundred kids here.

Austin and his friends, maybe they're partying with older siblings—they seem too young for this crowd. They're at the side, in their own small group, and Austin seems to be the center of attention, others moving around him in an orbit. Some on bikes.

Maybe, as I've still got the butterfly stitches on my face, they'll give me a free pass today.

But as I approach, I feel the atmosphere shift when Austin spots us. Someone whispers in his ear and he nods.

We slow down. We can't help ourselves. I hear myself swallow. *Just walk past*, I think. Ignore them.

Up ahead, I see a figure approaching from the other side.

A girl striding up the grass, toward the tree. She's taking big, decisive steps. Most of the crowd is looking at us. So maybe they don't see her. But I see her. Matthew sees her. It's Rosie. Wearing a black jacket, pale-denim jeans.

She knows a few people here and greets them as she pushes through, turning between shoulders, smiling at a couple of boys her age. Even with all this fear, I think to myself that she is just so pretty.

Austin is coming for me, slowly but surely, he's rolling closer on his bike, his friends trailing. I stand and wait.

But Rosie is still inbound; she's behind his group now.

"Austin," she says. Calm. Polite. Strangely mature. How a teacher speaks. He turns to her. "Leave James and Matthew alone."

The crowd's excited. Maybe they can already smell a fight.

And that seems to be the end of it. She turns away and begins speaking to a few other kids. But Austin's angry. He climbs off his bike. Stands there behind her. A girl. A fucking girl telling him what to do? His friends are waiting. He can't let her get away with this.

"Or what?" he says. The tone of the situation changes, and people stop talking. I see Rosie's shoulders rise slightly as she takes a breath. It's hard to tell, because she's facing away, but it really seems as though she's relieved. Rosie is so happy he said that.

The silence lingers, and I notice her right hand moving.

A metal crowbar slides, almost by itself, out of her sleeve.

She grips it like a bat and turns and hits him in the face, so hard—so hard people gasp and he falls.

Matthew flinches, steps forward to help—help who?—and stops, and we watch as she swings the metal down onto Austin's skull again. And again. A thwacking sound—a thin line of blood flows almost instantly down his face like a tear.

Austin is so shocked and hurt and lifts his hands, and she's on top of him, mounting him, pulling his clothes off. His T-shirt is gone, torn in half.

And the crowd is on her side now. They laugh and cheer. They point. Austin is rocked. He struggles and grabs her wrists, but she carries on. Rosie tugs at his belt and yanks it out, flinging it like a whip over her shoulder—it's gone and she's up and pulling his jeans down. The audience can't believe it. They're clapping, howling. Austin crying, begging, and rolling over as she wrestles his pants over his boots. One falls off. He's trying to crawl away. She's just calmly undressing him like a mother undresses a lively toddler.

He's down to his underwear and surely it's over. Austin rolls to his back, touches his face and wipes the blood and mud, and apologizes—hand up.

"Sorry." Both hands up. "I'm sorry."

The rumble of excitement in the crowd as Rosie grabs his underwear.

"No—no, please."

But she tilts her head because it's too late to negotiate. He had a chance, and he blew it. So now it's all coming off.

She has to rip them.

"Get up," she says.

Rosie grabs him by his hair and forces him to stand. He's cupping himself, but she gets him in a full nelson hold, his arms held up. His naked body facing us, both their backs to the jeering crowd. Austin is crying hysterically now.

He looks at me, blood and sweat in his hair, and it seems as though he's asking for my help.

I turn to Matthew, who's just smiling, swept up by the atmosphere. The baying mob wants to see.

And in one motion, she swings him around and shows the crowd. It's like a home run. They go wild—laughter, cheers, clapping—kids bouncing off each other as they scream like chimps. Hands over mouths. Fingers extended. Someone throws his torn underwear at him—it dangles from his head. One of them pretends to frame his penis, and someone else winds up a camera—there is a flash.

Rosie drops him on the ground. He falls to a seated position, his knees together in the dirt, his shadows long in the headlights of the parked pickup trucks. He's sitting where the beams meet, like spotlights. He's center stage.

"Or," Rosie says, "I'll do that again."

Austin doesn't bother anyone too much after that night. He's quiet. Everyone calls him worm-dick. Every time he sees me, he looks straight at the ground. Like a young dog that's learned to feel shame.

Austin's dad calls the police about the incident, and they come to Matthew and Rosie's house to take a statement.

Me and Matthew are sitting in the living room, watching TV. Nickelodeon is bright but quiet as we turn the volume down to listen.

Rosie's put at the end of the kitchen table while two uniformed officers ask her questions.

I hear her recite the entire attack. She's completely honest. She even confesses exactly how many times she hit him with the crowbar.

At the very end of the interview, one of the cops says, "Why did you do it?"

And she looks at him like he's just asked her the dumbest question imaginable. The frowning judgment, the scrunched lip of disapproval that teenage girls do so well.

She speaks slowly, like he's a child. Like this cop hadn't even been listening to the story.

"He was a bully," Rosie says.

Chapter Five

There's a cold reality about today. The surreal chessboard flashing behind my eyes, black and white. The squares and blood. The thud. The sleepless night. The mud. It's all adding up—it's painting a picture that almost looks real enough to believe.

Before sunrise, I get up and go into the yard, where I cut holes in the bottom half of a trash can. I put everything inside—clothes, rags, cleaning bottles, gloves, everything—and set it alight. Bright flames fling shadows, bringing the night back and burning away the sky's feeble attempt at dawn.

Once it's all gone, I sweep the ash into a pile on the paving stones, then take the blackened trash can into the shed and use a hacksaw to cut it into manageable pieces.

I bag it all up and put it on the path at the side of the house.

Now I'm clean, I'm in the kitchen, and Rosie is up and dressed.

"Ready?" I ask.

We leave our phones at home, load up the car, and set off to the country, toward the lakes at Treaston Mills. About ten miles from the city, on the winding lanes that skirt the hills, I pull over at an empty rest stop, parking alongside a sandy bank beneath tall, straight trees. Looming firs and fat red cedars with bushed moss on every outstretched limb.

Rosie is holding Frank's phone in her latex-gloved hand, his wallet on her lap.

"How many?" I ask, glancing down at the glowing screen.

"Thirty missed calls. Sixty-three notifications."

"Mark them all as read." I turn away.

"Done. For the ticket, should I register with his work or personal email?" she asks.

I'm staring outside, into the woods, my elbow resting on the window, my palm pressed into my mouth. There's a low damp fog, tinted green, thin black branches and fallen trunks crisscrossing in the mist—they're losing their color the deeper I look, through the creeping twigs, the mulch hills and rocks.

He was face down.

"Which email account?" Rosie says.

In the mud.

"*James.*"

"Use his personal account," I say, still staring.

"OK." She types on his phone, waits a moment for it to load, then asks, "What kind of ticket? Should I get a day pass? And where to?"

"No," I say, looking back into the car. "Get a week. A multi-ride one."

"Why?"

"It's feasible to check a day's worth of train CCTV. But a week's worth? And buy two of them."

"Two?"

"Look at the apps on his phone . . . Frank has a Tinder account."

"Huh. You think he was cheating on his wife?"

"It doesn't matter what I think." Another wave of shame—the privacy, the violation.

"What about arrival?" Rosie asks. "His tickets would be logged? Scanned through a machine?"

"With a multi-ride he could go to a hundred different stations. Plenty without modern gates."

She frowns.

"It's about seeding doubt," I explain. "Spreading resources."

"I understand." She thumbs Frank's credit card details into his phone, then waits as the order goes through.

I look out the window again, into the trees. Out there where the brown wood turns gray, where Mother Nature is the only authority that has any right to judge you. Wilderness seems inviting today.

"He was face down," I whisper.

"What?"

"In the ground. Frank was lying on his front."

"So?"

I sigh. "At least pretend, Rosie. Please."

"What do you want me to say?"

"I don't know." I blink slowly and take a breath.

"You said last night, we have made our decision." She touches my arm. "We're all in."

"It's going to be a high school."

"What is?"

"That's what they're building there."

"I can't see how that's relevant."

Something moves out in the woods—a deer maybe. Antlers bounding off into the haze.

"You think it'll be possible to drive down South Clark Street and not think about him? Will our kids go to that school? Will they learn math above the man we buried?"

"No," Rosie says. "We're not staying in the city. It'll get easier with time. Right now, worrying isn't going to help."

I nod. She's right. Solutions.

"Shall I turn it off again?" she asks, holding up the phone.

"Give it ten minutes."

"When will they start looking?"

"I'd imagine he's been reported missing already." I start the engine. "They'll be taking it seriously later today. And very seriously tomorrow."

We switch the phone off, then drive for another hour or so to get some real distance between that crucial location and the final resting place for all this physical evidence.

I pull into a track, the rough terrain tilting the car side to side as I roll down toward the water. Here we're shielded by rocky cliffs and a thick canopy of evergreens. Birds sing high above us, in the sunshine—the fog's long gone now, clean air and blue sky making a high-resolution stock photograph out of the lake.

We climb from the car and tie the weight to the bag of ash and metal. I step to the water's edge and throw it. Rosie wipes Frank's phone clean, hands it over, and without a word I fling it as far as I can into the middle of the idyllic picture in front of us.

It splashes and sinks.

And it's gone.

"Now what?" Rosie whispers, arriving at my side.

"You were one of the last people to speak with Frank." My attention stays out there on the water. "Nothing we've done changes that fact. The police are going to interview you. It goes without saying that you absolutely must get your story straight."

"We'll go over it, get it ironed out."

"Funnily enough, that's the one part of all this I'm least worried about." I turn and head back toward the car.

"What does that mean?"

And I stop and sigh. "You're a fantastic liar."

◆ ◆ ◆

The next part of the plan is simple. We act normal. In every way. So the following day, I smile and wave at Mr. Thompson, who's cleaning his car outside his house in the unusually warm morning air.

"Lovely weather," he says, looking up from the bucket, wringing out his big yellow sponge.

"Glorious," I agree.

The paperboy throws the heavy Sunday edition onto our front lawn and stands high on his pedals to cycle off further up the notoriously steep Singers hill. It's so steep that the yards behind Mr. Thompson's house look, from here, like the edge of a cliff. Sometimes, when the fog is low, the world ends just beyond that crest.

In the evening, I cook spaghetti, we drink red wine, and our commitment to the role is worthy of an Oscar. We're performing like we believe, method acting as though really, truly, nothing is out of the ordinary.

But later, in the bathroom, it comes creeping back. I stand alone at the mirror and watch my hand shaking above the faucet. I turn it on, brush my teeth, head down to rinse, back up, and now both hands are trembling away as I drop the toothbrush into the ceramic cup.

Another night where I'm not brave enough to close my eyes for too long, or else I go back to that red grid—like a roadmap of a brand-new city, where every street is soaked in blood.

I'm not one to count sheep—the only reliable way I fall asleep is to repeat Matthew's suicide note in my mind.

When you're growing up there's constant change. But when you're an adult, it all plateaus. A period of stasis that you'll ride for the rest of your days. And it dawns on you. The question. A horrifying realization as you ask yourself, "Is this it?"

There's just nothing left. No change. No joy. It shouldn't be a mystery why I want this life to end. The mystery is why you don't.

It usually gives me comfort to have such focus. To remember why I do all the things I do—why I took the job, why I'm taking care of Rosie, why family, future, and any glint of hope is worth fighting for.

Although after fifty full recitals, I realize it's no use. So I watch videos on my phone—a recipe for a complicated rainbow cake, how hot glass is blown, and all the ways this brash guy pranks his Barbie Doll girlfriend—until the stripe of yellow above me disappears as the streetlights go out. It returns an hour later as bright-red sunshine.

They say it's always darkest before the dawn. As though the warm light of day hides your problems. Really, you can just see them clearly.

Now though, it's time to pretend I can't.

Monday morning, and we begin the charade again.

Teeth. Shower. Shave. Button up my shirt. Fasten my watch. Tie my shoelaces in double bows and take my jacket off the back of the chair.

Sip coffee with Rosie in the kitchen—both dressed smart for work. She starts an hour later than me. She'll go in as normal. And she'll act surprised when someone tells her Frank hasn't been seen since Friday.

A slice of toast, a glass of orange juice, and it's time to go.

But not before I bid goodbye to Rosie through our waving window.

Although it might be an unnecessary risk, I drive toward South Clark Street on my way to the office. It helps to actually see the thundering convoy of cement trucks pass me on the freeway, their bulbous tanks always turning. I picture them reversing onto the Taylor–Samson building site, beeping, hissing, pumping ton after ton of wet concrete into the ground.

It'll be flattened out, patted down, and on its way to solid by the end of the day.

Arriving at work, I park, turn off the engine, and head toward the door—strolling into normality, swinging my keys without a care in the world.

This world.

Maybe I should whistle?

A freight train trembles the glass as I step inside and head straight to the kitchen, saying good morning to Foster at his desk.

Nell's sitting at the lunch table. She's wearing desert cargo pants and her navy-blue DEA T-shirt tucked into a high waist.

"Shit, look at you," she says, folding her newspaper and standing. "You sick?"

I pull the carafe from the coffee machine as she leans on the countertop and then places her empty cup in front of me.

"Tired." I fill it, then pour one for myself.

"Been keeping up the good work, soldier?"

"I . . . um . . ."

"Don't make me spell it out."

Then I realize what she means and push a smile onto my face. Rosie and I have been trying for a baby for the last year or so. Seems a lifetime ago that I thought about this.

"Yeah," I say. "Still, uh . . . still banging away at that problem."

"This is the fun part." Nell pats my shoulder. "Enjoy it while it lasts. You still on top of ovulation dates?"

"She's got an app."

"What you guys talking about?" Foster asks from the doorway.

"Unprotected sex," Nell says.

"Nice." He comes inside.

"In order to procreate," she adds.

"Ah, never mind then," he says. "You still firing blanks there, James?"

I just stare at him. I'm too exhausted for his shit. In fact, both Rosie and I are totally healthy. Fertile. The doctor said the delay might be stress related. If that's true, I'm guessing the last few days won't have helped.

"Nah," I say. "Just takes time."

"Well, you'll get there. Took us a fair while to have ours." Foster picks up the pot of coffee. "Gonna be good-looking kids."

"Thanks," I say, although I know this is the setup for a joke.

"Assuming, of course, they look like Rosie and nothing like you." And he laughs—obnoxious, too close to my face.

"Very good," I mumble.

Foster's wearing his leather jacket and a plain white T-shirt. With his gelled black hair, his straight-cut sideburns, he looks like a T-Bird. And his hands are dirty with motor oil stains. He is literally a greaser.

"How's the bike coming along?" Nell asks him.

"We're getting there." He whips his phone out, sidles up to her, and begins flicking through photos of an old Harley he's been restoring with his dad. Any opportunity. He's obsessed with that bike. When he shows me one, I make a polite humming sound like I care. But I pitch the tone just right so he knows I don't.

Foster isn't a bad guy. But he's hard work to be around for any length of time. Like a buzzing insect. Almost certainly harmless, but really fucking annoying.

On the table, a few photos are spread out—half of them were in the presentation we gave to Rob Sanders on Friday. Pictures of the high-end equipment we seized from that warehouse. No idea where it all came from—the forensic team is *still* working on tracing it. But it definitely illustrates how sophisticated they are.

"Any update from the units watching the Leyland & Lang building?" I ask.

I'm so fucking tired I could fall asleep—I'm speaking on autopilot.

Nell looks over, passing Foster's phone back. "Nope. No movement. No intriguing visits. Edward's acting like he always does."

"And the *Hamburg*?" I wonder.

"On course and on time." Nell gestures to the table. There are some sheets of paper—a map of the city port and an aerial photo of the cargo ship. "Also got the official green light from Sanders for Thursday morning. And we're keeping the port in the dark. We can't trust anyone working there. I wouldn't even be comfortable using their arrival times. We stick to our system. Our data. We have a GPS tracker on that container. Might as well use it."

Did that final dose of heroin, the one that took Matthew away, arrive in a container aboard a ship just like this one?

"That's good," I hear myself say.

The words just appearing in my mind. My words. His words.

This world.

I'm so sorry to say goodbye. I know you tried. Now, you only have one person left to worry about.

Take care of Rosie.

It's worrying to recite Matthew's note during the day.

Nell said, when he died, that I should use it as fuel. Motivation. Because, she explained, grief takes you to dark places if you're not careful.

And here we are—the dark place grief has taken us.

The fallout. For me, Matthew's addiction hijacked my career—it pushed me down this path. It gave me all the anger and drive to punish those who profit from these substances. To leap headfirst into this pit and start killing snakes.

But for Rosie, I think Friday night was the first time grief truly showed its dark hand.

We're all victims of this epidemic in one way or another. You can trace the red lines all the way back to a poppy field.

We have to get away. This city is no place to start a family.

Catching Edward is going to close the door. And I'm going to keep it locked.

They say suicide is the cruelest way to lose someone you love, because there's no one left to blame. But that's not true. I blame him. I blame Edward fucking Lang.

God, we're so close now.

◆ ◆ ◆

Aside from beer and the occasional cigarette, I'm pretty straightedge. But by 2 p.m. I'm drinking coffee to the point of intoxication. Pulsing stars and blind black holes in my electric head-rush vision. And by night, I'm sober again. Anxiety comes in similar tides—sometimes slow and creeping. Other times you turn away and, when you look back, suddenly the water's around your neck.

I park in the driveway at home. It's dark. Maybe 8 p.m.. The fog is here again—streetlights making clouds of gold all the way down the hill.

Inside. Food. Wine. Normal things.

Rosie tells me about her day—she was just another member of staff surprised to learn of Frank's disappearance. Watercooler speculation. Did you hear? She fades into the theories and gossip. The plan is working.

Upstairs. Bathroom. Undress. Shower. Shower. Shower. Mirror. Teeth. I brush them until it hurts and I spit blood.

It spirals, white and red, down the drain.

My heart pounds. Hands firm on the sink for balance. Jesus. I keep my eyes open—looking at myself in the glass until I'm someone else. Like a word you say so many times it sheds its meaning and you realize it's just noise. Like me. I'm just matter. Atoms. Inexplicably assembled and aware.

I stand there for what must be over an hour. Just breathing. Shaking.

Eventually I decide to face it. I close my eyes and relive the entire night again. Here, in these memories, I manage to find solace. All the possible loose ends were tied up.

Still, I allow my mind to catastrophize. Entertain the devil and see all the ways it could go wrong.

But I feel confident in my abilities. Even now, with fear given total dominion over my imagination, I can't envisage any plausible ways this might come undone.

Or am I lying to myself? No, no. It's true. It's true.

All the scenarios that end in disaster involve unlikely elements of chaos. With all our hard work accounted for, the chance is surely low. There's always risk. Every mouthful could choke you, every passing car could swerve, every heartbeat could be your last.

One day, you'll do everything for the final time and you won't even realize it. Your final meal, your final kiss, your final glimpse of the sun. I just can't wait anymore.

It was a clean job. If it is possible to get away with murder, and I know it absolutely is, we took every necessary step.

There it is again—the glinting light, off in the distance. A tiny spark of hope. Like a firefly. Still alive. Rosie and I have a future. By the ocean. Time will hide the remorse. Shame will wash away with every other forgotten thing, in the soft waves we'll hear from our back porch on the sand.

I'm so exhausted now that I might even be able to sleep.

Finally I open my eyes and recognize myself. Then I head into the bedroom and sit on the edge of the mattress.

Rosie breathes quietly behind me in the dark as I touch the scars on my legs. They still ache from kneeling down, from all that cleaning. All that hard, hard work.

It's going to be OK. I say that in my mind. *It is going to be OK.*

We did everything we could. We planned it all so well, we scrubbed it all away and now—

A glowing light on the bedside cabinet. My phone. I pick it up and it tells me I have eight missed calls and three voicemail messages. It's always on silent but, still, I'm surprised Rosie slept through the vibrations.

I press for voicemail.

First message, received half an hour ago.

"Hi, James, it's Nell. Call me when you get this."

The second message, eight minutes after.

"It's Nell. Call me back."

And the third message. Breathing more and more, I hear the words in a timeless, weightless tidal wave of terror and dread.

"James, listen," Nell's voice whispers in my ear. "I would obviously rather tell you this in person. I don't want to worry you, but we may have a problem."

I'm coming out of the bedroom now, barefoot, down the stairs.

"You know all that high-end surveillance equipment from the warehouse? Well, just got the full forensic report back. One of them . . . it has a, a plastic thing. Made to replace a dial on a radio. Another can fit inside a gearshift. These devices . . . They're meant for cars."

I'm dizzy at the front door. I stop, lean on the wall, look at the floor.

"Then I wondered and . . . and I looked. And, well, I found one." Nell sighs. "A fucking bug, in my car. These guys, Lang's guys, they're serious. They're big time."

I'm outside.

"I'm not saying you've definitely got one," she says. "But I guess it'd make sense. We've been using your car. You said he even recognized you."

My heart is hitting me.

"I'm heading to the office now to do a sweep." I can tell that she was driving while she left this message.

I'm desperate, dying, too panicked, too sick, drowning now as I come down the steps, into the damp, gold, foggy night, holding the phone against my ear as I open the driver's door.

"It was just under the steering wheel."

I climb inside. My hand scrambles, searching—scraping the plastic so hard, so fast that I hurt my fingertips.

Leaning down, I look, I feel—down the sides of the seat, under it, the air conditioning vents. I search. The car's ceiling. I search. I search. I squeeze the sun visor. I hold the phone with my shoulder. I swap ears. Open the glove compartment. Lift things. Move things. I search. And I search.

But I . . . I slow down, looking around . . . there's nothing. I find nothing.

And I rest my head on the steering wheel and breathe. God. My chest heaves. My bare feet are dirty, gravel pressed into my soles. Nell's still driving, still talking.

"It's bad, James," she whispers. "They have . . . they have been listening."

End of messages.

The phone slips from my hand and clatters between the seat and the door. For a few seconds, I feel like I'm going to be sick, so I close my eyes, hold the dash for balance, and take slow, deep breaths.

As I calm down, I place my hands on the steering column, trying to center myself, trying to process—

Eyes open.

The plastic casing, behind the wheel. I lift my head. I look. It's hollow.

Gripping the edge of the paneling, I click it aside with ease.

And I reach under, inside, and I pull out a small microphone—the black wire attached to a metal, coin-sized transmitter. It dangles from my trembling fingers.

High-end surveillance equipment. Exactly the kind used by associates of Edward Lang.

Nell's words echo in my mind. They. Have. Been. Listening.

Slowly, I lean back in the chair and stare at it.

And for the first time in my entire life, my hand finally stops shaking.

Chapter Six

I'm sitting on the floor in the kitchen, on the tiles, cross-legged, like a little boy. Our big silver fridge is directly in front of me. I think I might have been here all night. It seems like morning now.

Nell's been calling a lot. But I've ignored them all. I had to disconnect the landline. I'm not even sure how she got that number. I just can't speak to her. Not yet.

The bug is on a white tile to my left, its wire coiled—the black microphone is no bigger than a Tic Tac, the rest of the device contained in a metal disc, like a poker chip. I've pulled out the battery. Whoever is on the other end now knows it has been found. The clock is ticking.

My phone, screen up, is on my right-hand side, also framed in a white tile.

Now I just sit and stare at these two objects.

"James?" Rosie whispers from the doorway.

I turn, my vision's blurry, but I see she's fiddling with an earring—dressed for work. Her hair, her makeup, it's all perfect. She steps along the internal wall, her heels loud on the floor, and picks up her keys from the windowsill.

"You look nice," I say. "When you wear smart clothes."

"Thanks?"

"You're really, really pretty."

"Did you manage to get any sleep?"

"Nope."

"What are you . . . what are you doing?"

"Waiting."

"For?"

"A phone call."

"OK . . . Do you want to wait on a stool?"

"No." I turn back and face forward again.

"Well," Rosie says. "You know what I always say about being on the floor."

"Yeah . . . A different perspective."

"You should lie down."

"Maybe I will."

"I'm gonna go now."

"Rosie?" I say.

"Yeah?"

"Don't you want some coffee?"

"I'm running late. I'll get it on the way."

"Oh, that's cool. Have a nice day."

Rosie leaves the kitchen. I hear a gentle tapping and I turn again and she's at the window. Smiling, I wave.

Normality. We must act normal.

And the front door clunks shut.

A patch of sunlight creeps over the kitchen, across the breakfast bar, straight lines of yellow reflected in the chrome legs on the stools—glinting at my side.

It's impossible to tell how long has passed when my phone finally vibrates across the tile.

I pick it up, press the little green icon to answer, and slowly lift it to my ear.

"Hello, special agent James Casper," he says. "Edward Lang here."

"Hi."

"You gave me your card. Said I should call if I hear anything that might be . . . of interest. Maybe we should meet and have a chat?"

"Sure."

"You know Nelson's Diner?"

"I do."

"Well, that's where I am."

The line goes dead. I gently place the phone on the tiles and, lifting my head, look directly at the tall, silver fridge. And Edward's drawing of a tiger, pinned to the metal with a magnet I made in high school, looks right back at me.

Nelson's Diner is a huge, single-story building with a wide glass front, a standalone neon sign in the parking lot, and a Hollywood theme that seems like it'd look better at night. Big, round ground lights run around grass banks on either side. The life-size replica of a great white shark's head bursting through the bricks lacks a certain charm when bleached out in the sun.

Inside the door, an animatronic model of the alien from *ET* greets me. The voice box hisses and crackles, like a breaking radio. Once upon a time, it may well have said "phone home."

The wood above the bar is adorned with old, framed movie posters, some dating back to the days of black-and-white cinema. And each of the booths appears to have a particular theme—all the tables and the red leather seats are the same, but the walls host paintings and various pieces of mounted memorabilia. There's a black umbrella over the Mary Poppins table, King Kong's silhouette hangs from the Empire State Building nearby, and the scorched tire tracks from a time-traveling DeLorean take you down a yellow brick road that leads, I see, all the way to the bathroom.

One door for "Guys," one door for "Dolls."

And there he is, directly in front of me at the far end of the otherwise empty diner.

Edward's waiting in the Disney booth beneath a collage of wall art shaped like Mickey Mouse. He's sitting in the middle, his arms spread wide across the back of the red seat, the iconic ears rising like an angel's wings above his shoulders. And he lifts his head and looks straight into my eyes with a warm, welcoming smile.

I take a breath, then walk to the table.

Edward stands, shuffles around, and gestures to the seat opposite.

"Good to see you again, James," he says.

We shake hands.

Today, Edward is wearing a white shirt with a blue embroidered vest—dressed like a barman in a Wild West tavern. He's a ten-gallon hat away from full cowboy chic. And he's trimmed his beard, now he looks neat and preened—his hairline cut with a barber's blade. I imagine the metal scraping, close up, zoomed in, over his thick, tanned skin.

"Hope you don't mind speaking in here?" he says as we sit down opposite one another. "I love this place. They do these ice cream shakes. I'm getting the Buzz Shake."

Edward slides a menu toward me—I can see that he's excited. But I'm feeling absolutely nothing. Exhausted. Numb. I think my adrenal glands must have exploded from overuse.

"I invented it," he adds. "They made us change the name because although you can have all this stuff on the wall, all this memorabilia, when it comes to selling things you can't use registered trademarks, do you understand?"

I nod.

"So it's just called the Buzz Shake on the menu, see." Edward points, his eyes lighting up with an almost-childish delight when he sees me reading the ingredients. "But really it was the Buzz Lightyear Shake."

Swallowing, I whisper, "I think I'm OK."

The waiter arrives. "Who are you?" Edward asks, looking him up and down.

"My name's Brendon, I'll be your waiter today."

"Brendon?" Edward frowns. "What movie are you from?"

"Oh, we . . . we don't dress up anymore."

Bang—Edward slams his hand onto the table. I flinch, knives and forks clink. "Not even a fucking pirate hat."

"Sorry, sir."

"Ah, it's not your fault."

"Can I get you guys some drinks?"

"Two Buzz Shakes," Edward says. "And did you say you want fries?" He points at me, then tilts his hand. "Share some maybe?"

I simply stare at him.

"Just the shakes then."

The waiter jots down the order and takes the menus.

"And"—Edward sits up and leans over, conspiratorially lowering his voice—"it's not really James's birthday but it's his first time trying the Buzz Shake, so I was wondering if you'd be able to put a sparkler in?"

"I'll see what I can do," the waiter says with a smile.

Edward places his hand on his chest, on the vest's ornate stitching. "You have my gratitude."

There's a strange silence once he's left. Edward looks around the booth, pouts his lips, looks back at me, and widens his eyes slightly.

"So there are questions." He turns to the collage on the wall by our side. "One of which is . . ." He searches the artwork. "I can't find it now . . . it asks what's your favorite—there." He puts his index finger on Mickey's chin, on a tiny line of printed text. "'What is your favorite Pixar movie?' I'd say probably *Toy Story* is the best. Do you agree?"

Still, I just look at him.

"James," he whispers. "Do you agree?"

I blink.

"You . . . no." Edward shakes his head. "You don't think *Finding Nemo* is better, do you? It's good, it's real good, don't get me wrong. Of course, it's a compelling arc, and the seagulls, the stoned turtle, these are iconic in their own way, but the narrative? Boil it down, and it's just a missing fish. *Toy Story*—you've got Woody's neurosis, the whole theme of Andy growing up, Mr. Potato Head's turbulent marriage, that charming homosexual dinosaur. And then Buzz believing he's really a Space Ranger. It's so rich, James. His entire identity, called into question . . ." Edward makes a fist. "He doesn't realize he's a toy."

"Shall we play that game again?" I say.

"Which game?"

"The one where we learn what the fuck I'm doing here."

Edward's eyes crease with a smile.

"I knew it. I fucking knew it." He jabs a finger toward me, bangs the table again, and looks across the empty diner. "You're a Nemo man."

The waiter returns. "I'm sorry, sir, but I've just spoken to the chef and we are out of sparklers."

Edward lifts his hands as though this is a disaster. "There's only so much disappointment a man can take. This is James's first ever visit." He leans to the side to remove his wallet. "I'll give you a thousand dollars if you can get a sparkler before we're finished."

"Um." The waiter seems confused, looks over his shoulder at the kitchen. "Well, I . . ."

"Five hundred now, five hundred on delivery." He holds folded bills between his fingers like a cigarette. "But bring the shakes first or the deal's off."

Realizing he's serious, the waiter takes the money and heads back to the swinging kitchen doors.

"When I was growing up, I used to spend summers with my grandparents. My grandpa." Edward strokes his beard with his thick fingers—he has a faded tattoo on his wrist, an abstract gauntlet pattern. "His first wife, my real grandma, she died from cancer when she was quite young. This must have been in the twenties." He gestures a timeline with his finger. "But he married a Japanese lady who the family welcomed, and soon I just called her Grandma. She had this strange scar, down the left side of her face and neck, like a . . . like a kind of rash." He touches his own cheek. "And there was no hair. She wore a wig and makeup, she was very glamorous so tried to hide it, but you could still tell. I asked her one day what happened."

The young waiter arrives. Edward sits up straight and nods as the two tall shakes are placed on the wood in front of us.

"Enjoy." The kid holds the tray to his chest, bows, turns on his foot, and sprints toward the door—the tray and his apron thrown onto the counter as he leaves the diner.

Edward takes a sip. "My goodness," he says. "That is so fucking nice. James. Try it."

I lift the glass and put the straw to my lips. The top of the shake has cream, white chocolate shavings, and bright-green lime sauce. I taste.

He spreads his hands, lifts his brow. "Not bad, hey?"

"Delicious."

"She caught fire," he says. "The left-hand side of Grandma's body burst into flames when she was a young woman. Out on her bike. She'd stopped and leaned against a tree. In a park in a city called Hiroshima. Nice normal morning, she was heading off to work and pulled over to look at the birds. And the sky changed—she said there was a new sun on the horizon. She'd been standing in the shade, but everything in the new sunlight was on fire. Hair gone, clothes stripped from her body. You imagine an explosion, destroying buildings, turning brick to dust and people to shadows. But that's just the red zone, the epicenter, zoom out and you've got a radius of destruction. People in the orange zone, they're blown to bits—arms, legs gone, torsos cut in half, cut in quarters. Few hours screaming in the rubble, but they're as good as dead. Then zoom out a bit more and you've got thousands of human beings in the yellow zone. You don't hear many stories about them. They're blind, deaf, burned, buried, skin coming off like old wet gloves. Injuries you might associate with hell—but not all of them fatal. Can you imagine, walking around on a sunny day and then having the left-hand side of your body catch fire from the sheer radiated heat of an explosion in the sky?"

Edward scoops out some whipped cream. "Really," he says, licking it from his straw. "This is one of the best shakes I've ever tasted. Do you like the taste of it, James?"

"Yes."

"My grandma, she said it was the scariest time of her life—the decades after that. Because she was always wondering if it might happen again. If she might be outside and then, without any warning, catch fire. She might blink and be in hell. She might have to roll around, naked, on the ground, putting herself out, and listen to the howling screams of terror and confusion."

Slurping again on his straw, Edward swallows and dabs his beard with a napkin.

"That would be what I'd describe as a 'bad day,'" he goes on. "And that was a risk. A nuclear first strike. While America had the technology, there really was a chance that we might use it again.

Take a few Russian cities off the map. Flex our muscles. Only when other nations developed similar capabilities did my grandma feel safe again. Mutually assured destruction. There is nothing more dangerous than a single force having the ultimate weapon. But give it to everyone?"

Edward gestures to the window, around the diner. "Notice," he says, "that we haven't seen an atomic attack since 1945. It's counterintuitive, but, aside from luck and diplomacy, we have nuclear proliferation to thank for this. If the president wants to nuke Russia, shit, he can. But it means the end of everything."

"You're not very good at the game," I say.

"Oh, James, I'm one of the best. But fine. I'll speak plainly. I thought it might be a good idea to let you know that, the other day, I lied. Truth is, you are absolutely on the money. It's difficult to judge, because you can only go by law enforcement data, but I would wager I am one of the most profitable traffickers of narcotics this country has ever seen. We import heroin, mainly, but also fentanyl, cocaine, and a fair bit of methamphetamine. And, of course, the legal side of Leyland & Lang also opens up some extra revenue streams. We overproduce opioids, benzos, and so on and then sell them on the streets too."

"Ryan Payne worked for you?"

"Uh, yeah." He scratches his temple. "In a roundabout way, yes."

"And when he got busted, you had him killed?"

"Um . . . yes, yes, that's correct."

"And the money laundering?"

"Huge. Biblical. We clean a great deal of it through the employment agencies, mainly on construction projects, as I think you already know. But a lot is done in old-fashioned ways. Look at this place."

Sighing, I turn and glance around the rest of the empty diner. We're the only customers in here.

"What do you see?" he asks. "Notice how the place is full? Notice how many people, how many families are ordering shakes? Buying pancakes? Look over there at Timmy and all his friends eating hamburgers for his big double-digit birthday. Ten years old. Maybe they'll go play laser tag after. I own a hundred places just like this, each turning over thousands of dollars a day."

I'm not even recording this conversation. I'm just a deer in the headlights.

"You're evil," I whisper, dazed.

"Why the fuck would you say that?" He frowns, genuinely offended. This is the first time I've ever seen him look angry. "That's too strong. Retract it."

"You know how many people die every year from this shit? Just in this city. You know how many addicts you've created?"

"None. That's how many."

"You can moralize all you want. You're killing people."

"Drugs are not the enemy," he says, his eyes wide and mad again. "The enemy is hopelessness. The enemy is empty lives. You think those lost souls under Blue Bridge would be smoking junk if they had something better to do? Addiction is a lot more complicated than chemical dependence." He smiles slightly. "You know this. You have firsthand experience. Tell me about Matthew."

"No."

"Careful." Edward points. "That will be the last time you use that word with me. From now on, that is not something I want to hear from you."

The ice cream in my shake has started to melt, the lime-green sauce sinking and mixing with the white milk.

"Here's the thing," he says. "You guys know what's coming in on Thursday. Now, I'm aware that while you have colorful theories about me and my operation—which incidentally happen to be largely true, though I must say you've dramatically underestimated it all—you still need hard evidence. You need to seize that container. Am I right so far? The case hinges on that?"

I nod.

"The sensible thing would be for me to stop it. But I imagine if I attempted to do that, the authorities would seize it earlier. Plus, I don't really like the idea of retreating. So you have two choices." Edward takes a small USB drive from his pocket. It has L&L printed on the side. He places it carefully on the table between us. "Choice number one, you plug this into your computer at work—or any computer at your office for that matter. The software will do the rest. An associate of mine created it, he's very clever—bit of a wizard on the old tech side of things. As I understand, it's malware that will effectively duplicate the marine traffic program you're using . . . but it'll swap two ships around. Apparently, you have an internally vetted log of movements?"

"We do."

"Well, that's fantastic. So, basically, our container will come into the north dock, around 6 a.m.. But the computer will make it seem like it'll arrive on the south dock, just before 9 a.m.. Even when they realize, it'll be too late. You'll be all geared up to seize a container that'll already be long gone, driving away on the back of a truck."

"What's choice two?"

"Very simple. The nuclear option. That's the beauty of our new business relationship, we both hold the detonator. At any point, should you feel the urge, we can both go to prison. Totally up to you. For the record, I do not want that to happen, and I'm willing to work very hard to ensure it doesn't."

"What if I just arrest you now? With everything you've just said."

"Yep, you can. I wouldn't even resist. I know how strong your case is. I suspect without your help I'm in serious trouble . . . Of course, though, there is a recording of you talking to your wife about Frank McBride, who she murdered and you buried on Friday evening. There is that . . . It will go on YouTube within an hour of my arrest. Or within an hour of my death, in case you guys are doing a *Bonnie and Clyde* type thing?" He looks around the diner once more. "Don't think they've got a *Bonnie and Clyde* poster . . ."

"How long were you listening?"

"Since you arrested Ryan. We were on the ropes. We'd been using the devices to gather dirt on the cartel." He's still distracted, searching for that poster. "Knowledge is power. But, obviously, we needed to know what *you* had on *us*. You and Nell, parked at my office for those long stakeouts. I was in the car with you the whole time. Nope, they haven't got any *Bonnie and Clyde* stuff . . ."

I just stare at the table. I'm just a little boy.

"I can't tell you how excited I was when I heard that recording." Edward's attention snaps back to me. "I stood up. I literally clapped. Anyway. Don't make up your mind now. Just take the drive." He slides it across the table. "Sleep on it."

"This is blackmail."

Edward thinks for a moment and nods. "Yeah. Yep. That's one more charge for your sheet. This is a classic case of blackmail. Textbook. You're absolutely right."

"I can't help you," I say. "Even if I wanted to. They'll figure it out."

"You ever see *Prisoner 99*?" He looks toward a poster across from us. An old black-and-white movie. "Main character escapes from his maximum-security cell during a riot. Stays out of sight all night. He hides in the yard, directly beneath the biggest searchlight. That's the blind spot. Right in the center. Right in the fucking bullseye. You *will* help me, James. The stakes are just too high for anything other than peaceful coexistence." He puts the USB drive in my palm, closes my fingers around it, and pats my hand. "Mutually. Assured. Destruction."

Standing, I feel dizzy and head for the door—ET hisses a long goodbye as I step outside, back into the sun, across the parking lot, and to my car.

I pull the door open, climb in, and sit for a moment. Staring, thoughtlessly staring at the steering wheel and feeling oddly calm and serene and—

Thud. Something hits the door at my side. I turn to see the waiter, panting, at the window—he gestures for me to roll it down.

When I do, he produces a lit sparkler from behind his back. It crackles and smokes as he holds it out for me. "Happy"—he gasps, catching his breath—"happy birthday from all of us at . . . at Nelson's Diner."

I look straight ahead and lift the switch to close the window.

As I drive away, I see the shrinking waiter in the rearview mirror, standing alone in the middle of the empty parking lot, still holding the sparkler in his slack, disappointed hand.

Chapter Seven

Driving away from Nelson's Diner, I find myself unable to think about the future. Only the present and the past are available to me. My mind is so deprived of sleep that it seems to have insufficient resources to speculate. Imagination simply demands too much energy.

I think about Rosie in these newly dimmed lights. She's at the window in our kitchen. Waving goodbye. Impossibly young, wearing a black T-shirt with a white image on the front. Just me and her. Although she's been a feature in my life for as long as I can remember, it wasn't always just us.

Growing up in Treaston Mills, Matthew was a natural best friend for me. We lived opposite one another, went to the same school; when you're four years old, that's pretty much all you need to form a bond. Mutual interests are a bonus. And we had plenty.

Rosie was his big sister. At first she was an anonymous extra—so ambient her name wouldn't even appear in the credits. But before long I realized she was more than that. She was the main character. The love interest. It's all about Rosie. I knew that long before hormones dialed my infatuation right up to eleven.

I lived on Green Street with my Aunt Beatrice until I was ten years old. My English mother died giving birth to me, and my American father, drunk on liquor and grief, drove his pickup truck into a boulder at about eighty miles per hour. No one knows if it was an accident. I'm not sure anyone cares.

So that left me alone with no family besides Aunt Beatrice, who raised me with, well, I suppose you could call it a hands-off approach. She'd feed me, clothe me, make sure I finished my homework on time, but that was about it. Sometimes I felt like she was taking care of me out of nothing more than a sense of duty. Like a conscripted soldier—they'll only ever fight so hard. When I grazed my knee, she would patch it up with a Band-Aid and a pat on the back. Kisses, she said, did not heal wounds.

Still, she was a decent enough woman. There was nothing stopping her from saying no when it came to custody arrangements. For that first decade of my life, she did her best. And that's all you can ever ask.

She'd tell me my mother would have done an incredible job—as though that might make me feel better about the cold limits of her own maternal disposition. When I was young, I mistakenly thought her regret that she wasn't an ideal guardian proved that she loved me. Really, all it confirmed was how much she'd loved her sister.

And when I asked about my dad, she said his death was a stroke of luck.

"It's better to have no father than a man like that," she'd say.

We lived opposite a couple called David and Mary. They were upstanding citizens—pillars of the community. David had served three terms as mayor. He was a well-regarded family doctor and, in retirement, the street's most capable handyman. Mary was Treaston's pastor. A firm, conservative woman.

Aunt Bea told me they couldn't have children, which is why they'd adopted Rosie and Matthew, a young pair of orphaned siblings. But biology didn't seem to matter. To me, they just looked like a happy family.

Their willingness to take care of kids who were not their own worked well for Aunt Bea. It meant she could open the door, send me out to play, and happily not see me until dinner was served.

When summer came, me, Rosie, and Matthew would venture to the woods—into the hills. A ten-minute walk took you out of town; ten minutes more and you couldn't see or hear anything like civilization.

The forest, the river, the rocks—we'd lose hours out there without crossing paths with another soul. That kind of wild country is rare. But it seemed the residents of Treaston Mills didn't care that they lived on the edge of nowhere. For most it was all the more reason to stay put. Only children have things to learn in the shadows of tall trees or the glisten and thunder of sunbeam waterfalls.

We'd get told horror stories about hikers who disappeared over the rocky ridge. The rule was that we shouldn't play any further than Hunter's Lake. Even though it was a good mile trek from the nearest road, that was the line in the sand. A line we thoughtlessly crossed almost every single summer's day.

It must have been August when we found the cabin. Deep in the woods—a long abandoned shack, hidden in the foliage. We'd pushed through the weeds and leaves and snapped thin branches to clear our way. And then we'd climbed over the rotten steps and onto the half-collapsed veranda.

Now we're inside. We've been here for a while. Rosie, sitting on the wooden floorboards against the wall, creeping plants coming through the empty window frame above her. Dappled sunlight across her legs and the hiss and rustle of nature outside.

She's throwing pebbles into a rusted tin can across the room. I'm sitting on top of one of the old hunting tables. Huge and wide, with strange black stains in the middle of the wood. I stroke my fingers over the dust and sweep off flecks of mud.

Matthew and I must be ten years old. I can hear him in the bedroom, looking through a closet. The cabin smells like an old shed. Warm, dry. Insects crawling beneath anything that moves. Lift a log and they'll scurry and spread, like beads you've spilled.

Dink. "Yes," Rosie yells as the tin can tilts, wobbling with a successful shot.

She's twelve now—enjoying the last few years where she's taller and stronger than me and Matthew. Her hair is thin, natural brown, and tied in a ponytail—her cheeks freckled and tanned—a few strands passing her eyebrow. She curls them over her ear or sweeps them back with her palms from time to time.

Her knees. She's wearing shorts, then, and a black T-shirt. And there's an image across her chest, a white motif—it might be a skull, maybe the Misfits face, but my memory can't seem to get it into focus.

"You know what that is, right?" she says.

"What?"

"That table." Rosie looks up at me from the floor. Her left hand is full of stones. She throws another. It goes over the can, onto the wood, bouncing to the wall.

"Yeah," I say. "It's a table."

"Do you know what it was used for?"

"No."

She points at me with a pebble. "That was used to chop up dead animals." She looks ahead again. *Dink*—it pings off the side of the metal.

"Like deer?"

"Deer. Boars. Little kids."

"Oh, I get it. Another story . . ."

"I heard the killer's still out here," she whispers. "Shhh. He waits out in his treehouse and watches the cabin with binoculars. When a victim arrives, he creeps in with an ax."

Floorboards creak—Matthew still searching in the adjacent bedroom.

"Uh-oh, here he comes."

"That's Matthew."

"You better pray it is."

"Rosie, I'm not scared." I am scared. "All those stories are bullshit."

"I suppose you don't believe the legend of the Stone Ghost?"

"Never heard of it."

"The rumor is . . . there's a ghost out here," she says, shuffling around to me, now cross-legged on the floor. "A young girl. She looks beautiful. I mean, she is stunning. Like a supermodel. But it's a trick because . . . wait . . . you hear that?"

"*It's Matthew*," I say again—perhaps to myself.

"No, not that. Seriously." Rosie closes her eyes, tilts her head. "You can't hear that? Listen."

"Shut up."

"Close your eyes, James."

"No."

"Are you scared of the Stone Ghost?"

"No."

"Then close your eyes and listen."

I pull a face and play along, closing my eyes.

"Some people say you can hear her breathing. Or a footstep. Or maybe scratching on wood." Rosie rubs her fingernails on the floorboards. "But you can never see her. Because if you see her . . . you die."

"OK." I nod, eyes still shut.

"And James," she whispers, "do you know why? Why they call her the Stone Ghost?"

"Why?"

"Because that's how she curses her victims. And some say, if you concentrate, you can even feel it happening. You just have to close your eyes and . . ."

One of Rosie's pebbles hits me in the face. "Ouch." Flinching, I open my eyes.

"What happened?" she says, hiding her smile, beginning to snicker.

I grab the stone from my lap and throw it back. She shields herself and turns to the wall, her boots kicking out into the sunlight as she laughs and laughs.

"Look what I found," Matthew says, coming back into the room.

We both turn to the doorway.

"Aw, cool." Rosie stands, brushing dirt from the back of her shorts.

"What is it?" I ask.

"Cigarettes." Matthew opens the half-crumpled, faded packet.

"They must be so old—check out the label," Rosie says.

He slides one out. "Still dry, look." We all marvel at the crinkled white tube. "Give me the lighter."

"What? No," I say. "It's for campfires."

"Just give him the lighter," Rosie says.

"You can't smoke it." I look at them like they're crazy.

"Why?" Matthew shrugs. "I'm not gonna tell anyone. Are you?"

"No, but . . ." I appeal to Rosie.

"Well, I've already tried one," she says. "You little dorks can do whatever you want."

"Give it to me." Matthew holds out his hand.

"Fine." I pass it to him.

He thumbs the wheel, holding the flame over the end of the cigarette.

"You have to suck on it at the same time," Rosie huffs.

She snatches the lighter, takes the scorched cigarette, and puts it in Matthew's mouth. Then she cups the flame, just like she's probably seen in a movie.

He takes a drag and instantly blasts it out with a heavy, shocked cough. "Aw, aw, that's horrible." Wincing, he shudders.

Rosie tries a quick puff. She manages to stifle her tickle, croaking slightly. "Yeah . . . it's nasty."

Then she holds it out for me. The smoke curls in the cabin's still air, glowing in the patches of sun, rising from her hand. I hesitate, shaking my head.

"Come on," Matthew says. "We've all done it."

"And you said it wasn't good." I frown.

"You won't know until you try," he says.

Rosie juts it closer. "Smoke, bitch."

There's a long pause. "I . . ."

"I'm fucking with you, James," she says. "You don't have to smoke if you don't want to."

She drops it and twists it out with her boot. "Come on, let's head back, before the Stone Ghost rapes us."

Rosie grabs her sweater off the window ledge, throwing it over her shoulder.

"Wait," I say.

She turns.

Three kids standing together in the abandoned shack.

I hold my hand out and Matthew passes me another cigarette. Carefully, I place it between my lips, spark the flame, and, right on cue, I cough and cough and wipe tears from my cheeks.

"You're cool now, ten points." Rosie gives me a sarcastic thumbs-up. "Let's go, losers." And she runs out through the cabin's wide-open doorway, leaping off the broken steps and into the woods.

On the way back, we walk over the ridge and toward the wide meadow just down from the old steel mill.

Me and Rosie have wandered off ahead.

"Two, or maybe even three," she says. Somehow we've got onto the topic of children.

"You've planned it all out?" I say.

"Hey, wait for me," Matthew shouts, jogging to catch up. "What you guys talking about?"

"Having babies," Rosie explains. "When we're adults."

"Why?" Matthew curls his lip. "Kids are expensive."

"How else are you going to have a family?" she asks.

We're approaching the wooden fence at the bottom of the next hill.

"You got a family," he insists.

"David and Mary don't count." Rosie climbs over. "David's boring and Mary's a stupid fucking bitch."

"I meant me," he says, placing his foot on the wooden bar.

She turns back and waits. "Well, you definitely don't count."

"Why?" Matthew looks offended—even from his big sister, this seems especially mean. He lands on the grass.

"We won't live together when we're grown up, dumbass." She picks a tall flower and waves it as she explains. "You have to have children or else you'll be all old and lonely. How about you, James? Do you want kids?"

"I don't know." I swing my legs over the fence. "I guess?"

"Way I see it," she says, as we carry on walking, "if you haven't got something you should just make your own. You need money, make some. You need a family, make one. This world doesn't give you anything. It only takes stuff away."

"You have to find someone to marry first," Matthew says. "And who's gonna marry you?"

"Shut up. Loads of people would marry me. James, you'd marry me, right?"

I hesitate, and Matthew frowns as though this is a disgusting idea. "I . . ."

"Too slow," she says. "You lost your chance. Hey, who's that?"

Someone is sitting at the top of the hill. A silhouette on the high horizon, black against the endless blue sky, the light summer clouds seeming perfectly still behind him. We walk up and up through the long grass toward the figure, and when we're close I see a square shape.

"It's Patrick," Matthew says, shielding his eyes from the sun.

Patrick Quincy-Jones. He's a big-time artist. Paints portraits, boats, and, on nice afternoons like this, landscapes. He owns Treaston Gallery, one of the town's few tourist attractions, where he stores and exhibits all his work. Much of it features famous people—presidents, pop stars, that kind of thing. Many modeled live and, I'm sure, spent a lot of money for the finished piece. I know of at least three of his works that sold at auction for well over a million dollars.

He painted a snow scene. It has holes in it, but I can't remember why.

"Howdy," Patrick says, lifting his brush as we approach. "You kids enjoying the weather?"

"Yes, sir," Matthew says.

"What are you painting?" Rosie asks, stepping around to look at the canvas on his wooden easel.

"This wonderful vista here, see." He gestures at the view.

"It's really good," Matthew says.

"Thank you."

"But you've left out the steel mill's chimneys." He points at the rusting buildings down the hill.

"I only paint beautiful things." Patrick taps his own nose.

His young, handsome face is half covered by long black hair. His dreamy eyes peep through when he shakes it back. He must be in his early thirties. But he looks younger.

His painting is good—he's captured the valley, the trees, the sky and clouds. But my memory's made it like a photograph—given him more talent than he could have ever had.

"Will you paint me?" Rosie asks.

"No, duh," Matthew says. "He only paints beautiful things."

She kicks him in the shin.

Patrick laughs. "I'm sure you'll be a star one day and then I'll paint a glorious portrait, six feet tall."

Rosie smiles and touches her hair, staring at him in wonder.

"Will you put holes in it?" I ask. "Like your snow painting?"

He seems confused, ignoring my question. And then Patrick leans closer, smells the air, and looks at each of us. He raises an eyebrow. "Would you like some gum?" he asks as he places his brush on his stool and pulls a foil packet from his bag. "For your breath."

He hands a strip of chewing gum to me, then to Matthew and Rosie.

Matthew holds his palm to his mouth, breathes out some air, and tries to smell it. Then he sniffs his fingers.

We all chew as Patrick says, "You know smoking's bad for you. I'll keep it to myself, this time. But you kids owe me one, OK? You should be especially kind to the man who knows your secrets."

And we leave him there on the top of the hill, painting only the beautiful things he could see.

It was that summer Aunt Beatrice told me she was leaving. My mind has made it the same day we found the cabin, the same day I tried to smoke, but it can't be, because the dates don't tally. This was later. It must have been September.

I knew something was wrong when I went into the kitchen. Aunt Beatrice was standing at the table, paper spread out around the fruit bowl.

"Sit down," she says.

I'm there now and I sit. Ten years old. Just a little boy at the dining table, listening to his Aunt Beatrice.

She tells me she's moving away. It's all so cold and matter-of-fact. She hands me some forms. It's happening so quickly.

I'm ten years old and she's handing me forms.

There's a choice of boarding schools, she says. In the city. I should look and pick my favorite, because she'll be gone before Christmas.

"Gone where?" I don't understand.

She says it's for work. They want to relocate her. And she's already agreed.

"Can I come?"

"No."

"But . . ."

"It's better this way—I'm going to be traveling a lot. Won't fit in with school."

"Can't . . . maybe . . ."

"Really, James, it'll be OK."

I look at one of the sheets of paper, and no one speaks for almost a minute. Aunt Beatrice starts drying dishes at the sink. The conversation is over. My chin begins to tremble.

"Please don't go," I whisper, my voice cracking.

She sighs, still facing the window. "Why are you crying?" she says. "I said this is for your own good."

"But . . ."

"You can always call me. I'll visit when I'm in town."

"I just . . . I'll be alone."

And Aunt Beatrice turns, a bowl in one hand, a dishcloth in the other, and tilts her head. "We're all alone, James," she says.

That night I lie wide awake in bed, thinking about what Rosie said on the hill. We were walking up through the meadow, right in the middle of Patrick's beautiful painting. She wanted to make her own family, because the world hadn't given her one. I'm up all night long, thinking about what she asked me.

A little boy in bed, looking at the ceiling, his arms rigid, his fists at his sides.

Would I marry her?

I toss and turn and wish I were brave enough to have said yes. But I was too scared.

It feels like the whole universe is falling apart around me—like I would only get one chance with Rosie and I'd completely blown it. And now I'll have to leave town forever.

Eyes open and bolt wide as the ten-year-old boy makes a plan.

Because he knows what she said is true. This world doesn't give you anything. It only takes stuff away.

Chapter Eight

Nell's at her desk, head in her hands, when I walk into her office. There are red finger marks on her scalp—if her hair was long enough, I imagine she would have pulled some out.

I've put the bug in a sealed evidence bag, which I hold at my chest like a gift.

She looks up at me, then at the device. "Where have you been, James?"

"I'm here now."

Standing, she steps around her desk and comes closer.

"Pretty sure that's all of them," she says, taking the bag. "I've done a comprehensive sweep of the office, so I think we're all clear now."

"I suppose we send them to forensics." I'm staring over her shoulder at the wall.

I've been in a haze. A trance. As though I'm floating. It's like a dream. One where I'm driving in the fog. I think this is the longest I've ever gone without sleep. My thoughts come in jumbled snippets, little soundbites—half are nonsense, the other half are gentle, devious introductions to nightmares.

"Maybe," Nell whispers, checking outside her office, then closing the door behind me. "Or maybe not."

I hear myself ask, "Why?"

"The container is still on its way. Nothing's changed. I can show you on a map—on our very own map—where that cargo ship is at any moment." She points to her computer. "Just because they're listening, doesn't mean they heard."

"So we do what? Pretend it hasn't happened?" I agree, we're in uncharted territory, but this seems unusual for Nell.

She's always done things properly—image, she says, is important at the agency. Especially with a new taskforce like this. Any unfiled paperwork, any discrepancy, could play against her in the long run. It's a tight operation.

"We're still on top," she says. "But let's imagine that—" She stops. Her phone's vibrating across her desk. She looks.

"It's Sanders." She sighs. "Fuck. I called in a panic last night, but . . ." Nell takes a deep breath, steps over, and lifts it to her ear. "Mr. Sanders." Her voice is bright and normal. "Yeah, and you too . . . OK . . . Well, that's good. We'll take the reins from Wednesday evening. Yeah, sure, it's all . . . No, no . . ." Smiling, she fakes a laugh. "Everything is still under control. No, nothing like that—total false alarm . . . yeah, just . . . exactly, crossed wires . . . Great . . . Thanks for letting me know."

Nell hangs up and chews the inside of her mouth. For a few seconds, she doesn't look at me, as though I might disapprove. She seems so old today—creases in her skin that used to trace a thousand smiles. Now they only speak of strain.

"James," she finally says. "No one else besides you and me knows about the bugs. It might be best if we keep it that way. If it proves to be immaterial, there's no benefit to sounding the alarm."

"And when Sanders finds out?"

"If it's after we seize the container . . . well, it's embarrassing, but we'll be heroes. If it's before, it could unravel everything. Rob's vouching for us—if they catch wind that we fucked up this badly, they might withdraw the teams for Thursday. We could go back to square one. We're on a knife edge. Let's be real, if not for those drugs, what have we actually got? Scrutiny is the last thing we need right now."

Maybe she's right, I think, as I slide my hand in my pocket and feel the Leyland & Lang flash drive. It could unravel *everything*.

"There's also a very real chance that Edward isn't on the other end of the devices," she adds.

"That seems . . . unlikely."

"Remember when we interviewed Ryan Payne?" Nell shakes her head and sits on the edge of her desk. "We asked him what they were doing with all that surveillance equipment. He wouldn't answer."

Nell and I had sat across from Ryan a few months ago as, arms folded, he slouched in total silence and ignored a hundred questions. His attorney had recommended he plead the fifth but, at one point, he couldn't resist.

"You know, whoever you're protecting, whoever you're working for," Nell had said, leaning closer, "we're going to get them."

The bright strip bulbs above were reflected on the silver table. He sat between two glowing white lines, proudly framed against the glass behind. Ryan, hands flat on the table, had looked at each of us in turn. Then he'd laughed. "No," he'd said with genuine amusement, bordering on pity. "No, you're not."

"He laughed at us," Nell says. "He laughed in our faces. Like he knew something we didn't."

"And now he's dead," I say.

I leave her office, make some coffee, and head to my desk. Sitting, I lean down to turn my computer on. Password. Blank screen. Desktop. I double-click the real-time marine traffic log and see the GPS coordinates updating every thirty seconds. Looks like a screen at an airport—arrival times and destinations listed on the right-hand side. Our ship's ID number ends in 454. The *Hamburg*.

On board, wrapped neatly inside an L&L container, there is around one point five tons of heroin. I had thought it was brazen, bordering on downright stupid, to move it all at once. But the more I get to know Edward, the more sense it makes.

I rest my head on my forearm, looking across my blurred desk. The black mouse. The white cup of coffee—the eagle logo, the letters *DEA* fading in and out of focus. Phones are ringing out there in the fog. People are talking, moving; things are happening all around me and I'm closing my eyes and it feels like a dream . . .

I jolt awake—a skeleton's face inches from my nose.

Laughter erupts. Nell pats my shoulder as I sit up. Foster's crouched in front of me, wearing a ski mask with a skull on the front—the kind you wear beneath a motorcycle helmet. He pulls it off.

"Very good," I say, rubbing my eyes.

"Thought you were dead." Foster smiles, folding the black material in half. "I was looking forward to taking your chair."

"Maybe you should go home." Nell inspects me with real concern. "You look awful."

I feel awful, I think. Have I been . . . was I sleeping? I check the time. No more than five minutes have passed.

Everything's still offline. The mist of insomnia still clouding my thoughts, still hiding reality's searing glare. Even through the haze, something inside me knows it's still there. Fear lingers just out of reach, like a word, a name, something you know that you know but can't quite get a grip on right now. I've lost precious time. I stand up, grab my jacket, and leave.

Driving, I click open my third . . . fourth . . . maybe fifth energy drink held between my legs, then slurp it empty and fling it in the back with the other cans. I need a plan. What am I thinking? I'm wired. Bright, bright, bright lights. Little stars pulse in my vision. My head throbs with every one of my fast, fast heartbeats.

I decide to tell her. I decide to tell Rosie everything.

At home I'm finishing another coffee when I hear her key in the door. She's dressed smart from the office—white blouse, black skirt—kicking her shoes off the second she's inside.

Now she's short again. Small.

I sit her down in the living room, take a breath, and tell her the entire story.

"Wow," she says when I finish. "That's . . ."

"Yeah." I'm standing in front of her, on our rug. She's on the couch, leaning forward, elbows on her knees.

"Was it good?"

"What?"

"The milkshake?"

I'm made of electricity now, so I don't care about her jokes. "It was OK, yeah." She's just trying to cheer me up.

"So the hidden microphone was under the steering wheel . . . that means they must have broken into your car?"

"Well, yeah."

The USB drive Edward gave me is in the middle of our coffee table.

"What will that do?" she asks.

"It's malware. It'll change the shipping logs, the marine traffic, on our system."

I pace in front of her, on our rug, onto our wooden floor. My jaw aches.

"So the container will still arrive?"

"Exactly." I turn. Pace back. "But earlier. We'll be waiting for the wrong ship."

"Fuck . . . But won't the people at the port know?"

"They will, yes, but they're out of the loop. We don't trust them. That's why we use our own software. Our own data. Because we know it's secure. Uncorrupted. It's the only trustworthy way to track the cargo. From Wednesday night, we'll be the only ones watching that boat."

"Huh."

"We've worked so hard, it's been years." I stop. "I just . . . I simply cannot do it."

"The alternative?"

When I imagine this, I feel strangely ashamed. Not guilty or sad to lose my freedom. But the way Nell, Foster, and the others will look at me. They'll shake their heads. They'll pity me. "You helped your wife bury a body?" They'll tell their friends about it for years to come. An old colleague who fell off the rails. They'll laugh. "How did he think he would get away with it?" Fuck, they'll *laugh*.

"I know," I say. "But . . . it's too much. It's too far. I'd be complicit. I could receive the same charge as Edward."

"You're considering it."

"We're exploring options."

"There might be another way."

"Go on."

"Well, I don't exactly know what it is yet," Rosie says. "But we have two days until Thursday. Let's look at it rationally. Solutions."

She's right. Solutions. *Bang*. I clap my hands.

"OK," I say, walking to the window.

"What will happen if you do nothing?"

"We'll seize the shipment," I say, turning back, pacing. "A special response team will raid it at dawn. We'll arrest Edward later that morning." Rosie watches me from the couch. "He'll be convicted of trafficking a schedule one substance. He'll probably spend the rest of his days behind bars. Which is what he deserves."

"And what will happen to us?"

I stop, stand still for a few seconds. "He said he'll post the recording online. We said enough to expose ourselves."

"Expose ourselves how? What does a conversation prove?"

"It proves that . . ." I start to pace again. "We talked about Frank's death. Mentioned where he's buried."

"Is that evidence?"

"Maybe not, but they'll dig him up. It'll piece together. They'll come here. Find traces."

"So that path leads to us going to jail, no matter what?"

"Yes."

Rosie hums in thought. "What if we move the body?"

"It's below concrete now, foundation rods . . . It's not possible. Whatever we do next . . . I just don't know. We need . . . I just need more time."

"Then . . ." Rosie sighs, "do what Edward says."

I look back, standing opposite her, the coffee table between us. The flash drive dead center.

"Listen, you said it yourself, the case is rock solid," she adds. "It's inevitable that he's going down eventually. It doesn't need to be on Thursday."

"That's the problem with blackmail, it probably won't end there. I don't like the idea of being his pawn."

We share a moment of silence.

"It's kind of funny in a way," she says.

"I don't think *funny* is quite the right word."

"I just mean . . . of all the people on earth who could know what we did . . ."

"Yeah. It is a predicament."

"As long as we stay strong." Rosie stands, walks around the table. She takes both my hands. "As long as we stay together. Hey," she says, "your hands . . . they're not shaking."

I look down at them, Rosie's fingers resting on my palms. "They stopped when I found the bug."

"Why?"

"Maybe because . . . well, there's no more doubt. If the worst thing imaginable actually happens, I guess there's nothing left to worry about."

"James," she says. "Look at me. I'm here. We will get through this. Lie down. Lie down with me, on the floor."

We both sink to our knees, then lie flat on our backs on the rug, looking up at the ceiling. She nestles into my shoulder. "See," she whispers. "Things look different from down here. I have a secret. I can see the future."

"What does it look like?"

"There's going to be children, dogs." She lifts her hand and paints this in the air above us. "By the ocean. A big house. I'll own a bakery. You'll be the sheriff. Keep the small neighborhood in check."

"How small?" I ask, rolling my head to look at her. "Treaston small?"

"Yeah, but nice."

I smile.

"There's firefly lights in mason jars draped around the big tree in the yard," she says. "And late at night, we're on the porch, on our swinging bench, under a blanket—the kids are all fast asleep. And that's the best time. When we're together. Just me and you."

It's past 10 p.m. now and I'm driving to the office, through the city. It's dark—neon signs and flashing eyes of lost souls shuffling down the sidewalk. They're red in the lights of traffic ahead of me and white in the light of cars behind. Waiting at crossroads, I see a young kid with his hood up over his head. He's sitting on a bike on the corner.

Music blares from a shiny pickup truck that pulls up alongside him—it thumps louder as its window comes down. The passenger whispers something to the kid. And the kid scratches his ear, clearly holding up three fingers.

The black pickup truck glistens with gleaming stripes of red, white, and blue from the store across the street. These colors move and morph as the truck pulls away around the corner and, closer to me, stops again.

A woman emerges from the shadow of a nearby alleyway and approaches the window. The passenger shakes her hand. *That was the money*, I think. Then she reaches into her back pocket. And she passes over three bags of powder.

All this happens before my light turns green and I drive away.

Two miles later I'm turning into the parking lot at work. I get out and stroll across the asphalt.

My keys rattle as I shoulder open the sticky office door, like I would on any other night. Like I might have forgotten some paperwork.

Inside I go through the hallway, leaving the lights off.

Place is empty. Quiet. This is good.

I move quickly through the doorway and to my desk, sit down, reach inside my pocket, and—

I pause, looking instead across the room. Foster's laptop comes gently into focus. Fast now, I stand, push my chair back, and swoop to it, tilt the lid and turn it on.

On my feet, I lean on his desk and wait for it to boot up.

Username. I type "Foster_Gray." A few weeks ago, he trusted me with his password when he needed me to forward him a file. It's not particularly cunning. His first daughter's name and a single obligatory digit, "Belle1." As I assumed, he hasn't changed it.

So I hit enter and I'm in.

Staring for a long while at the screen, the drive in my fingers, resting against the USB slot. My chest feels tight—maybe it's doubt clawing at the inside of my ribs.

But there is no time, no energy, no way to get off this ride now.

So I close my eyes, take a breath, and . . . *click*. I've done it.

A black box appears, lines of code flicker and slide up the screen. They stop. Three dots flash. And some more code.

It says something about the system. I see the word *Administrator* appear—wants to make changes to the "Shipping.Trafficmap01 data." Something about protocol. Execute. White text. Numbers. An error. It solves itself. Code. Code. Another box appears.

"Installing," it says. "Do not remove storage device."

Then a small bar arrives on the screen. It begins filling with blue. One percent. Two. Three. I check my watch. Four. Five.

At sixty percent, I grab the drive and *so* nearly pull it out. The fear. It comes hard and sudden. But it can't win. My hand is steady. I know what's going to happen.

I leave it in, stand, stare, and watch it climb higher and higher.

Sixty-eight percent. Come on.

Seventy percent.

Seventy-nine. Eighty.

My heart.

As the installation bar creeps into the mid-nineties, I have to look away. I shield my eyes as though from the sun.

And in the blue gloom of the lightless office, I see Foster's skeleton ski mask on his desk. The one he wears beneath his motorcycle helmet. The face he scared me with just hours ago.

In my peripheral vision, a new window has appeared on the laptop screen.

And I know it's done.

But I can't take my eyes away from the black material.

It reminds me of something. Maybe a dream I had?

That skull. I've definitely seen it before.

Chapter Nine

It was a dream about death. The Treaston Mills Choir singing at Matthew's funeral, led by a tall woman with a powerful voice, filled with light, hope, and the kind of sadness that echoes beyond language. I do not know the song—it's not in English. But it makes me cry. I look to my left, down the church bench, and see that I'm not alone. Matthew's colleagues, suited men in black, with big beards and thick fingers—every eye forward, red, and glassy. Neck tattoos and deep creased foreheads, ten heavyset foundry workers, all brought to tears.

To my right, Rosie gives me a sighing smile and squeezes my hand. She swallows, keeps her chin high as if to stop the tears from falling.

The choir's tribute seems impossibly loud against the gray church stones, in the stained-glass colors beaming in behind them. So bright and beautiful, like the light you see and the sounds you hear as you glide up to heaven in the arms of angels. I'm adding poetry to this memory. I must be. Is every single person really crying?

The pastor stands high at the wooden lectern, wearing his white frock and superior tone with pride. Couple of thuds and rustles as he bends his microphone down to his mouth. He addresses the thirty or so guests. Gives us all a potted history of Matthew's life, his troubles mentioned only in subtext—euphemisms everyone will understand, kept vague in case God really is listening. As though he doesn't already know about our catalog of sins.

"Matthew was a longstanding member of the Treaston Choir," the pastor says. "And in recent years, while he did not take part as often, he remarked that the unity of singing alongside his fellow choristers brought him a unique connection and peace.

"The circumstances of his passing are especially tragic. But as I look around this room, and as I hear the love," he turns to the choir, "I feel reassured that even at our lowest moments, even when we feel alone, there is always someone who cares. In Matthew's case, I can see that he will be missed." The pastor looks at Rosie, then at me. "To say goodbye to someone well before their time is difficult for any family. But Matthew's struggles in this world will only make his rest seem all the more peaceful. And I do pray that there is some comfort in knowing where he is. He will wait. He will wait in a glorious place that gives him everything he could not find here."

The sermon ends with more singing from the choir—they sing and sing as we file out through the big oak doors. And in the churchyard, in the sun, Rosie and I stand at the foot of Matthew's grave. The grass is short, golf green, and flowers have been laid around the brand-new headstone.

I spent almost all of the service repeating his suicide note in my mind. I can remember snippets clearly—but I've yet to learn the whole thing by heart.

"You'll look around when you mourn me and you'll feel a unique regret," Matthew wrote. *"You might think, if only I knew how much people cared, how much I was loved, maybe I'd have made different choices. That's the thing you need to understand. I know exactly how much I'm loved. And it doesn't change anything.*

"So do not entertain remorse. Commit to your life. Never, ever feel regret. Never feel that you could have done something differently. You

did everything you could. There's only one person who's at fault here. And it's me."

But I stand there in the afternoon sun, watching people dressed in black, people I don't even know, walk past and offer condolences, and I feel only one thing.

I committed myself to making Matthew better with every ounce of effort I had. And I wish, *I wish* it could have been enough. If I could turn back time, I'd do *everything* different. Despite what he told me in his letter, I'm the very embodiment of regret.

The pastor approaches. He steps close, standing in front of a tall, granite angel—her stone wings half-crumbled, her chest and arms green and white with moss and lichen.

The choir's still singing inside, their haunting voices pouring out of the open door. High-pitched, swaying, sweeping sounds that seem to rock the trees with the wind.

"Your brother's in God's embrace now," the pastor gently whispers, his hands clasped together at his waist.

But Rosie frowns, as though genuinely confused. "No," she says, "he isn't." And she points to the fresh earth at our feet. "He's in there."

◆ ◆ ◆

It's like an alarm in my mind. But instead of the sudden synthesized drums from my cell phone or the clattering drone of a bell, I'm drawn awake by a feeling.

I'm aware of nothing besides regret.

Steadily, though, other things begin to appear in this new universe of mine.

There's breathing. A creaking sound. Maybe it's Matthew. He's shivering again. When he was getting clean, he did that. I'd lie, half-awake, listening to him shudder his way through the cold hell—calming down long enough to puke or cry or a desperate combination of the two. But he died five years ago, so it can't be him. I think about Matthew a lot.

There's a rhythm to the breathing. And I sense that the creaking is a floorboard.

Finally I open my eyes and look across the rug—past the table leg. The living room. It's sideways. I'm lying down.

The breathing almost sounds like counting. I turn my head. It's Rosie.

She's wearing her yoga pants and a tight fluorescent-pink gym top. I see her doing squats in the corner, next to the window—the flowers I got her are in full bloom now. Still on my front, head slack, it looks like she's standing on the wall, pushing the whole room away with her legs, like everything's moving apart from her. Whole world's upside down, a shroud of petals and green leaves bursting up from a glowing hole in the floor.

Last night I got back from the office and drank half a bottle of . . . something. Dry mouth, pounding headache. Bourbon, maybe. Now, I'm fully dressed on the couch, one numb arm folded under my chest, the other hanging straight down, my limp hand like a dead spider on the rug.

And in this fleeting, creaking, breathing moment, maybe for less than half a second, I feel peaceful.

But then I'm struck by an overwhelming nausea. Like sudden withdrawals from a drug that's kept me blind. Now I can see everything all at once.

I sit up fast, the room shifting back upright, but it keeps going—tilting the other way.

Pressing a fist to my lips, I take a breath and try to hold it all still.

"Morning," Rosie says, at the top of her last squat, puffing out some air.

"Yep."

Her face is slightly red. "I tried to wake you up last night, but you were gone."

That was the first time I'd slept since Thursday, I think. No surprise it was a deep one.

"Feel better?" she asks.

I groan, because no. I feel much, much worse.

All these colors, lights, sounds, and feelings, but it's still there. The regret.

"I'm powering through," she says, wiping her forehead with her wrist. "Felt a bit strange this morning. Queasy . . . maybe something I ate?"

"Yeah . . . or, I don't know, maybe because of . . ." I spread my arms. "Last few days have not exactly been serene."

"Hmm, true."

Rosie picks up her phone, leaves the room, and gets ready for work.

I'm still on the couch when she kisses me goodbye.

Deciding I can't face it, I call in sick. Then, still dressed in yesterday's clothes, I pace the whole house. I almost start crying when I stop at our bookshelves, pick up a framed photo of us on our wedding day. Rosie looks incredible. Nell and Matthew—our only two witnesses—standing either side of us. I put it down and sigh.

In this new clarity, I know I have to undo it.

Plugging that USB drive in, it was a moment of madness. Brought on by panic and insomnia.

I have to tell them the ship will arrive earlier, at a different dock. If they ask why . . . I'll . . . I'll just tell Nell to trust me. Even if we split the forces. Even if what I did last night comes to light, I'm not playing his game. We're seizing that container. Edward Lang is going to prison.

That is the only fact I know in my heart about the future. Whatever happens after Thursday, however Edward reacts to his arrest, well, I'll cross that bridge when I come to it. I am not corrupt. I am not a criminal. This is *not* who I am.

◆ ◆ ◆

Over the next eight hours I almost call Nell more than fifty times. I just need to find the right words.

It's Wednesday evening now and I'm in the kitchen. I've been biting my fingernails red raw—each one stings as I rinse marinara sauce off our nicest plates.

Rosie arrives at my side and begins drying the dishes. I hold back my tears as she smiles. The path I've chosen might mean losing her forever. It hurts me so much to think that I'm risking our future. It's the perfect nightmare. But it's time to wake up.

She's telling me about the detective who came to her office today—asking about Frank.

"All the questions you said he'd ask. It was like a script," she says.

She looks at me in our dark reflections—both our faces gloomy in the black window ahead. The backyard invisible through the glare of our kitchen lights.

"You sure he said Ray?"

"Detective Cohen. Gray hair. Tall."

"Yeah, that's him."

Rosie crouches down to put some bowls in the cupboard near my knee.

"How long were they speaking to Leanne?" I ask.

"Longer than anyone else." She stands.

"What did she say?"

"I don't know, I wasn't in the room."

I stare at the two of us in the glass. Our black faces—reflections standing outside looking back in. "It's going to be OK," I say.

"Who are you talking to?"

I realize I'm looking into my own eyes.

There's a *knock-knock* at the front door. We both freeze, then slowly turn.

"Who the fuck is that?" I whisper, holding a dripping sponge.

Rosie drops the dishcloth and heads across the tiles, through the doorway, and down the corridor. I wash my hands, dry them, then I wait, standing at the breakfast bar, peering through the internal window. She opens the front door, and I see a male figure on the step. I lean sideways to make him out in the porch light.

Realizing it's Detective Ray Cohen, I close my eyes and compose myself. Maintain the lie, play the charade until it stops working. No sense in coming clean if we don't need to.

It's going to be OK.

He walks toward me, appreciating the decor with polite admiration. "Lovely," he says, standing in the doorway. He steps back to take in the wall. "So all this," he waves a hand into the kitchen, "is new?"

"Yep," Rosie says. "Used to end here." She pats the bricks. "They were halfway through the renovation when we bought it. We left this door so the new kitchen could be finished. But when it was, we decided we quite liked the wall."

"An outside window on the inside." He nods. "Well, I think it's charming."

Then he looks at me.

"Detective Cohen, this is my husband, James." Rosie guides him into the kitchen. "He's with the DEA."

Lifting a finger, he frowns, as though he's remembering something. "You work with Nell Walker, over near the tracks?"

"That's the one."

"How's it going? We hear rumors at the station about the taskforce."

"We're getting there."

Rosie pulls a stool out for him. He sits to my left at the breakfast bar. And she perches directly opposite me. The low metal lampshades hanging from the ceiling between us make three big, round patches of light.

"Pleased to hear that. I've said for years that the DEA needs to get a firm grip on this city." He takes a notepad and pen from his jacket pocket, places them on the countertop. "These dealers are brazen. Half the time they're not even subtle."

"Oh, yeah," I say, "they're ballsy all right."

"There was a girl." He clicks his pen, opens the pad. "I shit you not, couple of weeks back, I'm pulled up on the street and she asks me if I wanted a bag. I was driving a squad car."

I laugh knowingly.

"How much did you buy?" Rosie asks.

Detective Cohen shows teeth when he smiles. "I got five, it was the weekend."

The joke lingers almost flirtatiously between them. This is good.

"Do you want a drink or anything?" I ask.

"Nah, it's OK, I won't be here long. Just wanted to double-check a few things about Friday."

"I'll leave you to it," I say, tapping the breakfast bar and stepping away.

"Ah." He raises his hand slightly. "No, it's . . . it's fine. I understand you were here too? Maybe you can shed some light?"

I nod and lower myself onto a stool.

"So Frank was dropping off some files?"

"Yeah," Rosie says. "That's right."

"And his assistant said he was acting . . ." Detective Cohen refers to his notes. "Unusual?"

Something lost in translation, but Rosie's call seems to have landed. All these lies, all these seeds sprouting consequences, blocking paths, spreading doubt.

"Yes," she says. "A bit, I don't know. Stressed, maybe? Like there was something on his mind."

"Any clue what that might have been?" He flips his hand over and shrugs. "Work related or . . . ?"

"No, no." She shakes her head. "When it's work related, he lets us know. He's a firm boss."

Rosie's use of the present tense sounds natural here. She waits, allowing Detective Cohen to mention it first.

"Trouble at home?" he suggests.

And she nods. "It's hard to say, but I know he'd had issues with his wife. She can be"—Rosie inhales through her teeth—"not sure of the best word . . . A bit tightly wound?"

Detective Cohen smiles again. "Oh, yeah. I can confirm that. Mostly that's the reason I'm here."

"How so?" she asks.

"Well, Mrs. McBride's kicking up a fair old fuss because we haven't declared him *officially* missing."

"Why not?" I say.

"Thing is, and keep this under your hat," he looks from me to Rosie and back, "Frank had been using dating apps. And he bought two railroad tickets on Saturday. So . . ." Another shrug.

We're getting an open book—Detective Cohen is speaking to me like a colleague.

"Huh." Rosie frowns. "Maybe . . . I hate to say it, but maybe he left her?"

"To be honest with you, ma'am, that's uh, yeah, that's where my money is." He tilts his head, wincing slightly—an awkward pill for Mrs. McBride to swallow. "Parked his car down by the old fairground. We're thinking he traveled on foot from there—possibly met someone. Does he strike you as the adulterous type?"

Rosie pauses expertly, then simply says, "Yes."

"Anything unusual about the car?" I ask.

"Nothing. Though I am sad to report he left the cakes behind."

"Last time I give him a gift," Rosie says.

"Hmm. Fact is Frank switched his phone off," he adds. "Probably ditched it. Now, only reason he'd do that is if he didn't want to be found. All the tells of a runaway. Happens more often than you might think. But try explaining that to his wife."

"What does she think's happened?" I ask.

"She's adamant something *real* bad. And maybe she's right, maybe he has been murdered."

Rosie hums again, as though this is the first time she's considered this.

"But if that's the case," he adds. "I tell you, the killer's *pretty* smart."

Her eyes flit sideways and meet mine. I manage to ignore her.

"So he came by, you gave him some cupcakes, then he left?"

"That's basically it, yeah," she says.

"You bake professionally? As well as working in admin at Limehouse?"

"It's a hobby, but I make a few extra bucks on the side."

"My door's always open for bribes. Anything chocolate will sweeten me up just fine."

"I'll remember that," Rosie says softly.

"What did you guys do for the rest of the evening?" He has his pen ready to take notes.

"Nothing." Rosie glances briefly at me. Delivering her lines perfectly.

"Yep, no," I add, keeping our alibi as clean as possible. "Just watched some TV. Had an early night."

This can be verified by checking our phones, both of which were here all evening.

Detective Cohen runs through another ten minutes of general questions—none too invasive. All formal. He's ticking boxes.

"OK," he says, coming to a conclusion. He jots some final words down, then closes his notepad and clambers off the stool.

He's literally standing where Frank's corpse bled empty—I can't help but imagine a chalk outline around his shoes. He's in the middle of the torso.

"Oh, hang on." Rosie leaps to her feet.

She leans in and touches near his neck—he hesitates as she plucks something from his collar.

"Aw, shit, that's embarrassing," Detective Cohen says, now holding the tag from his brand-new shirt. "I've just come from a press conference. Needed to look my best. Mrs. McBride knows a producer at Station 6—they're making a song and dance about Frank's disappearance." He buttons up his jacket. "Tune in. I'm on at 9 p.m.."

We say our farewells, and he leaves the kitchen. Rosie escorts him to the door, closing it behind. She doesn't say a word as she returns, looks at me, and nods.

I go to the downstairs bathroom to catch my breath. The tides of panic are turning.

◆ ◆ ◆

By the time 9 p.m. arrives I'm shaking again. Sweating. But I have to. I have to watch the news. I have to see what they're saying.

Rosie's gone for a bath, so I sit alone on the couch and point the remote at the TV.

It's all so clear when I see Frank's wife on the screen. A broken woman, clutching a tissue. She's crying as she looks into the lens and begs anyone, *anyone* who knows anything to come forward. Please.

Lauren McBride is talking to me. Through red eyes, down wires, she's asking me to end her suffering. It hurts so much, she says. She can't live with not knowing.

I hit pause and sit for what feels like a lifetime.

A tear rolls down my cheek. This is the end. Now that I know for sure what I'm about to do, I play out the worst-case scenario in my mind.

We're both going to prison. Me and Rosie. But maybe we can soften the blow. She was grieving the death of her brother—that's why she snapped. Frank was threatening. Rosie Casper was driven to kill by a cruel boss who bullied her relentlessly—that sounds like a story that might fly. We'll get a good lawyer to sell it. Shave some years off her sentence. As for me, I'm ready to face the music.

What I did on Foster's laptop . . . I'm not going to muddy the water. I'll just confess. God's honest truth. It was a fleeting, desperate dance with insanity. Hand on heart, I regret it with every part of my soul. My clean record says as much.

This is me undoing it all. Putting it right. Tomorrow morning, when Edward Lang's shipment arrives, we *will* seize it.

"James," Rosie shouts from the kitchen. Muffled. Sounds like she's in the downstairs bathroom now. I didn't even notice her walk past. "Come here."

But I can't. I'm busy.

So I pick up my phone from the coffee table, still face to face with the newly widowed Mrs. McBride, paused on the glowing TV.

I scroll down to Nell and thumb the call icon.

"Hey, what's up?" she says.

"Listen to me." I sniff. "I just want you to . . . I want you to know that . . . Just, listen. Tomorrow. The container."

"What about it?"

"The ship is coming in . . ." I feel it falling apart, tumbling down like a house of cards, my whole life, my whole future disappearing in the words I am about to say. I'm pressing that red button. I'm going nuclear—a brand-new sun lights up the sky.

"Yeah?"

"The log says it's arriving at the south dock."

"That's right—9 a.m.."

I take a long breath and sigh. Here we go. "Nell . . . I have something to tell you."

There's a tapping sound to my left. I turn.

And I see Rosie. She's crying too. Wearing her bathrobe, she's standing there, crying at our waving window. One hand clamped over her mouth. And in her other hand, she's holding something. A plastic object—straight and white.

She nods at me. Tears rolling down her cheeks—just like mine.

Then I realize what she's holding up. And I realize why she's nodding.

"What is it?" Nell says in my ear.

"I . . . I thought there was another way," I hear myself whisper. "But I was wrong."

"Another way? What are you talking about? What do you want to tell me? James?"

"It's Rosie." Inevitable resignation in my voice. There she is, standing at the window. I just stare at her and she just stares right back, the positive test against the glass. "She's . . . she's pregnant."

PART TWO—LIBERTY

Chapter Ten

We wait on the asphalt at the cargo port—dawn already shaping up to be a warm day. Behind Nell, I see the row of tall container cranes stretching off hundreds of yards down the shoreline. Straddle carriers beeping in the distance. Gulls squawking somewhere beyond the metal. The expansive flat of concrete, the hissing machines all in perfect lines. Reminds me of an airport. Low morning sun makes sheets of summer gold and mirror glass on the ground—long puddles shine white.

"This must be him," Nell says as a man wearing a hard hat and a high-vis jacket strides toward us.

"Good morning." He waves. When he arrives, we both shake his hand.

"Special agent Nell Walker," she says. Nell never gives her full rank, unless she's talking to fellow law enforcement.

"James Casper," I add.

"You're . . ." she begins.

"Stephen Evans, I'm head of logistics. I can show you what's what. Follow me, some of your friends are already here."

We step along a yellow paint grid on the ground, and Stephen's pointing out a large ship docked nearby. It's huge—red, white, brown, blue containers stacked high into the sky above—like a windowless apartment block made of steel. He's telling us some trivia about it. Seems it's got a story.

Then we pass under the cranes—most sit dormant, though a couple off toward the sunrise are slowly swinging cargo onto a neat stack. They cut long shadows, the sun still touching the ocean behind. We walk toward this seemingly endless horizon that glints on the flat water, casting every shape between us either orange or black. A steady stream of darkened trucks carries containers away like bees taking nectar.

On our left, a couple of warehouses. As we approach one, I see "4" stamped above the tall shutter door.

"They've set you up in here," Stephen says. He walks to the side access door and starts thumbing a code into the keypad. "Do you guys need to see our arrivals? We can get some tablets down from the office."

"It's OK," Nell says. "We'll stick to our tracking map if it's all the same."

He pauses at this—wondering why that might be, realizing, then taking slight offense all in the space of a second. The convenient irony of trusting our own software over his is not lost on me.

"Suit yourself," Stephen says.

We go into the warehouse. The cool air smells like cardboard and rubber. A faint hint of gas—oil, some other fuels maybe.

They've set up desks with laptops and radios. A few faces I recognize. Rob Sanders is sitting on a chair in the corner, dressed in a smart suit. The place looks like a movie set. The amount of equipment surprises even me.

"Can we open up these doors?" Nell asks. "They're nearly here."

Stephen obliges, walking to the wall and pressing a button on a hang-down control terminal. The huge gray rolling doors shudder and slide up, letting the morning light flood the warehouse.

"Here they come," she adds, stepping back outside.

Following her, I see a convoy driving down the port strip toward us, windshields catching the sun. Silhouetted seagulls make way for the vehicles, erupting into the sky and threading out over the water's glare. Two special response trucks and three, no, wait, four black SUVs shimmering like a mirage in the hazy air.

Stephen looks at me and Nell with disbelief. "That seems like quite a lot of men."

"Chopper's on its way too," she says.

"What exactly are you expecting to happen?" he asks, slightly concerned now.

I step to her side and say quietly, "I have to agree. Why so many?"

"Probably overkill," Nell explains. "But we can't know which members of the crew, if any, are part of the operation. Better to be prepared. Desperate people do desperate things."

I turn and head back inside as the convoy rounds the warehouse and parks behind, out of sight.

The whole team is here now. Half the agents I don't even know. Word gets around though—and you can feel the excitement already. Anything that costs this much, involves a force this large—it's got to be worth seeing, right? Records will be broken. Headlines will be made.

A few of the special response guys are preparing weapons in the corner. One of them sits on the back of their big black armored truck and laces up his boots. Then he stands, adjusts a buckle on his vest, bounces it higher, and puts his helmet on. He takes a couple of magazines from a box, slaps one into his Rock River LAR-15 carbine and slides another into his pocket.

I'm on autopilot for the next couple of hours—answering questions, helping with the prep work. But mostly I'm an extra in this montage of dark figures checking sights, holstering side arms, adjusting rifle scopes, clicking everything into place.

These men look like soldiers. And me, Nell, Rob Sanders—we're the well-dressed generals, coordinating everything from the safety of our desks.

Nell's explaining the log to Sanders. "Here it is," she says. "The *Hamburg*. Container is still on board, we had visuals confirmed just last night. It's been on course ever since. And we've got the live feed from inside, here, see. Still no activity."

He nods, reassured, though his arms stay folded—he's already taken off his blazer and loosened his tie.

The special response teams disperse, all taking their positions at various locations around the port's dock.

"Five minutes and we'll see her," Nell announces, her voice charged. The anticipation is infectious. All our hard work over the past few years—it's all been leading to this.

Three of the men in the first team have headcams so we can watch it all unfold from here. Radios are crackling—countless voices exchanging details, times, confirming what they can see. There are men on the roof. I picture black shapes, their twinkling scopes flaring like Christmas stars.

Out on the water, there's a fishing boat with more agents on board. And closer, one of the crane operators, wearing blue overalls, checks in on his radio. He confirms visuals on the ship.

Passing my gaze across the row of monitors on the long desks in front of me, I see it too.

Deep, loud blasts from the horn—unseen metal *clonks* echoing as it approaches. The port's own security cameras show the ship arriving. Turning like a creature from the deep, slow and heavy, it lines up with the gray dock wall.

Nell's eyes sweeping left to right—CCTV on the top of the warehouse, the headcam from one of the snipers, the chopper high enough to seem silent. It films the port from directly above—the sprawling concrete and machines and shapes, monochrome in the zoomed footage, like drone shots from war.

"Got eyes on the ramp," the radio says. "Two men."

"Hold off until it hits the concrete," someone replies.

"Roger that."

The special response teams are orchestrating all this themselves—we've told them what they need to do, but how? That's their business. Our job now is to stand back and watch them work their magic.

There's some interference. "—ffst about—is that? Psss—cshh, over."

"Say again?"

"—an a—*Starliner* is—fee—operators, confirm?"

"He's right—*Starliner*."

"Unit—sscrhh—say again?"

"Ramp's coming down now."

"OK, here we go. Stand by . . ." The ship's wide metal ramp tilts, tilts, opening up like a whale's mouth. We all wait until, slowly, slowly, it touches the ground. "Move."

A conga line of black helmets, an arm's length apart, snakes out from the side of the warehouse—the chopper's camera pans slightly, zooms out, back in, and follows them across the gray expanse, beneath a crane, toward the ship.

Nell and Foster to my left, fixated on the screens, Rob Sanders on my right, leaning in, squinting. No one says anything. We just watch.

Shaky footage from the headcam—the first man up the ramp. We get a nice view down his sights as he lifts his rifle. Looks just like a video game. The two guys on the gangway, confused, terrified as they're ordered to get "down, get down on the ground."

They comply, hands up, panicked eyes. Gloved fingers pointing them lower. "Face down."

“OK, move up through the stairwell on your left,” the radio says. “Get to the top deck . . . container is on the portside, about sixty feet from your current location.”

“Thought it was a bigger ship,” Nell whispers, looking between the screens. The first inkling of doubt on the edge of her flattening voice.

Someone with ear defenders is checking a clipboard as the team turns a corner and orders him to hit the deck. But he doesn’t move.

“I said down,” the voice roars, the camera juddering, then perfectly still—we’re looking down the iron sights of a black carbine rifle. “*Down on the fucking ground.*” We’re gliding toward him, smooth and always aiming.

“Uh, yeah . . . I don’t think he can hear you . . .” the radio says.

The entirely oblivious man is still facing away, looking down at his paperwork.

On another screen, another headcam, he turns as a pair of gloved hands gripping a yellow Taser make the decision for him. He’s shaking, rigid and shocked as the rest of them step past and turn again, down a long line of containers. Fast. Fast now.

“Not too many. Should be obvious.”

They arrive at the slot and pause. “This it?” someone asks.

“Uh . . . Four . . . Four . . . uh, yeah. Psssh—rawl. Over.”

“Copy that.”

They bunch up at the side, then fan out. One of them sweeps his strapped rifle to his back, then cuts the tag and, shoulder against the steel, lifts the long bolt lock.

They’re all around the front of the container—guns up in a semicircle, like a firing squad—a bird’s-eye view from the chopper as the doors spread open.

I look back to the headcam screen.

It’s dark inside. Pitch black.

And then, *click*, *click*, flashlights shine and show us the contents.

The container's full of horses—huge plastic horses. A stack of twisted, spiraling metal poles at the back.

"We got ourselves some fairground shit down here."

Rob Sanders is glaring.

"That's . . ." Nell's beginning to panic. She snatches up a radio. "What's the serial number on the side of that?"

A camera leans down and shows us. Nell tilts her head to read from the screen.

She looks at me. Then at the hidden camera feed in the actual Leyland & Lang container. It's still closed, sealed.

"Have they moved it?" she whispers, then lifts the radio to her mouth again. "What's the next one? We're looking for a white label—Leyland & Lang on the side."

Stephen's shaking his head, checking the tablet in his hand. "Ain't no L&L containers on there," he says.

There are a few seconds of confusion—overlapping questions on the radio. Someone asks if they get to keep a carousel horse.

Sanders is looking at Nell, waiting for an answer.

"It's . . ." She appeals to Stephen for an explanation. "This . . . can you search the container serial . . . the registration numbers?"

"For which vessel?" he says.

An awkward pause. A lingering silence. I break it by whispering something I've known all morning. A fact that everyone must have wondered about by now. "It's the wrong ship."

"Just . . . just search, on the *Hamburg* for . . ." Nell looks at our marine traffic data, checking the container's ID.

"That is not the *Hamburg*," Stephen says, astonished.

"Yes, it is," Nell snaps, as though enough conviction might change the truth. "Look at the map." She jabs her finger into the laptop monitor—at our very own detailed log. "It says it, right there."

"Uh, control, we'd like some orders," the radio crackles.

Stephen seems to enjoy the ceremony of drawing her attention to a screen across the desk. Crane CCTV shows a perfect view of the ship's bow.

"Sure," he agrees. "But it says *Starliner* on the side." Then he lifts his tablet—the one we didn't need to check. The one we didn't trust. "*Hamburg* arrived two hours and fifty-seven minutes ago. At the north dock. Your container is gone."

"Seems like we might have missed the boat on this one," someone on the radio says. There's a quiet ripple of electronic laughter.

"We gonna shoot these creepy horses or what?"

"All units stand down."

The next five minutes pass me by in silence. I can tell people are shouting. Pointing. Arguing. But who can they blame? The technology? The chaos? The inexplicable disparity between our screen and reality?

Nell grabs a desk and tries to flip it, but all the wires get caught, so she just slams it against the wall. And then she storms off behind me, turns, and wraps both hands around the back of her head.

Rob Sanders is rolling his eyes at a couple of agents from his office—as though the skepticism he'd spent years batting away had all been justified. The days of him defending Nell and her outlandish theories have come to an end.

I look over at her. She's squatted on the ground now, her eyes in her palms. Part of me wishes there was a way to offer comfort. But I know nothing I can say would change how she feels. Even honesty would only hurt her more.

As people begin to clean up—like the saddest part of a good party—the atmosphere in the warehouse simmers. Dull disappointment now, anger and accusations proven to be little more than cathartic foreplay for the very real consequences taking shape in senior minds. Fuck-ups like this do not go unpunished.

Foster is the only other person still sitting down at the row of desks, six empty chairs away. We make eye contact, and he gives me half a shrug—a shit-happens wave of his hand.

I nod in silent agreement, then look away.

"Hey," he says. And I turn back. "Congratulations."

I show absolutely nothing on my face. I must look shell-shocked, blinking, waiting. What the fuck is he talking about? Does he know what I did?

"You'll make a good father," he adds.

My relief becomes a gentle tilt of my head—an unspoken thank you.

And then I just sit for a while, glancing around the room.

Look at these people—fifty or more—flying above, pitched on the roof, armed to the teeth. Strong men and women, all of them capable of killing with the softest of squeezes. All of them trained for moments like this. Capable. Adaptable. Intelligent. Masters of their trade. They've all just been rendered totally helpless by the absolute, uncompromising nature of expired time. And none of them has the slightest idea why.

No one here has any power. No one besides me. Matthew was right. I did everything I could. I should commit. Regret makes no sense.

Something strange is happening. All the anxiety that comes from doubt is gone. I don't feel guilty or scared. No. Honestly, I feel liberated. Unburdened by inconveniences like truth or choice. I feel free.

Chapter Eleven

The ten-year-old boy, alone in the world, rises from a sleepless night. He gets dressed, sits on the floor in front of loud cartoons on a small TV and eats a bowl of colorful cereal. And then he goes back upstairs, straight to the desk in his bedroom. He writes a letter in his very best joined-up handwriting.

It takes me a long time to find the right words, and by 11 a.m. I have a trash can full of scrunched-up attempts. But eventually I finish a final draft and sign it carefully. I lay the pen flat, fold the paper, slide it into an envelope, lick and press it down as neatly as I can.

Then I go downstairs and lace up my shoes.

Outside I head across the street with serious purpose to my step. I push open David and Mary's gate and walk up the path with the letter in my pocket. On the front step, I lean down and, without a moment's hesitation, slide it under their door. *This is better than leaving it in the mailbox*, I think. I want it to be personal. It needs to get to their hearts.

I hear a sound behind the house, so I climb down off the porch and head to the backyard.

Matthew is on the swing, standing up, yanking the ropes and thrusting himself higher and higher.

Rosie is standing to the side, leaning against the frame, her arms folded. She looks unimpressed.

"You're going to die," she says, glancing at her fingernails.

"James, James, check this out," he yells at the top of the arc. Then he zips back again, his head and torso rising well above the bar.

There, at the peak, he looks weightless—his clothes filling with air.

And then he sweeps down so fast and up and when he's at the highest point, he leaps off the swing and does a wild, flailing flip, somersaulting and falling and somehow landing on his feet—but then crumpling to the ground.

Miraculously uninjured, he laughs. "I'm getting pretty good," he says, clambering upright. "I'm gonna add a twist by the end of the day."

"There's a reason you've been told not to do this." Rosie shakes her head.

"Mary said I shouldn't do flips off the roof—she never said nothing about the swing."

Part of me wishes Rosie wasn't here. I want to tell Matthew about Aunt Beatrice and my plan in private. But then I need to discuss it before Mary or David read the letter. I scratch my arm and ask if he wants to go get some ice cream or something.

"Two more tries and then we'll go," he says, climbing back onto the swing.

He starts slow, getting a good rhythm. "Wait," I say, stepping in front.

Matthew lowers himself to a sitting position and drags his heels in the dirt—the swing comes to a stop. He turns and shifts side to side while I begin to explain.

Although Rosie listens, she can tell this is more a conversation between me and her brother. She doesn't speak at all.

"So Bea's just leaving?" Matthew asks. "Forever?"

"Yeah."

"But why?"

"It's for work."

"Doesn't she do insurance or something?" Matthew draws lines with his toes, his shoes scraping across the dry mud and dust in the swing's shallow trench.

"Medical insurance," I say.

"Why can't she do that here? On the phone?"

"I don't know." I shrug. "But she's made up her mind."

"And you have to go to some Oliver Twist school? Asking for more porridge and picking pockets?"

"I hope not."

"Seems messed up," Matthew says. "After all these years of taking care of you, suddenly she's just decided she's had enough?" Then he turns to his big sister. "What do you think?"

And Rosie looks slowly from him to me. She's heard the whole story and she's had time to process all the details. "I think Beatrice is a *fucking cunt*," she says.

Our eyes are wide at this—of the many, many words banned in their household, that is surely the worst. The anger in her voice would be scary if she wasn't on my side.

"But I have an idea," I whisper. "I thought . . . David and Mary . . . well, they adopted you guys. So I was wondering if, well . . ."

"They could adopt you?" Matthew says, a smile spreading. "That'd be awesome."

Rosie winces. "I don't think you'd enjoy it here. You don't know what she's like."

"Mary's not that bad," Matthew says.

"Not to you," Rosie snaps. "You're a good little church boy."

"Maybe if you stopped cussing and slamming doors?"

"She's a psycho."

"She seems OK to me?" I say.

"Annie Wilkes *seemed* OK." Rosie draws a cuckoo circle at the side of her head.

"Who's that?" Matthew asks.

"The crazy bitch from *Misery*."

And Matthew laughs. "Yeah, she is a bit like her. She likes books too."

The truth is, I am scared of Mary—I can see that she's strict and always talking about Jesus and the Bible. That's why I call her ma'am and try to be polite whenever I visit.

I hope David reads the letter first. He's gentle. Kind.

"So if you don't mind lying in bed with broken legs then—" Rosie stops.

"I already know what that's like," I say.

It's been two years since I fell from the tree, but I still wear jeans to cover the scars on my knees. Even now there are long white lines, with red around the edges, like a few bits of string are buried under my skin.

We'd stayed up late to watch *Misery* together a while back, despite being told we were too young. Matthew and Rosie found the violence and cruelty funny. But they've never broken any bones. I didn't enjoy the movie at all. I don't like remembering all that time in the hospital—all the screws and bolts they put in my legs.

"Well, I think it's a great idea," Matthew says. "Though I bet Beatrice won't even let you ask."

"I thought that too," I say. "Which is why I've already done it."

◆ ◆ ◆

The plan works. David finds my letter and comes around that evening to speak to Aunt Beatrice. I watch them from the living room doorway, praying she'll say yes. There is no answer there and then, but I see David's smile—his white mustache creeps up his face when he makes eye contact with me. And he nods. I feel like crying happy tears, because the plan works.

I move in with them, and we wave goodbye to Aunt Beatrice from the doorstep, her car packed to the windows, cases strapped to the roof. And off she goes. This is a photo in my mind—me, Matthew, Rosie, shoulder to shoulder, David and Mary close behind.

We're standing out on the porch. We look so much like a family.

My infatuation with Rosie grows as my body begins to change. I stare at her whenever I get a chance. I love the way her room smells. Like clean, sweet things.

I'm eleven years old now and she's thirteen. She's getting prettier. Even if she has a pimple on her cheek or her forehead shines. Even when she slams her bedroom door in my face and tells the whole world to fuck off for an almost endless list of reasons.

We have a cookout. I'm twelve.

It's Rosie's fourteenth birthday and it's a hot summer. She's wearing a red bathing suit and we fight with water guns in the yard. Ducking, running, aiming, laughing.

David's the proud owner of a brand-new Gasmax 3000 Grill. Or something like that. He stands in his checkered shirt, shorts, and an apron and cooks—turning over loud, hissing, spit-sizzle pork chops and hamburgers. Big frankfurters with seared black lines across tight, split skin.

Rosie's wearing a red bathing suit.

We eat, and by the time we're finished the warm sun is behind the trees and all the grass is in the shade—suddenly cold on my bare feet.

The shiny black Gasmax 3000 is still hot, the lid closed, a few wisps of smoke creeping from a vent.

"I'm freezing," Rosie says as David and Mary begin clearing the plates.

"More juice?" David asks. I turn and see him holding a pitcher.

"Sure." I lift my cup and he fills it.

Rosie bundles up her clothes from the ground, stands, and turns—she has lines across the back of her thighs from sitting on the lawn chair. She goes around the side of the house, between the fence and the gate, out of sight.

"Don't let her come indoors, OK?" David whispers.

Then he and Mary take stacks of plates and cups up the back stairs and into the kitchen.

Now that they're gone, Matthew leans over to the cool box and pulls a beer from the water, the ice long since melted. He checks through the kitchen window, then turns toward the end of the yard as he clicks it open.

Matthew takes my cup, pours the last bit of juice onto the grass, then, as though this is a high-stakes covert operation, fills it with one of David's expensive German beers. He opens another and hides the contents in his own cup.

Then, slouched back in our lawn chairs, we tap our drinks together. "This is called a formative moment," he says. "Our first beer."

"I've tried beer before, Matthew," I say. "And so have you. We tasted it like years ago."

"Yeah, but . . . shut up . . . this is the first time we get to drink a whole one."

"Sure?"

"Happy birthday to Rosie," he says—speaking in a deeper voice, like an adult might, lifting it and taking a sip.

I do the same. "Tastes like juice mixed with beer," I say.

"I like it," he replies. Though obviously he doesn't.

The cold bubbles are just touching my top lip when, out of the corner of my eye, I see movement on the side of the Gasmax 3000. Shiny black metal, like a mirror, reflecting something. I can see Rosie at the side of the house. She's getting undressed. The red bathing suit rolled down to her waist and now coming off—she's stepping out of it and picking up a towel. I don't know why, but I can't stop looking. I try to turn away, but my eyes creep slowly left again and I stare. I see her completely bare back. She leans down and picks up a bra.

"It's not as fizzy as I remember," Matthew says. "Last time it—aw gross, Rosie," he shouts, "we can see you in the grill."

I pretend like I've just noticed too.

"Well, don't look then," she yells back.

"Get ready for the cake," David whispers from the door.

Matthew and I turn, place our beers on the table, and look up as Mary comes down the steps. "Haaappy birthday," she begins to sing. "Rosie, where are you?"

"Sorry," she says, coming back around the corner, buttoning her shorts, then pulling a scrunchie from her wrist. She ties her hair up as the singing continues.

David stands high on the steps, Matthew and I are reclined in the lawn chairs, and Mary's moving carefully toward the table. She's carrying a huge, homemade chocolate cake, shielding the glowing candles with her hand.

And as we get into the last lines, as Rosie's smiling, as we're all singing the final, drawn-out "haaappy birthday to—" there's a sudden smash and the song cuts out.

Mary's dropped the cake.

The glass tray has shattered—the brown sponge and icing completely ruined on the ground. There's a strange moment of silence, confusion, then Mary opens her mouth and frowns. It's as if she's trying to speak but can't.

And she grabs her chest and lowers herself to the grass.

David leaps into action, resting her on her side and ordering one of us to call an ambulance. I rush indoors, into the kitchen, and snatch the red phone from the wall.

I dial 911, then pull at the curled wire as I blurt out what happened. "And . . . and she's . . . she's lying down . . . she can't breathe."

Blue lights flicker at the front of the house and down into the backyard—glistening off the shiny black Gasmax 3000—flashing right where I saw Rosie. Paramedics come in and take over the situation. They give Mary some oxygen and check her heart, then roll her onto a stretcher.

During all this commotion, I see that Rosie's got some cake on her hand. As Mary's wheeled away, as David speaks frantically to a paramedic, as Matthew watches, pale and shocked, Rosie sucks icing from her knuckle and nods in approval.

The doctors tell us that Mary has an unusual heart condition—a problem with one of the valves. She makes a full recovery and returns home in no time at all. But we are under strict instructions to keep a close eye on her. We have to call an ambulance if she ever has any chest pains. Or if she ever starts to slur her words. Or if she ever faints. Basically, the rule is don't hesitate. It's always better to be safe than sorry.

And it happens twice more that year. Once at the store, a second time at church. As before, paramedics arrive, take her to the hospital, give her some shots, and she's back within a couple of days.

She says it's all a load of fuss for nothing. But David insists it's serious—and could even lead to a full-blown heart attack if she's not careful.

"Oh, come on now," Mary says from time to time. "I'm not gonna drop down and die. I've got too much to do."

◆ ◆ ◆

I realize why Mary is stricter with Rosie than she is with Matthew and me. It's not just that Rosie talks back, uses bad language, and forgets to do her chores. It's because she's a girl. Mary says she is protecting her.

Still, even with the slack of being a boy, I stick to my bedtime and do all my chores without any question. Not just because I'm scared, but because I want to be respectful. Even after three years, I feel like I'm a guest, like maybe I don't belong.

They all have their own thing. On most Friday nights, for example, Mary and Matthew sing together in the church choir. And on Saturdays David takes him bowling. Sometimes they invite me, but I say no. I can't sing or bowl very well, but mostly I feel like I would be a third wheel.

Rosie manages to dodge this altogether by either hiding in her room or going out with her friends.

The downside is that sometimes I'm left stranded at the house with Mary. And as the rest of the family are doing family things, she says we should too. So usually we end up playing cards or board games or doing puzzles together. I'd rather just watch TV. But, like with my chores, I don't want to seem ungrateful.

I'm thirteen now. Rosie is fifteen. Though I look younger, and she *definitely* looks older. And it must be Saturday, because I'm sitting at the dining table, passing jigsaw pieces to Mary. She holds her broken glasses up to her eyes.

"OK," she says. "We need an edge piece that"—she checks the picture on the box—"It'll have a fox's tail and some of this tree."

Rosie comes into the kitchen and grabs her jacket from a hook on the door. She looks great—like she's spent the last five hours doing her hair and makeup. Good enough to be on the cover of a magazine.

Mary lifts her head from the jigsaw box, slowly lowering her glasses to the table. "Strike me dead," she says. "What *do* you look like?"

But Rosie ignores her. "I'm going out."

"Not like that you're not, young lady."

"What's wrong with this?" Rosie gestures down at her clothes—her outfit is usually the issue. She's wearing a long summer dress with boots.

"It's not your *attire* that's the problem, it's your makeup." Mary points with her glasses. "Only clowns and whores wear that much face paint."

She's had a couple of drinks. She gets even stricter when she's drunk.

"It's tasteful," Rosie whispers, more offended than annoyed. "Red lips are fashionable. You wouldn't understand, because—"

"You look like you cost ten bucks," Mary yells. "With change. Now go on upstairs and take some of it off."

I just sit patiently and wait. I've seen this show before, more than once. They argue. Some doors get slammed. Maybe Rosie gets grounded for a week. It's an endless cycle.

"But . . . I don't have time."

"This ain't a debate," Mary hisses through teeth.

"My friends are already waiting—"

"Your friends? You mean that Patrick man? You shouldn't go near him."

"I'm not going to, I'm just meeting the girls."

Mary slams her fist onto the table, bouncing some jigsaw pieces. She stands. "Go and change it."

But Rosie walks calmly across the kitchen and stops directly in front of her. I watch from my chair, trying to be invisible. Mary's already furious at this *outrageous* disobedience, her eyes darting in total disbelief.

And then Rosie looks directly into those wide, searching eyes—stopping them dead. "No," she whispers.

Mary hits her. I flinch. Hard. A palm across the cheek.

It seems like we're all shocked, even Mary.

"You don't talk to me like that, not in this house," she says.

Holding her face, Rosie snarls and looks back up. I sense that Mary regrets what she's done.

"Please, Rosie, please." She speaks gently now, like she can undo the slap. "I never said you can't wear some makeup. Just a little bit less."

"OK." Rosie nods. "I'll go and take some of it off."

She leaves, and I hear her feet on the stairs.

"Now, I'm sorry you had to see that, James." Mary sits back down. "But it's different for girls. Girl like that, on a Saturday night. She's got the body of a woman but the mind of a child. Boys would want to eat her for supper. I just want to keep her safe. You understand?"

I nod. The room is tense, but we return to our jigsaw.

"We need to find two more edges," she says. "Have you got them over there?"

I look at all the pieces spread out on the wood in front of me—green, blue, brown—and turn a couple over.

"I think one would have a fox's . . . maybe its foot and a branch, maybe some sky? It's for the corner, here, see?"

"I can't see any more edges," I say.

She laughs and flips over the lid. The picture we're making is meant to look like animals in a woodland. "Serves me right," she says, forcing normality back onto the table. "I knew it was a bad idea to have secondhand jigsaw puzzles at the church sale. Let's just do it as far as we can and see what it looks like."

"Good idea."

"We'll just have to imagine the gaps."

"Or we could cut them out from the lid?" I suggest.

"You're a bright spark, James." She points at me briefly. "We'll do that."

We continue with the puzzle for a while, about ten minutes of work—like this is our job. Like it really matters.

Then I hear the floorboards in Rosie's bedroom creak. My eyes tilt to the ceiling. Mary pretends she hasn't heard.

Then footsteps on the stairs, and Rosie comes into the kitchen, wearing a bathrobe. Her hair is tied up nicely, with a blue band, like she's ready for church. And she's got no lipstick on, just a light covering of natural makeup. I think to myself that she actually looks even prettier like this. I'd still put her on the front of my magazine.

"See," Mary says, smiling—everything is OK now. "That's more like it. Why couldn't you just look like that all the time? You don't want to hide that lovely face of yours."

"So it's acceptable now? This is good enough?"

"It's fine, and I'm sorry I got so worked up." Mary turns her attention back to the jigsaw. "I just want you to be safe is all."

"Great."

And Rosie removes her robe.

Now she's wearing knee-high, black leather boots, pantyhose like a fishing net, the shortest denim skirt I have ever seen in my life, and a tight top that shows off most of her stomach and the top of her breasts.

I'm staring—I can't stop staring, I'm astonished for a number of reasons, but Mary's focused on the table.

I wait.

"Right, now we need this tree trunk, here, then I think we can—"

She looks up. Does a double take.

"Are you *trying* to upset me?" she yells, rising to her feet, sweeping the half-finished puzzle across the kitchen floor.

"What do you mean?" Rosie seems genuinely confused—she's so good at that expression. Like she doesn't understand, like she doesn't know perfectly well what she's doing.

"You wanna go out there looking like a slut?" Mary stalks toward her. "You want to be grabbed and groped? You want creeps like Patrick to follow you into a dark, dark alleyway?" Her voice sounds mean and mocking.

Rosie retreats, stopping at the kitchen countertop.

"You want boys to put their hand up your skirt? Stick their tongue in your ear?" And Mary grabs Rosie's hip. "Is this what you want? Hands on you. Squeezing you."

"Stop. Get off."

"Oh no. They won't stop. They'll just carry on." Mary pushes her against the cupboard, squeezing her shoulder now. "This is what you want."

"Stop it." Rosie squirms. "Fucking hell, get off me."

"Why? You want to be grabbed?" And then she grips her by the throat. "You want to be strangled in a bush and—"

Rosie shoves her away. "Fuck you," she screams.

"Oh, so that's *not* what you want . . . that's not . . . you don't . . ." Mary groans. "You . . ." Her hand goes to her chest, she leans over. And, as before, she struggles to breathe as she sinks to the floor.

Now on her front, lying and moaning amid the puzzle pieces, she grinds her teeth in agony.

I know the routine, so I leap up and rush across the tiles. "It's OK, lie down," I say, putting her on her side. "Slow breaths. I'll call an ambulance."

Then I stand, turn, and reach for the red phone on the wall next to Rosie.

But just as my hand gets to it, hers does too. And they bump into each other, right near the tangled spiral wire.

Instead of picking up the receiver, she weaves her fingers in between mine. And, gripping tight, she looks deep into my eyes. I lean again toward the phone, but she's strong and she squeezes, keeping me in place. Gradually she lowers our hands, and I feel her warm palm as we both turn and face Mary. She's gasping, blinking, dying now on the floor, and no one is calling for help.

We just stand there.

We just stand there, side by side, my heart pounding. My skin tingling. An overwhelming sense of something . . . a feeling I've never felt before. Goosebumps and fear and joy and—*God.*

Oh my God. I keep thinking, *Oh my God.* That's all I can think. *Oh. My. God.*

She's holding my hand.

Chapter Twelve

There are a pair of bookends on the shelf behind Rob Sanders's desk—bronze statuettes shaped like bulls, their horns against a metal plate, pressing the covers together. Neat spines foil-stamped in gold. Leather-bound books for show. His whole office is like this: old-fashioned, clad in dark wood, with a country club feel. You can almost smell the cigars they'd have smoked in here back in the day. Crystal glass of scotch in one hand, a funny story about some broad in the other.

The deputy special agent in charge has, until now, taken little interest in *how* Nell runs the taskforce. That was part of her proposal—to have autonomy. Give the office the means and judge it only on its results. He had green-lit the unprecedented funding and personally vouched for her ambitious plans.

The opioid epidemic has created a fresh willingness to try new things at the agency—especially given the rapid spread across the Pacific Northwest. If you're fighting a war and losing every battle, it makes sense to change tactics. We've been riding that open-minded goodwill for four and a half years now, but in the afternoon shadow of this morning's blunder, Nell's claims are starting to sound absurd.

We sit in front of Rob's desk, the bulls and books high on the wall behind him. We're like a pair of children in the principal's office, waiting to be told off.

And he's suddenly very interested in the details. When all this settles into place, he will have to explain himself to those above. He needs answers to all the questions they will inevitably ask. First up, he wants to know how and why we came to the conclusion that Edward Lang was trafficking drugs on both sides of the legal divide.

"What exactly do you have to back this theory up?" he asks. "In terms of evidence?"

"He has previous convictions," Nell says, leaning forward in her chair. "He has connections to international suppliers. He's affiliated with Ryan Payne, the Leyland & Lang employee we caught a few months back . . . He had heroin in his truck. And the warehouse with all kinds of sophisticated equipment. They were dealing. Big time. You, you remember?"

"Is that it? One dead employee with"—Rob checks some paper on his desk—"two pounds?"

"Well, his cell phone records," Nell adds. "The first number Ryan called right after he crashed was a phone we believe belongs to Edward Lang."

"You believe?"

"Doesn't that seem unusual?" she says. "The director of the entire company. Why would Ryan phone him? And then," Nell gestures to me, "he denied knowing Ryan. James spoke to Edward, at his office. And he lied."

"He might—*might*—have told a lie. We really hanging it all on that?"

When it's framed like this—said in the open, all at once—it sounds so outlandish, so implausible. The kind of late-night harebrained stab in the dark you'd only make when drunk enough to forget it by morning.

"There are other things too," Nell goes on.

"Like what?" Elbows on the desk, Rob puts all his fingers together, steepled up to his chin. "Please." He spreads his hands briefly. "I'm all ears."

"We've found white prescription bottles, oxy and others, filled with heroin," Nell says. "Filled right to the brim. On the streets. Small-time dealers, but they're using Leyland & Lang packaging."

Rob throws his arms in the air. "So?" he shouts. "I'm sure they eat cheeseburgers too. Doesn't mean Ronald McDonald's smuggling drugs in the end of his clown shoes. Causation, correlation. Come on, Nell."

She accepts that point gracefully with a nod, showing her hand. "We had assets take photographs—which were dated, they were real." She makes a fist. "Edward Lang was directly connected to that stock. The product was on the *Hamburg*, in the shipping container. More than one and a half tons."

"The shipping container that's disappeared?" Rob shrugs. "The cargo you tracked across the ocean and then missed?"

Nell's almost bouncing in her seat now. "Don't you see—can't you see how powerful he is? To bring it in, under our noses?"

A streak of amusement flashes amid Rob's exhaustion. "It could mean that, sure." He laughs. "Or it could mean you're wrong?"

"We can find it." Nell sounds so desperate—like a person losing their faith in real time. She's grabbing at the empty air in front of her, clinging onto nothing. "We just need . . ."

"It's gone," Rob says softly. "Even if it was there, it isn't now."

"If we could get some help, work with the FDA's guys," she says, so far forward in her chair she's almost kneeling on the floor. "If we could actually *investigate* him from some different angles. The . . . the money. Or get into his house, his office."

"Nell, please. You want a warrant to investigate one of the largest pharmaceutical firms in the world, on a whim?"

"It's not a whim, sir. It's him. Really . . . it's him." Nell looks at me, waiting for me to agree. "It's him," she whispers.

I realize, aside from hello, I haven't said a single word during this entire exchange.

"Without a doubt," I say.

"I've known you both professionally for a number of years. Nell, in your case, it's been decades," he says. "I respect you both. But I'm not convinced. How on earth do you think a jury would feel?"

Neither of us respond.

"This morning was embarrassing for everyone, but especially for me," Rob adds. "I can't keep throwing in a good word for you and your team."

"We'll do better."

His eyes close for a second. "Please, Nell, read the tone," he says, lowering his head slightly. "We're doing a complete restructure. You two will stay in place, but your taskforce will be brought under the wing of the field division office. Accountability. Oversight."

"Yes, sir," she says, though I see she's already looking for another path—the gears in motion.

"Do you mind if I have a word with James alone?" he asks.

Nell hesitates but stands. "Of course." She leaves.

Once his wide mahogany door's closed, Rob leans forward in his tall leather chair and says quietly, "Listen, don't think we haven't noticed you. Even when a ship's sinking, there's still good work to be done. And we see that you're doing some of the best."

The compliment slides through me without even the slightest hint of serotonin.

"Well, thank you," I say. "I appreciate that."

"Is there anything you want to tell me?" he asks.

I pretend to search my mind for a moment, turning the sides of my mouth down. "No, I don't think so."

"Nell called me the other night concerned about something. Something she'd found? It was a pretty cryptic message, but she said after that it was nothing to worry about."

"I . . ." My cheeks fill with curious air that puffs out of my mouth as I sigh. "You'd have to ask her."

"Something to do with a car?"

I just shake my head. "I'm sorry, there's so much going on . . ."

Rob waves the topic aside and tilts back in his chair. "What's your *honest* opinion on all this?" he says, fingers on his chin. "Just, overall."

The trick to an effective lie is to build it entirely from the truth. "That would be very difficult for me to say."

"I get it." He nods. "Nell inspires loyalty. And that's good. It'll take you far. But I want you to rest assured that any of the task-force's failings won't reflect negatively on your progression. You're a good man, James. And a fine agent."

"I'm just doing my best, sir, just trying to do the right thing."

"And that's why I like you." He points. "What's that phrase you say? You fall in the bottomless snake pit—and you do what?"

"You start killing snakes."

He knocks on his desk with a knuckle. "That's it. I like that." He stands, picks up a piece of paper, signaling the end of the meeting.

Rising, I give him a single nod and flatten the creases on my shirt. "Thank you, sir."

Outside his office, I walk with Nell down the corridor—past the gray foam benches with chrome legs.

"What was that about?" she says, cautiously eyeing every person we pass.

"He was wondering if there was anything I wanted to tell him."

We arrive at the elevator, and she presses the silver button. A triangle glows green, points down. She waits for me to say more.

"About what we found in the cars," I whisper, standing up straight, shoulders forward. "Your call raised the alarm."

"What did you say?"

"Nothing. He doesn't know."

We step inside the elevator and turn around to face the doors. They slide closed. Our reflections blurred impressions, warped ghosts shifting in the metal. Faint piano music plays from a small speaker in the top corner.

"Thank you, James," she says. "That's . . . you shouldn't have been put in that position. But I appreciate it."

"It's fine. I was careful not to lie."

We sink slowly down through the building.

"The bugs," she says, thinking aloud. "They knew what we had planned."

"Yep."

"But I don't think that's why we missed the ship."

I turn my head to look at her.

"The map, the shipping traffic log," she adds, still facing forward. "It said . . . it fucking said 9 a.m., south dock. Our ship. The *Hamburg*. At that time. It said it."

The elevator's thick wires and rolling mechanism above and below hum and clunk, drowning out the gentle music.

"Unless we misread the number?"

Nell strains as though this makes her doubt reality. Like she's losing her mind. "We didn't. We just didn't. The computer swapped the ships."

My phone buzzes in my pocket. I pull it out, hold it at my hip, and read a message from an unknown number. It's an address, the words "green maintenance door" and "10 p.m.".

As I put it away, the elevator jolts to a stop.

I see that Nell has hit the red button. All the metal around us is still and quiet. Now the piano can be heard clearly—it's surprisingly loud in this stationary limbo between floors three and four.

Nell turns away, looks at her feet, wipes her palm down her mouth, then over the back of her shaved head. And she spins around again. "Marine traffic isn't a secret. We could have looked at a map online. Our data was supposed to be reliable and secure."

"What are you saying?"

"Everyone else, the guys at the port, anyone interested in when ships come and go, they would have all known what time the *Hamburg* was arriving. We were the only fools who got it wrong."

"So . . ."

"So whatever it was that tricked us? It must have come from the DEA?" There's a strange loss in her eyes—like she's certain of this, but asking for me to reassure her. Is she crazy? She wants me to tell her if she is or, perhaps more concerning, if she isn't. "What if Edward has someone on the inside?"

I swallow and pretend my fear is shock.

"The computers couldn't be hacked remotely," she says. "That'd show up. The IT guys and their firewalls." Nell can barely bring herself to even say this aloud. "It would have to be someone in our office."

And she stares at me—I see her thoughts racing, running through a list of possible suspects. It pains her.

"Who?" I manage to say.

"I don't know. But we should start by checking software—see if anything unusual crops up on anyone's hard drive."

"Good idea." I think of Foster's laptop, the skull ski mask on his desk.

Nell steps closer. The whole building seems like it doesn't exist; it's just me and her in this metal box. The dimmed red lights. The classical piano playing soft, sad chords above.

For a second, I think she's going to ask me outright—force me to lie to her face. But what she says is far worse.

"The only people I can rule out are standing in this elevator," she whispers—her eyes bloodshot, locked hard on mine. "So we don't say anything. We look at this together. I don't trust anyone else like I trust you."

Unlike the last one, I feel something when this compliment lands. I feel sorry for her. *Poor Nell*, I think. She's even more lost than I am.

Chapter Thirteen

The map on my phone takes me to a huge warehouse just outside the city. It's surrounded by a tall chain-link fence and there's an automatic gate with an empty security guard booth next to a yellow barrier arm.

Five streetlights spaced equally in the empty, sprawling parking lot—like a runway that leads all the way to what could pass for an aircraft hangar. Other than that, the place is dark. Closed.

But still, I proceed with caution, stepping slowly along the sidewalk, checking shadows and cameras around an open pedestrian gate in the fence. I pause, touching my gun.

And in I go, down the long walkway, through five orbs of yellow mist under each streetlight. At the building I step around to the green maintenance door mentioned in the text message. There's no handle. No box for a key code. But I notice a camera perched on the bricks above the door, looking down on me. So I stare into it for a few seconds, stepping back so they can see my face. I imagine myself, small, looking up, black and white and pale. I'm wearing a plain blue jacket and my college baseball cap. And they see me.

The door buzzes and clicks.

I push it open into a long, shaded corridor. At the far end, warm light pours out onto some barrels and cardboard boxes. Voices. Two men. Laughter. Or three.

Pausing, hesitating, I begin to creep toward the glass on the left and see an office. Inside, Edward Lang is sitting with his feet up on a table, reclined in a swivel chair. I tap on the door and he yells, "Come in."

As I open it, Edward sits up straight, holding a drink carefully and lowering his boots—his ridiculous, alligator leather boots with their deep-cherry pattern curling up the ankle—back down onto the concrete.

On my right, I see a younger man, maybe mid-twenties, standing against another internal window, arms folded. The warehouse behind him, through the glass, is pitch black.

And on my left, an older man I've seen before. A security guard from Leyland & Lang's headquarters.

"James," Edward says, on his feet now. "This here is Adam." He points at the younger of the two, who nods politely. "And this charming gentleman . . ." The older man, seated at the head of the table, hasn't looked at me once. "Stefan, please, it is customary to stand when someone of distinction enters the room."

Stefan takes a long while before he reacts. "I'm familiar with that tradition," he says in his low voice. He does not move a muscle.

Edward sighs. "You're making James uncomfortable."

"It's fine," I say.

"Stefan's in a bad mood because he was raised wrong . . . if I recall correctly, by wolves?" Edward smiles. "As such, he lacks basic social skills. But we forgive him, because he's got that Germanic blood and I don't pay him to be nice."

"What do you want?" I ask.

"That . . . well, that's an almost-philosophical question." Edward's eyes light up. "What do I want?" He lifts a finger. "You know, my partner sometimes asks me the same thing. Near my birthday. She'll look around the big house, at the art, the cars, the pinball machine in the bathroom," he spreads his hands, speaking fast, "I got a mammoth skull above the fireplace, you would not *believe* the size of these tusks. She'll say, 'What can you get for the man who already has everything?' Well, the answer's obvious. The answer's in the question. What *does* the man who has everything want?" He pauses, staring at me with an intensity that approaches threat. "More," he whispers.

I glance at Adam. He's wearing a hoodie, glasses, scruffy Converse sneakers. He's got shaved black hair and the demeanor of one of those Silicon Valley tech millionaires. I wonder what he's doing here—seems like he doesn't belong.

But Stefan, still seated, still refusing to even look at me, fits the bill. Tattoos on his hands, letters on his grazed knuckles, a tear on his cheek that's been lasered away. Short, thick blond hair that clings to his skull like sheep's wool is thinning on the top. And he's got the swelling and extra cartilage you'd expect to see around the nose and brow of a retired boxer. But he strikes me as the kind of man who doesn't care. All that bulk serves a function beyond aesthetics.

"Basic social skills," I say, turning back to Edward opposite me. "Like answering questions?"

"So stern and cold." He grits his teeth comically, makes a fist and shakes it. "So much angst and anger. What do *you* want, James?"

"I want to know why I'm here."

"You're being introduced to my business associates," he says, gesturing with both hands. "You asked to know more about the setup, so this is it. Young Adam here . . . he's formally employed as head of IT at Leyland & Lang. I suppose, with his technical know-how, he's the eyes and ears of the operation. And the psychotic man of stone seated on my right is my head of security, Stefan. He deals with the more complicated, ethically nuanced side of mass-market drug dealing. I suppose you could say he's the arms and legs of the operation. The muscle."

"And you?" I say. "You're the brains?"

Edward laughs with those mad eyes of his. "I'm the balls. Hence why I've decided to invite a DEA agent into my inner circle."

"So what would I be?" I ask.

"Oh, I don't know . . . to be honest with you, James, I already regret starting the analogy. Maybe you could be the heart." He raises a fist again. "Keep us moving. Keep us alive."

"Are we done?" Stefan says, unimpressed.

"You're free to leave at any point." Edward lifts an arm to the door.

And Stefan stands, picks up a heavy-looking gym bag, walks around the table, and stops at my side. He turns and stares into my eyes—a blank, empty stare. Then he leaves.

Adam glances between me and Edward, then nods, picks up his own gym bag, and says, "Nice to meet you," then follows him out.

Once we're alone, Edward turns around, like he's just remembered something. He lifts a third dark-gray gym bag, the same as the other two, and drops it onto the table. It lands with a hefty thud. "This is for you."

Tilting my head, I look at it, then back up. I grab the strap, drag it toward myself, and pull on the zipper—it rumbles down the full length of the bag. Then I spread it open to see cash. Lots and lots—I move a stack—and *lots* of cash.

"What is this?" I say.

"It's called money." There's a long silence. "It represents value. You can swap it for goods and services. It allows people to trade in the abstract . . . I'm sorry, James, but you must have come across the concept before?"

"Why are you giving it to me?"

"It's your fee. You more than proved yourself this morning. It's a square million. Seems fair. I was prepared to negotiate—I thought you might want double that."

"I don't want any of it."

"But . . . it's yours." He slides the bag closer to me. I take a pace back. "Look, James, it's either your money or it's evidence in a case against me. Either way, it's *your* responsibility. Burn it. I don't care. Just take it with you."

"If I do, we're done?"

"There's something else," he says, crouching. "This is a gift . . ."

Edward stands and hands me a wrapped package. It has a bow and everything. It feels like a picture frame.

I keep thinking about Nell. About how much she trusts me. And here I am, taking money and gifts from the man we're meant to stop.

Looking around the room, I ask, "What is this place?" I nod toward the dim window across from us. "What's in there?"

Edward steps over to the wall and flicks a switch. The warehouse appears. Rows and rows of pallets, stacked high, like a forest of squared leafless trees. Monoliths. The lightbulbs come on one at a time—a rhythmic *clunk, clunk, clunk*—and the products stretch further than I thought possible. Until the final light is a silent speck glowing in the distance. Each stack wrapped in plastic, the Leyland & Lang logo on the side. We both look down the tunnel.

"Just storage," Edward says. "We have a lot of stock, but this ships internationally, remember. And we overproduce by about ten percent. Expired pills get destroyed. And by destroyed I mean Stefan arranges for them to be sold on the streets. So it's all profit. But all this stuff is totally legit, we don't store anything illegal on L&L grounds."

"Would your father be OK with you using his empire as a front for selling illicit drugs?"

"My father's dead. But for the record, no, I don't think he'd like it very much at all." Edward's smile is warm. "He was not a nice man."

I step back to the table, zip up the bag, and lay the wrapped gift across the top, between the strap loops.

"Listen," Edward says, standing against the window, the warehouse lit up behind him. "If you ever need help with anything, don't hesitate to call me. We can make things happen. Big things. Small things. I have a lot of resources, people at various agencies, the police for example, and I want you to know they're all at your disposal."

"I think I'll be fine."

There's a short silence.

"Open it," he says.

Sighing, I pick up the gift, tear the glossy purple paper away, and drop the scraps on the table. It is a picture frame—I turn it over and see a face. My face.

"Do you like it?" Edward asks. "I did it from memory."

He's drawn me in ballpoint pen, shaded my features with neat crosshatch lines. I'm wearing a polo shirt, *DEA* printed in small text on my chest. There is a likeness, undoubtedly, but he's drawn me too young.

"I look like a child," I say.

Edward inspects me carefully, squints, leans closer.

Then he nods. "Yes," he says. "You do."

I collect my fee, turn, and walk out of the office, down the corridor and back outside.

The weight of the gym bag is making my shoulder ache, so I push my thumb under the strap and lean to the side as I cross the parking lot, waddling through the streetlights, out through the gate and along the chain-link fence.

Approaching my car, I notice another vehicle parked nearby, its hood propped open. The road is empty, quiet. I check behind myself.

When I turn back, Adam peers around the hood. "Know anything about cars?" he asks.

"Yep," I say, walking past.

"Think it's the battery." He follows me, wiping his hand on his jeans.

"Probably."

He darts back and grabs his own gym bag, then clutches it to his chest as he catches up.

"Hey," he says. "Do you mind giving me a ride back into the city?"

"I do mind." I haven't slowed down, even carrying a million dollars in cash. And guessing by the weight, it's mostly fifties.

At my car I open the back door and chuck the bag inside.

Adam's standing near the front wheel hugging his earnings. He looks vulnerable—small, young. Too young.

"What are you doing?" I ask.

"Come on, man, you're driving there anyway."

"No, I mean, generally. Here. All this. Why do you work for him?"

"Well, the money isn't bad." Adam places the heavy bag at his feet.

"Is it really that simple?"

"He offered me a position straight out of college as an IT consultant for the entire company," Adam says. "It's not the kind of job you say no to."

"It's not the kind of job you get offered straight out of college."

He blinks, rubs his arm. "My mom was sick. I . . . I had to raise some money. I committed some high-level crimes."

Part of me wants to get away from this entire situation as quickly as possible. But what's my plan? Learning more about them could be a good step to take, no matter which direction I'm heading.

"Such as?" I ask.

"Hacking," Adam says. "Mostly for fun. Payday loan companies, scrubbing their records. Resetting it all back to zero. That kind of thing."

"How noble," I say in a flat tone as I open the driver's door.

"I'd taken a . . . significant loan out myself, so I'm hardly Robin Hood. That's how I got caught." He shrugs. "Confessed to some stuff, helped the FBI with their cybersecurity. Managed to avoid prison."

"Get in," I say.

A surprised smile spreads across his face, and he awkwardly lifts his bag and takes small, bouncing steps out onto the street, past the hood of the car, then around to the side. With our bags of money next to each other on the back seat, Adam climbs into the front.

I watch him wrestle clumsily with the seatbelt.

"Thank you," he says, clicking it in.

Hand on his headrest, I look out the rear window as I turn the car around and head off back toward the city.

"So it's the kind of job you get offered straight from college, but only if you're especially qualified?" I say.

"And the career counselor always told me a criminal record would look bad on my resume." Adam adjusts his glasses, his eyes big behind thick lenses. "What about you?"

"What about me?" I grip the steering wheel.

"Why do you work for him?"

"I don't."

Adam nods quickly. "OK," he says, keen not to offend. "Sorry, I was . . ."

I get the impression he's not trying to call me out—he doesn't point to the very real bag of money sitting behind me, boldly disproving my claim. He's just taking my word as gospel. Just being respectful of the lies I'm telling myself.

"You seem an intelligent person," I say. "Do you know why life expectancy in the US is falling?"

"There are a number of factors, but drugs, suicide, and obesity are largely to blame."

"Any moral alarm bells ringing for you?" I ask.

"If we weren't selling in this city, it'd be overrun with Carrillo guys. And trust me, it'd be a whole lot worse."

"This shit kills thousands, millions of people. It destroys lives. It saps the soul out of innocent men, women, children."

"You don't get hooked on opioids unless your soul is already gone," Adam says.

Matthew said in his suicide note that something crucial was missing. It was him against the world, this world, and he'd lost so much ground.

"Concerns about the law?" I wonder, pushing Matthew out of my mind.

"The law has no relevance if we're discussing morality. The . . . the business sells drugs. You're the one making distinctions between legal and, and, and illegal."

"I think it's *all* highly unethical."

Adam seems nervous defending himself, but continues nonetheless. "It's supply and demand," he says cautiously. "If no one wanted drugs, there'd be no, no business. Don't be offended, but a lot of the harm is caused by people like you, pushing it underground."

I laugh. "Yeah. You're right. I'm the bad guy."

Adam swallows and shifts anxiously in his seat. He picks at his thumbnail. "I'm sorry if I'm . . . if I'm speaking out of turn but . . . this high horse you're trying to climb onto bolted a long time ago."

For a brief moment there, I almost forgot what he knows about me. "You're the one who put a bug in this car?"

"It was my idea, but Stefan planted it. I'm not really the breaking and entering kind."

"Proved fruitful, hey?"

"I was surprised to hear you guys actually stormed the wrong ship." He laughs, turns to me, then instantly stops the moment he realizes I don't find it funny. "Edward doesn't like cancelling plans. He says you have to march forward no matter the cost. I knew if we tried to abandon the stock, the DEA would know. It had to come in as scheduled. You were the perfect solution to an impossible problem."

Sighing, I remember what Nell said in the elevator—suspended between floors, serenaded by that sad piano music.

"The USB drive Edward gave me," I say. "Did you write that software?"

"Yes." He seems proud.

"They're going to look at all the computers in the office. Trying to trace it. What will they find?"

"There will be evidence of malware. But it won't be possible to identify the source. I assume you used someone else's computer?"

A tiny crackle of sorrow, like a spark that burns out just as you realize how bright it could be—now just a fading stain on my vision. Foster doesn't deserve to be framed for my crimes. But it's dark and done. "I did," I whisper.

Adam's knees are together—skinny legs in baggy jeans. "Good." He folds his arms tight. "I am worried about it all," he says. "I trust Edward, but sometimes he's reckless. It's like we're spinning plates. I get the impression he doesn't care if he lives or dies."

"Do you?"

"Yes," Adam says. "You're judging me, but I've got plans for all this money. For my family. And I'm finding ways to donate it to charity, to do good things. Help people."

"You do all the mental gymnastics you need. If it gets you to sleep."

He looks down at his lap and doesn't speak for a good minute.

"I get it, by the way," he eventually says.

"What?"

"Why you did it. You love your wife. That means you'd do anything for her. Even help her get away with murder. It's not complicated, psychologically, I mean."

"You don't know anything about me."

Adam turns and blinks—innocence and sincerity emanating from the very depths of his soul. "I know *everything* about you, James."

We don't speak again until I pull up at his apartment building. He thanks me, climbs out, and leaves.

I watch as he disappears inside, then my attention shifts to the remaining bag on the backseat. Edward was right—it's my responsibility.

So I drive fast down to the harbor and pull into an empty parking lot behind one of the countless restaurants. It's past midnight now, and they're all shuttered for the night. There's some outdoor seating enclosed by a low wall made of loose bricks. I crouch and pick one of them up.

Carrying the heavy bag, I go along the boardwalk, around the railings, and down some steps.

Now standing alone on the rough concrete wall, I look into the dirty black water below—bits of old seaweed, cigarettes, and leaves floating on the surface, slick like oil. Boats bob and masts tilt. Gentle splashing sounds as the small waves lift and fall, lift and fall.

I double-check there's no one around, then squat, open the bag, and swap the framed drawing of me for the heavy brick. I zip it closed again and rise to my feet.

Holding the portrait, I look a final time at Edward's artwork before I drop it into the ocean six feet below.

Then, without hesitating, I do the same with the money—tossing it out in front of me. A loud splash, and it sits on the water for a few seconds, half-submerged. But then, like a ship with a busted hull, it rolls over, bubbles glug to the surface, and just like that it's gone.

With my head bowed, I close my eyes and take a minute to breathe. To contemplate. To assess my decision. To think.

"Shit," I whisper to myself, wholeheartedly regretting this foolish stab at righteous symbolism.

Twenty minutes later and here I am walking up the driveway at home—my wet pants hanging over my shoes, slapping on the concrete with each step. Like some kind of sorry-looking penguin. Over my shoulder the bag of cash, soaked through, drips a trail of dark, salty water behind.

Of course, I leaped in to get it. But that picture? That drawing of me as a little boy? I left that down there. I let it sink.

Chapter Fourteen

"Oh, James, look at this one," Rosie says, lifting another item of miniature clothing from the bag. "So cute."

Nell is kneeling on the rug next to the coffee table, searching through suitcases and a couple of backpacks. Me and Rosie sit opposite her, side by side on the couch.

"I brought a carrier too," Nell says, nodding toward the window—her car parked outside on the driveway. "I won't be offended if you don't want any of it."

"No, no," Rosie says, looking at me. "It's lovely, it's a lovely gesture."

Nell's visit was unannounced; she decided to bring around all her old baby stuff she'd had in storage ever since her own children—who are now adults—grew out of it.

She's dressed in a smart gray suit and even has a bit of makeup on, which is a rare sight. Though I'm not surprised she's stopped short of a ball gown. Tonight is the annual city police awards dinner. A big, glossy charity event that only a select few people outside the force attend. A handful of agents from our office have been invited the past two years. For obvious reasons, I'd feel more comfortable not going but, in the interest of appearances and our pursuit of normality, I've dug out my tux and shiny shoes.

“Some of it is old, I know,” Nell explains, touching a bag. “But the clothes, they’re timeless. And a lot of it is still in its packaging—Joe’s mother bought us a ton of new products with each pregnancy. Things like these.” She produces a tiny pair of pink . . .

“Sweatbands?” I ask.

“They’re leg warmers,” Nell says.

“For a baby?” I smile.

“I think leg warmers are pretty pointless no matter how old you are,” Rosie says. “I love them.”

“It’s all yours.” Nell looks around the floor, surrounded by open bags. “Anything you don’t want you can donate. I just want it to go to a good home. Been holding out for grandkids, but first come, first served.”

Nell’s three daughters are all in their twenties—and each one lives at least a day’s travel away. Strange to think she sees us more than she sees them.

“And then there’s all this.” She stands up and unravels a long maternity dress. “Stretchy, stylish, comfortable.” She holds it against herself, modeling. “Spacious.”

“Looks like a big sack,” I say.

“Well, yeah, that’s exactly what you want.” Nell reaches down and rummages through the clothes. “Got some pants and stuff too.”

Rosie’s just staring at her. There’s a short silence. And then Rosie stands up and steps forward. “Thank you, Nell,” she says. “Really. It means the world.”

Nell’s surprised by her hug, but returns it all the same—the long green dress on her arm hanging from Rosie’s lower back.

“Yeah,” I agree. “We appreciate it.”

Rosie beckons me over. “Come on,” she says. “Group love.”

I rise and put my arms around both of them.

When we release each other, Nell has water in her eyes. She covers her face and laughs. "Oh, it's so stupid," she whispers. Then she composes herself, sniffs, and nods. "I'm just . . ." She pauses, swallows, looks at the ceiling, as though only gravity can hold the tears in. "I'm just happy for you guys." Sighing, she looks back down, her eyes glassy but not enough to smudge her makeup. "I know it's been tough over the last few years. It's going to get so much better. You have no idea."

"Well, that's true," Rosie says, now holding one of Nell's hands. "I don't have a clue what I'm doing."

"No one has," Nell laughs. "But I've had no clue what to do three times. Was a while ago, but I understand the physics of it remain largely the same."

"As long as you're happy to answer all my stupid questions?" Rosie says. "I don't . . . we don't really have anyone else we can speak to about all this."

Nell seems simultaneously honored and horrified that this is even a question. "Of course," she says, gripping Rosie's hand affectionately. "You snap your fingers, and I will be here every step of the way. As much or as little as you need."

"I guess we should start getting ready," I say, checking my watch.

"I'll leave you to it," Nell adds. "Bad timing, I should have called. I'll see you there?"

"No, don't be silly," Rosie says. "You're already ready. Stay, help me pick my dress. This might be the last time I get to wear something other than a sack."

"You sure? I don't want to intrude."

"It's fine," I say. "We might as well share a ride."

"I've got a few options," Rosie explains as she heads toward the stairs. Nell begins to follow.

Sudden panic jolts me up straight. "Ah—wait," I say. "Um. Clean up first?"

"I don't mind a bit of mess," Nell says.

"Yeah, it's mostly your mess anyway, James."

"No, really," I insist. "All the wet . . . water . . . water leak."

And Rosie remembers too, her eyes widening. "Yes." She points at Nell. "You wait here, I'll shout when I've picked out some choices."

"I suppose we should talk about work anyway." Nell turns to me.

"I suppose we should," I say, as Rosie rushes upstairs to hide the million dollars in cash we currently have spread out and drying across every surface in our bedroom.

Held at the old city hall, with its grand stone arches and high ceilings, the gala dinner looks more like an awards ceremony for movie stars. Round tables of six, dotted throughout the wide spiral patterns on the carpet. A big stage with bright lights and curtains. Champagne sticking out the top of silver ice buckets in the center of every table.

The DEA guests are seated in the corner—like at a wedding, we're grouped together by family. Foster's here, with his tall red-headed wife, Zoe. Nell, me, and Rosie are seated on the next table with a few other officers I know from the force. Rosie ended up wearing a black dress with straps at the back, her hair in a loose bun. She looks great.

Before the presentation, we stand around and I smile, give thumbs-ups and fast rounds of small talk to anyone who catches my eye.

We sit, we eat, and then the ceremony begins. Awards for heroism see officers on crutches limp up onto the stage and explain how they were just doing their job. But we all stand and clap.

The first part of the evening ends with a charity raffle. They sell donated items, including a gigantic bottle of whiskey, an experience day driving sports cars, and even some memorabilia from cases mentioned in the presentation. Sergeant Smith's bullet-hole badge, lot number five, sells for two-and-a-half thousand dollars.

Later, in clusters of standing suits and gowns, firm handshakes and single cheek kisses, I see Donnie Rhodes across the crowd, flashing between shoulders and faces. He's holding a champagne flute in one hand and a bottle in the other, pouring drinks and stumbling.

"Hey, you want a smoke?" Foster nudges me with his elbow, lifting two fingers to his lips.

I've had a few drinks, so "Yeah, sure," I say. "I'll be back in a minute." I touch Rosie's forearm, but she's deep in conversation with someone I don't know.

Outside, in the dark parking lot, the dynamic reminds me of a high school reunion—five men standing in a circle, suited and booted, smoking and laughing. The conversation's crass, charged by alcohol and camaraderie. Good-natured rivalries from the office turn to crude jokes and well-told stories about one another. Stories you've heard before, but nod along to as if you haven't.

"How about you, Foster?" one of the officers (Neil? Nigel?) says across the group. "Hear you're moving on? Greener grass?"

"Yeah," Foster says. I turn to him. This is the first I've heard of it. "I meant to tell you, I've been reposted over with Mike Ward and his team—working on the cartel operation."

"Going undercover?" Nigel—it is Nigel—says.

"Something I've done before," Foster explains, speaking through smoke. "Years ago."

"Well, you've got the face for it." Nigel toasts his glass to a gentle cheer.

He's right—Foster has sharp features, creases, the scars and edges you might expect to see on the face of a career criminal. His greaser sideburns only add to the image.

"It has its pros." Foster shares the laughter, stroking his cheek.

"And you, James?" Nigel says, before drawing in enough smoke to make him squint. "You ever been tempted to inflict those good looks on the city's criminal underworld?"

"I think a pretty boy like James might raise just a few too many eyebrows," Foster adds.

It's always better to roll with these jokes, even the ones that sting. "Hey," I say, spreading my hands, "if the charge is being too handsome—lock me up, motherfuckers."

And there we go—I score the biggest laugh of the whole conversation.

The door slams open, spilling warm light and music out into the parking lot. We all turn to see Donnie stumble at the top of the hall's stone steps.

"Fuck me," Foster whispers.

Donnie's still holding a champagne flute, lifting it high above his head for balance as he begins the seemingly momentous feat of coming down the stairs. We all stand and smoke, keen to see the inevitable.

As predicted, he slips on the first step, and there's a low hum of anticipation from the small audience. Donnie wobbles and spills half the drink, his ankles buckling like he's wearing high heels. But then he recovers and sheer luck carries him to ground level with a slight bounce—and we let out a cheer as, still on his feet, he bows.

"And I'm OK," he announces, lifting his arms, losing the last few drops of champagne.

"You still driving tonight, Donnie?" someone jokes as she leaves the party behind him.

He turns to see who said it, but she's gone. "I'm . . . I'm getting picked up. Ssssays. Too drunk to drive my car. End up in." He points. "Woodland." He looks back at us. "Hey," he shouts, as if we haven't all seen each other already tonight. "It's you guys."

"Anyway," Nigel says, "good to see you."

"You too," I add.

And one by one the group breaks apart and people head their separate ways, until Foster, me, and Donnie are all that remain.

"For the road," Foster says, passing me another cigarette. "I have to go shake some hands and pretend to know who I'm talking to."

He heads inside, patting Donnie on the shoulder as he passes. Even this nearly topples him.

Once the door is closed, Donnie lowers himself carefully to the curb and sits down.

His hiccups sound comedic, like he's doing an impression of a drunk—the way Tom hiccups when Jerry tricks him into drinking liquor. But I can tell from how he's swaying, even when sitting, that it's the real deal.

Groaning the long night away, I perch next to him.

"You got a light, Donnie?" I ask.

He strains his eyes to make me out, then seems to sober up slightly, centering himself on a familiar face. "James Casper," he says. "There you are."

"Yep, me again."

Donnie leans close, holds his hand near his chin and points. "You're a good guy," he says. "You're a good, good guy."

He pulls his jacket aside, frowning, confused, and reaches inside for a lighter. He passes it to me. I light my second cigarette of the night, look up and watch a long plume of smoke disappear into the black sky above. A faint orange haze from the city's street-lights, out there, hiding all those beautiful stars.

"You too," I say. "Maybe a glass of water and a nice rest?"

"Nah, nah. I'm . . . I'm . . . fuck it, yeah. I'm drunk. I can't pretend anymore."

"You weren't doing a great job, I'm afraid."

I pass him the cigarette and he takes a shaky drag.

"No, no, don't say that, you're doing a great job, James," he mumbles. "And I'm honest. You know I'm honest."

"Sure."

"But you're a good guy." He holds the cigarette vertically in my vague direction. I'm careful not to burn myself as I pry it from his fingers.

"Again, you too."

"So you have . . . you have nothing to worry about."

"Oh, you'd be surprised, Donnie." I tap some ash away, resting my elbows on my knees.

"No. No, I mean it. Don't worry about him . . . Detective Cohen . . . he's just . . . I think he's just curious, you know. It's his job."

Donnie now has my complete undivided attention. I turn slowly to look at him.

"So . . . I will tell Detective Cohen," he adds. "But you're a good guy . . . so . . . you don't have to worry."

"What do you mean?" I say quietly, checking over my shoulder.

"He was . . . well, he was . . . speaking to your wife tonight, like, like, like they'd met before. Friendly. Like friends. I said, 'Hey, small world, small world.' We laughed. But, no, it's . . . it's because he interviewed her about the case. His case. It was . . . well, it was a Friday. He asked . . . He asked about Frank Mc . . . McBride?" Donnie waves a hand. "He's gone. He's . . . he's the missing one. On the news. They got all the posters. Find Frank. Your wife . . . she works with him, right?"

"She does."

"But me and Cohen, we're colleagues, you know. We talk and we say hey. And he had asked *me* if *I* saw Frank's car on . . . on *my* shift. Detective Cohen . . . he said . . . he said Frank might have driven on the freeway. I don't know . . . I don't have a dashcam so who knows?"

"What else did he say?"

"He said nothing. And I said nothing. It only just clicked. Just today, just in . . . in there." He points behind at the hall doors above us. "And I'll tell him what . . . I tell him. But it's OK, because you're a good guy. So don't worry." Donnie leans against me, pats my chest, his hand slipping down and landing on my leg. "I pulled you over, on the Friday . . . same night. You were . . . you were going home. You were driving home from a party. Polish . . . Polish party? Do you remember? When I pulled you over, on the freeway?"

"I remember."

"Rosie, your wife, in the black dress, the classy black dress. Anyway." He sits up and flaps his hands theatrically. "She was there that night. And you were . . . on the freeway, that night. I pulled you over. That night. Tail light."

"We were driving home from a party."

"Yeah, that's right. You were driving home. All made sense. It's just, in there, I just heard her say that you live in Singers. But . . ." Donnie points at me again, like we're sharing a joke, one eye half-closed. "You were driving *south*. So . . . you can't have been heading home. See?" He spreads his arms, like he's just solved a riddle. "Wrong way." And he sighs, his limp hands hanging down between his legs. "You were driving the wrong way . . ."

"I think maybe you're misremembering; you've had a lot to drink."

"James." He stares at me, puts his hand firmly on my shoulder. "You're a good guy, so don't worry."

A cab pulls up and honks its horn. Donnie lifts his head, and it rolls back slightly, his neck muscles loose. "Oh, this is me, this is me, this is me."

He stands, and I catch him before he falls, then walk carefully with him to the taxi. The driver climbs out and opens the back door.

"No puking in my car," he warns.

"No," I say, without any evidence. "He'll be fine."

"See," Donnie says, both hands on my chest, patting it again—face close enough to kiss. "Good guy. Good. Good . . . *Good* guy."

I bundle him inside and watch as the car drives away, red lights disappearing into the night. I'm fighting fires. This investigation has to stop. We're the weak link in Frank's story. Detective Cohen has a narrative—the lies we wrote. We were home all evening. That's the line. It was perfect. It was working. Who knows if Donnie will remember all this in the morning, but if he does . . . An anomaly could change the plot in wild, unpredictable ways.

A thousand thoughts hit my mind all at once. I imagine the suspicion growing, swelling, exploding with the only lead they have. Rosie. Me and Rosie.

We absolutely must not become suspects in this investigation.

I have nothing more than an outside influence on the police—I can suggest directions, I can even give them a false roadmap. But I can't make them follow it. What I need is someone on the inside. Someone with resources. Someone like . . .

And I remove my phone from my pocket and, standing alone in the dark parking lot, stare down into the screen.

Take care of Rosie.

I press call, turn around, and look back at the hall doors, the muffled music and laughter silenced by the speaker against my ear.

"Good evening," Edward says after just two rings. "What can I do for you, James?"

"We have a problem."

Chapter Fifteen

The little boy is wearing a black suit that's two sizes too big for him. But David says he'll grow into it. As though he'll have plenty more opportunities to wear a black suit over the next few years.

I stand in Treaston Mills' church, my jacket sleeves hanging down past my knuckles. Today, we remember Mary. I'm thirteen years old and I'm saying goodbye to my adoptive mother.

David cries during the service and I feel strange. I've never seen him cry—or show anything other than a tough smile. Even when she was ill, even when he'd crashed his car and ended up in a neck brace. It was always like everything was going to be OK. David is a big, firm, outdoorsy man. He has a white mustache and arms like trees. He fixes his own car and chops his own wood.

But he's crying like a child at Mary's funeral—hugging his old mom, clinging onto her clothes, breathing into her tiny, frail shoulder. It sounds like he's suffocating.

Rosie and I never, ever discuss what happened in the kitchen. We made sure we didn't lie—but we certainly didn't tell the truth.

It went like this:

Me and Mary were at the table. We were doing our puzzles. And Rosie came in and they had a fight about her makeup, her clothes. Mary was angry, furious. Then she fell over and grabbed her heart. Just like she'd done plenty of times before.

And we called an ambulance.

But it was too late. She was already gone when the paramedics arrived.

Without ever saying so, me and Rosie agreed it was best not to mention the minutes we waited before dialing 911. Soon as we heard a final gasp, we did what we should have done straightaway.

Matthew's sitting on the bench across from me. He's crying too. His suit is too big as well.

After the funeral, we go home, and David sits me and Rosie down on the couch and tells us we did nothing wrong.

He's holding a bottle of beer, perched on the edge of the coffee table opposite, still wearing black. Rosie's fifteen and I'm thirteen. But he speaks to us like we're half that age.

I'm extremely aware that our thighs are touching. I can feel her warm, soft skin against my leg—the slight weight of it when she shifts in the cushion. I can feel it through my suit pants and her thin, silky dress.

"You two did everything you could and . . ." David sighs, takes a breath. He's got the sore, red eyes you get from crying all day and then suddenly deciding to stop. "And you should never blame yourselves. Mary's heart condition was serious. More serious than we thought. Sadly, it . . ." His thin lips press together, his thick mustache twitches. "It was just her time to go." His voice cracks a little on that last word. "You understand?"

Rosie nods.

"James?" he says, looking at me with concern. "You know that, right? When the clock's up? It's just the way it is."

"She would have died no matter what we did?" I suggest.

And David nods. "Exactly."

She would have died no matter what we did.

Life goes on. David sits alone in the kitchen most evenings, listening to the radio and staring at the wall, or at a drink in his hand.

During the day, he works in the shed—restoring old tools, sanding furniture, repairing appliances for neighbors. Sometimes I wonder if he's looking for broken things—like he's trying to fix them all. But they break so much faster than he could ever dream of working.

He's always there at night though, when I remember him. He's always in the kitchen, by himself. I see his big hands. It looks like he's waiting for something. Counting down the days.

And they just fly by.

I'm fourteen and Rosie is sixteen.

Now, with far less discipline in the house, she goes out most weekends. She disappears, and me and Matthew just hang out. We watch TV. Wrestling. We play video games and rate the girls at school. As always, Becky Marci comes out on top. The universally accepted hottest girl not just at our school but any school, anywhere, any time.

I never tell him I think Rosie deserves the crown.

Mary's theory about Patrick and Rosie's relationship turns out to be absolutely on the money.

She's been spending a lot of her time at Treaston Gallery. She tells me one evening that Patrick is her boyfriend but they've only kissed, even though she could pass for eighteen. I simply do not reply to this. I just feel angry and sad.

Their relationship is not even a secret now that she's seventeen. He picks her up in his shiny car and takes her to the movies. Matthew makes jokes.

We call him Patrick the Pedo. He's twice her age. But, in his defense, he looks younger and she looks older.

Rosie starts wearing nice designer clothes. Because he's rich. All from art. From selling paintings.

I remember when we saw him up on the hill—he told us he only ever painted beautiful things. Not just that, but Rosie insists he only *sees* beautiful things too. Like he's blind to all the ugliness in this world. Which sounds to me like a curse, not a power.

The idea of Rosie and Patrick stops being creepy and steadily becomes reality. Just how it is.

He's holding an exhibition tonight.

Rosie is eighteen and I'm sixteen.

We're all smartly dressed, walking along the wooden floor at Treaston Gallery. Rosie's talking to guests like she's an adult. We stop at a painting and nod.

"Oh, my, yes, very good, very good," Matthew says at my side, sarcastically stroking his chin, one arm across his chest. He's putting on a posh accent—sounds like a British woman. "The composition is stunning. Oh, oh, hmm, yes."

I laugh a mean, mocking laugh.

Patrick—literally wearing a black turtleneck sweater—is at the front of the tour, explaining the wide painting, lit by a brushed-bronze strip light. Trees and houses or something, I don't know.

Me and Matthew giggle like schoolboys at the back of the group, against a white marble pillar.

"This is so fucking boring," he whispers to me.

"Stop messing around," Rosie hisses.

We're only here as a favor—she said Patrick wanted to have as many people attending as possible. Didn't matter who. But we're testing whether he really meant that.

A half-empty gallery might have been a safer bet.

I can see that Rosie's torn between being the Rosie we know and this mature version. This new Rosie that wears black cocktail dresses and impresses her boyfriend's rich customers.

We pass a staircase, which is cordoned off with a red velvet rope.

"Hey, what's up there?" Matthew asks.

Patrick breaks away from a conversation and steps over. "That's where I keep all my work in progress. And all the pieces I've painted over the years."

"Stick 'em up, man," Matthew says. "Should be proud."

"Oh no." Patrick shakes his head. "Some of it is far too good."

"Too good to show off?" Matthew wonders.

"Too good to sell."

"What's the most one of your paintings has ever sold for?" Matthew asks.

Patrick is patient with these questions. Even though there's an obvious lack of reverence—sincerity being a tricky trait for a sixteen-year-old stoner like Matthew to fully grasp. Especially if you're sleeping with his sister.

"Let's just say . . . enough to buy a couple of nice houses in a couple of nice places."

"How much would you get if you sold everything?" Matthew adds. "Even the stuff that isn't for sale."

"I don't know. But I do know that it isn't about the money."

"What is it about?" I ask.

"Art?" Patrick takes a moment to think. "It's about beauty."

Some guests with real questions step close, so Patrick shows us a hand and departs.

As he goes, Matthew leans over to me and whispers, "Cringe."

We spend the rest of the night snickering and making fun of how seriously these people are taking it all. This is what they mean when they talk about the power of youth. To be a teenage boy, unburdened by anything as lame as caring. The limitless freedom of absolute apathy. Not even the fact we're pretending matters all that much.

◆ ◆ ◆

The little boy has got hair on his face and he's almost as tall as David.

Now I'm seventeen. Rosie is nineteen. We've drifted apart over the past few years. But some days, like today, we end up alone together. Talking how we used to.

I walk into the kitchen and see her, lying on her back, looking up at the ceiling.

"Um . . . what are you doing?" I ask.

"Lying on the floor," she says, arms by her side.

"Why?"

"You get a different perspective."

"Whatever floats your boat, I guess." I step over her and pour myself some orange juice. Rosie rises to her feet behind me. Turning around, I add, "You've been weirder than usual lately . . ."

I'm standing in the kitchen and grinning like a clown as Rosie tells me she and Patrick have broken up.

"Why is that a good thing?" she asks. And then she turns her head away and smiles slightly.

"It's not. I'm . . . I'm sorry."

"James Casper? Have you got a crush on me?"

"Oh, you wish."

"Then why are your cheeks as red as my lips . . ." Rosie whispers in a jokey, breathy, seductive way. Slowly her eyes close as her mouth opens. And she shows me her tongue.

I try to laugh my blush away, but it's got nowhere to go.

"I'm sorry," she says, returning to normal. "I shouldn't make fun. But . . . it's pretty fucking obvious."

"How?" I ask, kind of concerned but mostly just curious.

"You've been staring at me for the past ten years."

Sometimes her front catches me off guard. Rosie has a special ability to cut through bullshit and just say it how it is—to announce things that normal people leave unsaid.

"You either really, really like me or you really, really hate me." She raises an eyebrow. "Maybe we should go out together sometime? If you like me, then we'll call it a date. If you hate me, then maybe we should iron out why?"

I smile. "I don't hate you, Rosie."

"Friday," she whispers. And she steps past me, so close I feel the breeze on my skin. It's enough to give me goose bumps.

Three days later, I'm at the mirror in my bedroom, looking at myself as I button up my best shirt. I haven't worn it for months, and I sniff the air, lift a sleeve to my nose. Smells a bit dusty.

So I step out and stand at the top of the stairwell, listening to the radio downstairs. Whispering voices. A football game. *Touchdown, touchdown*. When I'm certain there's no movement, I sneak across the carpet and into David's bedroom. Past his bed and toward his small bathroom, pausing once to make sure I've not made any sounds.

I push the door open and jump.

"Whoa." Matthew is standing there. He turns, a shocked, guilty look on his face, his hand coming down from the bathroom cabinet above the sink. "What are you doing?" I ask.

"Nothing."

He's holding something. We stare at each other for a few seconds.

"What's that?" I say.

"I'm . . ." Matthew shows me a bottle of prescription pills—David's depression medicine. "I'm stealing a couple of these."

"Why?"

"Don't worry," he says, flashing a hand to lower my voice. "He's got loads."

"But why are you taking them?"

Matthew shrugs. "They feel good."

"It's medicine to stop him from being sad."

"Maybe I need medicine to stop *me* from being sad?" There's a long silence. "Relax, it's no different than drinking a couple of beers or smoking some weed. Maybe you should take a few—chill you out."

"I'll be OK, thanks."

"What are *you* doing in here?"

Now it's my turn to be embarrassed. "I was . . . I was going to steal some cologne."

"Why?" He looks me up and down. "Why you so dressed up? You going on a date?"

"Yeah, don't shout it."

"Well, then you sure as shit don't want to smell like David. Old man musk? Fuck that. Follow me."

We leave David's bedroom, walk across the landing and down the hallway to Matthew's room. It's cluttered, messy—used cups and half-peeled posters. Skateboard against the wall. The sheet on his bed has rolled off the corner under the pillow.

Matthew moves a baseball bat aside so he can close his closet door—now we're both standing in front of his full-length mirror.

"What time?" he asks.

"Meeting at seven."

He checks the alarm clock on his bedside cabinet. "Great, so you got time to put on some nice clothes?"

"Fuck you." I neaten my collar and turn sideways.

"Here it is," he says, producing a bottle of expensive-looking cologne. "Be careful—two sprays and she'll be riding you like . . . wait, I assume it's a she? Never known you to have a date before."

"Yes, you have. I dated Lucy? Melina?"

"Melina?" He hands me the bottle. "That weird chick from France?"

"She's Greek." I make a point of spraying my shirt three times.

"Wow. You could be in real trouble there. Who is it?"

I hadn't even imagined how awkward this part would be. I decide to confide in him. "You know what, Matthew, it's really hard for me to say. Because you won't like it."

I head out of his bedroom and back toward my own door.

"Is it someone I've dated?" he asks, following me. "I won't mind. That's on you. You want to go where I've been, you be my guest."

"No, you definitely never dated her." I step into my room. Matthew leans against the doorframe.

"Then why would I care? Unless . . . if it's Becky Marci then we really can't be friends anymore."

"Aw, imagine." I look around the bed for my wallet, find it, and push it into my pocket. "But, no."

"Who else would I . . ." And he stops, dares to think. "No. Rosie?"

Turning back to him, I sit down on my mattress. "I said you wouldn't like it."

"What the fuck?" He comes further into the room as if this is top secret. "Have you been smoking meth? She's, like, your sister."

"She absolutely is not like my sister," I say, lining up my shoes. I slide my feet in, leaning down to adjust the heel.

"Well, I guess not but . . . she's like your friend?"

"Yeah, she's like my friend." I stand, adjust my buttons, check my hair in the small wall mirror. "That's fine. Going on dates with friends is reasonable?"

"I don't like it," Matthew says, as though this somehow ends the debate.

"Clearly." I'm clasping my nice watch now. "But I wonder why?"

"I'm not sure . . . I can't explain."

"Protective? You're worried I'll break her heart? You want to give me a macho pat on the shoulder and tell me to watch myself?"

"Nah, that ain't it . . . I just . . . Why? Why do you want to go on a date with her?"

"Why not?"

"Uh, well, for a start, she's crazy."

"But you have to say that." I smile.

"She's going out with Patrick?"

"Nope," I say, snatching my jacket from the bed. "They broke up last month."

"And she's not good-looking. I mean . . . Rosie?" Matthew seems astonished by the idea that I don't see her like he does.

"I'm really sorry to be the one to report this to you . . . but yeah, she is extremely good-looking." I put my jacket on and step toward the door. Matthew moves aside.

"This is so fucked up. I'm gonna have to take five of these pills."

"You knock yourself out," I say as I leave him standing, shell-shocked, in my bedroom.

◆ ◆ ◆

I arrive at the restaurant ten minutes early. This is the first time I've ever been on a dinner date—all the others usually consisted of a simple trip to the movies. Or an evening rendezvous up by the old elm tree. So I'm not entirely sure whether I should go in or wait. I decide it's more chivalrous to wait.

It's 7:23 p.m. when Rosie finally emerges around the corner of the building.

"Oh, hi," I say, turning, surprised, having expected her to come from the other direction.

"Hey," she says, slightly out of breath—perhaps she'd rushed.

"You look nice."

She's wearing a short, flowery dress, a small leather jacket, and a pair of low-heeled boots. Her hair is tied back, except for a wide section at the front that she's pinned in place.

We hug.

"And . . . wow," I add. "You smell nice too."

This is half true—Rosie is actually wearing a crazy amount of perfume. Way too much. And suddenly I feel less nervous about overusing Matthew's cologne.

"I . . . the bottle's broken so loads came out," she says, waving a hand. "Shall we?" She gestures at the door.

"After you," I say, opening it for her.

Inside we're guided to our table in the corner, near the window. The restaurant's logo—a bull's head with "Treaston Steakhouse" written beneath—is a backward watermark in the glass to my right. The waiter pulls her chair out, then lays a cloth napkin across each of our laps.

"Would you like some bread to start?" he asks, lighting our candle.

"Yes, please," Rosie says, smiling up at him.

He reads the specials, we order beers, then he leaves us alone with the menus. We know the steakhouse is by far the most expensive restaurant in town, but still, some of these numbers are alarming.

"We are *not* ordering from this side of the menu," I say.

"Check out the Wagyu." She leans over and points.

"I wouldn't pay that for a whole cow."

"Down at the bottom," she says. "Two-course set. That's more our range."

"Yeah, definitely."

There's a long silence, and when I glance up from the menu, Rosie's looking at me, over the warm candlelight. "What?" I say.

"Nothing . . . it's just . . . not awkward."

"Did you think it would be?" I ask.

"Did you think it *wouldn't* be?"

"I don't know. I hadn't really questioned it. We've had dinner together lots of times."

A basket of fresh bread arrives on the table.

"Not like this," she says. "Thanks."

"Guess who isn't keen on the idea."

Rosie smiles. "What did he say?"

"That it's weird. I think he was just shocked." I break a roll in half. "Did you know he's taking David's pills?"

"Yeah. He's been doing that for ages. You know what Matthew's like; you've seen that three-foot bong."

"But . . . prescription medication for depression?"

"It's anti-anxiety too—they feel amazing."

"Is everyone popping pills?"

"Yes." Rosie nods, tearing off a piece of crust. "He'll get over it."

"I'm not sure. He's . . . I think he might be . . . I don't know, a bit down?"

"No, I mean about this. About us. He's definitely fucked up generally. That goes without saying."

"He's gotten worse though."

"Hmm. You ever feel bad? The way, like, we used to hang out as kids? And now we don't?"

Part of me does miss Matthew—our friendship has diminished in recent years. But, "No, not really. Sitting around smoking weed is fun for a while . . . But not every day. Do you?"

Rosie shrugs. "He ain't *my* best friend."

"No, but he's your family."

"Exactly. Nothing can change that—we'll always be brother and sister. Have to love him by default."

"Maybe I should make more of an effort?"

"I think you might have to, after this. He's never liked any guy I've dated."

"He certainly likes me more than Patrick the—" I stop.

She glares at me in mock disapproval. "Go on, you can say it."

"Patrick the Pedo."

Understandably, Rosie's not a fan of that nickname.

"What exactly happened there?" I ask.

"With Patrick?" She holds a fist to her lips, chewing her bread. "He's just a . . . he's a prick. He's seeing someone else now, so."

"It wasn't the age thing?"

"Bothered him more than it bothered me." She shrugs.

"Did . . ." I bend the corner of the menu, wondering how to approach this question. "When did you guys actually . . .?"

"I was seventeen. So yes, technically a felony. But pedo is a stretch."

"Seventeen, so that would make him . . ." I pretend to do some calculations in my head. "Sixty-five?"

"Ha ha. He's thirty-nine."

"You remember his snow painting, the one with holes in it?"

Rosie seems confused. "No?"

"Oh . . . I could have sworn—" The waiter arrives with two bottles of beer. Then he takes our orders and leaves.

"Did he ever paint you?" I ask, before taking a sip.

"Why are we talking about Patrick?"

"We don't have to . . ." I place the bottle back on the table. "I was just wondering."

"No. He didn't. I asked him to, but he refused."

I hesitate, reworking the cheesy compliment I had planned. "Well, that makes no sense," I say. "He only paints beautiful things. And you're the most beautiful thing in the world."

Rosie stares at me for a few seconds and then bursts out laughing, covering her mouth. "I'm sorry."

"I thought that was good." I'm laughing too. It's easy to be silly together. Nothing needs to be serious. We're just being ourselves.

There's a siren nearby—blue and red lights flicker across the window, across the bull horns, as a fire engine passes the restaurant at top speed. But we're too engrossed in each other to comment.

"No, no, it was." She wipes a tear away from the corner of her eye with a knuckle. "Super smooth. You're sweeping me off my feet, James."

The busy open kitchen, clad in wood with black bovine imagery burned into the front, bursts into life as two chefs prepare our food. Steam and sizzling sounds serenade us as we drink our drinks and make our jokes.

Two courses of expensive, gourmet dining later, we're full and softened by our third round of beers. All the while talking, laughing, and totally at ease. *She's right*, I think. It isn't awkward. Not at all. There's no pressure. From the moment she arrived, I haven't felt nervous even once.

The waiter begins clearing our plates away, gestures out the window. "Apparently there's quite a big fire in town," he says. "Down at the bakery."

"Yeah?" Rosie dabs her lips. "Saw the lights."

"You can smell it out the back," he adds. "Probably flour. Goes up like a bomb. Anyway, how was the food?"

"It was great," I say. We ask for the check and I insist on paying—Rosie agrees that she'll cover the cost of our next date.

Outside, in the late dusk light, I can see a thick cloud of smoke chugging into the sky from down the hill.

"Want to go check it out?" I say, offering my elbow.

"Sure." Rosie slides her arm in mine, and we walk off together along the sidewalk.

"I think the waiter liked you," I say, looking over my shoulder.

"I doubt it. That was Tommy Preston."

"Shut up, really?" I hadn't recognized him. "I haven't seen him since middle school. He looks so different."

"You know he's married to Austin's cousin?"

"This fucking town." I shake my head.

We keep reminiscing while we stroll toward the fire. But our laughter simmers down as we get closer. People are leaning out of windows; others are leaving storefronts to check. A crowd has amassed at the top of the hill, looking down main street.

And as we join it, we see why. It's not just the bakery; the whole row is alight. Half the street. The flames are huge, roaring columns disappearing up into the bottom of a black cloud. It's fierce and glowing, and we can feel the heat from here. Three long straight lines of water are being squirted into the blaze.

"Jesus," I say.

Treaston Gallery is the worst hit—fire coming out of its collapsed roof like a tornado. The clock tower's skeleton exposed; charcoal beams crumble amid flares and falling debris.

Three fire crews, an ambulance. Police. The drama of pushing onlookers back, shouting, evacuating every building. Parked cars with melted tires—a couple already burning.

The bakery, the convenience store, half the gas station—even the old bike place is going up. A canister of something explodes, and the inferno seems to creep out even further.

"This is fucking crazy," I whisper in disbelief.

There's a strange sound coming from the commotion.

Like a woman screaming. Howling.

"Oh my God," I say, weaving through a couple of people for a better view—Rosie still at my side. "Is that Patrick?"

I point down toward the bottom of the hill. It's not a woman making that noise, it's him. He's being held back, restrained, like he's trying to run into the building.

"All his work's in there," I say. "All his art."

Rosie nestles closer to me, her arm wrapped around mine. She holds her hand out and catches a couple of flakes of falling ash.

"Look," she says, rubbing her fingers together, taking in the scene. "He could paint this. It's kind of beautiful."

"Huh, yeah."

"I had a good time tonight, James," Rosie says.

"Yeah, me too." I'm still staring down at the chaos. It's glistening off all the windows nearby, everything turned black behind the bright orange glare. Every piece of glass has become a mirror. And the embers floating up, so high into the sky—it looks like a volcano.

"What will you say?" she whispers. "When people ask about our first date?"

"Um . . . Nothing. I'll say we had fun."

"We did, didn't we? We met at seven and then had dinner."

"Well, actually, you were pretty late."

"Nah. I was early." Rosie presses herself against my arm, rests her head on my shoulder. We just watch the fire together. "You've been with me the whole night," she says.

And my eyes widen. I can still smell her perfume, even over all that smoke.

Chapter Sixteen

I'm driving fast and—I shift gears, foot down—faster, my teeth clenched together. I hit the steering wheel. Punch it again and again, so hard the metal inside seems to bend.

"Fuck, fuck," I say. "Fuck."

I am pure rage. Blood hissing in my ears. Arms locked straight. I want to put my elbow through the glass. I want to inhale black smoke and taste raw flesh. I want to burn it all down.

"Fuck."

I grab my gun from the passenger seat and lift it as I grip the wheel. Pushing myself back into my chair, teeth showing, shaking. I come to a hard stop at a red light.

The radio's saying the news again. I turn it up, loud, louder, louder than the engine. Louder than my breathing. And I literally shout—as though part of me doesn't want to hear the name.

The more the story progresses, the harder I squeeze the pistol in my right hand, the steering wheel in my left.

"Tributes have come pouring in this afternoon after the body was identified as officer Donnie Rhodes, thirty-eight," the radio says. "Colleagues have described him as a kind, fun-loving man with a zest for life who dedicated his career to making the city a better place for all its residents."

I groan as tendons tighten and stretch the skin on my neck into wafer-thin tents.

They killed him, I keep thinking. They fucking killed him. Donnie. Drunk Donnie who remembered too much. He figured out we were driving the wrong way.

And now he's dead.

I slide between screaming fury and stomach-churning dread.

Turning slowly to my left, I see a woman in a car at my side. We make eye contact, and I lower my pistol and look straight ahead. She's right to be concerned.

And the light turns green. A screech of rubber—steam wisps off the asphalt below, behind, spreading across the sidewalk in the afternoon sun.

I swing the car down the ramp and into the underground parking lot, sticking it between two spaces near the stairs. I'm up and out and striding and not even closing the door.

Then I'm yanking the handrail as I go inside, up the stairs, around the corner, into the Leyland & Lang lobby.

"Move," I say to someone standing in front of the elevator.

A suited man turns, holding a folder, eyes me up and down. "Who are you?"

I snatch the folder from his hands and fling it across the marble floor. A few people nearby stop and stare. The man almost says something but chooses instead to step aside, allowing me to enter the elevator. I hit number six. Before the doors close, I glimpse two security guards coming across the lobby, one speaking into the radio on his shoulder.

And up it goes.

That blonde woman on the TV in the elevator wall. She's back again. Smiling in her yard. Look. Look how happy these pills are making her. The oxy, the fucking benzos. I turn away and there's a poster with an even happier woman—it says, "A life without pain."

Spinning back to the glossy, looping commercial, I punch the screen three times, hard, cracking the glass and freezing the frame. A black line goes from corner to corner now, the Leyland & Lang logo emblazoned across where her eyes would be, leaving the bottom half to flicker with her perfect white smile. Perfect aside from the smudge of my knuckle blood smeared over her lips.

And the doors spread open.

Storming down the corridor, scanning, searching through the tall glass of the conference rooms, empty, empty, empty, *there*, I find a meeting in session. Edward Lang at the top, chairing a committee of ten, maybe fifteen men and women sitting around a long, varnished table.

"Um, sir," a worried voice from behind as I tear the door open.

Everyone looks. Edward doesn't seem in the least bit fazed.

"Can we have a word?" I say, the wrath coiled inside me, moments from striking.

"This is special agent James Casper," Edward says. "He's investigating some very serious allegations about nefarious members of L&L's workforce. Got some real bad eggs in the system, you know who you are." He points at one of the seated men. "I'm looking at you, John." There's a small, lighthearted laugh—corporate Edward's charm going down like honey.

I wait, then tilt my head toward his office.

"If you'll excuse me," he says, standing, buttoning up his red vest with a single hand.

Faking a smile, I shut the door behind him.

Edward dismisses three security guards gathered near the elevator. "It's cool," he says.

We don't speak again until we're inside—I make sure his door's closed and the internal blinds are drawn.

Edward casually rounds his desk and sinks into his chair. When he looks back up, I'm pointing my gun at his head.

He kind of half frowns, hesitates, checks over his shoulder, then shrugs to himself. There's a long pause before he picks up a newspaper and begins reading the front page, as though he's bored. As though I'm invisible.

"Be scared," I say.

"I . . ." The paper falls slack in his hand. He thinks for a moment—"no"—and starts to read again. "I don't believe you'll shoot me, in an office full of witnesses. And on the off chance you do, you're aiming at my head, so it'll be instant. Really nothing to worry about."

I lower the gun, pointing the barrel at his gut.

Edward huffs, folds the newspaper, and places it on the desk. "You're going to shoot me in the stomach? James, that's insane . . . Fine. You have my attention."

"You fucking killed him," I say. "You killed Donnie."

"No." He scratches his eyebrow with his thumbnail. "I haven't killed anyone. You're getting confused."

"I wanted you to help. To stop the investigation. I called you to—"

"Exactly, *you* called *me*. There was a problem. It has been solved."

"You killed a cop," I shout. "What do you think's going to happen?"

"Absolutely nothing. Please, speak more quietly."

"You think those detectives are just going to forget about it?"

"Forget . . . no. But nothing will come back to us. I assure you. The Carpenter is extremely professional."

"The Carpenter? Who the fuck is that? Some hitman? That doesn't make it better."

"Calm down."

"You can't kill police officers, you stupid fucking . . ." I trail off, because I simply don't know the right word.

"You know what I think's happened, James?" Edward says. "I think you got yourself all worked up on your way over here but you didn't actually have a plan. Like a dog chasing a car," he wiggles two fingers like little legs, "has no idea what to do if it actually catches up."

"It is not a smart move," I say, as though disciplining a child.

He takes a long breath in, then whispers, "Woof."

Finally I stop aiming my pistol at him. I pinch the bridge of my nose and sigh.

"Oh, wow . . ." Edward's expression changes, like he's just heard the most incredible news. "*Wow*. You're not upset he's dead." Every hole in his face slowly spreads open, something between joy and fascination drawing his mouth into a cartoon smile. "You're upset because you might get caught." There's more white in his eyes than any other color.

"Fuck you."

"That's why you're so angry." He stifles a laugh. "You think it was a bad decision. You don't give a fuck about deputy Donnie. Wow, James, you," he points, "*you* are something else. I really, really like you."

"No. That's not—"

"Who are you really angry at? Who's this little performance actually for?"

"I didn't want you to kill him," I whisper. Maybe to myself.

"OK. Sure. Whatever. Listen," he says, like this discussion is over. Forgiven, forgotten, swept under the rug. Time to move on. "While I've got you, I have a detailed business proposal for us going forward that I'd very much like to discuss. It'll be hugely beneficial for all involved. Are you in?"

My top lip twitches as I consider my next word very carefully. *Yeah*, I think, *let's move on*. Let's try something else for a change. Something I know Edward just hates to hear.

Leaning closer, hands on his desk, I look him square in the eyes and speak as clearly as I can. "No."

And then I turn around and walk out of his office, leaving the door wide open behind me.

Chapter Seventeen

The coffee grinder shakes and rattles on our kitchen countertop. Rosie's making a fresh pot—our morning routine continues to appear normal. She's wearing her white blouse, gray skirt, her hair tied up loose with a pin—ready for work.

I'm sitting at the breakfast bar, finishing my toast and reading the newspaper. They're blaming Donnie's death on the Carrillo cartel. I wonder if this is by design.

As Rosie walks past, I smell the wisps of coffee steam following her and, a moment later, her sweet perfume. She goes into the living room. I hear the high-pitched hiss of the TV coming on. Voices on the news. But from here it's only a whisper.

"Uh, James," Rosie says. "You want to come and see this."

Dabbing some crumbs from my mouth, I climb off the stool and leave my plate behind. And I'm transfixed when I look through the window and see Edward Lang on our TV. I keep my eyes locked on the screen as I walk fast through the door and into the living room.

"It touched my heart," he's saying, his head and shoulders on the right-hand side of the frame. He's wearing a three-piece suit. He's even neatened his beard and combed his hair.

The news anchor, on the left, asks, "And what would your message be to viewers? How can people help?"

Across the bottom, the scrolling banner reads "Leyland & Lang director donates funds to 'Find Frank' campaign."

The footage cuts to a long street, with the "Find Frank" posters pinned up on every other streetlight. I remember his blood crawling between the chessboard tiles. A red grid that just keeps on growing.

"I'd say that people should donate if they can," Edward says. "And use the hashtag to raise awareness." His face appears on the split screen again.

"And I understand you personally reached out to Mrs. McBride following our piece on Frank's disappearance?" the anchor says.

"Yes." Edward looks right into the camera. "She was very grateful." You'd be forgiven for thinking he was addressing the whole world. But no. He's speaking only to me.

"Why is he doing this?" Rosie whispers.

"You've been accused of acting with ulterior motives in the past," the anchor adds. "Saying popular things for good PR. How would you respond to that?"

"Good deeds do not hinge on motive," Edward explains. "Would you feel more or less comfortable if your surgeon was working for free, out of the goodness of their heart? But, honestly, I feel . . . well, it's solidarity. Frank McBride is a fellow city businessman, just like me, and I like to think if I ever disappeared, I'd receive similar support. We will find answers. We will find Frank."

And then the news moves on to its next item. Rosie and I just stand, side by side, and stare at the TV. She slowly points the remote and turns it off.

Finally, I say, "He's warning us."

"Why?"

"I said something he doesn't like to hear. I told him no."

"What now?"

There's a sound behind us, and I look over my shoulder.

And Edward Lang is standing in our living room, leaning on the wall next to our waving window, looking nonchalantly down at the cell phone in his hand.

I tell him to "get out." Rosie flinches when she sees him.

"Hmm. I think I'll stay," he replies.

"You can't just walk into my house," I say.

Edward pretends to be confused, gesturing at his body, at his obvious location. "I'm afraid I have to disagree."

"Rosie, go into the kitchen."

"Oh, come on." Edward laughs. "What decade are you living in?"

"Go." I turn to her.

"No," he says. "Don't. I want to speak to both of you."

"I'm sorry, but we're busy," I explain. "Get the fuck out."

"Take the morning off and come for a drive with me. I want to show you something."

"We're not going anywhere."

"Fine." Edward sighs. He notices the carrier Nell brought, the baby clothes, the hanging mobile, all piled up at the end of the couch. "Well, isn't this wonderful news." He places a hand across his chest. "Congratulations. You thought about names?"

"Leave."

"If it's a boy, you could call him . . . what was his name? That guy?" He snaps his fingers. "The one you murdered . . ." Edward acts like he's straining his memory. "It's on the tip of my tongue. He was Rosie's boss and . . . you buried him. It's been on the news?"

"I'm not going to tell you again."

"Of course." He spreads his arms. "I apologize. I've got places to be anyway. Going down the police station to speak with . . ." Reaching in his pocket, he pulls out a card and reads, "Detective Ray Cohen." He points through our window, then turns to look.

"Get some forensics in there," he says, casually waving across the tiles. "Full sweep."

"James," Rosie whispers.

"He's bluffing," I say—though I sound like I don't believe even myself.

"Sure, *maybe*." Edward nods, looks back. "Maybe James has a rock-solid case against me—it'll be exciting to see how it all plays out. Anyway, lovely to meet you, Mrs. Casper." Edward bows. "I hope prison isn't too unpleasant. And I hope they find a good home for little baby Frank." He lifts a finger dramatically. "*Frank*, that was it. That was his name. Frank McBride," he says, like he might forget again. "Frank McBride."

He turns to leave, his footsteps in the corridor, the front door creaking open.

Rosie has fear in her eyes.

And I tilt my head to the ceiling and sigh. "Wait," I shout.

Edward's personal driver takes us all out of the city. Me and Rosie sit in the back, on tan leather seats, gloomy thanks to the tinted rear windows. Up front, Edward fields business calls—most of which sound legitimate. And the ones that don't are wrapped in euphemisms—words like "product," "persuasion," and "territory" peppered throughout a particularly tense exchange with Stefan. I get the impression his driver is not kept in the loop.

Eventually, it becomes apparent where we're heading. Familiar landmarks, like the great boulder at the T-junction, the old "Welcome to Treaston Mills" sign, and the ever-denser coniferous forest—uniform trees growing straight up out of the steep ridges over the road's edge.

We follow the weaving lanes all the way down toward the lakes, which, although sharing the name, are a good twenty-minute drive from Treaston itself.

"What are we doing here?" Rosie wonders, shadows flashing over her through the window, dappled sunlight on her smart work clothes.

She was speaking to me, but Edward responds with, "You'll see."

We pull over at a large iron gate between two brand-new brick walls. Behind it, the woodland is thick and dark.

Sensing the car, the gate opens automatically and we drive through. The road's rough beneath the wheels as we turn down past the trees and then, suddenly, the woods open up too, like a magician's cloth has been whisked away. The huge, sweeping lake comes into view—a sprawling expanse of water, glinting white and deep blue. Small, fast ripples across the surface in the wide-open breeze.

A neat wooden fence appears to grow out of the track's edge and guides us further down the hill, onto the grounds of a house. It's surrounded by short, freshly cut grass, flower beds with low rock dividers—a rose arch and even a solitary tree. A tire swing spins gently, its shadow switching between a perfect circle and a perfect line. Zero to one and back again.

I wonder if this is Edward's house—it's certainly striking enough. But it feels too empty, like a display model. The building itself looks relatively old, though it's clearly seen a recent renovation. Maybe it's been spruced up to go on the market.

We park in the center of the driveway, and Edward climbs out of the car, his door thudding quietly behind him.

Rosie looks at me, slightly alarmed, and I respond with nothing more than a shrug.

She reaches out and holds my hand as we crunch over the gravel and toward the front of the house—I'm on reasonably high alert, checking the area and leaning to see through the window.

"Security system is all off," Edward says, putting a key in the door. "But you've got cameras and alarms." He points above him at a small black lens. "Motion sensors and so on."

Inside he drops the keys on a table, walks across the open-plan tile floor.

"You got your living room here, with some pretty nice views."

We follow him, turning full circle as we go. At the back of the building, floor-to-ceiling windows show us the long green slope that leads all the way down to the lake at the bottom of the yard.

There's a giant corner couch on my left. Edward leans over and straightens a cushion.

"Automatic doors open up onto the veranda at the flick of a switch, which is pretty cool." He turns, nodding ahead of him at the fireplace on the other side of the room. "And then there's this." His boots are loud on the floor as he strides excitedly past us. It's like he's a rookie real estate agent behind on his commissions. "For home security, but also, let's face it, looks great too."

He proudly presents a vintage double-barreled shotgun mounted on a varnished slice of wood above the mantel.

Stepping closer, I see that the silver receiver is engraved with a delicate pattern. I lean in and read the words in the middle: "For James Casper, a dear friend."

"So what do you think?" he asks.

"Thanks, but I already have a gun."

"That pistol isn't stopping anything. But this." He picks it up, turns it over, cocks it in half—it's loaded—then slams it shut with a flick of his wrist. "This'll turn bone to dust. Only shoot bad people with it, OK?" Edward puts it carefully back on the wall. "I meant, what do you think of the house?"

"It's very nice," Rosie says sincerely, looking across the kitchen worktop.

"Bought it a while back from a Swedish property developer," Edward explains. "Prices around here have fallen off a cliff—on the outskirts of small towns like Treaston, even mansions change hands for pocket change."

"Lot of unemployment," I say. "A lot of drug addicts with nothing to do. Rich folk don't want to live too close to all that."

"Exactly," he agrees, like this is a good thing. "But we're miles away from all that trouble. Taints the address, I guess. Spent a fortune on renovations." He swirls a hand around the room. "Good way to clean money, you know how it is. In terms of paperwork, that's all covered—I've had my lawyers tweak a few dials here and there. Incredibly, you inherited the land from a great uncle—Roger Ayrton. And Adam is a pro—because you actually *do* have a great uncle called Roger Ayrton who owned land around here. It's very clever. Absolutely watertight. There's a minor, token mortgage negotiation, but we'll cover those costs."

I make a special effort not to look at Rosie as I realize what's going on.

"You can't buy us," I say.

"Why on earth would I try to buy something I already own?"

I smile. "The answer is no."

"What do you mean?" Edward frowns.

"We do not want this house," I say.

Rosie lets out a small, doubtful humming sound.

"No, James, you're not paying attention again." Edward looks at her. "Is he always like this?" Back to me. "It's your house. It is legally *your* house."

"Then I'll sell it for a dollar to a pack of junkies."

"I'd advise you not to do that, as it may draw unwanted attention," Edward says. "Also, going forward, I am able to assist where I can when it comes to laundering your money. I've got an investment portfolio for startup businesses, and we're always on the lookout for any opportunities. So have a think if there are any ventures you might be keen on, something with reasonable cash flow—an air of legitimacy. It's got to make sense, you know. An airline might be a red flag. We can look at premises in Treaston or even back in the city. How about you, Rosie? What would *you* do if money were no object?"

"I'd open a bakery," she says, distracted by the expensive decor in the living area.

"Perfect." He claps his hands once. "You find a suitable location and we'll do it."

"If you already own us, then what's going on?" I ask.

"Vinegar. Honey. Flies. I want you to see everything you'd be giving up. Please, sit down. Listen to my plan."

Tilting my head, I make sure he watches me stride over to the huge couch. Once I'm seated, Rosie follows suit and perches by my side, the wide lake behind us.

Edward opens the double-door fridge and removes a pitcher of water, with slices of lemon and lime floating on the surface. A mechanism churns, and a deluge of ice chips fly from a nozzle into the drink.

"Ice machine," he yells over the noise.

He carries it with three glasses. It's like a traditional Chinese tea ceremony as he carefully places the cups equidistant on the table mat, then pours a precise amount into each.

We sit patiently as he finishes, then he passes a glass to Rosie, oddly pleased with himself.

"Thanks," she says, sipping it.

I just stare, and he shrugs, placing my drink on the table in front of me.

Edward leans back in the couch, his big arm over the cushion at his side, his legs crossed. "So peaceful here, isn't it?"

Sighing, I roll my eyes.

The way he reacts is strange—like he's genuinely hurt by the fact I have no interest in friendly small talk. For a split second, I feel sorry for him. Like a lonely kid at school.

"It's lovely," I say. "Please, let's speak about the plan."

"I want you to understand how unique our relationship is," he says, leaning forward. "The lengths I go to in order to keep my identity secret. Not even my partner knows about this side of the business. It's just me, Stefan, Adam, and now you two."

"I'm honored," I say.

"Crazy to think that an empire as big as this can be operated with such a small team. You know how many people work for Leyland & Lang? More than thirty thousand. And the profit per head? I can assure you, it's not as good."

"It can't just be about money," I say.

"It's about winning."

"You can win without breaking the law."

"You sound like my father. We're too far along now. No retreat. No surrender. If you're going to be found dead on a battlefield, might as well be facing the right way."

"What the fuck does that even mean?"

"It means we're marching forward."

"Well, then, eventually you'll get caught," I say.

"You're right." He sits up straight, points. "You're absolutely right. Adam says this all the time. And that's where *you* come in. It'll work like this. We will continue trading virtually as normal, but we will cost in, let's say, a ten percent attrition rate. I will assist you in arresting our competitors."

"You mean the Carrillo cartel?"

"Yes. I'll also facilitate a series of larger seizures, for which you will take full credit. We'll get drugs and cash placed in the possession of various businessmen."

"You want to frame people?"

"Well, yeah, people who are already deep in the game though," he says. "We'll just make it look worse than it is. You'll exceed your arrest quota. And you will be a hero. This will in turn keep us out of the limelight. The DEA has always been the biggest risk. And you can single-handedly neutralize it."

"So I work hard, make countless arrests, and the amount of heroin on the city streets remains exactly the same?"

Edward smiles. "How is that any different to normal?"

"What do I get out of it?"

"Freedom . . . and a fucking obscene amount of money," he says. "There's no reason why we can't all win." Edward stands. "Don't decide now. Sleep on it. I'm sure you'll realize this is the best option for everyone." He heads toward the door.

"We walking back?" I ask.

"There are three brand-new cars in the garage," he says, turning in the doorway. "We weren't sure on color, so got a selection."

Once he's gone, me and Rosie sit quietly for a while.

"Do you want to talk about it?" she says.

I watch small droplets on the side of the cold cup begin to run. Then I look around the room. "Not in here."

We stand up, and Rosie presses a button on the wall. Our new automatic glass doors slide open on smooth runners. The mechanism is almost completely silent. And then we walk all the way down the yard, stopping at the water's edge.

"It is perfect," Rosie says, the small waves creeping up the silty ground near her feet. "It's like the dream."

I think about him again. My chest aches. And Rosie must spot something because she's suddenly concerned.

"God, are you OK?" she asks.

My eyes sting and I feel the blood leaving my face. I realize why. It's because I'm considering it. "People like him," I whisper, pointing back up the hill. "People like him killed Matthew."

"It's more complicated than that," she says, holding my hand. "Matthew was depressed."

I bow my head. "He was a drug addict."

"I know it hurts. No one likes to swallow pride. But . . . what's the alternative?" Rosie gently places my palm on her stomach. "Hmm?" She searches for eye contact.

"It's untenable," I explain, looking at her. "It just doesn't work long term to be in his pocket. Edward Lang is on borrowed time. And you've seen, he's fucking, I don't know, autistic or something. He's not right. We can't always be at his mercy. Blackmail does not go away. He'll demand more and more."

Rosie stares across the lake, her loose hair swept back by the breeze. "Nothing has changed," she says, narrowing her eyes to the cool air. "The goal is the same. It's just harder now . . . Earn his trust. Get close. Keep him happy, keep him out of prison. You can still get him. There will be an opportunity."

"An opportunity for what?" I lean to see her face. "Edward will have a copy of that recording, so will Stefan and Adam. If any of them go down, the others will respond accordingly. Maybe they all have the file on laptops and phones. External hard drives. The aim is to get our hands on that recording . . . it has to be, but . . ." I puff out a lungful of air. "It'd be a miracle if we covered every base before they could expose us."

"What if there was a way to have all that stuff—all their devices—come to you?" Rosie wonders. "It's all evidence in a case you've been working on. If you got all three of them. Edward. Stefan. Adam. All at once."

"Even if I could orchestrate something like that, get all three of them off the streets, all at the same time, have all their devices bagged up in an evidence locker, it still wouldn't be enough."

"Why?"

"They *know* what we did," I say. "They could make a phone call, pass a note to their lawyer. They could shout it out in court. Even if I managed to arrest them all at precisely the same moment."

"James," Rosie says softly, as though I'm being naive, like I've missed something obvious. She turns and steps closer, holding both my hands now. "We're not talking about arresting them."

Chapter Eighteen

"Matthew," Rosie yells, cupping her hands around her mouth, all the vowels drawn out in the shout. I hear his name echo back at us across the valley.

We're standing high on the stone ridge, at the edge of the trees. I can see the pointed canopies on the hills opposite, but everything in between is hidden by a thick, low fog. Like a series of floating islands.

Down there, below the clouds, the river and rocks and endless wilderness are cold and lonely. A thousand places to get lost and die.

"Why?" I ask. "Why did he get so upset?"

"You know what he's like," Rosie says over her shoulder, leaning away from her megaphone hands.

"What did you say to him?"

"Loads of stuff, I can't remember." She shakes her head and turns. "I think he was embarrassed."

I'm seventeen. Rosie is nineteen. We're outside in the woods. It's late autumn, the crisp, damp beginnings of winter creeping into every morning, freezing blades of grass, killing final flowers.

Matthew has run away. It sounds stupid to use that term, as he's turning eighteen in a matter of days. But here we are. What else can we say?

"What was he wearing?" I ask, because it's much colder than it should be.

"Not enough to be out here."

This is not the first time Matthew has disappeared. When we were thirteen, he got caught shoplifting and, instead of facing David's inevitable disappointment, spent the entire day hiding under a bridge. The following year, having recently discovered weed, he ate a full tray of brownies at a midsummer party. They found him asleep on the altar around 4 a.m. after residents reported "strange singing" coming from Treaston Church.

Matthew's turbulence correlated with puberty. But if I'm honest, I think Mary's death is where it really started. It's not that he necessarily misses her—more that he misses his relationship with David. And *he* has changed in fundamental ways since he lost his wife.

It's like his grief is contagious. The fact that Matthew steals David's depression pills adds a certain layer of credence to this theory. He's grown to be quite the drug connoisseur in his teenage years.

But heroin? This caught me completely off guard.

"And you're sure?" I ask, as Rosie steps back toward me, over the soft woodland floor.

"It was light-brown powder," she says. "In tinfoil. Wisps of smoke. He was sucking it up with a straw." Her jawbone clenches slightly. "It was heroin, James, trust me."

"You got angry at him, didn't you?" I say. "It's a red day?"

She looks at her feet. "I may have used some sharp words, yes."

Rosie and I have been on at least five dates. But it seems like the intimacy has plateaued. We'll sit close on the couch and hold hands beneath the blanket. We'll hug longer than friends, far longer than family. And last week we even slept in the same bed.

Yet we still haven't kissed.

It's almost like something is missing. Or maybe we're both so comfortable that neither wants to make the first move. Either way, it's been about six months now and I'm worried I've missed the window. Six months is too long to date a girl without a kiss or more.

We trudge down the hill, and in the fog it's hard to tell what time it is. I check my watch—just after 5 p.m..

"It's going to get dark soon," I say. "He's probably gone back anyway."

Rosie's walking ahead, over the mulch and sticks. She's wearing a thin jacket, jeans, and gloves. Faint white puffs of breath fade instantly into the mist around us.

But she doesn't slow down. I'm guessing, from her concern, that she said something pretty bad to her brother. I can't begin to imagine how spiteful it must have been for her to care this much.

It's quiet too. Things that buzz or growl have gone to sleep, so when leaves rustle or twigs snap, they're usually beneath our feet.

"We're reaching the point of no return," I add. But still, she just hikes on.

So I keep following her.

We take our minds off the matter at hand by talking about the news—even after a couple of months, the TV is obsessed with the World Trade Center coming down. I must have seen that second explosion a thousand times.

"It's really fucked up," I say. "If you actually stop and think about it."

"Uh, yeah," she agrees. "That's kind of the consensus."

"I mean, just on a human level. Psychologically. Can you *imagine* doing that?"

Rosie clambers over a wide tree stump. "Vividly."

"Yeah?"

She looks back at me. "Don't you wish you believed in something enough to die for it? Hijack a plane and slam it into a building?"

"That . . . that is a strange way of looking at the situation."

"I just understand the anger, the hatred. You never get any impulses like that?"

"Never been tempted to hijack a plane," I say, "no."

"Not necessarily that extreme, I mean . . . You're never tempted to go to the shed, grab David's revolver, and just burst into math class and fire until it goes click?"

"I wouldn't start in math class—too many windows to escape through."

"I'm just saying, I get it. I get the appeal of just . . ." Rosie puts her hands on her chest then spreads them out quickly. "Just fucking exploding. Complete and utter fuck-everything annihilation."

"I think you should be on a list somewhere."

"No, that's my point." Rosie sighs. "I wouldn't do it. I have all the passion but no cause."

"Sounds like one of his T-shirts."

"Whose?"

"Matthew's. Killing snakes, you remember, when he went through his goth phase. He used to make his own shirts with the funny mottos."

"'I know all the words, but I've got nothing to say.'"

"Yeah." I laugh. "That's the one."

"My favorite was always, 'Dance like nobody's watching, sing like nobody's listening, die like nobody cares.'"

"He did some pretty fly nihilism. I've forgotten most of them—some were great."

"'Beauty is skin deep, so go to the bone.'"

"Ha ha, yeah."

"Or," Rosie says, the quotes flooding back to her, "'Gunshots speak louder than words.'"

"I liked the surreal ones too. 'Blood is thicker than water.' And then on the back it said—"

"'But not as thick as jelly.'"

I laugh. "He should have gone into business."

"*Matthew*," Rosie shouts suddenly, startling some nearby birds.

"He could be anywhere by now, let's go back."

"I'm worried about him, James. What if he does something stupid?"

We both know what she means, but it doesn't need to be said. "He wouldn't."

"You know, he was talking about leaving Treaston the other day."

"Good," I say.

"To find our biological parents. Apparently there are agencies that'll do it."

"Oh. So? What's wrong with that?"

Rosie slows down, turns to look at me. Behind her, the fog is so thick—three trees and then endless gray. It could pass for smoke. "It's not going to do him any good, is it? Meeting those pricks."

"Why are you so angry at them?"

"Your parents died, James," Rosie explains. "My parents gave us away. No wonder Matthew is so screwed up. Imagine that hanging over you."

"Are you not curious?"

"Yeah, slightly," she says. "It'd be nice to hear that they died in some horrible way."

"There are complicated circumstances. You don't know what was happening in their lives when they had you."

"Can you envision a scenario where you'd have a two-year-old daughter and a newborn son and then get rid of them?"

"Money troubles?" I suggest. "I don't know."

"Well, don't fuck unless you can take care of a baby—it ain't rocket science," she says. "They had a family. A *family*. And they gave it up, on purpose? I don't have time for weak shit like that. They don't deserve to meet me and Matthew. Honestly, I hope they're both dead in a ditch."

"Are you OK? Is this like hormones?"

"I feel like this all month."

"So if you got pregnant, you'd keep it no matter what?" I ask. "What if you were homeless? What if you had nothing?"

"You can always abort the thing—I'd rather be clawed out with a coat hanger and flushed down the toilet than abandoned."

"Jesus."

"If I had a baby—yes, James, I'd do absolutely *anything* to take care of it."

We arrive at a crossing over the river. It's been faintly raining for the past hour and now every branch is dripping. A tree has fallen, creating a bridge. Though it looks slippery and too old to walk across.

"Come on," she says, stepping up.

"That's a bad idea."

"Why?" Rosie pushes down with her boot, testing the wood's strength. "It's fine."

"We're a two-hour walk from civilization." I have to speak louder over the splash and rumble of a nearby waterfall hidden in the mist. "It'll be dark in about five minutes. And I'm freezing. Let's go back."

She turns around and beckons with her hands, inviting me to follow. "Come onto the log."

Rosie steps backward, turning, her hand held above her head now like a ballerina—like a tiny girl in a music box. And her foot almost slips. "Whoa." She laughs, wide-eyed and wide-armed for balance. Then she carries on, turning full circle again as she crosses the tree trunk. Dancing.

I lean over the rocky edge and look down into the fast-moving water, maybe fifteen feet or more below. Craggy stones and gnarly roots. It's almost black and white in the sunless fog.

Halfway along, Rosie stops, turns back, and gracefully lowers her hand—holding it out for me. "Come on, James," she says. "I want to dance with you."

But I just stare and shake my head.

"It's rock solid," she shouts, standing up straight. She bends her knees and bounces slightly. Jumps. "See? It's not going to break."

And she jumps again and the wood gives way and she's gone.

"Fuck." I reach forward, even though she's too far, then fall to the ground as the end of the broken trunk swings up into the air in a haze of wet mud and bark.

A loud, crunching splash, and I look and catch a shaded glimpse of her jacket. She's face down, being carried away on the water.

Rising to my feet, I stumble and go fast over the rough terrain above, making sure not to lose sight of her.

"Rosie," I yell.

It's so dark—I squint as she moves in and out of my vision, the river taking a gentle corner up ahead. Clambering over a boulder, I slide down the bank, my jacket riding up, soil and leaves on my back as I thud to the ground at the water's edge.

Now that it's flatter, I can run—I round the corner and she's there, sitting, still submerged to the waist.

Putting my hands under her armpits, I feel her soaked jacket. Water oozes out like I've squeezed a sponge. It's cold enough to make my fingers ache as I drag her back onto the pebbles.

She's breathing fast, eyes locked ahead. I can't tell if it's the gloom of dusk or if her skin really is a pale shade of blue.

"James," she says, showing me her trembling hands, looking down at herself.

The river is splashing, spitting nearby, and the light rain has taken a turn. It patters on my jacket, so I fling the hood up onto my head.

"OK," I say. "Rosie, you need to stand up. We have to be quick."

Her shivering becomes a nod as I lift her to her feet.

Again I notice her clothes. She's soaked through. "We should take this off," I say.

"No." She pants. Sniffs. "I'm too cold."

"You're in shock. You're wet."

The rain is coming down hard now, loud on the flicking leaves above us. They bounce and sway—glossy even in the narrow twilight.

Unzipping her jacket, I see she's only wearing a thin T-shirt underneath. Even in this state of panic, I realize the clock is ticking.

"It's not that windy," I explain. "I think it's safer not to wear this."

"I'm . . . really . . . cold."

"I know." I take her jacket off and drop it on the ground.

Then I remove mine and drape it across her shoulders. She hunches over, her teeth chattering, her hair clumped and stuck to her face.

"We need to move fast, OK?" I say.

It takes a good hour or two, in daylight, at a brisk pace, to get back to safety. Already, I feel *I* might be too cold to make it. Now that the sun's gone, it must be close to freezing down here in the dark, damp air.

As we take our first step, my arm around Rosie's waist, she grunts and pulls her right foot off the ground. She just stands there, shaking, on one leg.

"You've probably sprained it," I say. "But we *have* to go."

It takes us five long, painful minutes to get back up the steep bank. I pull out my cell phone, flip it open, and see there's no reception. Lifting it high, I stand on a nearby boulder. Nothing. So I fold it, slide it back in my pocket, and turn. Rosie is sitting on the ground now. She's stopped shivering.

Again we begin to walk—her arm around my neck, my arm around her waist. And an hour later, it's pitch black—I'm using the faint glow from my phone to light the way.

Rosie hasn't spoken for a long time. Her eyes are closed and her breaths are fast and shallow—I only hear her inhalations, two gasps a second.

"I know you don't want to hear this," I say, forcing a jittery laugh. "But I'm really, really, really cold too."

She doesn't react.

"We're nearly . . ." I whisper, my heart sinking at the tree line. The rocks. It's . . . wait . . . "Oh no."

We've gone the wrong way.

The very moment we stop, Rosie collapses. A sudden ragdoll, crumpled at my feet.

As I try and get my bearings, my phone's battery dies, dropping us into a black abyss.

I've lost track of time. Distance. I'm just . . . lost. My clothes are drenched. It's agony to unfurl my cramped fist—I watch it twitching in the shadow like a time-lapse flower opening up to the sun. The sun that left us hours ago.

And now I'm dragging something. Her.

I'm dragging Rosie. Walking backward. Stumbling. Falling.

Is she dead?

I blink and we're both sitting on the ground. She's between my legs. I'm hugging her. It reminds me of last week, when we shared a bed. We hugged for the entire night.

We're there now, so it's OK. Just asleep, under a blanket. Comfortable. Safe.

Maybe I can give her some of my warmth. But my skin feels like stone. All I can hear is whimpering and rain.

I realize I've closed my eyes. No. Back up, I drag her. Drag her. Drag. We're going backward up a hill, and I'm whispering the word "help."

I'm thinking, *help*. *Help*. Praying. *Help*. Asking for—

Something trips me and I groan, thudding onto my back yet again.

I'm on a log or . . . wait. Steps. I manage to shuffle, look over my shoulder. And there's a black shape cutting the faint glow of night between the trees. A silhouette. I wipe my eyes. It's a cabin. Our cabin.

Abandoned, half the roof collapsed, hammering rain running off in long streams, creating sheets of falling water, rivers in the mud.

I'm pulling Rosie by her arm now, too tired to be careful.

Once I've got her inside, I kneel and check her pulse. But my fingers are so numb I can't tell if she's dead.

There's an iron woodstove in the corner. I crawl over, grab the rusted handle, and it squeaks on old hinges. Empty.

The back and side of the cabin are gone. The remaining patch of roof is about half the size of my bedroom. All that's keeping us from the elements are the nearby walls, two of which are made of rain. The kitchen is even worse—the ceiling has fallen in and rubble and debris have created a dark swamp.

My eyes are closed as I feel my way into the bedroom. Everything is damp—grit and splinters sticking to my fingers. The wide-open window howls and sprays. But the ceiling appears to be intact. I search inside a drawer.

I'm looking for something. Something to eat? Or . . . I sink lower on my knees and pull open a cupboard. There's a box of matches and a few sheets of paper. I grab it all and crawl back into the living room. Rosie is on her side on the black floorboards. Perfectly still.

I try to say a word but I can't.

Some small, thin logs are piled behind the woodstove. I pull at them until they fall and tumble, digging through to the ones in the middle. I take a fistful of tinder and bark and push it inside.

Squinting, I carefully pull open the matchbox and whimper. There are two matches.

I try to strike one, but nothing happens. I try again. My fingers are shaking too much.

Finally, squeezing the matchhead, I drag it down the side and it lights. Panicked, shallow breaths as I cup it and—

A drip from my hair hits it perfectly. It fizzes out.

"No."

For the second, final attempt, I put my hands inside the woodstove, my head resting on the front. And, as before, it barely sparks alight. I hold my breath as I gently lower it to the edge of the paper. A tiny blue orb struggles, flickers. Then, after a lifetime, it grows to the size of a candle flame. And then the paper catches, and I nurture it with small strips and the short puffs of air escaping my mouth automatically.

Even this slight warmth feels like it's saving my life.

A few broken planks, a log, and the fire is going. It's really going.

I lean down, rest my ear near Rosie's face, and feel the lightest stroke of cold air.

She's still breathing.

Faster now, I leave her and crawl, dizzy, confused, across the room. Then I push the table closer, tip it over onto its side, and drag it toward Rosie, enclosing her between the legs, her back pressed against the underside.

It takes me a long time to strip her to her underwear. Then I undress myself.

With our clothes hanging up next to the woodstove, I feed it log after log, blowing and blowing until it roars. Until the heat hurts my face. Until steam rises from everything, everything orange and glowing like we're in a furnace.

The rain behind us, over the table, hammers and rumbles in my chest, splashing out in the pitch dark. But here, it's so bright. There's so much steam.

I go to the bedroom again and find a few damp sheets that I hang over the table, creating a tent of sorts, sealing us in. Three new walls—the fourth full of fire.

The chilling air creeps through every gap, but the heat inside just blasts it away.

My skin is bone dry now. Hot to the touch. And I'm thinking clearly as I lie behind Rosie and cover her with a warm, dry blanket—tucking half of it beneath us. The inferno is almost too fierce to look at.

We're in a cocoon. An oasis in the storm.

Rosie just wearing an off-white bra and panties. I feel life coming back into her body. Within half an hour, her heart's beating against her ribs.

I stroke her dry hair, touch her red cheeks—her skin's so soft and clean.

And, with her head on my arm, she gradually opens her eyes, blinking in the firelight.

She hums, sleepy and comfortable. "It wasn't," she whispers.

"What?"

"That tree trunk. It wasn't stable."

I laugh. "No."

Rosie smiles and glances at the fire. "James," she says, rolling her head back to look at me. "I'm so warm. I'm so . . ." She frowns. "Naked. Did you take my clothes off?"

"It actually was a life-or-death situation."

"Then I forgive you." She reaches up, puts her hand on my neck, and pulls me down to her face.

And, lying right there on the floor, we kiss.

"I'm not usually into this kind of thing," she says, our lips still touching. "But this is pretty fucking romantic."

We laugh. I rest my forehead on hers. "It was, until you said that."

"I'm sorry." Her eyes creased and glassy.

"I forgive you."

"Where are we?" she asks.

"In the abandoned cabin. The one we found when we were kids. Honestly, I can't remember how we even got here."

Rosie closes her eyes, bites her bottom lip, and sighs. "Who cares?" she whispers.

Chapter Nineteen

Driving our brand-new electric car through our brand-new electric garage doors, I turn and smile at Rosie in the passenger seat. We leave our brand-new house behind.

Both still dressed for work and many miles from where we should be, there's that uniquely exhilarating sense we'd get when we were young and out of school—the excitement, the disregarded inevitabilities of truancy. All the consequences are out there somewhere, waiting for us. But here, now, we're together and we're safe.

She looks out through the back window, then notices the antique shotgun on the backseat.

"Why did you take that?" she asks.

Edward's gifts are mounting up. The house, the car we're sitting in, the million dollars in cash we've dried and bagged.

"It's got my name engraved on it," I say. "Best not left lying around."

Up the long, winding drive, the house and lake disappearing in the rearview mirror as we weave back into the trees, through the shadows of leaves, up and up and out onto the main road.

And then it's foot down, the near silent acceleration as we're pressed back into our seats. Back into the city. To the concrete and smoke, the lights and filth.

I'm thirty-four years old and Rosie is thirty-six. We're in trouble again.

Only now I have a clear plan of action.

I'm going to kill them. That's our play for all this. It's a simple, blunt instrument. But it really is the only way out.

Just like with everything else, Matthew's words arrive to guide me. I recall another one of his T-shirts. Printed in white letters across black cotton. "Become something far worse than the monsters who torment you."

So that's what I'll do. And the clarity is liberating.

The evidence of what we did is stored in a number of places. On wetware, hardware—on minds and hard drives. A private conversation about burying Rosie's boss. It really does all hinge on that single piece of information.

That recording needs to be deleted. Every available format needs to be wiped off the face of the earth.

I know now which direction I'm heading. There's no uncertainty. I can see it. This is what they say—this is how you succeed. You have a vivid image of precisely what success looks like—let it grow so bright in your mind that it burns away all the pictures of failure you mounted in your darkest moments alone.

I will strengthen my position at the DEA, with Edward's help. He's right, a series of arrests will make it appear as though we're having an impact on the city's drug supply. Ironically, this will cast further doubt on Nell's abilities and our theory about Leyland & Lang's involvement in illicit activities. Carrillo cartel men will seem to fill the Edward Lang-shaped hole.

In tandem, I will secure Edward's trust—and find a way to kill him, Stefan, and Adam, all at exactly the same moment. The timing of this move is key. Then, using the very real fact—and established suspicion—that Edward has men in the city's police department, I will demand that all the evidence is delivered promptly to our office. Their sudden death will cement their criminality and, like clockwork, all their devices—all their hard drives—will arrive untouched, sealed in evidence bags.

It's the only safe way to get a true reading of what these men were doing. I am the only person trustworthy enough to handle something this sensitive. Me. Rob Sanders will green-light it all.

That power I felt at the port is back and tingling in my arms. The inevitability. Like the comforting rules you have as a child. Structure. So much anxiety comes from not knowing. From doubt. But now there is no mystery. Now the weight of choice has truly been lifted. Now it's fate.

"Pull over," Rosie whispers, removing her seatbelt.

"Why?"

Still wearing her tight, gray, corporate work skirt, she shuffles in her seat, rolling the material up her thighs. She wrestles it above her waist, then leans toward me—perfume and breath—as she pulls her underwear down to her knees, ankles, and over her shoes. One falls off and she unbuttons her white blouse.

The car has slowed down on the quiet road. And it rumbles on the gravel and stones and comes to a gentle stop in the shade of these straight, dark trees. I try to check there's no one around, but Rosie is already climbing on top of me.

That night—after Edward told me to sleep on it—I do. Back home in Singers, I sleep like a baby. I think I'm only halfway through Matthew's note before I'm gone.

I dream of a beach, maybe, or somewhere else with water. Bare feet. Birds turn black against stock image skies. Filter applied.

I know I'm asleep. But my mind will keep pretending there's no control here, in the sandy paradise, in the surreal sunset flare and glare flashing on lenses that don't even exist. The modern world, with all its gloss and screens, has made my dreams cinematic.

And Matthew's words still find me in these private places, on these secret shores, as they do in waking hours.

True fear does not dwell in things that happen. But in things that might. And, almost always, in things that never will.

His letter was a masterpiece. Looking back on myself and considering the paths I've forged, I can trace it all the way to his writing. Could I ever admit this to anyone, though? The greatest influence on me? Not the Bible, not the sonnets of Shakespeare or the wisdom of the Greeks. The Dalai Lama's soundbites don't resonate here. And how could I possibly know the kinds of things my father used to say?

But my best friend's suicide note? That's found its way into my soul.

This cannot be a healthy way to deal with grief. But I've tried everything else.

Matthew can join me on the beach, with a lighthearted shrug. If the dream was lucid, I'd tell him I'm doing my best. I'm taking care of Rosie, just like he asked. And I'm punishing those who profit from the chemicals that took him away from us. He'd understand that this will come at a cost. But it's not lucid. So I just sit with him on the sand and enjoy one of the thousand conversations I wish we'd had.

And, for the first time in a long while, I wake up feeling refreshed.

Rosie is looking at me from her pillow, the sun warm on our white bedspread. Distorted squares of morning yellow, the window behind her bright and blurred in my vision. She reaches out and touches my cheek.

"It's not real," she says softly.

"What?"

"You were having a nightmare."

"No," I say. "It was a nice dream."

"What was it about?"

"All my dreams are about Matthew."

Rosie blinks. "He'd have made a good uncle."

I sigh. "He would have been great."

She strokes my neck with her thumb.

"Are you still sure?" she asks.

"Yes," I say. "This is how we win."

I reach under my pillow, pull out my phone, and call Edward Lang.

Still lying on my side, facing Rosie, I look into her eyes as he answers.

"Good morning, James."

And I smile. "I'm in."

Adam's apartment is deceptively large—a narrow corridor opens up to a sprawling living room. I think it's two apartments—maybe three—joined together. He's got a panoramic view of the park—long, weaving paths with joggers and pigeons. Grass mounds for picnics and pouting, peace sign selfies.

It looks like a deluxe hotel room, the honeymoon suite, with ornate pots and bowls, marble flooring, and eclectic antiques. Also modern things, like limited editions of toys still in their boxes, figurines, Japanese characters from cartoons I've never heard of, which no doubt boast an audience the size of an average country. Blue hair, big eyes, overly sexualized girls and feminized boys. On an archway that separates the kitchen from the living area, he's got a framed comic book, with a black signature across the glass.

"You want a drink or anything?" Adam asks.

"Sure," I say. "Coffee."

He guides me further inside. Adam's wearing a baggy hoodie, jeans, and gym socks. One of which is loose, so it hangs slightly from the end of his toes. The back of his hair is spiked up from his pillow.

There's a small green bong on his coffee table. Adam darts forward and snatches it, hiding it at the side of an armchair.

"Sorry, I . . ."

I give him a tired laugh. "I'll let you off."

"Sure. Yeah. Right." He fiddles with his glasses, then turns and heads into the kitchen. "Take a seat, man," he yells through the doorway as a coffee machine drones into life.

I stroll past the leather couch and his gigantic TV mounted above an impressive collection of electronic devices. A full library of books, films, video games on three sets of expensive-looking shelves at the side.

And next to a tall closet, with hand carved edging and what look like solid silver handles, I see a painting on the wall.

A snow scene. Frozen water, trees just black smudges in the white haze. Up close, the imperfections in the paint, the mounds and dips and brush marks, form waves of dried liquid. But step back and it's stunning. I recognize the work immediately, but confirm my suspicion when I lean in to check the corner.

Adam places two cups on the table behind me.

I look around, and he's unfolding a large paper map.

"This is a Patrick Quincy-Jones piece," I say.

Adam peers up at the painting, at me, then back to the map in his hand. "You a fan?" he asks.

"I used to know Patrick, back in the day." I return to the snow.

"Yeah?"

"Yeah. My wife dated him for a while, before we got together."

"No shit." Adam steps over and admires it with me. "I bought it at an auction. I know nothing about art, or antique furniture, or any of this stuff." He knocks on the closet door—sounds hollow. "All I know is that if it's worth a lot of money, it's a good investment."

"Saving for the future?"

"For my ma and my sis, yeah," he says. "I just want them to be comfortable."

"They know what you do?"

"No, God no. They . . . they can't. That's why I got all this stuff. Piles of cash raises suspicion. But crystal lamps? First-edition comic books?" He raises a hand to the winter landscape. "Ridiculously expensive paintings? I really like it though. Will be a shame to sell it someday."

"Hmm." I nod. "She burned down his gallery."

Adam hesitates. "Excuse me?"

"Yep, whole thing, years of work. Gone."

"Uh . . . Why?"

"I'm not entirely sure," I say, still eyeing the painting. "I think he cheated on her. She was quite young when they first met. Complicated times." I remember our date. Rosie said she asked him to paint her. But he never did. He refused. "Anyway, that's why remaining pieces like this are worth so much."

"Kind of, uh, kind of makes them more beautiful?"

I smile. "Maybe."

"This might sound like a rude question but . . ." Adam picks at his sleeve. "You sure about her?"

"Who? My wife?"

"Just going on the few stories I've heard."

"She's the only thing in this world that I am sure about."

We sit down at the coffee table, and Adam runs me through the city's drug-dealing networks. I learn more in thirty minutes than I have in over a thousand official briefings.

He explains how they move the product, where they sell it, ship it, the levels of detachment Edward insists on maintaining.

"Like an airlock," Adam says. "Stefan is hands-on—people know his name, his face. But Edward's involvement is kept quiet. Same with me. That's why it's been so difficult for you guys."

"We were getting close," I say.

"I know . . ." He sighs, concerned. Vulnerable. "OK," he says, shifting gear. "Saturday night. Couple of guys have been bulk buying and then cutting our product—working with Carrillo dealers. I can give you a time and a place. There's going to be a car, owned by a man called Wesley or Warren or some shit. Doesn't matter. Inside there will be a substantial sum of money and whatever's left of the heroin."

"And what if he talks?"

"He knows nothing about us," Adam says. "If he talks, it'll be about the Carrillo cartel. And he will know better than to do that."

"Why so sure?"

"Do you remember that guy hanging over the freeway last summer?" Adam says. "They took out his eyes and his teeth, cut his dick off, and strung him from a bridge. They shot his girlfriend, her mother, and even his dogs. He worked for the cartel. And he was an informant. He was speaking to the FBI. That's what they do to rats. The people you bust won't say a word. I promise."

"And you're not worried about fucking around with them?"

"I'm extremely worried." Adam's eyes are huge behind thick lenses. "Which is why we need caution from now on. We do not meet up for friendly debriefs at L&L warehouses. After this conversation, me, you, Stefan, Edward . . . there is no need to ever be in the same room again. We have to distance ourselves from illegal activity wherever possible. In every conceivable sense."

"How much cash will this guy have?"

"About a quarter of a million."

"How can you be sure of that?"

Adam frowns. "Stefan is going to plant it."

"Seems expensive?"

"Getting rid of the competition and simultaneously diverting attention away from us?" Adam shakes his head. "It's a bargain. It needs to be substantial enough to make it seem as though they're major players. You're looking for big fish, right?"

"We are."

"Well, this guy is affiliated with Raymond Avery himself . . . so . . ."

"Who's that?"

"You've got to be kidding." Adam laughs like I just said I'd never heard of the Rolling Stones. "Raymond Avery owns the Eagle Hotel—he launders money for the cartel. Handles things for them around here."

"So he's your main competition?"

"Yes, I suppose he is."

"Why don't I arrest him then?"

"You're welcome to try. But let's start with this first. Baby steps."

"I'll need a paper trail."

"Of course." Adam reaches down into a folder on the plush Persian rug. "This is an email exchange."

"They'll want to know where it's from."

"Anonymous tip-off. It doesn't matter. When he's in custody and you've got the money, who's going to care about how you found it?"

"And if he claims it isn't his?"

Adam's eyebrows lift as he spreads his hands. "Has that defense ever swayed you in the past?"

He's got an answer for everything. So this is what we're doing. Framing low-level dealers for Edward's crimes.

For the next ten minutes Adam outlines all the details, using the physical map and street view on his laptop. All the while, there's a creeping shame poorly hidden behind his hesitant mannerisms. A good, sensible boy running with a bad crowd. Working with the kind of men his mother should have warned him about.

He reminds me of Matthew. Innocence corrupted far beyond repair. If only he could put these talents to better use.

I'm not really one to talk, but Adam appears dangerously out of his depth.

"You seem like the voice of reason in all this," I say. "What's your view on killing police officers?"

"Broadly, I'm not . . . I'm not a fan of any violence. But what did he know?"

"He pulled us over, me and Rosie, on the night we . . ." I don't need to say it. Adam knows what we did. That's why I'm sitting here. "We told him we were heading home. He figured out we were driving in the wrong direction. That's it. And now he's dead."

Adam seems genuinely unsettled by this. He knows it's wrong. But what can he possibly do? "It would have been fast. Clean."

"Well, that's good," I say, giving sarcasm free rein over my voice.

"I'm sorry. But, the guy who did it . . . he is highly skilled."

"You ever met him?"

"The Carpenter? No." Adam shakes his head again. "No one has."

"But he works for you guys?"

"Nah, he works for no one. Stefan has a contact, who has a contact—we have absolutely no direct involvement. He does not know who we are. As I say, it's an airlock. And, to be honest with you, I'd rather not cross paths with him."

"Why?"

"The idea of somebody who murders people for money scares me. The Carpenter's got no morals, no loyalty. He'll kill *anyone* for cash. I'm not even sure he's got a limit on age."

"Seems like a monster."

"Yes," Adam says. "That's exactly what he is."

I keep my face still as I repeat those words in my head. A highly skilled individual without loyalty, a monster who's willing to kill anyone for the right price. That sounds like the kind of man I'd like to meet.

Chapter Twenty

"I was right," Nell's saying. "I was absolutely right."

She hands me a piece of paper, checks there's no one outside her office, then closes the door.

"About?"

"Read it," she says, stepping past.

I look down but before I've taken in a single line, she adds, "They found malware on our system. It was changing the marine traffic log. It tricked us." Leaning close, she glides her index finger across the bottom of the sheet. "See. Swapped these two boats. *Hamburg*. *Starliner*."

Nell's excited, vindicated, her face lit up with new energy. But then she frowns—clearly, I'm not reacting how I should.

"It says it right there." She taps the paper.

So I take a deep breath—as though my silence has been surprise. "Shit. Is . . . I mean, is there . . ." I pretend to read. "Any clues where it came from?"

"Foster's laptop."

I think I strike the balance between shock and confusion, because Nell's eyebrows lift as she gives me a sympathetic, knowing nod.

"They sure?" I ask.

"These digital forensics guys don't get this kind of thing wrong," she says. "It's zeroes and ones."

Staring through her window, through the thin trees and chain-link fence between the office and the rumbling train yard, I wince as I compose my next words. Using Foster's computer was an impulsive decision. It wasn't so it could be traced back to him, but so it *couldn't* be traced back to me.

"We . . . me and Foster," I say, holding my chin. "We've not always seen eye to eye. But I just can't see him doing something like that."

Again I remember that the easiest way to sell a lie is to say true things. You can build a terrible house out of impeccable bricks.

"There's a new internal affairs investigator looking into it." Nell steps backward, perches on her desk, and folds her arms. She's wearing her dark-blue polo shirt with khaki pants. She crosses her feet, resting one black boot on top of the other. "I'm expecting a callback any minute." She checks her chunky watch. "When it all went south, he was first in line to be reposted."

Chaos is good, I think. The more noise, the more distraction, the more likely I am to stay under the radar. But pressing too hard on Foster will likely only expose his innocence—and then that spotlight would come swinging around the room again.

"He'd wanted to go back undercover for a long time," I say. "He's got all the contacts; he's got a good front, with his scrapyard."

"Foster's convenient ties to criminality can be read in a number of ways."

"True. But is it," I say, as though this is just coming to me, "is it possible the software originated from outside? Just arrived via his computer?" Adam told me there would be no evidence to disprove this—and it appears he was right.

"Yeah." Nell sighs. "They said it could well have come from an external source—an email, a clicked link. He might not have even realized. I don't know."

"Well, that strikes me as more likely."

She draws some air in through her teeth and concedes, because it's true and she knows it. But this just sends her straight back to the confusing world of unanswered questions. "If not him . . . then who?"

"Now that it's out—we could start interviewing?" I suggest. Chaos. Noise. Division and suspicion.

"I suppose," she says. "When all else fails, just ask." Nell looks at her boots, then back up to me. "Was it you?"

Smiling, I let out a short laugh and shrug. "Yep. I'm working with Edward Lang."

And Nell's mood lightens—because of course I must be joking.

"What if Rob Sanders is right?" I wonder, bringing us back down. "This whole mess . . . it's made me doubt everything."

"Don't let him get into your head."

"No, no," I say. "It's more than that. What if . . . what if we *are* wrong about Edward?"

Nell hesitates, narrows her eyes. "But we're not."

"I just think we should keep an open mind." I've said enough. Just this single drop of doubt cuts her deeper than I'd expected. It's so much worse to hear it from me. Her closest ally—the one person who's always been in her corner. She presses her lips together and nods. Years of work, coming unraveled.

"I might have something else," I say. "Got an anonymous tip that sounds worth checking out."

Reaching into my back pocket, I remove and unfold the email exchange Adam provided. Again, like everything else, I want to put some distance between myself and this arrest. Feels safer to let Nell take the lead. I hand it to her.

She glances down the lines of text, lifts her gaze. "This Wesley character, you think he's one of the cartel's men?"

"Could be—sounds like they're expanding."

"As it stands, I think this should come from you," she says, passing the paper back. "I'm not exactly flavor of the month."

"We could just send it up the chain—get them in cuffs, then jump in if it's worth our while?"

"Whatever you think is best." Nell's lack of enthusiasm for any investigation that deviates from the Lang case is, while inconvenient, entirely justified. She tilts up to her feet, moves around her desk, and sits on the leather swivel chair.

This signals the end of our conversation, so I step away.

"Hey," I say, casually turning back from the door. "You ever heard of someone called The Carpenter?"

Nell's attention is on her monitor. She types something. "Like Jesus?" Hits enter.

"No, he's a . . . a hitman."

Her eyes snap back to mine. "Yeah," she says, lifting her head as she remembers. "There was a long-running case. You remember Brett from homicide? He had a theory that a load of gang killings were connected. He was obsessed."

"But they never caught him?"

"No, he . . . apparently it was decided that The Carpenter is fiction. Abstract. More of a symbol. A concept. Probably a few different people. The romantic days of classy men in suits with silencers are long gone. Folk who kill for cash in this city are usually exactly what you'd expect them to be. Why?"

I pout as though it doesn't matter—just making conversation. "Heard the name, sounded interesting."

"Speak to old Brett," she says. "He'll talk your ear off all night about that one."

◆ ◆ ◆

Five long, hard days of good old-fashioned police work later, and I'm sitting on the couch at home with a yellow Post-it note on the coffee table.

I spoke to Brett from homicide, and, over a few drinks in a quiet bar, he was very keen to tell me everything he knew. In fact, I think he was downright cheering me on. He assumed, as you would, that I was looking to make contact with The Carpenter as part of an official investigation.

And Brett explained the man was the best in the business, speaking with all the manic zeal of a retired detective who'd wasted years chasing a myth.

"But he is real," Brett had said. "Apparently he dresses like shit, wears a green jacket. And he's got this guarantee." He paused for effect, like he was telling a campfire ghost story. "He says, he promises, that his targets will never, ever see him."

"How would we know?"

"Exactly." Brett had laughed and banged the table. "It's all part of the color. The romance."

"Sounds like some admiration."

"Credit where it's due—some of these murders . . ." Brett looked deep into nowhere, recalling a hundred horrors. "Connected to countless cases across the country. High profile too." His face brightened again. "I've heard all kinds of figures. Quarter, half, even a full mill. Someone said you can only pay him in solid gold." A short, nostalgic laugh as Brett shook his head, sipped his drink. "Hmm." Those were the days.

"Why was he so hard to track down?" I'd asked.

"He wasn't. I think I spoke to him on the phone a few times. We set up meetings. Stings. But he obviously did his research after the initial calls and steered clear. Somehow he always knew if clients were genuine or not. He's just a perfect, cold . . . well, he's a psychopath. I suppose it goes without saying that, if you're looking for him, you might live to regret it. He's a dangerous man."

"Well," I'd said, lifting my glass. "So am I."

Brett gave me a list of names. This led me to meet four more people—including a librarian, a convenience store manager, and a street cleaner who tried to sell me a bag of meth the size of a football. Until, finally, I arrived at a tattoo parlor to meet a woman with a split tongue, black contact lenses, and enough ink on her face to render her ethnicity a complete mystery. She sounded Russian but looked like a lizard dressed for Day of the Dead. In the neon-blue light, she told me the password and wrote down the number.

And now I have those digits in front of me. I've been staring at the Post-it note for a long time.

"What is that?" Rosie asks, coming into the living room.

"It's a number," I explain, my eyes still locked on the square of yellow paper. "Apparently if I call and ask for a 'black elm rocking chair with brass rivets,' I'll get to speak to a hitman called The Carpenter."

Rosie smiles, raises a skeptical eyebrow. "Really?"

"So they say. I may need some help further down the line. Want to get this sorted out sooner rather than later."

"You're sure it's legit?"

"Let's see," I say, picking up the burner phone I've bought especially for the occasion.

Holding the Post-it, I dial the number on the plastic buttons and lift the phone to my ear.

"Hello," a voice says.

"I need a . . . a black elm rocking chair with brass rivets."

"Excuse me? Say that again."

"A black elm rocking chair with brass rivets."

"One more time." He speaks slowly. Each word deliberate, polite, almost as though he's reading. Sounds East Asian, maybe, old, like a wise martial arts guru.

"Do you sell them?"

"No."

"Can you put me in contact with someone who does?"

"I could have a look for you, but chairs are not really my specialty."

I sigh. "What is your specialty?"

"Sorry, who is this?"

"A customer."

"What is your name?"

"Jonathan . . ." I hesitate. "Blackwood."

"Blackwood. Black. Wood. Are you sure? It sounds like you might have made that up."

Fuck it. "James Casper."

"I am not sure I believe that one either."

"Well, then we're in trouble, because that really is my name."

"I will get someone to give you a call about the chair. Can I get you on this number?"

"Sure."

"One more thing, has your phone got a camera?"

"Uh . . ." I check. "Yeah. Not a great one."

"I do not need to see your face, but could you turn it on and show me the room you're in?"

"Um. It's new, so . . ."

"You have ten seconds."

I scrabble quickly with the phone, find the option, and click the video-call button. The screen flashes and then a small window appears, displaying my ceiling. The footage is grainy, blurred with motion.

Teeth clenched, I gesture for Rosie to duck.

"Pan around slowly, please," he says.

I hold the phone up and rotate it, showing him the living room.

"Great. Now show me the floor."

I glare at Rosie, who's lying on her back in the middle of the rug. "The what?"

"Three, two, one—"

I point the camera down, straight at her. Not knowing how to react, she waves.

But he doesn't seem to mind. "There is a doorway to your left with a window. Go there immediately and show me what is inside. Please be fast."

Again I comply, letting this stranger see into my kitchen.

"What is in the fridge?" he asks.

"Come on," I say. "You've seen enough."

The line goes dead.

Lowering the phone, I turn around and sigh at Rosie. "Think we blew it."

But an hour later, we're about to eat dinner when I hear loud vibrations coming from the coffee table. We clock eyes, and I dive into the living room to answer.

"I can get you that chair," he says. "Are you free now?"

"Uh . . . yeah. Sure."

"Stay on the line. Please get your car keys."

He takes me on a long drive around the city—a scenic tour—before finally telling me to pull over at the side of some derelict basketball courts.

"See that bench—near the edge of the park?" he says. "Go there and sit down."

I do as he tells me.

Again the line goes dead. So I just sit and wait, surrounded by weeds and grass growing up through the broken sidewalk at my feet.

Across the street there's an eight-story apartment building with more than fifty windows. To my right, behind some treetops, another series of possible vantage points. And even behind me, through the park, there are probably a thousand places he could be. At any rate, I'm sure he can see me.

A minute or so later, I feel something buzzing near my leg. I slide across the bench, reach down, and find a phone taped on the underside of the wood. Peeling it free, I check over my shoulder as I answer.

"Apologies for the caution," he says. "What do you want? We can speak freely now. No euphemisms, please."

"I need you to take care of something for me."

"Such as a pet? Are you going on a vacation? Speak plainly."

"I need you to kill someone."

"The price is $333,333 a head."

"Well, it's actually . . . it's actually three people."

"I make that $999,999 in total."

"Call it a million?" I say, rolling my eyes, assuming I'm being played.

"No. We will call it $333,333 for each target."

"That seems a little steep."

"This is not a haggling affair. That is the cost."

I frown and change my mind. It is a ridiculous amount of money. It's so ridiculous, no undercover cop would ever dream of using such an outlandish figure.

Too crazy to be anything other than real. Still, I check. "How do I know you're legit?"

"You do not. You will have to trust me. And, of course, pay in full up front. If it is out of your price range, I understand."

"No. I actually have a spare million dollars, as it happens."

"Good. I will need names and approximate locations."

"There's no rush . . . I don't need this done immediately."

"That is fine."

"I want to meet you," I say. "To make sure."

"I am afraid that is not an option. You will never see me. And neither will the targets."

"So I've heard. What makes you worth all that money?"

"I am able to orchestrate a complete disappearance or an unexplained murder. Or, on some occasions, leave clues implicating another perpetrator. Although that comes at an additional cost. I specialize in fast, clean jobs with minimal suffering."

"That's very nice of you."

"You have an unexpectedly high level of attitude, special agent James Casper."

There's a short silence as I look across the street, searching over the roof's edge, checking windows at random. Drapes, faint flashing TVs, and dark, empty apartments.

"For future reference," he adds, "it might be sensible not to connect your burner phone to a domestic router."

I close my eyes at the stupid mistake.

"You're worried it's a sting?" I say.

"No, are you?"

I smile. "No." My incompetence has given me credibility, just like his outrageous pricing. "Anyone you won't kill?" I ask.

"My preference is adult men, but I am willing to discuss any contract."

"There are some complicated circumstances."

"Explain them."

"The three men in question need to die at exactly the same time."

"That is doable, if they are all in the same place."

I grimace, recalling Adam's comment about staying apart. "They probably won't be."

"Then a delay is inevitable."

"No, no. No delay. Can't risk that."

"I am not using explosives and I only work alone, so I suggest you re-evaluate. Perhaps you kill one of them and then—"

"No. I'm not killing anyone."

"Why?"

"What is it with you people? Murder is not a simple crime to get away with."

"I could give you some pointers."

"Things will be clearer closer to the time. But I may need you on short notice."

"Well, I would suggest you pay for all three—I will remain in the city until you are ready. You let me know when a suitable window opens or, alternatively, what kind of delay is permissible. That will entitle you to three, two, or one, depending on the circumstances."

"How do I pay you?"

"Cash. Exact money—$333,333 a head." He says the sum slowly, as though I might forget. "Not a penny more. Not a penny less. There will be no change. There will be no refunds. I will give you a location. A courier will collect it and take it to a safe place. A second courier will then arrive. The process will take one hour. If at any point they are followed, by you or anyone else, even coincidently, our business relationship is over, I keep the money, and you will never hear from me again."

"Sounds like a deal," I say.

"Only use this phone to contact me. I am available twenty-four seven."

"What's your real name?" I ask.

"Jonathan Blackwood. What are the chances, hey?"

And, alone on the bench, I listen to the dial tone.

It feels good having someone like this at my disposal. I'm a phone call away from solving all my problems. And now I'm ready to get to work.

Chapter Twenty-One

David has made a roast pork dinner with steamed vegetables and a pitcher of juice—ice and slices of fruit floating against the glass. He sits at the head of the table, Matthew and Rosie to his right, me on his left. The chair at the other end—where Mary used to sit—is always empty.

Matthew is pale, dark bags under his slow, cautious eyes. He has a plate of untouched food—I've seen him eat three peas with his fingers and sip some water. Aside from that, he's just hunched awkwardly, fidgeting and sniffing.

We all know. Rosie and I certainly do. But we pretend. Especially David. He's happy to go along with Matthew's story. He's just got another cold. Maybe it's the flu?

I'm seventeen. Rosie is nineteen. It's my birthday tomorrow.

"Thanks for this, David," I say.

He forces a smile. "It's all good. I can never get the potatoes quite right. Not like Mary."

David mentions her all the time. Every film he sees, every song he loves, every new experience that leaves enough of an impression on him to recount at a later date—it's all set against that ever-present litmus test. Would Mary have liked it?

She'd have loved this pork. But she'd have some reservations about the length of time David steamed the broccoli. He acts as if these imagined comments are real, even defending himself against the kind of criticisms we'd hear from Mary.

"It's a big milestone," he says, nodding. He nods too fast nowadays. Something's off. As though he's sped up slightly. The calm, slow, docile man—the gentle giant I remember from my childhood—has steadily become a frail husk. In the last few years, like Matthew, he's lost a lot of weight. His skin hangs. His thick mustache is now just thin, curled wisps. "James, turning eighteen."

Rosie smiles at me from across the table, her foot—covered by a long, black sock—touches my leg. Her small toes wiggling against my knee. Physical contact seems natural now. It's like she just wants to touch me for the sake of it. And I don't mind one little bit.

"I know it's been difficult," David adds, his gaze drifting slowly to the empty chair as it so often does. "But . . . I want you to know that adopting you was a good choice."

"Well, thanks," I say.

"I agree," Rosie whispers, looking over the food on her fork, looking at me with her smoky eyes.

"Yeah, it's been great, bud," Matthew manages.

"You're good kids," David says. "Mary would have been proud."

Over Rosie's shoulder, I see the red phone on the wall. The phone we didn't pick up. The phone that could have saved her life. But it wouldn't have made a difference. She'd have died anyway.

"You're all going to be adults," he adds, with a grand sense of pride but also something else, maybe regret. Like he's going to miss us.

"You're still my dad," Matthew says, picking at his fourth pea of the evening.

"Yeah," Rosie adds. "We're not going anywhere yet."

"You'll all be off at college, in the city," David says. "You'll find your way. I want you three to know that I'm . . . I'm so sorry that I couldn't do a better job."

"Hey." Rosie frowns. "Don't be stupid, you've done amazingly well."

I shift uncomfortably—it's rare to see David show even a glimmer of weakness. He's the kind of man who says he's OK, he's just fine. And any implication that he might not be needs to be stamped out with some off-the-cuff masculine bravado. I think family occasions like birthdays are harder for him—anything that shines a light on that vacant chair.

Still, David takes the compliment, but nods as though he doesn't really believe it. "I got you there. All three. Eighteen." He looks at each of us. "That's what she would have wanted."

"And, hey," Rosie says, trying to lighten the mood, "that's probably the legal minimum requirement for the adoption agency anyhow. You're off the hook. You're a free man."

David gives us a smile—one of the hollow, empty masks that fit his old face so poorly. "I'll always love you kids."

We finish the surreal dinner and, again uncharacteristically for David, he says he's going out bowling with some friends.

"We'll clean up," Rosie says, taking his plate away.

He wipes his mouth and leaves the table. Carrying a stack of dishes, I follow Rosie to the sink, where I wash and she dries. David puts his jacket on, checks his keys, and heads out the back door.

When we've finished the final cup, I dry my damp hands—my fingers crinkled and soft—as Matthew reappears. He sits down to put on his shoes.

"I'm going out too," he says. "Just meeting a couple of guys for a . . . a beer. Maybe. We might go up to the old elm tree, for old times' sake. You guys are welcome if you want."

Rosie glances at me from the side of her eyes.

"Nah, think I'm cool just hanging out here tonight," I say.

Standing, Matthew steps between us and turns his back on me, speaking exclusively to his sister. "Rose, thing is, I get paid at the end of the month."

"My purse is on the chair."

He stopped asking me when I started saying no.

"You're a hero," he says, removing a couple of bills from her wallet—something he's done before, both with and without permission.

And just like that, me and Rosie are alone together in the kitchen.

"I don't think that's beer money," I say.

"You should be a detective." She acknowledges my disapproval with a quick nod. "He'll get his hands on cash no matter what," she explains. "Might as well keep him out of trouble."

Maybe she's right. Matthew has been caught shoplifting, stealing from parked cars; I'm fairly certain he's been draining my jar of coins.

We go into the living room and sit at either end of the couch, each holding one of the raspberry cupcakes Rosie baked earlier. They're meant for my birthday tomorrow, but she made a couple of extras.

"Like a preview," she says.

When we've finished, I squeeze the paper into a ball and put it on the coffee table.

"So . . ." she says after a long silence, arms wrapped around her legs, resting her head on the cushion as she gazes across at me.

Rosie is wearing some of her best makeup and a casual black dress that ends at her knees.

These moments—where we pretend to be awkward, even though we're not—have become a game. It's like we're acting out all the key landmarks of a normal teenage romance. The subtle flirting, the mutual, unspoken embarrassment about the things we both know. An inevitable closeness growing, like two stars in orbit falling into one another.

Except it's not like a regular fling. Because we're friends. The mystery of whether or not we like each other has been solved. So now we're free to simply enjoy the dance.

All the impulse, none of the fear.

"So," I repeat.

"What do you want to do?"

I point to my mouth. "You have icing on your lip," I say.

Rosie blinks. "I know."

And she holds her small hand out and takes mine, guides me out of the living room to the stairs, her black dress fluttering above me as we go up and up. She turns and we're kissing as she's walking backward into her bedroom.

"Lie on the floor," she says.

"Why?"

"Do it."

We get on her carpet with a pillow each. Lying on our backs, we stare up at her ceiling.

"See?" she says, her hand resting in mine. "Things look new from down here."

"I feel small."

"You should try and lie on the floor in every room," she says. "You get a different perspective when you're lying on the floor."

"What about, like, stores?"

"They're the best. Just have to be fast."

"What's the weirdest place you've laid?"

"Huh." She thinks for a moment. "I fell over in the middle of the ice rink once. Everyone thought I was hurt, cos I just lay there for ages. But it was because it looked so cool."

Rosie spends a short while listing various floors she's laid on. " . . . and the library, that one's good. Peaceful."

I turn to her. "My back aches."

"Yeah," she says. "That does happen."

We decide to move up onto her bed. Now face to face, we spend the next few hours making out or simply hugging each other, talking, and stroking necks and shoulders.

Around 11:30 p.m., Rosie stands up, turns off the main light, and flicks on her bedside lamp. Then she heads to the bathroom. So I sit on the edge of her mattress and wait.

When she returns, I see she's taken her socks off and now stands barefoot on the carpet in front of me. Warm in the dim orange light. She pulls some pins out of her hair and throws it forward, then back, as she puts a knee on the bed at my side and swings the other over.

"You're going to be eighteen in half an hour," she says, sitting on my lap now, our noses almost touching.

"Yep."

"You know what that means?"

I smile, my hands on her sides, on the laced upper part of her dress. "Yes, I do."

She kisses my cheek, pushes me back a little more onto the mattress. "Tell me."

Leaning in, I whisper against her ear, "I'm going to be able to vote."

"Oh, James." She sighs, her elbows on my shoulders.

"Deep in the ballot box."

"You're making me blush."

"Draw a little cross next to a name." I laugh as I trace an X on her neck with the tip of my finger.

"What else can you do?"

"Hmm." I pretend to think for a moment. "Buy fireworks?"

Her eyes light up. "And cigarettes."

"Great big cartons of them."

"Aw, we're forgetting the most important one of all . . ." She presses her lips into my ear now. "Jury duty," she breathes.

I lean back to look at her. "Oh my God. That'd be amazing."

"It's a tricky case." Rosie takes my hand and slides it slowly up her thigh, under her skirt, around and up to her bare hip. "Someone stole a young girl's underwear."

Kissing me—no more talking—she reaches down and unzips my pants and I'm breathing heavy and she lowers onto me and grinds her hips forward and looks into my eyes and *no more talking* and I was holding her hand in the kitchen and she was getting changed in the black reflection of the Gasmax 3000 and I shut my eyes as hard as they will go as she pulls my head into her chest and rolls her dress down and—

"Oh, fuck." I lean forward and hold her still. And it's all over. When I finish shivering, I fall back onto my elbows, come around, and look up through narrow eyes. Rosie smiles in the soft amber light. "Sorry," I whisper.

"No." She laughs. "I'm sorry, it's my fault." She pulls her dress back up over her bra. "Too sexy."

"Exactly."

"To be honest with you, James, I'm impressed."

"I'll be back in the game. Twenty minutes."

"And they say romance is dead." She leans over, enclosing my face in her hair, and looks behind me, her chin at my forehead. "But then it won't be a crime."

I crane my neck to check the clock—I'm going to be eighteen in sixteen minutes.

We lie on the bed, side by side again, and she asks how old I was when . . .

"First time ever?"

"Yeah," she says.

"Well, seventeen."

"Who?" And then she realizes. "Oh, James, I'd have put more effort in if I'd known."

"I've done stuff. But."

"What kind of stuff?" She smiles.

"All the stuff, aside from . . ."

The gloomy bedroom lights up slightly as a car pulls into the driveway outside. "David's back," Rosie says.

We both know this, just from the sound of the engine.

I hear the car door slam, but he doesn't come into the house. "Late-night shed times."

"Who knows what he gets up to in there," Rosie says.

"He's probably scored some broken things to fix."

A second car rumbles on the street—and Matthew says goodbye to a friend.

"Maybe I should go to my room," I say.

"I think you should sleep in here tonight." Rosie moves closer on the pillow, facing me. "We'll just have to be very quiet."

"Shh." I put a finger on her lips. She licks it and we both laugh.

"You taste like raspberries."

Rosie rolls onto her back and looks at the ceiling, listening to Matthew come in through the back door. And then the fridge opening. Jars. The silverware drawer.

"Munchies," I say. "Well, that's a good sign, right?"

"I guess so."

We lie there and listen. "Sandwich?" I wonder.

"Peanut butter and jelly?"

"Maybe."

Then we hear the microwave door. "Grilled cheese," Rosie says. "Nice."

And she looks over at the red glow of her alarm clock. It's two minutes past midnight. She turns again to face me and begins to whisper the song. "Happy birthday to you, happy birthday to—"

Bang. A gunshot rings out. She stops. Unmistakable. Loud in the quiet night.

A dog barks outside.

"The fuck was that?" she says.

It barks and barks.

"Sounded like it was in the yard."

We both sit up, listen. Out of her bedroom window I see a couple of lights come on in our neighbor's house. I go to the door.

"Matthew?"

Silence.

Rushing down the stairs, through the kitchen, the back door now wide open.

Rosie close behind.

Outside, I peer cautiously around the corner, holding her back.

That dog is still barking.

"Matthew?" I shout as quietly as I can.

He's walking across the yard. He pauses at the shed. There's something white on the door.

"What is that?" I think aloud. It looks like a piece of paper.

Matthew pulls open the door, enters, and—as we're halfway to the shed, the grass cold on my bare feet—steps back out and looks at me with complete bewilderment.

"What's going on?" I ask.

Over his shoulder, the wooden door clatters closed, and I see a note pinned at the top, right in the middle. It says, "Don't come in. Call 911."

And Matthew stands there in the gray moonlight and cries without making a sound.

The only noise is that dog.

I turn to Rosie, and she's still not figured it out. But then she does. Her mouth opens and she clamps both hands over it and I hear a high-pitched sound. I think she whispers, "No."

Tears pouring now, Matthew looks from Rosie to me and back again, his chin dimpled, his nose glistening.

And he shrugs. As though the horror of what he's just seen is par for the course. What else would you expect from a world like this?

Rosie comes forward to hug him, and he almost accepts it. But then he looks over at me again. And he pulls away. Steps back. "No," he says. "No, no, no."

Shaking his head, he walks around us both and just goes. Just runs along the side of the house and out onto the street.

"Matthew," Rosie says. "*Matthew.*"

But he doesn't slow down.

She turns in the colorless dark, on the black grass, and looks back to me.

"It's your birthday." She says. "He did it on your birthday. Why would David do that?"

My eyes are wide as I stare at the silent shed. It seems so still. Lifeless. "I don't know."

"Why today? Why?"

I go over the last few things he said to us at the dinner table. We're all eighteen now. That's all he had to do. "I think he's been waiting," I say. "All these years."

Rosie takes a lungful of air, glares as she processes this. She doesn't like the thought. She breathes through her nose, fists clenched, hair hanging down like she's possessed. She rocks slightly—she looks like a child at the start of a tantrum. And then she shouts, "Fuck." And then again. Louder. More lights come on across the street. She screams.

"Rosie, calm down."

Two more dogs are barking now—somewhere out there, beyond the midnight houses, everyone on the street awake and calling 911 so we don't have to.

"Please, stop," I say.

But she storms back inside and starts to break anything in her way.

Twenty minutes later, the dogs finally stop barking.

And now we're outside in front of the house, on the driveway, a police officer asking questions.

Rosie and I are sitting on the sidewalk, watching the commotion.

A black body bag, zipped up and bouncing rigid on a gurney. Blue lights flashing over the plastic as they slide it into the back of an ambulance. I wonder why. This doesn't seem like a paramedic's job.

The officer closes his notepad.

"We'll get someone out tomorrow to take a full statement, OK?" he says. "And we have some squad cars looking for your brother."

"Thank you," I say.

Rosie looks up at the cop, hugging her legs to her chest. "It's his birthday," she whispers, chin on her knees.

"What's that?" the officer leans closer to hear.

"It's his birthday," she repeats, pointing a thumb my way.

He sighs. "Jesus. I'm . . . I'm so sorry."

But she shakes her head. "It. Is. His. Birthday."

"Rosie." I touch her shoulder, but she flinches away.

The cop doesn't know what to do.

"It's his fucking birthday," Rosie hisses. She springs up to her feet like she's ready to fight. With his belt, his wide arms, his cuffs and gun, he's more than twice her size. Still, he takes a step back, visibly scared, and stumbles as his boot slips from the curb. "Say it," she yells.

After a long pause, the big officer swallows and slowly turns away from her, now looking down into my eyes. "Happy birthday," he says, with the flat, empty tone you'd expect.

PART THREE— THE PURSUIT OF HAPPINESS

Chapter Twenty-Two

"What kind of similes are you guys into?" the midwife says, her attention fixed on the screen.

"We've been doing fruit and vegetables." Rosie looks at me from the raised bed, her brown cashmere sweater lifted up over her round stomach.

"Well then, about as big as an eggplant," the midwife adds. "And if we go here, we should be able to get a better view . . ."

She slides the sonogram probe over Rosie's taut skin, the transparent lubricant adding a gloss to the bulge. Then the midwife leans into her monitor and tells us she's getting a good look at a healthy baby. Switching machines with quick, adept hands, she holds another device lower down, pressing it gently beneath Rosie's waistline.

The speaker hisses with the internal ambient noises you hear when you're wearing earplugs. Biological static. And there it is again—that fast *wow-wow-wow-wow-wow-wow* heartbeat. It sounds like it's coming from a distant, alien planet. Underwater. Otherworldly.

They're saying something about the rhythm—it's normal, it's all good, I can tell from her expression—but I'm distracted. I'm just staring past the paper-lined bed, past the bare white wall, through the slatted blinds and sterile air.

Nell's voicemail repeating in my mind.

"The lawyer specifically requested us."

What does that mean?

Has Stefan fucked up? Have they handed me a dead end? Even so, why would Nell be so concerned about that?

I'm tuning back in, my own white noise fading out as the room comes into focus.

"What do you think?" Rosie asks.

"Um, well . . ." I appeal to the midwife.

"It's totally your choice," she says. "I understand we couldn't confirm sex at the last two scans; now it's pretty clear."

Rosie grabs my hand and squeezes it. "Shall we?" Then she turns to the midwife. "Just tell us."

"You're sure?"

I nod.

The past six months have been a lot of hard work. Between them, Adam and Stefan have delivered a steady stream of arrests—from mid-range dealers to last month's frankly ridiculous raid that saw police seize almost a hundred thousand dollars, one of the cleanest-functioning meth labs I've ever seen, and five crates of unregistered firearms from a warehouse that claimed to make soap. Despite the testosterone and chemicals in the air, the place smelled great—everyone was singing my praises, and I took a box of bubble bath home for Rosie. Vanilla and cherry steamed from our bathroom for the next week.

But the haul was not what I had expected. When I asked, in a panic, which part of that cash-ridden meth festival we'd planted, Adam seemed confused.

"The heroin, the oxy?" he'd said. "The rest is all them. Did you check the roof?"

And, sure enough, there it was—all bagged up and ready to sell. It's a simple scam that flies well when the victims happen to be prolific drug dealers anyway.

Edward's plan is working. In the last few months, we've made enough significant arrests that it appears, at least to an untrained eye, that the DEA is making a real dent in the city's heroin supply. We're finally getting a grip on it all. They've been coming in so thick and fast that, more often than not, I've left them for the city's police department to handle. As long as arrests are happening, the consequences are the same. I don't need to take all the credit.

The sacrificial lambs are, according to Adam, mostly affiliated with the Carrillo cartel—money men, traffickers, falcons, that kind of thing. Though a couple have been on the fringes; Stefan's got plenty of enemies. In one particularly unpleasant bust, we took down an elderly car mechanic who'd overcharged Stefan's teenage niece for repairs. When she complained, he was alleged to have offered a sizable discount in exchange for, well, the rest of the story was implied.

The mechanic's punishment was to be arrested with fifty thousand dollars' worth of heroin hidden beneath the spare wheel in his Winnebago. Poor guy.

One of the hardest parts is writing the lies that lead us to these places. Adam has some clever tricks up his sleeve, though "anonymous informants" have been doing a lot of the heavy lifting.

The process is simple. They plant drugs and cash. We go and find it.

This kind of thing has been happening week in, week out, the relentless sirens and cuffs and bags and cash and guns and defense—"It's not mine, man, it's not mine."

That's what they all say.

All this gives Edward's product a clear run, makes me look good, and moves us safely one step toward winning.

And the sheer amount of heroin he's brought in through the city—truck after truck, spreading out like cells in veins, crawling across the country. I picture the map, all lit up with new lines.

Sweeping markets with the economic dominance of scale and speed. An unstoppable march.

We're literally changing the street value. And, as before, Edward has paid me in cash. I have five bags—there's a million in each, but he owes me so much more than that.

I sometimes imagine the harm—the spectacular cost I've had to bear. But I knew what I was doing when I signed that deal with the devil. Of course I'd have to sin.

And it had all been going so well. Until today. Maybe something has gone wrong?

Nell's message. The lawyer.

I'd wanted to have this all wrapped up long before the due date. But twenty-eight weeks in and it's already as big as an eggplant.

I should have done it earlier. I could have gotten out with clean hands. Every time I solve a problem, new ones sprout up.

They all need to die. Soon.

"Congratulations," the midwife says, having just announced the sex of our baby.

Rosie makes a fist and grins so madly I can see all her teeth. She holds an arm out and we hug.

"Aw, look at him," the midwife whispers to her. "He's speechless."

I am. Because there's nothing to say. I'm angry that these milestone moments are being stolen from me. I just hold my head on Rosie's shoulder, smell her hair. Oh, God. I wish I could stay here forever.

But I'm being dragged back out there. Out into that cold, violent world. Away from all this beautiful, precarious safety and comfort. I don't want to do it anymore.

My eyes are shut, my hand on Rosie's stomach.

"Are you OK?" she asks, stroking my arm.

"Just . . ." I bury my face in her neck and hold her like she's a lifeboat and I'm drowning.

The light. The hope. Just hold on. I'm so close. It's just there, right at the edge of my reach.

And I open my eyes again and lean away.

"I'm fine," I say.

Back to work.

After the scan, I drive Rosie to the new house by the lake. She's been spending time there lately, finessing the decor, sorting out a nursery, getting settled.

Then I head straight back into the city to meet Nell in the police station parking lot, near the lockup steps.

"Sorry I'm late," I say, slamming my car door and striding across the asphalt.

Nell's let her hair grow longer; now it's spiked at the front, halfway between a pixie and a crewcut. It shaves at least a decade off but makes her seem somehow softer than the number three-guard job she used to sport.

I first noticed this transition around the holiday season. She spent Christmas Eve at our place, and there was a moment late in the afternoon when she was sitting on our couch in her bright-red, holly leaf sweater, full of food and drink. And it was like that hard, ex-military woman had been put to rest.

She's not far from retirement. But I feel as though the last few months, the setbacks, her colossal failure to arrest Edward Lang, have fast-tracked the whole process.

Now, with Rosie's pregnancy and her increased presence in our domestic life, Nell seems ready to wind down. She just wants to be a gentle grandma.

Of all our victims—the network of people we've hurt and left—I feel stealing this from Nell, blunting the final edge of a razor-sharp career, is perhaps the worst.

She deserves better. I've lied to her more times than I could possibly count. Because it's so easy. Because she believes in me with all the passion and unconditionality that you should only ever receive from a mother.

She deserves the truth. But I've gone too far now for that to be an option. I passed that window a long, long time ago. It'd hurt her too much.

We go in through the dark corridors, along the shiny floor, past the thick metal radiators and disgruntled men in cells shouting angry things. One of them spits, but it misses. At the end of the hallway, the interrogation room door is propped open and a suited lawyer greets us both with a warm smile.

He introduces himself, says his name, but I forget it almost immediately.

Then he holds a hand to the room and we enter.

Sitting at the table is an underweight man, no older than twenty-five, dressed in his orange jumpsuit and a clean white T-shirt. He eyes us with familiar disdain as we sit opposite. Apparently his name is Sammy Gibson.

His lawyer rounds the table and unfolds the chair by his side. Then, seated, he adjusts some paperwork, moves a pen, and looks between me and Nell.

"My client has prepared a written statement," he says. "Which he is happy for me to read on his—"

"No, I'll tell them," Sammy interrupts. "I want to do a deal."

His lawyer squirms slightly, then leans close to him for a whisper, but Sammy refuses to listen.

"If he wants to speak," I say, "let him speak."

The lawyer retreats, sits up in his chair, shoulders back.

"So, listen, this is all the truth," Sammy says, leaning forward. More than half of his remaining teeth are gold. "If I tell you, if I tell you all about what we're doing, you can help me?"

"It would depend on a number of factors," Nell says. "Why don't you start by telling us what you know."

This is unprecedented. A Carrillo man opening up. Low-level too. A bottom feeder. The barbaric things they do to rats go beyond the realms of horror. We're talking missing eyes, flayed torsos, intestines dragged from the guts of screaming men—tug-of-war with slippery ropes. You read the coroners' reports and, if they're lucky, the cause of death is cardiac arrest. Unbearable dread and panic.

But Sammy doesn't seem scared of that. This is a good sign. It means he has no idea what he's doing. He is an amateur. And he's out of his depth.

"I don't care about my sentence," he adds. "I will do every day of it. Head down. No problem. I'll confess, whatever you want . . . You busted six men from the soap factory."

I remember Rosie in the bath—her shiny leg lifted out of the warm water, over the thick vanilla bubbles, the froth hiding her belly and reddened chest.

"That's right," Nell says.

"Three of them, including me, were involved in the ice and the guns," Sammy says, his eyes flicking between us to make sure we're with him for every word. "Three others were hardly involved—one, Jonah, he's nineteen years old. He only ever helped make soap. Is that justice? Do you even fucking care?"

His lawyer opens his mouth but resists the urge to speak.

"We'll look at the evidence," I say.

"Yeah, you look," Sammy says, his brow lowered in a hateful frown. "Because this next part is important. I have cooked meth and sold guns. I'm confessing that right now. But you guys found heroin and a big bag of oxy on the roof." He holds up a finger, like he's telling us off, and we indulge him enough to stay quiet. "That was *nothing* to do with us. That was *not mine*."

"You know," I say, scratching my neck, "this is not the first time we've heard that defense from a drug dealer."

Sammy leans forward again, his chest against the table. "Why would I lie? Hmm?" He taps his index finger on the surface four times as he repeats, "Why, would, I, lie? What would I have to gain?"

"Well, equally, why would you care?" I wonder—I really *do* wonder. "We're splitting hairs now."

He nods fast, smiling with his mouth but not his eyes. "Yeah, that's right, why would I care? I care because in the last five months, my uncle," he holds up a thumb, "my cousin," a finger, "my sister's ex-husband," he's counting these people off, "me, and add little fucking Jonah," he's holding up a full hand now, "and I make that five fucking people who've been busted for dealing heroin."

I clear my throat. "It's not unusual for criminal families to be—"

Sammy slams his palms onto the table. "None of them deal that shit," he yells, his upper body tensed tight, the veins and tendons in his neck bulging. "The pigs have been fucking *planting* drugs on people." He snarls his lips and points at Nell and then at me. "That's why I needed you. The feds can investigate them, right?"

There's a short silence, and Sammy winces, tilts his head side to side.

"Or," he adds, sniffing, wiping his nose, "maybe someone else, I don't know. But it's . . . someone is fucking framing us."

"You appreciate it's difficult to believe a person in your position," I say.

"I do. Which is why I'm going to prove it. We got these dead drops, OK." He lowers his head, like we're hatching a secret plan together. "For drugs and cash. For *all of it*. They'll be emptied tomorrow morning—11 a.m.. Right now, they will have small amounts of ice, maybe some coke—I'm talking small, for a few neighbors who use, that's it—and maybe two thousand bucks, max, across all three. You won't find heroin, you won't find gigantic sums of money that make me look like Pablo fucking Escobar. That's how we move it."

Sammy leans back as though he's said his part.

Checking he's finished, his lawyer perks up. "My client is willing to disclose details of his and his associates' connection to the Carrillo cartel, which can be corroborated by you at your discretion. And the individuals mentioned earlier will be willing to go on record with similar statements. Assuming we can arrange witness protection."

"With what aim in mind?" I ask.

"Mr. Gibson here is confessing to his crimes, but a couple of the others are facing lengthy sentences based entirely on their possession of heroin and prescription opioids which, as discussed, they allege were planted."

"Even if there isn't heroin at these dead drops . . . I can't see what that'd prove?" I'm speaking only to his lawyer now.

"It would add substantial weight to our claim," he says.

"How?" I'm being sincere.

"If these individuals were indeed dealing heroin, one would imagine the police would have discovered more than a single out-of-place bag—in this case quite literally *hidden* on a roof," he says. "They'd have found reams of supporting evidence. Because that's what a jury will expect to see when we lay out the defense. We're giving you their whole operation on a plate here. It is in everyone's best interest. And as we've said, it does nothing to Sammy's sentence—the DEA still wins. This is about the truth. Which is why we're not talking to the police right now. When all this is wheeled out in court, and it will be, the DEA will come up smelling like roses."

I swallow. It does sound flimsy when you say it like that.

"I see." I nod. "Well, I suppose we could look?"

Nell agrees, clicking her pen. "You tell us where these dead drops are and we'll be on them first thing tomorrow morning."

In the hallway, out of earshot, Nell steps close. "What are you thinking?"

"I don't know." I look back up the corridor. "Seems a strange move." I need to kill this. I need to stop it.

"There was that other guy, few months ago." She squints as she remembers. "He said the same. He was adamant the drugs weren't his. And he didn't fit the profile."

"It's the oldest line in the book."

"Yeah, but imagine if it were true," she says. "That's exactly how I'd react. Just keep promising as hard as I could. Begging for anyone to believe me. And, if someone *is* messing with the cartel's business." She puffs out some air. "They're playing with fire."

"Talking to us is playing with fire?"

"You heard what he said—members of his own family. Maybe he's more loyal to them than he is to the cartel—I mean, I didn't see any Carrillo tattoos on that kid. I say let's grab those dead drops. Sounds like their defense is lined up with this either way."

Fuck. Shit.

"Nell," a voice says from a nearby doorway. "Got time for a quick five minutes?" We both turn. It's Nigel, from the awards night. "Oh, hey, James. Cheer up," he says, "it might never happen. You want to come upstairs for a coffee?"

"No, no, I'll wait outside, need some air."

Outside, armed with three addresses, I pace up and down in front of the parked patrol cars. I stop from time to time and stare through the blue siren plastic, or at the brick wall behind.

Sammy doesn't strike me as a particularly bright spark, I think, pacing out of the huge shadow that splits the parking lot in two.

I'm guessing his friends and family are similarly impaired on the intellectual front. But still, with a slick lawyer conducting the ceremony, all that could sound pretty good if the dots were joined in court. I turn in the sun and walk back into the cold shade. Then what if others catch wind? What if they come together? What if they figure out all their arrests have one stark similarity? One glaring common denominator. I stop.

It all comes back to me.

When I turn around, the plan arrives fully formed—it's obvious what we need to do. We need to make the story stick.

I snatch my phone from my pocket and scroll right past Edward, down to Stefan. I'm in too much of a rush to go anywhere other than the source.

"Yeah?" he says.

"You fucked up," I hiss into my phone.

"Excuse me?"

"I've just been speaking to some toothless simpleton called Sammy." I look over at the back of the station, a sheer brick face with wide doors at the top of stone steps and windows clad in metal bars. The word "POLICE" written in bold capital letters across the old sign.

"Good for you," he says in his deep voice, sounding like a boxer who's been hit too many times.

"Talking about his friends and family all being busted with heroin and cash in the space of a few months," I say. "They're figuring it out, Stefan. They've got a lawyer."

"That last place was a meth lab. I don't think a flat denial is going to cut it."

"No, one flat denial won't. But five or more? With no other evidence? You know what that's going to look like? We can't frame a whole family. You need to do some more research on these people."

"You need to watch your fucking tone, boy."

"I've got three addresses. Dead drops. I want a substantial amount of product planted at each. Tonight."

"And I want your mother to sit on my dick."

"My mother's dead."

"See, James," Stefan says. "We don't always get what we want."

I clench my jaw. "Please," I say. "It's important. For everyone's sake. I can't keep the DEA away from Edward if these cases fall apart. They'll connect them. The convictions have to hold."

"It's too short notice, too risky."

"No, no, no, it's not. There's distance. They think the police are behind it—we gave them this bust. He's specifically asking the DEA for help. We have the upper hand here, but not for long."

"We'd have to scope it out. See what's what. I don't know this guy. I don't know his whole crew."

"Exactly, he's a nobody. He's just a desperate junkie clutching at straws. Nothing more."

"Besides, I don't have men to spare."

I almost shout "do it yourself," but stop and turn it into a groan, realizing it'd be counterproductive.

"What would you need?" I ask, my hand on the top of a patrol car, leaning over, head bowed to keep me calm.

"If you want it done, *you* do it."

"I can't do it alone. We'll do it together."

"We're not even meant to be in the same place. What happened to caution?"

"Stefan, just . . . Listen, dealing drugs is your world. Convicting people for dealing drugs is mine. Please, just trust me. I'm asking you to trust me."

The doors spread open across the parking lot and Nell steps out.

"Fine." He sighs. "We'll start at midnight."

"Thank you."

Nell approaches as I slide my phone back into my pocket.

"I forgot to ask," she says, buttoning up her jacket, "how was the scan?"

For a second, I can't speak. I feel like if I do, I'll cry. "Good," I manage. "Size of an eggplant."

"Are you OK?" She touches my arm.

"God, Nell, I'm so sorry." I blink the tears away.

"For what?"

For everything. "I should have told you. We're . . . we're having a girl."

She can tell that I'm overwhelmed but she can't possibly know why.

I'm torn between all the ugly things left to do and all the purity and fragility. All the innocence glinting at the end of this awful tunnel. I can picture it.

Rosie, standing at our waving window, feeding our baby and smiling at me through the glass as she bounces her to sleep.

I'd do anything to see that somewhere other than in my fading imagination.

"I just . . . in there, all that stuff." I look over at the station door. "Work. Stressing me out."

"James, I know it's scary," Nell says, holding my elbow. "But there will come a day when that baby, your daughter, grips your finger with her own tiny hand for the first time and you look into her eyes. Trivial distractions will be gone. Because you'll get it. You'll realize what truly matters. And you'll be happier than you ever thought possible, I promise."

I nod. Because I know that's true.

All I have to do is get there.

Chapter Twenty-Three

The first two dead drops go smoothly. A wide storm drain near the docks and a loose slab of rock covering a shallow ditch behind the train yard—ironically, a ten-minute walk from our office.

It's 1:15 a.m. when we pull over near a low bridge alongside an empty gas pipe building site, a few streets over from the third spot. With the engine off, the wipers are still. Rainwater collected on the windshield, city lights ahead of us fractured and starred, blurred beams of vertical yellow and red and headlight white. It's cold tonight. Feels like it might all turn to ice.

"OK, Sammy said it's inside a vent directly beneath the fire escape." I show Stefan the map on my phone, the screen glowing in his dark car. "I'm guessing this is the alley here—opposite the nightclub." I zoom in with two fingers.

"Swanky phone," he says. "How you pay for that?"

"With money I earned legally. You?"

He shows me an old, banged-up flip phone. "You were in school when I bought this."

"Jesus."

"Don't need all that internet shit following me around everywhere," he grumbles.

"Maps are handy."

Stefan reaches to the back seat and grabs the backpack. Inside there's one remaining wad of cash and a brick of pale brown powder wrapped tightly in plastic.

"Expensive night," he says. "It better be worth it."

"It will be." I flex my fingers in a fresh pair of latex gloves. Then I put my cap on, pull my hood up, and flick open a pair of sunglasses.

"Some of these bars are still open." I lean lower to look out the car's window—through streaked glass, wet and red, clear in the thin wakes of dripped water. "And security cameras. Up on these corners."

High buildings. A thousand potential eyes.

We get out and cross the road, head all the way up the sidewalk, turn right, and see our target three hundred feet or so ahead.

The rain has stopped, but the ground is still damp, so the clubs and bars that stretch the length of the street glisten in the asphalt, doubled doorways and traffic lights drawn out as though they've rushed up into the world from below.

There are a few people smoking outside one of the bars, standing at high tables beneath fire grills, the totem flames of indulgent outdoor heaters flickering; further down the street a long line of costume party revelers wait at the nightclub. Big doormen in black jackets unclipping velvet ropes to let people in, one group at a time.

I stay just behind Stefan, who scans the area then nods toward the alley. Once in there and out of sight, we move quickly.

Over these past few months, me and Stefan have only crossed paths a couple of times. He still seems wary of me, though his distrust appears to have died down. I've more than proved myself. I'm part of this—there's no way he could deny that, even if the idea of working alongside law enforcement has never sat comfortably with him.

And while, of course, his survival is incompatible with my plan, I have to admit, I trust him too. He's capable. Strong. Smart. Cautious. All the traits you need when you're out late at night committing serious crimes.

Though, unlike Adam, I can't say I see much good in him—there's no innocence to be found. And if I were brave enough to go looking, I'm sure he'd hide it well. Stefan is a dangerous man. Out of the three, he's the one that scares me most. Even Edward exhibits basic human warmth. Stefan's just as crazy but has none of that charisma and charm.

Sometimes I reflect on my old life—look back at what I should do with all this knowledge. In some ways Stefan is as much a target for the DEA as Edward Lang himself. He's the muscle. The solid foundation. Hands-on. The whole operation falls apart if he's gone. But tonight he's my closest ally in the world.

Just the other day Rosie and I were sitting in the new house, the one Edward gave us. We've been visiting, spending weekends, like it's a vacation home. She still wants us to live there for good. But I'm not so sure. Either way, she laughed and said it was kind of a shame that this couldn't go on forever, as we're actually pretty good at it.

But I never lose sight of the light at the end of this tunnel. It's all about Matthew. It's all about justice. In fact, taking their money, destroying their entire empire, and making them pay with blood is a far better punishment than a lengthy prison sentence.

Rosie was right. We are good at this. I'm just playing a slightly different game.

"There," I say, spotting the metal fire escapes running up the bricks on the apartment buildings either side of the alley. "Should be below one of these." On the right there's a doorway and on the left two overflowing trash cans, flattened cardboard with broken crates piled on top. "Here," I say, "the one without the ladder."

I take my sunglasses off. Then I slide some of the trash aside, kicking a garbage bag out of the way; a couple of rats scurry quickly back into a shadow. The rusted vent is about the size of a pizza box. It's screwed in on the top right and bottom left corners.

Reaching into his jacket, Stefan pulls out a screwdriver and hands it to me. "Fast," he says, looking back up the alleyway, steam on his breath.

The sound of the street is distant as I click my flashlight on and hold it in my mouth like I'm chewing on a fat cigar. Then I unscrew the grill, pumping the spiral ratchet screwdriver and collecting the screws that fall into my numb, gloved hand. I lift it carefully away and lean it against the bricks.

Stefan takes the flashlight, holds it on me as I crouch lower and reach inside, pat bare metal and dust and—

"There's no—" But then I grip a strap and pull. A bag falls down, and I drag it out onto the concrete between my feet.

Pulling open the zipper, I see, like the others, it contains a modest amount of methamphetamine and maybe a thousand bucks in cash. I put that right, like the last two, placing the brick of heroin and the thick bundle of bills inside.

Tomorrow morning when agents do as Sammy suggested, they'll find that he was full of shit. If anything he'll be accused of wasting police time, and the Carrillo cartel will probably hear all about his big mouth.

I zip the bag closed and shuffle to—

"What's that?" Stefan says, aiming the cone of light at my hands.

I look up. "What?"

"On the side?"

Hesitating, I shift the bag, lift it, and see a small piece of dangling card—a price tag. The bag is brand new.

"Fuck," Stefan whispers. "I fucking told you. It's a trap. James, get up, we have—" He stops and stares back down the alley.

Still crouched, I lean around the trashcans and see two . . . three men. Dressed in black. Four now.

"They cops?" I ask.

Stefan clicks the flashlight off. Now the figures are dark silhouettes, backlit in streetlights, framed at the foot of a tall, narrow rectangle.

"No," he says, his eyes wide. "We need to run."

One of them pulls open his jacket, lifts a submachine gun and aims—professional stance as they come down the black track.

Stefan drags me to my feet and throws me into the doorway. I rattle the handle—locked. I turn, but then he comes shoulder first past me and takes it off the hinges. They shout at us to stop.

We go into a dark, dusty corridor, through a backroom, and slam another door closed behind us. I slide a bolt lock. Then into a gloomy convenience store. I follow Stefan along a line of fridges in the low blue light, humming and buzzing, to the front.

The back door's getting kicked open as Stefan smashes the window with his elbow, shielding his face from the falling, shattered glass.

An alarm wails.

He clambers through and we run across the street, toward the crowd waiting in line at the nightclub.

"Make a scene," he says over his shoulder as he jogs toward the doorman.

"What?"

And Stefan headbutts him and darts inside.

Behind, the men are coming fast across the road, their guns hidden. There are two more on the other side of the street, one of them on his phone.

So again, I follow Stefan into the club, shoving people aside as I weave amid the commotion.

A group of security guards are blocking the main door so I dive right and into a corridor, fliers and graffiti on the walls. I shoulder between men and women. Then I leap over a girl sitting against the bricks and run and push myself off the wall at the end. Turning, stumbling backward through another hallway near the bathrooms, white light and drunk, drugged, costume party faces inches from mine. Goths and gasmasks and sweat, and I turn and fall through doors and onto the dance floor. Music pounding out of speakers at the front, green lasers scanning the packed room, glowing beams in the smoke and dark, and dancing, bouncing, jumping people.

I spot Stefan. He snatches a glittery cowboy hat from someone, puts it on his head, then disappears into the throng. Staying close on the dance floor, I try to keep a hand on his big shoulder, the heat and humidity of strangers moving all around me. Pushing through.

The music drops and the room's pitch black and quiet enough to hear a cheer as the DJ says, "Hold on," and returns with a new song—fast, loud industrial techno starts with a sudden crash and a burst of strobe light on every other beat. Spinning spotlights and bass so deep I feel it in my ribcage.

At the speakers—my ears are ringing—*wow-wow-wow*. Freeze-framed figures, arms raised, appearing in camera flashes, everyone moving in the dark, cast still and vivid with each strobe. A photo, a photo, a photo—the music's like a scream now—howling and thudding—a revving engine.

High above, on the balcony, a couple of the men look across the sea of heads. On the other side, the doormen are also searching for us, reporting in on radios.

I nudge Stefan, bowing my head and subtly pointing.

He nods to let me know he's seen them, then gestures for us to go around the DJ booth.

Thunder and air raid sirens as the lights tilt up and the green grid spins and scans, turning blue, red, flashing white as it sweeps and pulses.

But then sparks and screaming as the music cuts out and panic takes over.

I duck. My hearing suddenly returns as a speaker spits out smoke and shards of plastic.

Jostling against the fleeing crowd, I look up and see one of them has fired a burst of rounds across the electronics and now even the doormen are evacuating.

Stefan drags me through another narrow hall. People shout as we pour out a fire exit and into a parking lot.

Everyone moves in a pack around the corner and back toward the street—women holding dresses on, running in high heels. Trying to get away from what they can only assume is an active shooter situation.

But me and Stefan make for the other end of the parking lot—his glittery hat flying off—and past a wooden fence down the next street.

"If they catch us, they will kill us," he says, with cold, blank eyes.

We cross two more blocks, sprint toward another alley, and skid to turn as, once more, three men join the chase.

But halfway down the narrow lane, we realize it's a dead end.

"Oh, fuck." Stefan steps left, right, turns full circle. There's a dumpster pushed against the bricks. He looks above at the low roof, quickly assessing an escape route. "Climb on, I'll boost you, then you pull me up."

It's doable, so I do as he says, get on top and place my foot in his cupped hands. I rest my elbows then my stomach on the edge, his firm grip pushing my heel higher. I swing a leg up, roll onto my side on the flat roof, and watch them arrive at the alley.

"James, quick," Stefan says, holding his hand up, asking for mine. He looks over his shoulder—they're coming. "Fuck, James. Come on." He sounds scared, his fingers splayed desperately. He bounces slightly, one foot raised ready to climb, his curly blond hair damp with sweat. And he slows down and looks up at me, glaring now as he realizes what's happening. I'm not helping him. I'm not giving him my hand. "James." There's so much disappointment in his low voice.

He turns to face them just as they slam into the dumpster, knocking him from his feet. They drag him off—the last thing I see as I back away, standing, is Stefan struggling—kicking and swinging his elbow as a bag goes over his head and one of the men pulls out some cable ties.

My heart's roaring in my ears as I cross the roof, suddenly filled with terror that I've made a mistake. If they *don't* kill him, I'm completely fucked. He saw. He saw that I let it happen.

But they will. They will. I tell myself they will.

What if they interrogate him? What if he talks? Shit, what have I done?

Behind some air conditioning units, I find a ladder and clamber down into a small courtyard. I pause and listen for a second. I can hear the panic from the nightclub, a siren in the distance. But I think they've given up the search. They got one of us. That's enough. It'll be OK. I'm still alive.

I catch my breath and stride quickly down the street, down a steep grass bank, and across the main road—all the way back to the bridge, checking behind the whole time, my hand never more than an inch from my pistol.

Walking backward now, leaning and inspecting shadows, I creep toward the car. I check all the routes behind me, panting, and no one is here. It's quiet. Thank God. I step slowly, edging away from all the places they could emerge.

Everything is still.

The only thing moving is a thin strip of plastic from the nearby gas pipe site, which has caught on the top of a chain-link fence opposite. It's faded white and flicks and curls in the breeze, like the long electric stingers that follow a jellyfish through the sea.

I'm stepping backward toward the car, backward to safety, backward to—I gasp when I bump into it. Standing still, I breathe and hold my chest.

"Jesus," I whisper to myself.

Reaching down for the handle, I turn and the coast is clear. I pull open the door, but a sound—

"Smart move," a voice says, rising from the other side of the car.

I grab for my pistol, but someone else has my wrist and the scruff of my neck, slamming me against the hood and hitting me on the side of the head. Dazed, I fall to the ground and reel and see there's two of them looming above. One has cable ties in his teeth and he's coming down and then black material across my face and metal on my neck. It feels like a Taser. I try to scream for help. But I can't.

Chapter Twenty-Four

" . . . piece of shit, you hear me, boy?" A voice is saying something. "Wake up, wake up."

Mumbling, I jolt awake and I can't see. I can't move. My hands are tied behind me. "What's happening? Stefan?"

I'm lying on a metal floor on my side; something's vibrating. An engine. I shift around and roll onto my back. A bump in the road bounces me, and I yell at a bruise on my shoulder. We're in a van, or a truck of some kind.

Something hits my leg. Someone's kicking me.

"Little, fucking." Stefan is angry. "You understand—I'm blowing it open." His voice is muffled. "That fucking recording is going online. I'm sending it to every newspaper, every TV show on earth. You hear me? You are done."

Shit. Why did I go back to the car?

"Where are we?" I ask.

"Tied up in the back of a fucking truck. They're cartel. I heard them talking. They're taking us to a . . . some place."

With a few breaths, I begin to think clearly. Of course they were watching the dead drops. Clever Sammy. It was win-win. Maybe it was always a trap. He pretended to trust the DEA. He appealed to our pride. Maybe they were just trying to isolate where the corruption lies, see who took the bait.

Or maybe not. It doesn't really matter. Either way, they were watching.

"Let's hold fire on our dispute," I say. "We're in this together."

Stefan sighs. "I knew it was a bad idea. I'm going to die, because of . . . *you*," he hisses that word.

"Look, I'm sorry. Just focus on the issue at hand. We can talk later. You need to think."

"I'm meant to be picking my daughter up in the morning," he says. "She'll be waiting at the end of her street. Holding her school bag. Her packed lunch."

"I didn't know you had a daughter. We're actually expecting a—"

"Shut the fuck up, James."

I fiddle with my restraints. Cable ties and . . . duct tape. "What are we going to do?" I ask.

"Die. Horribly . . . Oh, you've been waiting for this, haven't you? Waiting for a chance to fuck us."

It's hard to argue with that. So I don't respond.

After a long silence, I feel the ground beneath us change—the wheels crunching on new terrain.

I'd felt safe earlier following Stefan's orders. When he was still on my side. But now, blind and alone in the dark, fear is beginning to flex its muscles inside me. I swallow. "What will they do to us?"

"Very, very, very bad things." His voice sounds even deeper in the confined space. "Pliers. Hacksaws. All your favorite parts chopped off, fed to dogs."

"Why?"

"What do you mean 'why'? To make us talk before they kill us."

Focus, I think. *Focus on solutions*.

"What will they want to know?" I ask.

"Are you a fucking fool? They'll want to know who we work for, how it operates, why we've been framing Carrillo men."

I think for a moment. I'd do anything to get to that light. Anything. "Well . . . what if we tell them?"

"Rotten to the core." Stefan laughs in disbelief. "You're a fucking snake. A *fucking snake.* Don't you say a fucking word to them."

"If they're going to kill us anyway?"

He writhes again, and I hear his heels bang into the metal near me as he swings a few more kicks, but I shuffle and edge out of reach.

Eventually the truck rumbles onto even softer ground and comes to a stop. With the engine cut, it's completely silent—all I can hear are my own breaths, warm against the fabric over my head.

A door slams up ahead, then another. I turn my neck to listen. Mumbled voices. But then nothing.

"Where are we?" I whisper.

A long time passes—maybe an hour or more. Enough for my adrenaline to boil down and become something like anger. "Hey," I shout. "Hey, what's going on?"

"Be quiet," Stefan says.

"Help," I yell, banging the wall of the truck with my bound feet. "Help us."

"What are you doing?"

"Someone might be able to hear. Hey," I scream. "Hey."

There's a clunk and the light changes—I can make it out through the weave holes in the sack. Flashing stars, lattice light, breath closer than it should ever be. It moves and flickers as I pant and search.

"What?" a voice demands.

"I'll speak," I say. "I'll tell you everything you want to know."

"James, stop," Stefan says through his teeth.

"What do you want from us?" I ask.

"Shut up, James, shut up."

"Listen to your friend," the man adds.

So now that the doors are open, I shout again, "Help." And something hits me hard on the back. I struggle as a strong hand drags me closer to the light, holds my head, and lifts the bag over my nose.

"No," I mumble. "Fuck you, I'm a fucking—"

But before I can finish, he's wrapping thick duct tape across my mouth, around and around, tight enough to hurt. I hear more tape screech from the roll.

"Come on," Stefan grumbles. "I wasn't saying anything."

The doors hang open.

And now, both gagged, it's quiet.

Once more we're forced to wait. I listen to the men speaking. Smoking. Laughing. Sounds like there are four of them. A variety of accents. Rolling over, I can just about make out the bright sky through a small tear in the bag—and metal rafters of some kind. Like an old warehouse, but the roof, the ceiling, it's mostly gone. Birds flapping and leaping up there on the remaining frame. Pigeons. Gray feathers. White droppings down the girders.

Anxiety returns in sharp, sudden peaks. They caught us red-handed. It was never about the contents of those dead drops. Another terrible thought comes to me—they wouldn't suspect I'm a DEA agent. Even if they knew the details, which they probably don't, they'd assume the agent would feed information, tip someone off. Never do this dirty work themselves. They need to know who I am. It's the only thing that could save me. I start to mumble, trying to shout. I have to tell them.

"Shut up." One of the guys leans close. "*Shut. Up.*"

"Mmmm-mm-mmmm. Mmmmm."

And then he hits me so fucking hard I feel like he might have cracked my skull. It sounds like I'm snoring and then—*whack*—again.

I stay quiet now as what feels like warm shower water trickles down the back of my head. Another few minutes pass.

A phone rings. "Yeah," the main voice says. "Both of them . . . That's right. Made a bit of a scene, so we'll need to get out of town for a while . . . Across the border . . . Both still alive. We've got them tied up . . . No, no, we're at the new guy's yard. Yep. Real quiet . . . You sure? Well, it was just a lot of work and . . . yeah. No, no, I understand that . . . of course . . . I don't have an alternative suggestion, I was just . . . OK. OK. Fine. Will call you when it's done."

Stefan grunts. It sounds like fear.

"Come on then." The man sighs as two pairs of hands grab me and pull me out by my jacket.

My heels dragging in dry dirt and gravel—the sky, sunlight, rusted metal above. Little glimmers and flashes. My eyes focusing on the black fabric, on the world outside, on the bag again.

I'm lifted to my feet, then I feel a boot on the back of my leg pushing me to my knees. It hurts to kneel, it always has—since I fell from that tree in the snow—but I know they wouldn't care.

Fast, panicked breaths whistle from my nose as I turn to my right and see Stefan put in the same position. His black bag like a pointed hood. And in front of us, what is that? Dark. It's a ditch.

"Mmm," I whimper, fiddling desperately with the cable ties around my wrists. Hard, strong, unbreakable plastic.

There's some laughter. And another voice. "What did Avery say?"

A man paces near my feet. I hear the gun's slide rack back. "Well." *Clack*. "After all that, he told us to get rid of them."

I see, by my side, Stefan lift his head, kneeling upright. Like he's proud. Ready.

I'm in shock—it's too fast, no more talking—disbelief, it can't be happening, they're not going to just—

The gunshot is loud, echoing in my ringing ears, the black bag spitting string from his face. Startled pigeons flee above as Stefan's heavy, dead body thuds shoulder first into the shallow grave below me.

I hear myself mumbling—confused, desperate.

A light wisp of dust where the bullet hit the ground.

I'm trying to scream, trying to pull my hands apart and cutting my wrists and, no, God, no, no. Tears flow and I tense, like I'm bracing myself for cold water. I scrunch my eyes shut and hold my breath. At least if I'm still it'll be instant.

I can't see, but I sense his arm lifting, his aim straightening, the back of my head coming into focus. Square in the sights. His finger squeezing and—

"What the hell are you doing?" A new voice.

My eyes wide, my face hot, I try to slow my breathing to listen.

"These are the sneaky bastards—caught them at the dead drop. What are you doing here?"

"I was up in the office and I heard a gunshot."

"Maybe you should go back inside."

"So, what? You're just killing them?"

"That's what Avery said. We're following orders. Listen, man, this doesn't concern you."

"You're shooting people on my land. Yeah, it does."

"Well, look the other way. Came from the top."

"Who are they?" the new voice asks.

The man with the gun sighs. "This dead one is Stefan Fiennes—and this is his little bitch. Now, if you'll excuse me."

He moves again, taking aim.

"Wait. Wait, wait, wait."

Footsteps as someone comes toward me, at the edge of the grave. He steps close, in front of Stefan's body.

He crouches down and pulls the bag from my head. The bright dawn light makes my eyes ache. Wincing, I blink and look at him.

It's Foster.

We just stare into each other's faces—and, just like me, he's unable to speak. A lifetime seems to pass.

"You two know each other?" the guy behind me asks.

Foster's eyes dart quickly before returning to mine. He's working out what to say. "No," he whispers. "No," he says, louder. "I don't know this person."

Glaring, I groan. I can feel snot dripping down over the tape.

Foster tenses his jaw and swallows. "But I do know who he works for."

"Yeah, Stefan."

But Foster shakes his head. "You can't kill this one."

"Why?"

Foster sighs and looks up, over my shoulder. "He's a DEA agent."

"How the fuck do you know that?"

Still in character, Foster frowns. "I recognize him. He arrested me a while back." The lie falls off his tongue.

He's cut his hair, shaved his sideburns. He's wearing a white vest.

And my mind pieces it all together. Foster's undercover. These cartel guys don't know who he is. He's done well. He's done really, really well.

"You sure?"

"Check his wallet," Foster says. "His name's Casper."

I feel a hand slide into my pocket, followed by a short silence and then some hasty whispering behind me.

Foster stands and looks over my head, waiting for a response. "See?"

"So what the hell was he doing last night?" the voice asks.

Foster shrugs, taking my wallet from the man, slipping it into his own back pocket. "Exactly what it looked like. He was planting drugs."

"Why?"

And he looks down at me again. "Because he's a crook," Foster says. We share a silence. "But even so, we can't be killing feds. Especially not on my property."

"We don't play those rules. Order's to kill him, so we kill him."

"Don't you think, given what we know, he would be more useful alive? Doing this will cause nothing but trouble."

"The boss said—"

"Call him again," Foster snaps, being firm. "Explain. Tell him I'll handle it."

"He's seen our faces."

I shake my head, mumbling. Humming to say, "No, no, no."

Foster seems alarmed as the other man reaches around to grip the tape covering my mouth. After all, he's in just as much danger as I am. He rips it off.

"I haven't," I gasp. "Only his. No one else. I won't say a thing. I won't. I won't."

Everyone disappears behind me and has a quick crisis meeting. Weighing the pros and cons of their next move. I just wait, looking across the dirt and old car parts and derelict machines in this ramshackle warehouse. Then I look up at the pigeons. They've come back. The clouds moving slowly beyond.

Finally I feel a cold knife against my wrist as someone slits the cable ties. And my eyes fall closed with relief. They untie my feet, and I stand up slowly, carefully, trembling hands on show as they put the bag back over my head.

"I'll dump him in the city," Foster says. "He won't say a word. He's in our pocket now. But you need to get that body out of here."

He guides me by the shoulder, away from the ditch. We walk and walk. Neither speaking until we're well clear.

"Stop," Foster says, then he whips the bag from my head.

I check behind; we're standing alone at the edge of a scrapyard. Next to an outbuilding. Foster's pickup truck parked at my side. A stack of old, half-crushed cars piled six high nearby.

He steps around in front of me. "I just saved your life," he says, folding the black bag. "Do you know what I'm putting on the line? Do you know how hard I've worked to keep my cover intact?" He holds up his thumb and index finger. "I'm this close to Avery's inner circle."

"What now?" I ask.

"You say, 'thank you.'"

"Foster, listen, it's complicated, OK. I need you to understand."

"You fucking did it, didn't you? You put that shit on *my* laptop. They grilled me for three days about that. Accused me. And it was *you*."

I show him a hand. "It could have come from outside—you were never in any danger."

"How long, James?" He laughs. "How long has this been going on?"

"It's not that simple. Edward Lang is . . . he's a powerful man."

"So it's true? Lang is at the top. And you've been covering for him?"

"You don't understand."

"And now you're what? Framing the competition?" He points back the way we came. "Framing cartel men? So Lang can sell across the whole city, the whole country? And, shit, you look great at the same time."

Tilting my head, I give him credit for working it all out. "It's temporary and necessary."

"How, James?" he asks. "How did you fall so far?"

I take a long breath and sigh. "Incrementally."

"Nell's been looking," he says. "She's been looking for someone in the taskforce." He smiles in astonishment, maybe even awe. "It's you. James the golden boy."

"You can't tell her," I say. "You can't tell anyone."

Foster does a double take, dramatically turning his head as though he misheard. He must have. "What?" He laughs again. "Are you being serious?"

"Extremely."

"I'm going to tell Nell, Rob Sanders, everyone at the department. I'm going to tell the fucking media. You are finished. And you should be *grateful* you're alive. Now, get in the truck."

He opens the passenger door.

For a split second, it flashes again—the light. I see that beautiful image Nell described. A tiny hand reaching up from a wriggling body. Taking hold of my index finger. Her grip is tight. Tighter than you'd expect. Oh, it makes Rosie cry at my side. Maybe we kiss her warm head. The bone inside so soft, so delicate.

I'll have my whole life to fill the world with good. To undo all of this. To flood her empty mind with laughter and smiles. Nearly there.

But first.

Bowing my head, I think for a moment about how best to phrase this next sentence. "Foster"—he turns back—"think carefully about what you're doing."

"I'm doing my job." He grins. "They're going to throw away the key. An accessory to all that? You're dying behind bars."

"That's right," I explain, carefully, gently. "If you tell the truth about me, I'll go to prison for a very long time. But . . . If I tell the truth about *you* . . . ?"

The anger drops from his face and becomes total shock. Like he's seen a ghost.

I don't need to say any more—I don't need to mention his wife, his children. All the monstrous things the cartel does to rats. Foster already knows.

Then his expression shifts through disgust and settles on something unmistakable. It's working. He's scared.

Chapter Twenty-Five

I need to move fast. I've lit the fuse. Stefan's death is the beginning of the end. Edward is going to find out. It's just a matter of when. If he tries to contact him and can't. Or if he hears. He'll suspect foul play. I was the last person to see Stefan alive. The timeline shrinking from months to days, hours—we're minutes from midnight now. The doomsday clock is ticking.

Mutually assured destruction. Would Edward press the button? Would he blow it all open? I just don't know. But I do know that I can't risk it.

After a silent, frosty journey back into the city, Foster drops me off at the bottom of the Singers hill. He tells me I can walk the rest of the way. Then he turns his truck around and drives off quickly.

And I run, panting as I burst through the front door—Rosie slow to stand as I storm past to the stairs. Up.

"James?" she says.

She finds me in the bathroom; I'm washing blood out of my hair.

"What's going—Oh my God, what happened?" She steps inside, checking the back of my head. "I've been worried sick. Where have you been?"

"It's fine." I'm just making myself presentable. Scrubbing the mud from my hands now. "I need some clean clothes."

"You need stitches, shall I call an ambulance?"

"Just." I stop, resist the urge to shout. "Clothes, Rosie, please."

Spotting the alarm in my face, she nods and heads to the bedroom as I strip.

"Speak to me," she says, handing me a T-shirt and some pants.

Drying my arms, my neck, my wet hair, I take the bundle of clothes. "Stefan is dead," I say, stepping into the jeans. "Carrillo guys caught us. They . . ." I take a breath, realizing how fast my heart's still going—from the run, from the fear. "They were going to kill me too, but Foster was there." I zip up the fly.

"Why?"

"He's undercover. But he knows. He knows what I've been doing."

Rosie understands the fragile, elaborate house of cards we've built. "Will he talk?"

"I think I've bought some time, but"—I look squarely into her eyes—"it's today. It's all happening today."

"What can I do to help?"

"I love you," I say, grabbing her hand. "Coffee. Very, very strong coffee."

"OK."

She disappears as I put the T-shirt on, rub some of the persistent dried blood away from my temple, and gargle blue mouthwash. I spit reddish purple liquid out. Just need to look human. I've got a cut on my forehead, another deep gash on the back of my skull, and a fresh bruise around my cheekbone. But it's the best I can do.

Downstairs, I stride across the kitchen. Rosie hands me a cup of coffee, which I drink in one gulp.

"Wasn't that hot?" she asks.

"Yeah." I cough. I kiss her on the cheek, grab my car keys, and head down the hallway.

"James."

Looking back, walking backward, I see Rosie standing at our window. She smiles and waves. I blow her a kiss and leave. Through the city. To work. Fast.

"Nell," I say, erupting into her office. "I need your help."

"What . . . Jesus, what happened to your face?"

"Long story, I'll tell you later. Call Mike Ward. I need an update on Foster. What he's doing. Where he is."

"Uh . . . why?"

"I think"—I've rehearsed this lie all morning—"I think he's involved with Edward Lang. The malware was him, right?"

"Well, maybe. I . . ."

"I think he's been planting drugs. I think he really is behind it all."

"What? Internal affairs investigator gave him the all clear."

"I know, it sounds crazy. But I just need to know what he's doing. Tabs. We need to keep tabs."

Nell frowns, unnerved at my sudden, rushed enthusiasm. She hesitates. "Now?" she asks.

"Yes, right now. Immediately."

Wheeling closer to her desk on her swivel chair, she lifts her phone and dials a number. I pace, completing two widths of her office, chewing on my thumbnail, before she says, "Hey, Mike."

I stop and look. Listen. Then I gesture and mouth "loudspeaker."

"—s it all going over there?" His voice comes into the room.

"Oh, yeah, you know, all good." Nell leans down closer to the phone as she speaks. "And you?"

"Can't complain."

"Just a quick one," she says. "I need an update on some of your guys—the ones out in the field."

I give her a thumbs-up for being vague. Smart.

"Yeah, who?" I picture Mike at his desk, distracted by his screen.

"Uh . . . how's Foster Gray doing? He's with a Carrillo crew, right?"

There's a long silence. A terrible delay. "Why are you asking?" Mike's paying full attention now.

I freeze. Fuck. Why is he being cagey? Has Foster spoken already? Is it over?

"Honestly," Nell says, "I've heard a couple of things on the grapevine today and I was wondering if there was any truth to it."

"Well, yeah," Mike finally says. "It is true. I don't know the details yet—it's all happening very fast. Only found out about half an hour ago."

I stare at Nell and spread my hands—what does this mean? What's he saying?

"What . . ." Nell scratches her ear. "What exactly is happening?"

"He's pulled the ripcord." Mike clicks his tongue. "Poor guy. He says his cover is blown. They're moving his family out of the city as we speak. He's following them this afternoon."

Nell looks up at me, astonished by this bombshell. My hands are clamped on either side of my head.

"Full witness protection," Mike adds. "I think he could be in some real trouble. Damn shame. He's a fine agent."

She brings the conversation to an end.

"I don't understand?" she says.

I fucking do. Foster's just getting clear. Then he can blow the whistle. Fuck. He's gone all in.

"Can we find out where he's going?" I ask. Even though I know the answer.

"They do it through the agency, only Mike would know. We can follow it up—there's no rush."

Yes, there is. Foster's going to fucking do it. Today. "I've got to go," I say. "I have a plan."

"James?" Nell says, confused, but I'm already out the door and walking, now running, down the corridor, outside, across the parking lot.

I pull my phone from my pocket as I open my car door. "Adam," I say the second he answers, climbing in and starting the engine, swapping hands, phone on shoulder. "I need your help."

"Oh, sure," he mumbles. Sounds like he's just woken up. "What's on your mind?"

"I need you to get some information off a computer . . . or, shit, I don't know. A phone. Something." Reversing wildly, mounting the high curb, the wheels screeching off the road as I head toward Mike Ward's office.

As I drive, Adam tells me it'd probably take a while.

"No," I say. "Today. An hour. You have to do it."

"I guess . . . if you got the device to me, I could try."

"Are you at your place?"

"Yeah."

"Stay there."

I must be hitting a hundred on the freeway. I come off and run a red light. A mile later, I slam the brakes on at the DEA division building in the city. I'm out and inside, rushing up the stairs.

"Hey, James," someone says.

I smile but don't stop moving until I'm on the third floor and knocking on Mike Ward's door.

"Yeah?" he says, as I push it open and closed behind me. "Agent Casper?" He seems surprised. Maybe at the unannounced visit or at the damage and sweat across my face. "You OK?"

"Listen, I'm . . ." I swoop forward and sit down. I spot his smartphone on his desk. And he has a laptop. I need one of them. But I make sure not to stare. "I, well . . ." My legs are pumping, elbows on my bouncing knees. "You know what, Mike, can you get me a cup of coffee? I'm really, really thirsty and I need a cup of coffee."

"Uh." He squints. "Sure."

He presses a button on his office phone and it buzzes. "Hey, Dan, can you grab a couple of coffees?"

Fuck. Leave. Get out. "Um, yeah." I squirm. I need to get him to leave this room.

"So," he opens his hands, elbows on his desk, "what can I do for you?"

"I—" I stop. Stand up. The chair almost tips over so I grab it.

Mike is visibly uncomfortable. Concerned. "Have you been drinking?"

"No . . . You know, actually, hold that thought. I'll be back in a second."

I leave his office, walk down the corridor, checking behind me, checking no one's around. To the end, near a small janitor's room—a closet full of brooms, a vacuum cleaner, mops and buckets, and old filing cabinets.

I've gone completely fucking crazy, I think, as I pull the fire alarm and then step inside to hide.

Pulsing above me, a rhythmic honking, the alarm echoes through the entire building. I wait a good five minutes while staff evacuate, then emerge and walk quickly through the now-empty corridor back to Mike's office.

He's taken his phone, obviously, but not his laptop.

I snatch the mouse cable out, slam it shut, and bundle it beneath my arm, along with its power cord. Then I check the coast is clear, hit the stairwell, and at the back maintenance door slide the laptop into my jacket and hold it at my stomach like it's a baby. I'm able to use a low roof at the rear of the building to escape, falling hard back to the concrete outside, checking again that no one can see me. Then I break into a clumsy, desperate sprint as I return to my car. A hundred people gathered in the adjacent parking lot, waiting to hear that it was a false alarm.

Driving once more, I'm two minutes from Adam's apartment when I call him again. "Get ready, I'm coming to you now," I say, checking my mirror, steering one-handed.

He's waiting for me on the sidewalk—good man. I wind down the window and pass him the laptop.

"This belongs to Mike Ward," I explain. "He handles undercover DEA agents."

"Right?" Adam recenters his glasses to look at it. He steps closer to the car to let a woman with a stroller pass.

"They're moving an agent called Foster Gray and his family to a safe house," I say quietly. "I just need to know where. That's all."

"Will that information be on this?" he asks.

"Emails, messages?" I sigh. "I hope so."

"If it's not?"

"If it's not then . . . then we might be fucked. Call me. When you're finished, destroy it."

I leave him, and once again it's foot down.

Foster has to stay scared. He can't believe he's safe. The one thing I'm sure about is that he won't leave without his dad's bike. In fact, I'd bet everything I have that he'll be riding that vintage Harley out of this mess.

So I head to his workshop—it's out in the sticks, an hour's drive from the city limits. This is his private property. And it's easy to find—he's always talking about it in the office. I hide my car a few hundred yards away, then run through a field and climb over a fence to approach from the rear.

A wide, wooden building with thick, ivy-covered trees all around the back and sides. I step toward the small window on the front of the shack. And I'm dizzy with relief when I see the bike is still parked inside, surrounded by tables and tools. Shiny chrome.

Foster's pride and joy. He *won't* leave without it. This will be his last stop.

I go in. There's a folding chair in the corner, partially hidden by a shelving unit. I sit down, hold my phone, and wait. And then, just ten minutes after my arrival, I hear an engine rumbling outside.

Standing, I check through the dirty plastic window, a vignette of moss creeping around the edges. It's Foster. Through the shed's old Perspex, he looks distorted when he moves—stretched long and ripple-blurred. He's alone, dressed casually, and he's got a trailer attached to the back of his pickup truck. Maybe the bike's not ready to ride.

I call Adam. "Need it now," I whisper.

"I'm in, but," Adam hums, "he's got a few files on all the agents—it's really mixed up. And nothing about safe houses. Nothing about any witness protection."

"Keep looking. Please be quick."

My face pressed against the green plastic, hand on the frame. Ivy is growing inside through the gaps around the window—it clings and crawls like veins across most of the back wall.

Foster's approaching the building. I hear him moving outside, grabbing a box of tools that he places in the back of his truck. Then he turns and heads toward the door. I lose sight of him again and now he's rattling the handle.

"Adam." I turn.

"Found it," he says. "But no detail. Just a list of zip codes."

"Fuck."

Foster enters, closing the door behind him and walking toward the bike. He can't see me, but I watch him through the shelves, stepping sideways to get a better view.

"I think it's a list of possible options," Adam says. "Nothing to indicate which one."

I can't speak so I just listen.

"Wait." I hear Adam typing. "They're all in Alaska. That's the best I can do. Alaska."

Ending the call, I slide my phone into my pocket.

Foster's standing with his back to me, hand on his hip, looking at the bike.

Quietly, I stride out from the shelves and stand behind him—he's about twenty feet away.

"How much?" I say, now holding my pistol at my waist. Vinegar. Honey. Flies.

His head sinks as he slowly turns around. He glances at the gun, then up to my eyes. It looks like he feels sorry for me. Pity. "How much for what?" he says, sounding exhausted.

"For your silence. You're leaving anyway. What will it cost for you to stay gone and keep your mouth shut?"

Foster shakes his head. "A million dollars," he says.

"Done."

"An hour."

"Come on. Let's discuss this."

"James, there's nothing to discuss. You can't pay me off. I told you this morning. It's over. Just . . . stop."

"You trust them? These new identities? Can you hide from the cartel forever? They'll go after your family."

"You've fucked up my life." He's exasperated. "My career. And you have the fucking . . . the audacity to threaten me? Still?"

I shrug. "How much?"

"Fuck off." Foster turns his back on me and picks up a rag, leans over, and wipes the chrome fuel tank on the shiny bike. As if I'm not even here.

And I wish I wasn't. I wish I could smell fabric softener. See Rosie's tired eyes looking up at me as she sways, left to right, bouncing and whispering. Rock-a-bye, baby. Go back to sleep. We'd keep her safe. Protect her from things like this. From people like me.

But I am here. And there's just a little bit more work to do. I really didn't want to have to play this card—but part of me knew I'd have to.

"Alaska," I say.

Foster freezes. Then gradually stands up straight and turns around again. He wipes his hands, throws the rag aside. It lands on one of the old wooden tables nearby, clattering against tools. Then he takes a step closer.

I move the gun ever so slightly—not pointing it, but making sure he sees.

And he stops. "Yeah," he says. "That much. That's what it'll cost for my silence."

"Let's not go down that road."

"Those are your options. There's no one around." He lifts an arm to the door. "No one for miles. No witnesses. I can't see what's stopping you?"

Another step toward me. So now I have to aim it at him.

"There we go," he says. "That's the spirit." Then he taps his forehead. "Just, bang," he whispers. Closing the gap even more, Foster stops next to a table, now less than ten feet between us.

"I don't want to shoot you," I say. Which is the God's honest truth.

"Then why on earth would you point a gun at me?" Foster's rage clicks into gear. Pure hate in his face as he snatches a wrench from the table and throws it. I duck and aim again but he's at me, his hand on my throat, the other around my arm.

He pushes the gun down, his shoulder into my chin as he slams me against the shelves, items tumbling off as the whole unit tips.

Crashing hard and loud, we fall on top of the debris, smashing the wood, and the pistol is gone, somewhere above me—behind.

I roll off the shelves and turn and his knee connects with my nose. On the ground now, in the dirt, I'm gripping his jacket and scrabbling, slipping from his fingers as I hold my hands up and try to block and he's mounting me and hitting me and slamming my skull hard into the ground. Old leaves and dust when I reach to grab something. Anything.

He leans back for a screwdriver, and I'm able to get a leg free, kick his chest away, and get half to my feet, but he comes forward. And again he's on me—he's all over me—and I struggle, but his warm, strong fingers wrap around my throat.

I find the wrench and swing it up and he falls sideways.

Standing, I've got the gun and I turn but he's there—relentless and strong and snarling as he drives us back against the wall, against the ivy, in the creeping plants.

Damp and wrestling—I see flashes of glossed green leaves and his forearm, his teeth. Four hands on the pistol, held between us, at our chests, tilting up, the barrel pointing at my face, his face, the wooden ceiling. I wrap my hand around the trigger, shielding the guard, but he's stronger than me and the gun's coming up, slowly, steadily. He's pushing the barrel into my cheek, pointing up, pressing the metal so hard against my skin I taste blood and it's under my eye socket.

Grunting, I feel his index finger burrowing steadily below my palm, inching toward the trigger. He's nodding and it's happening and he's squeezing, he's squeezing, our noses inches from each other. The barrel, the trigger, the trigger. He's on it.

"No," I mumble. I let go and shove it away with the last strength I have and snap my head to—

The gun goes off.

A harsh flash blinds and deafens me. And we both fall again to the ground.

I'm sitting up, still against the wall.

My face is warm and wet, and for an awful moment I am certain I have been shot in the head and I'm groaning but I can't hear myself. My vision stays blurred as I look down at my shaking red hands like a little boy—a little boy who's fallen hard on the playground.

In a trembling state of desperate shock, I touch my face and feel my skull. My fingers in my hair, my eyes wide as I look across the floor.

Heavy, gasping breaths are the first thing I hear when my ears return to the room. And there, sprawled on the concrete, I see Foster, flat on his back, perfectly still.

His rolled, bulged eyes and the top of his head, his scalp blown apart—ragged strips of flesh. Wet death pouring across his face, adding emotion where there is none. He's crying tears of blood.

It's so quiet now.

Resting my head against the wall, still amid the leathery leaves, I take a few moments to compose my thoughts. I breathe. And think.

This place is a mess. I have to get away. I have to . . . what do I do?

Solutions.

It's a mess. But maybe that's a good thing. Opposite me, propped up against a table leg, I spot a hand ax. Stumpy yellow handle, razor-sharp edge.

Oh, fuck, I think, sighing.

Realizing what I have to do, I press my hand onto my knee and rise to my feet. It's messy. But it's not quite messy enough. This has to look like something far worse than it is.

So I grab Foster's body, roll it onto its front, then take a step back. I pick up the pistol and aim. I have to look away as I fire two more rounds into the back of his head.

Holstering the gun, I collect all three shell casings and every fragment I can see. I reach into my pocket, remove a pair of latex gloves, and put them on. Then I hold back vomit, tears, as I pick up the ax and stand over him.

I go somewhere else in my mind. She's growing up. It's her first day of school. She's talking. Asking me questions. Saying silly things to the silly world I'll have to lie about.

The ends will justify the means—I've done too much for them not to.

Remember what matters. Perspective. One more trivial distraction.

It takes another minute or so before I pluck up the courage to begin.

Just meat, I think. *It's just meat.* And I do to his body what the cartel might have done. All the things they do to informants. The brutality they inflict on rats.

Five minutes of butchery later, I'm cleaning myself at the sink—wiping everything I've touched. Fist to my lips, I almost puke again but somehow manage to keep it down.

There are a few dark-green jerry cans in the corner. I dowse the whole place in gas, splashing it over tables, the ground, the shelves, and ivy walls. I even unscrew the tank on the vintage bike and kick it onto its side. It thuds heavy onto the concrete.

I'm repeating Matthew's note in my mind, trying not to cry, hearing the choir at his funeral—their heavenly voices echoing out somewhere beyond this place. Singing from somewhere I'm never going to see.

Outside I look back at the wooden shack. Then I crouch and light the grass at my feet. The blue flame creeps across the earth, low and slow but then fast as it goes inside and spreads out and, with a sudden *woompf*, the whole place goes up.

Smoke is rising, black fog billowing over the tree line behind me when I arrive at my car. It looks like a plane might have crashed.

We'll buy a nice wooden cot for the baby. Handmade. I'll paint it myself. I'll use a fine brush to paint little stars for her.

I'm staring at the cloud and pulling my phone from my pocket. It's 1 p.m.. Tiny little stars.

OK. Next up on the list of people who need to die today . . . Edward Lang. I scroll to his name and hit call.

Chapter Twenty-Six

"James," Edward says. "I've been trying to contact you."

"Sorry, I was . . ." I turn and put a hand on the roof of my car, phone against my ear. "I had some things to do." The driver's window is like a mirror—a long line of black smoke streaked across the glowing sky over my shoulder. It's so thick now it's casting a shadow, blotting out the sun. "I think we have to meet up. Where are you?"

That's all I need to know. Where he is.

"What happened last night?" Edward asks.

"Uh." I look at the ground, kick some gravel. "Nothing. Dead drops went smoothly."

He doesn't know where they were, so even if he's heard about the commotion at the nightclub he wouldn't connect it to us.

"How did Stefan seem?"

"Um, fine." Fuck, why didn't I rehearse these lies? "Maybe acting a bit strange."

"Strange how?"

"Well, he's not exactly keen on me," I say, speaking faster now, getting a rhythm. "Plus he was really cautious about the whole thing—you know what he's like. Why do you ask?"

It's quiet here on the edge of the country road. Just the gentle rustle of trees, the faint buzz of insects in the nearby undergrowth. I can't hear the fire, but I can smell it.

"His ex-wife called me this morning because she couldn't get through to him. So naturally I tried to contact him myself, and still no answer." I hear a scratching sound. He seems distracted. "Then I asked Adam to see what he could do and he said Stefan's phone was turned off in the early hours. Which is unusual."

Oh no. This is bad. Shit. Think. Go hard.

"Listen," I say. "Whatever you're fucking accusing me of—I'd appreciate if you just come out and say it."

There's a silence. I went too hard.

"I'm not accusing you of anything, James," Edward says over the low scratching. "We're just having a conversation."

"I don't know where Stefan is, no."

"I didn't ask."

"You implied."

"Implied." *Scratch, scratch, scratch.* "And what does answering unasked questions *imply*?"

"Maybe that—"

"I'm drawing you, James," Edward says, cutting me off. "Right now. While we speak." I imagine him shading on a notepad, tilting his head, gazing, admiring his work. "Your eyes . . . and your mouth. Your handsome brown hair now. Hmm. Do you think I should add anything? A hat?"

"Listen, I—"

"Some horns?"

A slow breath. "I'm sorry," I say. "I've just had a stressful day."

"Sounds like it—Adam said you've been tracking down your colleagues. Foster Gray? Did he know something he shouldn't know?"

"Yes." Stay on track. There's only one objective here. "I think it'd be good to meet. We need to talk about it. Where are you?" I swallow.

This time he doesn't pause. He just simply says nothing. And every second of this silence feels like it's doubling his suspicion. Exponential inflation—approaching certainty now.

"Or," I add, looking down into my car, through the reflection of the sky behind, the long trail of black smoke hanging above like an approaching storm, "you could come to my place?"

But it's too late.

"What do you think the picture needs?"

"You have to trust me," I say.

"I'll ask Stefan about the horns. He's got a good eye for these things."

"Are you at your office?" I wonder—a last-ditch attempt.

"No, no," Edward says with a nonchalant sigh, still drawing. "I'm laying low for now."

Fuck, just tell me where you are, you piece of shit. "We really, really need to talk," I say. "Something serious is going on."

"Oh, I can tell." He's speaking slowly, like he's thinking aloud, attention on his artwork. "You can feel it in the air. An impending sense of . . . menace? Let's hope I hear from Stefan soon. I want to finish this picture. I hope it's a nice one."

The phone goes dead. Shit.

"Fuck," I yell, slamming a palm, then a fist—again and again—on my car roof. I spin and almost throw the phone. But instead I just squat low and press it against my head. I hit myself a few times with the corner and, *think, think, think*.

Gradually I lower my cell phone and stare at it. Then up to my feet, I turn and open the driver's door. Climb in. Clunk the glove compartment—the hatch falls to the end of its hinges and I reach inside for the burner phone. The Carpenter needs to know today is the day. Prewarning might yield critical time.

His old, raspy voice appears after just one ring. "Good afternoon," he says.

"Today."

"Please clarify what you mean by that word."

"I need your services now."

"Three targets?"

A quick flash of Stefan on his knees, that black string that sprayed from the bag over his head, like he'd coughed it up, spat it out. He put his shoulders back. He died with perfect posture. Dignified. Then the pigeon feathers fell.

"One is dead already," I say. "There are two left. Edward Lang and Adam Pearson."

And now Foster comes into my mind—people who trusted me, dropping like flies. But I never would have killed him unless it was completely necessary. Not after he saved my life. I'd be dead in that ditch too if it wasn't for him.

Why did he make me do that? Stupid fucking idiot. He's got kids. He's got a wife. And he just threw it all away. This was meant to be clean. Three deaths. *Three*. Adding him to the list is just an injection of chaos into a situation that needs order. Precision. Efficiency.

"Do you have an approximate location for the targets?" The Carpenter asks.

"I'm still working on that. Edward needs to die first," I explain. "And we'll have to move fast, OK? Really fast. Adam can't know about Edward's death."

"Understood."

I've paid this man a lot of money—$333,333 a head. Funny to think that Edward gave me that cash. He's bankrolling his own downfall. If this were a normal transaction, I might resent the fact I've paid for three hits and now only need two. But The Carpenter was clear, no refunds. And besides, it's not like I need it—I've made a lot more in the past six months.

"I'll let you know as soon as I do," I say. "Just want you to be ready."

"I am."

I end the call and sit for a while as a few tiny flakes of ash come swirling down around the car like snow.

It's going to fit. This is positive. Stefan, Foster, Edward, and Adam all dying in the space of twenty-four hours. It'll look like the cartel did it. Like they found out. All those seeds have been planted.

Then I look across at the passenger seat, at Foster's DEA badge. His ID. A photo of him in the top right-hand corner. What if they did find out? What if they knew everything?

Edward needs to believe Stefan is alive. Would the cartel help me tell that lie? It's a long shot, but I'm running dangerously low on options and even more so on time.

As I reverse, turn around, and pull away on the quiet road, two fire engines roar past with a blast of wind in their wake that shakes my car on its suspension; it wobbles side to side like a boat. Their red lights disappear behind and flicker in my mirrors as I drive in the other direction just as fast. This is, I agree, an emergency.

Within the hour I'm back in the city, pounding along the sidewalk outside the Eagle Hotel. At the front of the building, taxis turn, stop, drivers closing trunks and lifting cases, talking on the phone. Guests arrive and leave and check their watches.

Here on business. Here on pleasure. Here for something between the two.

I head inside, the doors sweeping open into the grand lobby. I stopped off at a public restroom on the way and did the best I could to make myself look presentable. The bruises ache, swollen and warm to the touch, skin stretched and split and dried scabs clumped in my hair. I'm pretty sure Foster broke my nose.

Even with sunglasses hiding my eyes, I'm getting stares from every person I pass. My face is truly fucked up. Onlookers stop, turn. Someone whispers to a friend.

The Eagle Hotel is huge, gold, and old, with red velvet curtains dressing high windows that aren't even there. Status. That's what you pay for when you stay in places like this. Nothing else. Expensive material draped across square patches of white wall that used to be, at least you'd hope, windows to the outside world. Even the carts have ornate metalwork, white gloves gripping brass tubes as porters wheel luggage past in their garish red blazers. These are the kind of scumbags who wait at the door, clear their throat. They'll do everything short of swinging a fist to make sure they get their fucking tip.

At the front desk, I lean on the polished wood and ask to see the manager.

"Mr. Avery is not available at the moment." This short, preened guy is wearing his uniform with pride. It's spotless. He looks like a toy. A little figurine of a man.

"Call him."

"Sir, are you a guest?"

I flash my ID. "Tell Mr. Avery that the DEA is here." The kid stares up at me. "Or I can come back later and make a real fucking scene with some door breakers and blame it all on"—I lean in to see his name tag—"Egbert? Jesus."

He picks up a phone and relays my message, though he's significantly more polite.

"Mr. Avery's office is just across the lobby." He points and smiles. I return with a fake grin, and his expression changes when he sees my teeth. I can tell from the taste that they're as red as his costume.

Turning around, I see a suited man is already waiting in a doorway opposite. He frowns at me as I stroll across the wide floor, then steps aside to let me into his office. Once in the privacy of the small room, I remove my sunglasses.

"Heaven's above," he says in a British accent. He speaks like the queen. "You look like shit, my man."

He's got jowly cheeks, like an old dog, and the side of his balding head is peppered with age spots. *Is this really the guy?* I wonder. He doesn't look much like he works for a Mexican drug cartel. But then again, I suppose I don't look much like a DEA agent, so who am I to judge?

"Thanks." Both seated, I waste no time getting to the point. I proceed on the assumption that this is the man I should be speaking to. "You work for the Carrillo cartel. I need your help."

"There must be some kind of mistake."

"Don't talk," I say. "Just listen." I'm past courtesy. Past fear. "The cartel has been moving drugs in the city. The DEA knows this. But in recent years, there has been a lot of friction with a domestic competitor. An all-American operation."

Mr. Avery is still frowning at me. Just like he'd frown if this was true or, equally, if this was the first he'd ever heard of it. The whites of his eyes are veined and discolored, the way paper turns yellow in the sun.

"This morning some of your men executed an individual called Stefan Fiennes," I say.

"I'm sorry, who exactly are you?"

"What did I just say about listening?"

Mr. Avery's posture changes slightly. It seems he's not used to this tone.

"Over the past few months, a lot of your dealers have been picked up," I add. "Associates—people working with and for the cartel. You've struggled, in part due to this sudden spike in arrests. This is because, as you already know, someone has been interfering.

It's that competitor. He's behind it all. I know who that person is—and I want to tell you."

"I'm afraid you really have crossed some wires here." He cups his thin, bony hands together.

"No. No, I think I'm right. I think this hotel launders Carrillo money." I glance around the office. "And I think *you* call the shots in the city."

"And you have some proof, I assume?"

"No, of course I don't have any proof—if I had proof then you'd be in prison."

"Is this to suggest you are not speaking to me in an official capacity?"

I look down at myself, then draw a quick circle around my face. "What do you think?"

"Nevertheless, it is of no concern to me who this mystery man might be." He waves his fingers. "But if it is your wish to inform me, then go right ahead. I'm always open to some good old-fashioned gossip. Who, pray tell, is this notorious drug baron?"

"Edward Lang."

For the second time, Mr. Avery's body language shifts. "As in . . . ?"

"Yeah, that Edward Lang. Dealing a shitload of drugs on either side of the law. He's the man who has been fucking with your business. He's your competition. He's the one undercutting your dealers. He's the one shaking the opioid market across the whole country. And this morning, your men executed one of his closest associates."

"Again, I must state clearly that you are surely mistaken."

"I saw it happen."

And now some gears turn as he realizes who I am. Mr. Avery ordered it, and he heard all about how one of the captured men was off limits. A DEA agent, deemed more use alive than dead.

"I didn't catch your name," Mr. Avery says.

"Yes, you did."

He smiles. "Well, Mr. Casper," he says. "I'm happy to indulge some friendly roleplay. If there was even a shred of truth to your frankly defamatory claims, I would surely be of the mind that you were not to be trusted, no?"

"Perhaps, but that doesn't matter."

"It is quite an accusation. It would seem you are submitting that Mr. Lang is, well, brazenly hiding in plain sight."

"You could say that."

"Sounds fanciful, at best."

"Let's pretend for this part of the roleplay that you *do* believe me."

"Then I would surely ask what you want in return for such information."

And I point at him. "Two things," I say. "I'm sure you'll dispose of Stefan's body well. But I'd ask that his death can be confirmed by law enforcement. But not for a few days. Sometime next week will be fine."

"Why?"

"It doesn't concern you."

"Yes, it does. That's why I asked."

"He's part of an active investigation, and confirmation of his death will be extremely helpful." If Stefan simply disappears, it'll make it so much more complicated to get my hands on all his hard drives. Every version of that recording has to be scrubbed from history. But that's a problem for another day. My immediate request is far more pressing.

"And the second thing?" Mr. Avery asks.

"I need Stefan's phone. I need it *now*."

"My, my." He squints. "That is a tall order. Again . . . you see, one might question the loyalty of someone who so flagrantly reveals the identity of his trusted allies. Such betrayal cannot slip by unchecked. Because, of course, if what you say is true and Edward Lang is indeed leading a nefarious double life, then the cartel would not hesitate to remove him from the equation."

"Well," I admit. "That would be ideal."

"Mr. Casper," he bows slightly in his chair, "this has been a wonderful experience and I wish you all the best in your future endeavors. But, please." He lifts his hand to the door. "Do fuck off now."

"This goes better if we're friends."

"Then you'll need to renegotiate your offer. Because a name is simply insufficient. You must of course appreciate that working with law enforcement is somewhat frowned upon in the community to which you so absurdly claim I belong."

"Funny you should say that." I lean sideways to remove the ID from my pocket. "How about I give you two names?"

He rolls his fading eyes.

"Foster Gray," I say.

Shaking his head, he frowns—has no idea what I'm talking about.

"Well, you probably know him by a different name," I add. "He's been working with your men. They've been using his property—he's got a scrapyard, lot of land just outside the city. They meet there. They store product there. They even, as of early this morning, execute people there."

I fling Foster's ID onto the desk. Those bold yellow letters printed on a blue banner. I imagine each character stamped, one by one, into his mind. D. E. A.

Even with all that British, stiff upper lip composure, Mr. Avery can't hide his reaction. His gaze seems to zoom in. He blinks slowly, but his left eye takes a moment longer to open again. Glaring hard at the card, then even harder at me.

"I mean, that looks bad, right?" I say. "Working with undercover DEA agents. You said it was frowned upon? At least I'm honest about who I am."

And this, here, is absolute proof. I am unquestionably not trying to catch him out. The entire facade disappears.

"Thank you for bringing this to my attention," he says. "But you must understand what it means for our mutual acquaintance?"

"Don't worry," I say. "It's already been dealt with. And you are welcome to take credit for it—if your bosses happen to find out about Foster's identity."

"You've played all your cards," he says. "What now?"

"Now, I hope you are honorable enough to return my kind gesture."

Mr. Avery lets out a short laugh. "It is lovely to meet a fellow gentleman," he says. "We're a rare breed in this city." And then he picks up his phone, dials a number, and brings it to his ear.

"What is the current status . . . ? Good. Yes. Excellent, that sounds perfect . . . No, no, continue. But are you in possession of his mobile phone? Superb. I need you to bring it to my office. Yes, yes, of course, leave it switched off. Thank you."

We both rise to our feet and shake hands. His trembles slightly from age, but mine's behaving itself. Steady as a rock.

I make sure I'm nowhere near any cameras, any witnesses, when I turn Stefan's cell phone on. A list of notifications pops up, and I ignore them all. Instead I sit in my car and spend half an hour composing a message for Edward.

I read back through their exchanges to get the tone right. It seems Stefan doesn't need to explain his actions—he appears to operate with a fair level of autonomy. Which suits me very well.

Finally, around 4 p.m., I send it.

Stefan tells Edward that the dead drops went well. I refer to myself, as Stefan had in previous messages, in an unfavorable light. That "little dickhead James" was demanding, but he proved himself surprisingly useful.

But Stefan says that he's gone out of town, because something has come up. He keeps it vague enough to let Edward speculate but detailed enough to seem like it's a serious matter.

And it goes like fucking clockwork—Edward replies within five minutes. He buys it. He believes it. He thanks Stefan for letting him know. He'd been worried. He'd even thought young James might have done something terrible.

"But, yeah, you're right," Edward writes. "I don't think he's got the balls."

I lock the phone; the screen turns black. And there I am, smiling in the glass.

It's all coming together. I'm so close I can feel the light on my skin.

The baby will need a teddy bear. Or maybe a floppy rabbit. One she can carry around until it falls to pieces. Rosie can sew it back together, though. She's good at that.

Chapter Twenty-Seven

I pull over down the street from the Leyland & Lang building and turn the engine off. This is where me and Nell used to park when we'd watch Edward's office. Surrounded by the tall blocks, the busy streets. Everything corporate and gray. Seems like a lifetime ago now. All this trouble from a tiny, electronic device planted in this very car, because it was parked in this very spot.

I wonder when Stefan actually did it. He must have come to Singers at night, broken into the car when I was asleep. It really makes you reflect on the things you say in private when you imagine, even for a moment, that someone might be listening.

The man who knows your darkest secret. There really is just one option. Killing Edward has been the only course of action since I found that bug. An inevitable march. Unstoppable.

As Matthew wrote. *The entropy that'll pull the universe apart and leave it resting cold and still until time itself ticks down to its very last moment. This makes our finite life precious if you can find joy and utterly meaningless if you can't.*

But he said he's already arrived at this final destination. And that's why he did it—he was stuck in a state, incapable of change.

That homeless vet is still sitting on the sidewalk, like he hasn't moved. He's got a new sign and a new leg, a big plastic thigh with a metal stick for a shin bone. The prosthetic is propped up against the bricks near his shoulder. And there he goes. Still drumming away with his bare hands, still hitting that watercooler bottle with his fingers and palms. A flick of his wrist to strike a bucket with his thumb. I roll the window down and listen to the traffic and the *thud-thud-thud-thud-thud* of his drums.

I feel vulnerable without my gun, having tossed it in the ocean on the way here. I was careful to retrieve as many shards as I could from Foster's workshop—but if there's one thing I know about getting away with murder, it's that there's no such thing as being too cautious.

I will need to figure out a good lie though. Losing a pistol is not exactly the height of professionalism. Mind you, as I look at myself in the rearview mirror, I see I've got a pretty convincing face to play the victim of a mugging. It doesn't matter. That's the smallest of my problems at the moment.

For today's events I don't need a gun. I've got a far more powerful weapon in my hand. The burner phone The Carpenter gave me. From here I can wield the necessary, inevitable death we've been falling toward since day one.

My cell phone died about an hour ago. But this old thing? It's got a battery that just goes and goes.

I try the L&L office. His assistant answers. "Is Edward Lang available?" I ask.

"Mr. Lang is out at meetings this afternoon, can I take a message?"

"No, I need to speak to him. Do you know when he'll be back?"

"I'm afraid he has a very busy schedule."

I look out the window, across the street—the homeless vet is performing a fast "thank you" drumroll for a couple of coins dropped into his hat.

"Do you know where he is?" I ask.

"Perhaps you could try his cell phone?"

How fucking hard can it be to find one man? "Maybe I'll send him an email."

"Good idea," she says. "Anything else I can help you with?"

I hang up, chew on my knuckle for a few seconds. The text message I sent from Stefan's phone has bought me some time—but not much. A day. Two at most.

I call The Carpenter. "Still working on a location," I say, glancing down the street, looking at the busy suits. Paper-cup coffees, hands-free ear pieces, walking fast, talking fast, weaving along the sidewalk. The upbeat soundtrack—drums and cars and honking horns. "We have a slightly wider window now."

"That is good."

To save time further down the road, I give him Adam's address. But I remind him, I insist, that Edward has to die first. If Adam hears of his death, there could be a delay before he suspects me. The other way around and Edward will know for sure. Then he'll be gone. And he'll have absolute control over my fate.

"You're the boss," The Carpenter says.

"Might have to be tomorrow at this rate," I say. Edward's clearly not at his office and even if he appeared I don't want to be anywhere near him when the hit happens. Distance is still essential. It's important never to lose sight of the severity of murder. "I'll let you know more soon. He can't hide forever."

I'd considered asking for help locating him—two pairs of eyes are better than one. But no. Nothing happens without my green light. I must remain in command of this situation.

"But don't hold your breath," I say. "To be honest, he might have even left the city. He could be a long, long way away by now. He could be settling in for a nice bowl of noodles in the middle of—"

Someone's at the passenger door. Opening it. I turn.

My fucking God, it's him.

Edward climbs in, closes the door, and looks suspiciously through the windshield, back toward the Leyland & Lang building. "Good boy," he says. "Didn't know if you'd got my message." He sees that I'm on the phone. "Oh, sorry," he whispers, fingers against his lips.

"I'll call you back," I say, hanging up.

"Crazy day," Edward says.

He's wearing a three-piece suit with another one of his colorful vests. A washed-out American flag—the stripes across his stomach, the stars covering half of his chest.

"Drive," he says, pointing ahead, nervous. "Go south out of the city."

What the fuck is going on?

Edward checks out the rear windshield, then glances at me. "Oh, wow, I want to see the other guy. Looks like you've been fucking around with bears. What happened?"

"Someone mugged me," I say, testing the lie, still completely bewildered. "They stole my gun."

"Ah, don't worry," he says. "I've got mine." He touches his chest, tapping all those stars. "What are you waiting for?"

I start the engine. Pulling away, the drums fading out as we join the heavier traffic.

"You know that guy's a fraud?" Edward says, scratching his beard. "He's always sitting on the sidewalk there." He flicks his fingers, agitated, moving around in the seat, his strange mannerisms dialed up to eleven.

"Yeah?"

"He's got two legs. Seen him walking around."

Small talk. Act normal. "Kind of admire the hustle," I say.

Edward smiles. "Yeah, if it pays." He looks out the passenger window. Groans. Thinking hard about something. "Hey, sorry about earlier." He swings back, inspecting me with those mad eyes. "I shouldn't have said that."

I swallow. Stefan's phone is in the glove compartment. Holy shit, did I turn it off? "It's fine," I say.

What if it rings?

"Stefan's safe, by the way," he explains. "I know how worried you were about him." And he laughs. Then he seems to get distracted by his fingers. "What are fingernails made of, James?"

"Uh . . . keratin, I think."

"Do you bite yours?"

"Yes."

"Keratin is the same stuff as hair?"

"Um, yeah, I'm pretty sure it is."

"Like rhino horns. They're made of keratin."

I nod slowly. "OK."

"You don't have horns, James. You're a good man."

The car comes to a stop in traffic. Where the fuck are we going? What did Edward's message say? "What exactly—" I stop. I can't ask, because if I'm not responding to an invitation, he'll wonder why I was parked outside his office. I steer the question somewhere else. "What exactly is the duration of this journey?" Jesus Christ.

Edward frowns. "I don't know, he's only just sent me the details."

Who? What fucking details?

"Ah, it's bad, James. It's really bad."

"Yeah."

"I mean, how the fuck . . . who could have spoken to him?"

I just shrug. "Hard to say."

"Only me, you, Stefan . . ." He thinks for a moment. "Adam's got a heart of gold. You trust Rosie, right?"

"Uh, yeah, of course."

"Maybe someone else then? Or maybe they've been watching? I've got Adam working on it."

We sit for a moment in silence, then Edward exhales. "Raymond fucking Avery," he says. My heart sinks. "Maybe this is what Stefan was talking about—he said he was getting out of town." Edward strokes his chin. "Keeping his head down for some reason. Has the DEA got much on Avery?"

"Nothing concrete," I say, staring ahead. "Sorry, I'm confused."

"Me too. Stuff he was saying . . ."

"You spoke to him?"

Edward's eyes widen. "Yeah, he's the one who called. He called my personal number. And, I mean, he knew *everything*." He makes a clicking sound with his tongue as he tries to figure it out. "I've worked so hard to keep my name out of all this. Meant to be a silent partner."

"What did Avery say to you?" Blinking, I don't need to pretend to be shocked and terrified. It's coming naturally.

"Oh," Edward waves a hand, "loads of shit. In his Mary fucking Poppins voice. Said he knows how it all works, knows that I've got a DEA agent working for me." Edward puts his index finger close to my face. "That's you. Avery's a sneaky fucker."

"And what does he want?"

"He wants to do a deal."

I sigh and feel my eyelids dip.

"James." Edward nods at the green light.

I pull away. "What kind of deal?"

"Wants to work together. Join forces."

"This is not a good idea," I say.

"I know. Don't worry, I've got no ambitions to work with the Carrillo cartel. Fuck that."

"So why are we going?" I'm too scared now to hide it.

"He said he'll explain who ratted on me. It would be beneficial to know. No offense, my first thought was you. But I *know* you're not dumb enough to trust him. That would be suicidal."

"Hmm." I feel sick. I'm driving to my own funeral. I'm walking headlong into the jaws of death. Falling into a trap I laid just hours earlier.

Avery has fucked me. A fellow gentleman? That prick. That snake. That *fucking snake*.

We cannot go to this meeting. "How do you know . . . what if it's a setup?"

"It's out in the middle of nowhere," Edward says. "Adam's at his place right now, coordinating a couple of guys. They're going up ahead of us. Scoping the place out. Either way, we'll be covered."

"No, no," I say. "This seems too risky."

"They'll see our men. It's fine. To be honest, James, I don't think we have a choice."

"We shouldn't go."

"We have to. He knows about me. He knows about you. We have to come to an arrangement."

"No, no, no. Please."

"James, relax, they're crazy. OK. They do not give a fuck. If they wanted us dead, we would be dead. The phone call means one thing: he's legit."

"I don't know. Why aren't you scared?"

"Pfft. What are they gonna do? Listen, if it looks like there's any fuckery, we'll turn around and drive away. Calm down."

He's right to be confident. He really isn't in any danger. But I am. Edward stares out the window as we drive and drive, leaving the city and heading deep into the hills. I try a few more times to talk him out of it, but it's no use. We are going.

"And if we can't reach an agreement?" I ask.

"Then we'll star in one of their internet snuff videos." Edward laughs. "String us up, you know, chainsaw job. Cut in half. Vertically. Bottom to top, real nasty shit."

I don't respond.

"I'm joking, James, chill out. They're businessmen. It's about money. It's all about money."

"I killed Foster," I whisper—but I don't know why.

"For real?"

My lip quivers. I'm just thinking out loud. Like this is a confession. "He was going to tell Nell about me . . ." I sigh. "So I shot him."

"Anticipate any blowback?"

I shrug. "Nah." It doesn't fucking matter now.

Maybe I'll pull over and snatch Edward's gun? Shoot him on the side of the road? And then what? I'll have another body. Besides, I don't really like the odds of going fist to fist with him. I've already had one fight to the death today. I'm not sure I've got another in me.

A new idea. I reach carefully into my pocket, slide the burner phone out, and hold it against my thigh. If I can give our location away, get a signal to The Carpenter. But when I look down, I see there's no reception out here.

I'm all alone. Unarmed. Driving toward the end of everything. The inevitable destination.

"It's cutting you up," Edward says.

"I was defending myself." My voice shakes. I sound like a little boy. "I had to do it."

"I believe you," he says. "I meant what I said. You're a good man. You're loyal. Reliable. Honest. All this . . . all this shit. You've done all this to protect your wife. Your unborn daughter."

Breathing, I manage a smile.

"Seriously," he says, grabbing my thigh. He pats my shoulder. "You'll make a great dad. I'd have liked to have some kids."

Edward leans against the car door, chatting like he's daydreaming. As though this is a normal road trip. "Think I'm scared. Like I've not grown up myself, kind of thing? I'm always talking about *Toy Story* and fucking around with . . . well, you know what I do."

"Sure."

"My old man always used to say that I was never going to be successful because I don't respect the rules. You know, if I'd cheat at board games, stow away some bonus dollars during Monopoly. Normal kid stuff. But the first time I got arrested, he was so . . . aggressive."

I just drive. I'm exhausted.

"Ah, he was mean," Edward adds. "Honestly, day he died, when they read that will—I was half tempted to burn it down. Destroy Leyland & Lang. Just out of spite. No point though. Can't get back at someone who's dead."

"No," I agree.

Edward looks over at me, leaning back on the headrest. "If this is the end," he says, "of my whole operation, I want you to know that you never have to worry. I'll delete that recording. I'll never say a word. Maybe we should just wrap it all up. Move on. Do something else with our lives."

"I would love that." If only such a thing were possible.

"Tell me about Matthew." This is the second time he's asked. I think back to that day, six months ago, in the movie-themed diner. Edward's Mickey Mouse backdrop. The birthday sparklers they didn't have. Our mutually assured destruction. I'd refused. I'd told him no.

I focus on the road for a few seconds, but then, with a big breath, I think, *why not*. "He was my best friend. Me, him, and Rosie—we grew up together."

"In Treaston Mills?"

"Yeah."

"He was Rosie's brother?"

I nod.

"Did you see it coming?"

"I think so, yeah, maybe. He was always troubled. He got worse, though, when his mother died. Well, his adoptive mother. And then . . . her husband, he shot himself. Matthew found him. He saw the aftermath."

"That's rough."

"I lived with them for a few years. It was a difficult time."

"You and Rosie were childhood sweethearts?" He smiles. There's so much warmth in his face. Like he's happy. Like we're old pals.

"We were."

There's a pause; he looks out the window again, at the trees, rocks, and hills sweeping past.

"Five and a half years ago," I say. "Matthew overdosed. Heroin. He was an addict for many years. Started on pills, moved up the ranks. His note." I've never mentioned this to anyone. "I know his suicide note by heart."

"Does it help?"

I nod. "A lot. I recite it in my mind. It's the only way I can get to sleep."

"I'm sure you did your best to help him."

"We did."

"I guess you just never know what's going on in someone else's head."

Slowly I turn to look at Edward. "You never know."

Another short silence. We're so far out in the sticks now, other cars are becoming a rare sight.

"You ever blame yourself?" Edward asks.

"No," I whisper. Hands firm around the steering wheel. Eyes locked ahead on the straight road. I can feel a tear on my cheek now. "I blame you."

The road opens up and we come out of the trees, down to a long stretch bordered on either side with wide, sprawling meadows, valleys that sweep up toward the horizon. It's so quiet around here. Empty.

"OK," he says. "There should be a trackway. There." He nods across me. "They said it's a private road, we need to drive on it for about ten miles."

This is it. The home stretch.

There's only one way out now. I'm going to crash my car. I'll aim for one of these boulders. Or maybe try and flip it. I glimpse down at his seatbelt. If I can hit that button just before the impact—who knows—maybe I'll get hurt and he'll get killed. And if not. If he survives. That's it. I'm done. Avery will tell him. Or he'll find out Stefan is dead.

About quarter of a mile ahead, I see a suitable rock. It's six feet tall, set at the edge of the road, surrounded by wild grass, settled dust. I slow the car down a little bit.

A dead stop at any speed is going to be very, very painful. But this is war. I'm fighting the war on drugs. This is what the war on drugs looks like.

There will be sacrifices.

Here we go. We're closing in. I glance over to Edward, look across his chest, past the American flag on his vest.

"Oh, shit," he mumbles.

Then I see what he sees. A car behind us. A patrol car.

Blue lights flicker, and I slow down even more.

Maybe I'll blurt it all out—tell this cop everything. Get us arrested. But then what? Prison suddenly seems appealing when held up next to certain death.

"All the way out here," Edward says.

I signal and pull over at the side of the empty, desolate road. Just grass, pitted asphalt, an endless line of utility poles disappearing ahead.

The patrol car crunches on the gravel close behind. I see the officer climbing out, strolling toward us.

He's got black mirrored aviator sunglasses on and a handlebar mustache over his top lip.

"Check this fucker out," Edward says. "YMCA."

Rolling down the window, I look up at him, blinking in the sunset over his shoulder. Desperate fear in my eyes as he steps between the car and the sun, his cold shadow falling over me. My small face in his black glasses. He peers lower, checking Edward.

"License and registration, please," he says. "And are you insured on this car?"

I nod, opening my wallet, passing up some ID. Edward squirms impatiently. He rolls a sleeve back to see his watch. The cop nods at my license, seems satisfied. Handing it back, he smiles.

"Now, I've been keeping an eye on this road and we've had no traffic all day," he says. "And then I get reports of a downright convoy headed south a couple of hours ago. What you fellas up to?"

Those would be the men Adam had arranged, I think.

"Just out for a drive, officer." Edward seems relaxed.

"I'm going to need both of you to step out of the vehicle," the cop says.

"With all due respect, would we be able to see some ID from you?" Edward asks.

There's a long, frosty pause. "Of course," he says, flashing a badge and another friendly smile.

Edward and I make eye contact. I nod. Just a state trooper with nothing better to do today.

With a resigned sigh, Edward unclips his seatbelt, and I do the same. Edward climbs out and stands near the hood.

Over on my left, at the side of the road, the craggy boulder I was going to hit casts a long shadow across the asphalt and onto the weeds on the other side.

"I'm going to go ahead and ask you to put your hands on the hood," the cop says.

We both do as we're told.

"Now, big man, I'm going to search you." He approaches Edward first, taking off his sunglasses and dropping them into his top pocket. "Am I going to find anything, anything dangerous, anything sharp?"

I nod, telling Edward to comply.

"I've got a gun holstered under my jacket," Edward says, spreading his arms so the cop can remove it.

I need him to arrest us. I need a plan.

Cautiously, the officer reaches into Edward's blazer and takes the pistol. Then, moving to Edward's side, he passes it behind himself, into his belt.

I frown.

The cop kicks Edward's legs apart and crouches, his hands sliding up and over his body, patting him down, stroking the length of each arm. Even passing fingers beneath his lapel.

"Officer, we've got places to be," Edward says. "How long will this take?"

"Not long." Then, as the cop leans sideways, I see it.

A small shape drawn on his neck, just behind the collar, just below his ear. It's a Carrillo cartel tattoo. This man is not a police officer.

He puts his hands behind himself again, as though he's reaching for cuffs, but instead he produces a length of piano wire. And he winks at me.

It's looped over Edward's neck in one clean motion, the cop spinning and using the stability of his own body to choke him. Back to back, the two men twirl as Edward kicks himself off the car. His arms flailing, elbows swinging into nowhere.

I can see he's trying to ask for my help—gasping, clawing at his neck—but his red face is swelling and he can't speak or scream. Veins bulging as he whips and bucks and falls and they both tumble to the ground. I move carefully around the car and see them rolling in the dust, in the dirt, onto the dry grass, the wire cutting in. And then the cop jolts him and gets in a really strong position, sits upright with Edward between his legs. Arms tensed, he thrusts back and applies incredible pressure. Spectacular pressure.

Edward's eyes stay locked on mine as he holds a hand out to me—a desperate, begging, help-me hand. Help me. Why am I not helping him? Why? He seems confused as I stand and watch. The tragic gloss of loss, of betrayal, of sadness too deep for anger.

And his outstretched hand sinks and falls slack and the wire digs, cuts, blood creeping from the slit and oozing—and then a pop, a burst as it pours down his front. It stains each star on his vest, each white stripe turning as red as its neighbor. The final gurgles and then his eyes stop, fixed ahead, staring out from somewhere else now. It's like he's looking at that boulder.

When he's dead, the cop clambers out and walks backward, hunched over, dragging him by the wire back to his patrol car, Edward's boots scraping over the ground, heels bouncing on small stones. He puts him in the trunk and slams the hatch.

I'm still standing there staring across the open grass when he returns.

"Mr. Avery will be in touch," the fake cop says. "You might want to get out of here?"

"Yeah." Then I look over to him. He turns to leave. "Hey," I call out. "Thank you."

"My pleasure," he says with a casual wave. "Have a pleasant day." He turns the patrol car around, sweeping past me, dust kicking into the air as he bumps off the road, back on and then he's gone.

◆ ◆ ◆

I climb into my car and hold The Carpenter's phone as I drive, checking the reception. Still none out here. Come on, come on. Finally, about four or five miles later, I get a flicker of one bar and hit call.

"Two down," I say. "Go to Adam's place. He's there."

"Now?"

"Now." I hang up.

Then I cruise back toward the city, smiling with relief and triumph and success. Waiting for confirmation, I take the big, arching corners against the ridges, against the trees.

I'm trying not to picture Adam. I'm grateful this one is happening miles from me. I don't think I could handle seeing that. He's the only good person in all of this. It's a real shame that it has to happen.

Again, it's Edward's fault. I just can't risk it.

Fifteen minutes have passed and I'm guessing it's over. I hope it was quick. I hope The Carpenter's promise is true. I hope Adam didn't see it coming.

When he returns my call, I even let it ring five times, enjoying these final seconds before it's made real.

But, of course, I have to know. I press the green button.

"He is not here," The Carpenter says.

"What?" I slow down.

"That is the simplest way I can say it."

The car rolls to a stop. I'm alone in the middle of the empty road.

"Have I been sold a lie?" I ask. "Like when rich folk pay a hundred dollars for a shrimp cocktail, a thousand bucks for a bottle of wine? And it's not even as good as the normal shit you find on the street?"

"Speak plainly."

"You're meant to be the best in the business and you can't kill a single fucking person? How did you even get this reputation? I've paid for three. I've paid *over the odds* for three."

"I will find him and I will kill him. You are the one that insists on time constraints. You wanted to micromanage this. I just thought you might be concerned to hear that there is a delay."

"I *am* concerned to hear that," I say. "I'm very concerned. Time is really of the essence here, you need—"

Buzzing. From the glove compartment? Stefan's phone is ringing. Wow. I didn't turn it off. I lean over, click the handle, and pull it out.

Adam's name is on the glowing screen. He's calling Stefan.

"He's calling me right now," I say. "Stay on the line." I put my hands-free ear bud into my left ear, then lift Stefan's phone to my right.

"I-I . . . shit," Adam murmurs. "I'm in real trouble. Something's happening, something really bad."

"What's going on?" I ask.

"James? Where's Stefan?"

"He's . . . busy." I look out the window, past the trees. The late sun is coming through in thin columns, jagged patchwork shadows swaying in the breeze, shifting over the car. Soft rustling and nature. I'm so far away.

"Oh, God, oh no." Adam's voice is barely a whisper. He's terrified.

"What's happening?"

"There's someone in my apartment," Adam breathes; it sounds like he's in an enclosed space. "He broke in . . . He's searching, he's looking or . . . I don't know . . . I-I-I didn't see him. I'm so scared, James. I can't call the cops. I'm so fucking scared." He's hyperventilating. "Please. I need your help."

The Carpenter is just listening to my side of the conversation.

"Where are you?" I ask.

"I'm . . . I'm safe."

"Did you get out?"

"No, there wasn't time."

"You're still in your apartment?" I hear The Carpenter's footsteps.

"Yes," Adam whimpers. "I'm hiding."

"Are you sure he won't find you?" I ask.

"No, I'm well hidden." His breaths judder. "In the closet, there's a sliding door, goes through into the wall . . . I'm in the wall cavity behind the snow painting."

I feel a tear trickle down my cheek. And I hold my hand over my mouth.

"Good," I say.

"Please, please help."

"It's OK." I speak softly. Comforting him. "Stay calm."

"I don't know what to do, James . . . I'm all alone."

"It's going to be OK. It sounds like . . ." I close my eyes, bow my head, pinch my nose. "It sounds like a really good hiding place. If . . ." I have to say it. I have to. "If I had a sliding door, inside the closet, I'd hide behind the snow painting too."

I hear footsteps in both ears. Decisive boots on the living room floor.

"What?" Adam's trembling voice. "James?" He's crying. "James? Ja—"

Two thuds—two fast rounds hiss and clack from the silenced pistol, pounding through the wall. Adam's phone clatters and rests still. A quiet hiss of static.

The closet door, a shuffling sound. Wood sliding against wood. A pause. Then another shot. A shell casing clinks and rolls to a stop. And a long silence follows.

"It is done," The Carpenter says.

Chapter Twenty-Eight

There are times when I remember things and I see myself. How I was and how I moved.

An eighteen-year-old boy walking through the mall with his girlfriend. That's what she is now. Rosie is his girlfriend. But it never needs to be said. Like so much of their life. Like all the other unspoken things they've left behind.

And here—in the white light, near the tall billboards, their plastic cups filled with milkshakes—the couple sit face to face in the mall cafeteria. Next to the glass balcony. Looking over at all the shoppers down below. They've been laughing and smiling. The boy rests his hand on the table, and the girl places her fingers on top.

It really does look like a love story.

Rosie's cheeks are still flushed from what we did in the changing rooms. When I lick my lips, I taste her perfume. She's wearing a flowery dress. Boots. Bracelets.

We've been having a lot of sex lately. Until today it had been confined to her bedroom—quiet and slow enough so that Matthew never hears. But I'm sure he has. Now, though, it seems we're branching out.

"You think she knew?" I ask. "The lady in the next cubicle?"

Rosie smiles. "Hmm. I would imagine so." She blinks. "Did you like it?"

I nod.

"What else would you like to try?" She sips her milkshake. Her cheeks dimple as she stares, sucking on the red straw. She's acting seductive ironically, which actually makes it more effective. Being fun and self-aware elevate her higher than good looks ever could alone.

"I don't know," I say. "Are you into anything . . . weird?"

"Oh, man." Her eyebrow twitches. "Almost exclusively."

"Such as?"

"You wouldn't like it."

"I'm pretty open-minded." I tilt my cup. "Unless . . . is it . . ." I frown. Wince. "It's not . . . bathroom related?"

"Never really seen the appeal."

"Thank God."

"It's . . ." Rosie seems slightly embarrassed. "Being rough."

"Yeah?"

"But properly," she adds.

"Like . . . you on me or me on you?"

"Both, but mainly you being firm with me."

"I can do that. Buy a horsewhip or whatever. Get a safe word."

"My safe word is 'more,'" Rosie whispers. "Jesus, fuck, more, more. Please, I beg you, *more*."

We're laughing.

"Maybe 'Eskimo' might be safer?"

"Good idea."

"I'll try anything once," I say.

"Not like this you wouldn't. It's fine." She shrugs. "I would never hurt you, James, and you would never hurt me. Those are the rules."

"Little spank? Some ripped clothes?"

"Nah. Kind of stuff I'm talking about ends in jail. Kind of thing you only do once."

We laugh again.

"Really, really dark, nasty . . . fucking," she smiles, "unforgivable shit."

As the laughter simmers down, Rosie looks at me and for a split second seems worried. Scared.

"What?"

"I just . . ." Her eyes are watering. "I just love you so much." It's the first time she's ever said that to me. I'm tempted to do a joke—make it funny. But it isn't. It's real.

"I love you too," I say. "I've loved you for as long as I can remember. I think that we—"

"Nachos," the waiter announces, placing a bowl down in the middle of the table.

We both smile at each other, and Rosie looks at him and says softly, "Thank you." When he's gone, she picks up a chip, dips it in the sour cream, and crunches it, staring off behind me in thought. I carefully load up a mouthful for myself.

"Should we, like, get married and have kids and stuff?" she asks.

"Well, yeah."

"When?"

"When we have stable jobs and . . . savings?" I hold a hand to my mouth as I chew. "Is that what normal people do?"

"Marriage first though, right?" Rosie says, wiping her fingers on a napkin.

"Well, of course, you can't have kids unless you're married."

"Good point." She picks up her milkshake, leans the straw my way. "Don't want to go to hell."

"When I'm twenty-five," I say.

"I'll be twenty-seven. Odd numbers."

"OK, twenty-six, twenty-eight. Marriage."

"Nice. Babies the year after?"

"Sure. Or the year after that? So it's exactly ten years from today."

Rosie frowns, doing a quick calculation. It adds up. "I like it." She smiles again. "Gives us plenty of time to change our minds."

"See, I don't think I will."

Her face straightens. Even she has to let go of humor now. "Me neither."

"You and me," I say.

"No matter what."

"No matter what."

Then she holds out her hand. And we shake on it. Behind her one of the tall billboards is displaying something that catches my eye. It's a photograph. Advertising suits and dresses. But the models look just like us. No, it *is* us. That's our wedding day.

"What the fuck, look at that," I say.

I'm there now. We kept the deal. I'm twenty-six, Rosie is twenty-eight. The years pass too fast. It almost feels like they're speeding up.

I'm wearing a gray suit. Rosie's smart blue dress swishes around her knees when she walks. Nothing about this wedding is conventional. We only have two guests. Two witnesses.

Nell is mine. It didn't seem strange to ask her. She's been my boss for five years, but I definitely think of her as more of a mentor. A friend. Even family. She's the closest thing to a mother I've ever had. Plus, who else could I ask?

Matthew is Rosie's witness—he gives her away.

We don't want a flashy wedding. We want it to be small. Just us four. And we read our vows and kiss and it's done. We're married. I married her.

Nell, wearing a suit, watches from her seat; she gives me a nod. She approves. It looks like she might wipe away a tear but she doesn't. I think she's too strong to cry.

But Matthew, sitting at the front on the other side of the hall—he looks truly lost. Sad to the core. A hundred empty chairs lined up behind him.

After the ceremony he rushes outside for a cigarette. He still smokes two packs a day but he's clean on every other front. It's been a rough few months.

He'd tried everything from counseling to rehab—even took up running last summer. In the end, it was a brutal bout of self-imposed cold turkey that clinched it. No matter how much he screamed and begged, we were not allowed to let him out of that room. The first couple of days were grizzly. But the rest of the week was much quieter. Matthew spent most of the time lying on our couch crying.

And steadily the life returned to his eyes. But some days, like today, it seems to fade away again. Gone as though it was never even there.

"What's wrong?" I ask him, stepping into the parking lot.

"I don't want to talk about it," he says, smoking hard—a drag on each breath. "Ignore me."

"No, come on."

Matthew shakes his head.

"It's my wedding day," I say. "You have to do what I ask."

He hesitates. "You ever think about when we were kids?"

"Sure."

"I used to hate it. You and Rosie going off together." He waves the cigarette. "I'd always prefer it when it was just me and you."

"OK?"

"It's like, she's my big sister, you know? And I used to get . . . well, I suppose I got jealous."

"You want to marry your sister?"

"No, not jealous of you. Jealous of her."

"Sorry," I say, trying to lighten the mood. "That's a hard limit. You're just not my type."

"I felt like, I guess, that you chose her over me. I was worried that today would bring all those emotions back. I thought it would be kind of . . . bittersweet."

"That's what's bothering you?"

"No. Not at all. I'm over all that. I was a kid. It was dumb."

"So what's the issue?"

"Honestly, today I walked my sister down the aisle," he explains. "She looks beautiful. She's married my best friend. And do you know what I feel? Nothing. Absolutely nothing. No resentment. No joy. It's all just so . . . boring."

"Jeez, should have booked the band, hey?"

"No, I don't mean the wedding. I mean everything. This world."

"What did the therapist say about time?"

"No, no, you don't get it," Matthew says.

"You're depressed. It will pass."

"It's not mental illness when you know why you feel sad."

"The answer is here," I say, gesturing at the door. "Friends. Family. Connection. They really are the key. You ever heard of rat park?"

"Nope."

"They did experiments back in the day." I turn to him. "They put rats in empty cages with a choice of normal water or water laced with drugs. Heroin. Cocaine. Whatever. The rats took the drugs again and again until they were fucked. Then they died. Run the experiment again, this time with an awesome cage. Full of food, drink, ladders, mirrors, other rats they can fuck and fight with—an ideal life. Rat heaven. And then they dabbled in the drugs from time to time, but pretty much they weren't really interested."

"Which cage am I in, James?" he asks.

"The second one. You've got friends. Family who love you. You've got a steady job, a nice apartment, safety, security, you said the other day about that date. You're talented, you can sing, you can write. You're smart, funny, you're not that bad-looking."

"Exactly," Matthew says, his glassy eyes blinking fast. "*Exactly*. I have everything I need to be happy. And yet . . ."

There's a long silence.

"I promise it'll get better," I say. "You know what would make *me* happy?"

"Go on."

"I want you to smile for the photo."

"No problem," he says.

And Matthew drops his cigarette on the ground, pats my arm, and heads straight back inside. I follow him, but instead of going into the hall he turns right and slips into the bathroom.

The photographer is preparing her tripod. "Ready?" she asks, leaning down to adjust one of the legs.

Me, Rosie, and Nell stand at the front of the room, with a backdrop of flowers.

"Light's good," the photographer says. "Just waiting for one more."

A few minutes later, Matthew reappears and comes over to stand at Rosie's side.

"Squeeze in," the woman says, waving us closer together, checking her viewfinder.

Nell's shoulder shuffles against mine, chin up, Rosie's hand clamped tight around my fingers. And on her left, Matthew's standing with his hands cupped at his waist. Perfect posture.

A flash of bright white light catches us here forever. We look so happy. Almost like a family.

And Matthew's got the biggest smile by far. His eyes are carefree, dipped, and glazed. Hollow contentment sitting empty on his face—a mask made of chemicals. But looking at the photo, who could ever guess it wasn't real?

Chapter Twenty-Nine

It's dark when I arrive home. I climb slowly from the car, limp up the driveway, and pause, looking back across the city lights. It's quiet tonight. I turn and open the front door.

Rosie leaps up from the couch when she hears me.

"Oh." She gasps, one hand on her pregnant stomach, the other over her mouth.

My left eye is swollen shut now—I haven't looked in the mirror for a while but I'm guessing it's not a pretty picture.

She waits for me to say something. To tell her it's over. To tell her that they're all dead and we're going to be OK. But I can't speak. So I just give her a nod, my face blank—I'm too tired to cry. Awe, sadness, relief, trauma. I'm just too fucking tired to show it.

We stand in our living room and hug. Breathing, eventually I find my voice. "I did it," I say, swaying, dizzy.

The plan works seamlessly. The very next day, cleaned up and composed, I go into work and tell my final set of lies. I was mugged. Badly beaten. Thugs. I tried to run and, oh, Jesus, they stole my gun. Nell buys it—she doesn't even mention the extra bruises—because there's something else on her mind. Something far more important.

She tells me to sit down as she delivers some very sad news that I already know.

"They got Foster," she says.

Yes, I think, *they did*. "The cartel?" I ask.

"Fucking animals. They chopped him up, burned his workshop to the ground."

It's not difficult to connect his death to Edward Lang, Stefan Fiennes, and Adam Pearson. I explain how it all happened. The story fits so well, it hardly matters how I know. Carrillo operatives must have heard about them. And taken decisive action.

I'm sitting at my desk, smiling as I picture the officers out there in the city, bagging up all the evidence. Breaking down all those doors. Closing them off with yellow tape. Questioning neighbors, relatives. The crime scene photos—the bright flash—the two bullet holes in the snow painting. Adam's corpse crumpled inside the crawl space.

Foster's workshop—charcoal, yellow evidence markers peppered throughout the chaos. Scorched bones separated by a brutal ax attack. The shape of an old bike fossilized amid the black ash.

Edward's and Stefan's bodies are found within forty-eight hours. Stripped, dumped, denied all dignity. Again, it's obvious they were executed. This vindicates Nell. As do the countless items seized from all their homes.

And the final piece of the puzzle falls neatly into place on a beautiful Wednesday afternoon, when detectives deliver all the electronic devices to our office. Box after box of bagged, tagged, untouched evidence arrives on a series of hand trucks. Nell personally signs off on it all, with Rob's authority to keep the inspection in-house. No one else can be trusted with all this stuff—no one besides me and Nell. It's just too hot.

"I guess we'll get to work tomorrow morning," she says, hands on her hips, looking at the mountain.

"Sure," I say. "Fresh eyes." But I decide, on reflection, to work a little late this evening. Catch up on some paperwork. There are a lot of reports to file.

I feel my face beaming as I say goodnight to Nell—she's the last person to leave the office.

"Don't work too hard," she says.

"Nearly done." I've got the twitching smiles, the kind that flirt and dance with laughter. And there I am. All alone with every single electronic device.

It takes me a few minutes to locate the files. I find them on Adam's laptop. I click open the folder and see he'd collected hundreds of recordings. Conversations me and Nell had in my car, in her car. Hours and hours.

Alphabetical order draws the one I need to the very top. He's named the file "***James and Rosie Casper chatting about murder lol."

They really did strike gold.

Idle curiosity makes me listen. Sure enough, we say plenty to incriminate ourselves. Talking about Frank's body, where we buried it. I even reference the kitchen—the epicenter, where the red grid grew on the chessboard tiles.

To be safe, I delete every single recording from that day. I wipe it from the face of the earth. And then I spend some time searching Edward's and Stefan's hard drives. Neither of them even had a copy. But they had the knowledge, which was enough. It's past 5 a.m. by the time I'm finished. I close the final laptop, slide it back into the evidence bag, stand, and grab my jacket.

Whistling, I stroll across the parking lot, looking up at the new day's sky. A brilliant carpet of pink and sunrise orange streaked over the sleeping city. Vapor trails. Vacation planes jetting off somewhere warm.

Once this is cleaned up, we're moving out of Singers—away from the shopping carts and litter, off that cracked hill. The new house by the lake, that's a better place to raise a family. We'll live there.

Aside from the money, that's the only memento I'll keep. I still need to dispose of the antique shotgun Edward gave me, which is currently propped up at the side of our fridge. I'll have to destroy it. After all, it's got my name engraved on the side.

Weeks pass, and all these seeds I've planted blossom.

There is enough evidence left over to cast Edward Lang in a whole new light—he's on the front cover of all the papers. The news can't get enough. They use all the terms—kingpin, trafficker, drug baron. How did the director of a giant pharmaceutical corporation become one of the most notorious heroin dealers on earth? Well, read all about it.

I get an email from a production company—some researcher. They're making a documentary. I say I'm happy to assist. I'll tell them everything they want to hear. And plenty more.

Nell takes all this very well—she's able to dial her pride a good few notches below smug. Though the contrition from senior DEA staff, particularly Rob Sanders and his colleagues, is something that never gets old. We both revel in the praise. It's great to see her happy again. She can bow out a champion. As Edward once said, there's no reason why we can't all win.

Rosie has three and a half weeks left before the due date, and Friday night sees me, her, and Nell enjoy a meal out together. Her retirement has now been made official. We toast this and we laugh.

As jubilant as things have become, we're still forced to endure the solemn ritual of Foster's funeral. His wife and children are unable to attend—they're holding their own ceremony somewhere else. Somewhere safe.

This means the whole affair can be carried out with all the formal bells and whistles. Men in uniform saluting his flag-clad coffin as it's lowered into the ground. Bagpipes and drumrolls echoing around the graveyard. His framed photo mounted on a pedestal surrounded by white lilies, a few purple petals peppered throughout. Irises, maybe. I don't know. A decorated hero. And quite rightfully so. Foster was a good man. I'm glad my accusations didn't stick.

After this we all head to a bar for the wake. Rosie is not in the mood for a long evening of polite small talk, and to be honest neither am I. So we bow out after two drinks, around 6 p.m., and head home for a nice early night. Just me and her.

We're sitting on the couch watching some reality trash on TV. It feels like old times. Rosie has a bowl of chips resting on her stomach. I reach in and take a few, rubbing the salt and grease between my fingers as I crunch and smile at her.

"We could open another bag?" she suggests.

"You're a machine," I say, beginning to rise.

"I'll get them." She huffs as she struggles to the front of the cushion and heaves herself up to her feet. "Have to go to the bathroom anyway. She's playing footsie with my bladder."

I put my feet up on the couch, lean back, cross my legs, and look at my phone. I'm going to buy a boat. Something big. Secondhand. I'll have to pay in cash. But, fortunately, I've got plenty of that left over.

There are some pretty crazy ones for sale, I think, scrolling through and zooming in on photos. Maybe I'll buy a few—good way to lose some money. The cash has become a bit of a burden; I've yet to spend a penny of the remaining five million.

A knock at the door. I check the time and frown. Then I stand and head down the corridor. Through the glass I see Nell's head in the porch light. Her short hair. I pull the door open. She looks sad.

"Hey," I say, "what's up?"

"Can I come in?"

"Uh, yeah, sure." I step aside and lift my arm. "You want a drink or anything—some chips?"

"No, thank you," she says, walking past me.

She pauses at the window—against the kitchen wall—and peers into the living room.

"What's going on?" I ask.

Nell turns and looks at me. She seems unsettled. Pale. Even ill.

"James, I . . . Foster's lawyer gave me a sealed letter." She pulls a piece of paper from her jacket pocket and holds it in her trembling fingers, staring down at the words.

Swallowing, I take it from her and, as though my eyes are searching for it, the first thing I see is my name. I don't need to read it to know what it says. But I do.

It says everything. I'm not reacting properly, I can't be, because Nell's confusion is becoming anger. Foster must have written this on the morning of his death—contingency in case he didn't make it to the safe house.

There's just too much information—too many details, too many lies I need to tell in the next few seconds.

"Listen," I begin.

But she reacts like I've said enough. This alone seems a sufficient confession. "What the fuck?" She shakes her head. "How the—"

"Nell, it's important to understand that this is very complicated. Let me explain."

"Explain what? That you were working for Edward Lang? That you installed that software? Is that true? Is it true?"

"It's not a straightforward matter," I say.

"How, why? I just don't understand. *How* did it even happen? Did he have something on you or . . . ?"

I don't react. But she sees that the answer is yes.

"What? What was it?"

Wiping my hand down my face, I pull at my cheeks, feel my lower eyelids peel away. I can't lie anymore. I've got to keep her on my side. I'll drip feed it.

"Rosie's boss," I mumble through my fingers.

Nell frowns and thinks. Calculates. Speculates. Suspects. Realizes. "Frank McBride," she says, her eyes snapping back to mine. "You know where he is."

Again, I don't need to say or do anything.

"He's dead," Nell states, as though for the record. "He's dead and . . . you killed him?" Another pause. "Rosie? Rosie killed him . . . and Edward knew? But how—" She stops. Thinks. Reads my thoughts. "The bug. He heard."

"It was blackmail. I had to. I had to take care of Rosie."

"You could have come to me."

"That wasn't possible."

"And that was . . . months ago." She's grimacing through these facts. "That was last year?" Presented all at once, it sounds too simple. All the nuance and circumstances getting lost in her shock. Swept aside like they don't matter. "You've been working with them all that time."

But they do matter. They do. "Please, you—"

"I thought I was going crazy. You lied. You're a liar. It all came unraveled. And those busts—framing Carrillo men. That was you?"

"Again, it was all necessary, and I always had the long game in mind."

"The long game? Which was?" Nell just figures it all out. "You killed them?" Wait, it's not a question. It's a statement. "You killed them," she says.

"No," I insist. "I didn't . . . I created a situation where—"

"James, you killed them."

"I arranged . . ."

"Fuck. My God." And then absolute rage flashes across Nell's face—all the compassion gone in an instant. "You framed Foster. You tried to frame him. James, did you have anything to do with his death?" She's warning me now, fresh and fierce from the funeral.

For the third time I stay still, I stay silent, and she hears the truth. It's singing out all around us. She stares into the living room, as though lost in thought. "You wanted to find out where they were moving him," she whispers.

"It was an accident. He . . . he was trying to get my gun and . . ."

"So." Nell half smiles, realizing something else. "You've betrayed . . . everyone?"

"Everything I have done, I have done for good reasons."

She can't even look at me with her bloodshot eyes.

"Nell, I'm . . ." My voice cracks, like a little boy getting told off by his favorite teacher. "I'm so sorry. But I'm speaking to you now as a friend. No, no. More. You're like family to me. Everything I have done has been for Rosie, for our future, for our baby, our daughter. I've done . . . I've just tried to do the right thing. That's all."

"Oh, James."

"Please, I'm asking for you to trust me. Have you said anything to anyone?"

"No, I wanted to hear it from you."

"Good. You . . . you have to keep this quiet. It's over now. I've undone it. I made sure of that. There's no reason why we can't all win."

"I'm going to be very clear with you, James. We are not friends."

"Nell."

"We are *nothing* like family."

"Please."

"You're going to prison. Both of you. For a long time."

"Please, please, please," I say. "Please." I hold my hands like I'm praying. I feel so small. "Please don't make it all for nothing." I reach forward. "*Please*."

Nell leans away, recoiling in disgust. She even takes a step back; she's against the window now.

"Fuck you," she says, shaking her head—looking me up and down like I'm a piece of shit.

"Nell."

"You're going to need a good lawyer for this one."

Something moves behind her. Over her shoulder. A shadow in the kitchen. A shadow in the glass, sliding into view. Silver glistens as metal tilts up, rising, rising to point at the back of Nell's head.

It's Rosie, in the kitchen, standing at our waving window. She's been listening.

She's holding the shotgun.

My eyes dart between them, my heart hitting my ribs. Everything seems to slow down, like in a nightmare. I can't speak. I can't move. Finally I manage a single, desperate, whimpered word.

"Don't," I say, clamping my eyes shut. "Don't."

"James." Nell touches my arm with the last bit of compassion she has left. "It's too late to turn back now."

"Don't do it. Don't do it."

"You know I have to," Nell says.

It's like I'm falling and falling and—

"Don't do it. Don't do it. Don't—"

Glass and dust explode past me, a sudden blast of damp storm wind speckles warm liquid across my face. Like a flicked paint brush. A heavy thud of thrown meat on the floorboards, loud even in my ringing ears. And when I open my eyes, the window is broken and the swirling smoke is beginning to clear.

Chapter Thirty

"Looks like glass," I say.

Matthew's sitting on the sand by my side. He's holding what he thought was a small green crystal. "It's so smooth," he says, rubbing it with his thumb.

And then he flings it into the water and leans back on his elbows.

It's Sunday afternoon and me and Matthew have met up for a beer on the beach. The sand is warm and dry in the sun. And the ocean's empty, calm, broken only by low waves and dive-bombing gulls.

"Rosie still stressed about work?" he asks.

She is. Rosie's been holding on at Limehouse—she's in line for a promotion and if things go well she should be bringing in enough money to push us over our total by the end of this year. We've been saving up to buy a house for a long time. I am twenty-nine, Rosie is thirty-one. Finally it seems we're on the verge of having a down payment set aside for a perfect place just outside the city. I know she hates the job. Mainly because of the new boss, Frank.

"You should just quit," I told her. "No amount of money is worth being unhappy."

"No. No more setbacks," she said. "We're already behind schedule."

She's right—we're meant to have kids by now. But I think we're both kind of relieved it hasn't happened yet. Nell said it'll never stop being scary and if everyone waited until they were ready, no one would ever have children. But still.

I have even suggested we could buy somewhere cheaper, in the city. But Rosie dismissed that idea. "Where?" she said. "You want to live in Singers?" We both laughed.

So she keeps working in a shitty role at a shitty advertising agency.

"Besides," she said, "it's normal to hate your job. We're nearly there. It'll all be worth it in the end."

Matthew's eyes are dim and dulled. I think he's been using pretty much nonstop since the wedding. He's thinner. His lips are always dry and sore. Rosie's worried about him—I am too.

"And you?" he says. "How's the new taskforce?"

It seems weird to go into the specifics. My job is now to investigate the supply of the very substances he's no doubt got in his pocket at this precise moment.

So I keep it short. "Good."

"Can I ask you a question?" he says.

"Fire away." I swig my beer.

"You worked really hard to get into the DEA. But growing up, I can't remember you ever saying that's what you wanted to do?"

I twist my bottle, pressing it into the sand near my thigh. "Rosie works in advertising," I say. "You work at a steel mill. Things don't always pan out how you think they will."

"Sure, but they're just jobs. You pushed for your position. Trained. Did all the research and tests. It's not about money. I think you'd do it even if you didn't have to."

I nod. "Maybe."

"Is it because of me?"

I'd done this analysis on myself years ago, so I don't need to spend much time on introspection here. "Yes," I say. "It is because of you."

"I'm honored, I guess."

"Forty thousand overdose deaths last year, most from heroin and opioid painkillers." We make eye contact. "That's not right, is it? Something really bad is happening."

He looks out across the ocean. "I just . . . I just need some help."

I've learned to stay calm. As tempting as it is to shout at the endlessly frustrating cycle, patience is always a safer bet. "We can get that."

"There's a place." Lying on his side, Matthew picks nervously at the label on his bottle, his elbow in the sand. "I've heard really good things."

"OK. Great. Go there."

"Nah, it's . . . No."

But this touches a nerve, wobbling my charitable demeanor. "What the fuck do you mean, no?"

"James," he says, holding up a hand. "I want to. I promise . . . It's just really, really expensive."

"How expensive?"

Matthew sighs and removes his phone, opens the clinic's website, and lifts it up for me to see.

"Pine Acre," I read from the screen. "Looks nice."

He points at the price.

"Holy shit," I say, leaning in. "I'd want to get superpowers for that."

"See." He shrugs. "It's fine. Maybe one day."

By the end of that week, me and Rosie are dropping Matthew off at the Pine Acre Clinic. I didn't even need to say it out loud. I just told her that he expressed an interest and then mentioned the cost—a very familiar figure. She knew what I was suggesting.

"OK," she'd said. "We can start saving again."

The clinic has something called contact days every month, where loved ones attend a group therapy session. Rosie and I sit either side of Matthew, and over the course of three of these we see him transform. His eyes come back online.

The final contact day is like an informal graduation ceremony. There's an impressive buffet—finger food and every soft drink under the sun lined along the white function hall wall. Pleasant paintings, fresh flowers on each windowsill. It's a warm day, so the windows are wide open to the world—the grass and bees of summer, the color and breeze whispering through the memory.

But it's not a memory. I'm there. I'm there now.

We're sitting in a huge circle on expensive velvet chairs. It's just like one of those AA meetings you see in the movies. Except instead of an indoor basketball court in some school gym, we're gathered in what looks like a five-star hotel.

All the guests—the clinic even calls them guests—take turns standing up and reading a statement about their time at Pine Acre.

Rosie's holding Matthew's hand on her lap, listening to the guest opposite us. When he's finished we all clap, and the guy wipes tears from his eyes and sits, gripping his medal, looking down at it like it's an Olympic gold.

The therapist stands and thanks him. She's a short, middle-aged woman, halfway between a hippie and a corporate CEO; her smart clothes clash with bright yellow earrings and a daisy in her hair.

"There comes a pivotal moment in every struggling person's journey," she says—they never use the word *addict*, because that implies the power to change is out of the guests' control. "It's a point in time. Sometimes it's triggered by an event." She looks around the circle, a well-trained public speaker, clocking eyes with everyone here. "Other times it simply occurs to them on an idle afternoon in a traffic jam. In the shower. Or in the middle of the night." She snaps her fingers. "An epiphany. A different perspective." And she spreads her arms. "When your relationship with a particular substance, or particular activity, a favored habit, whatever it may be, is suddenly cast in a brand-new light. Many who struggle find this traumatic. To have relied on something—searched for it, stolen for it, been prepared to kill for it—and then to realize that this thing is not good. Even though your behavior would suggest you love it more than anything else in the whole world."

She looks now across the circle, at me, Rosie, then Matthew. "Our next speaker," she says, "has been struggling for a long time. And his decision to come here, to seek help, was that fundamental shift. Matthew's journey, I have to say, his transformation over his stay here at Pine Acre, it's been nothing short of inspirational. And I know he will have prepared some special words for us this afternoon. So, Matthew, the floor's all yours." She sits, and there's a slightly awkward moment where we're not sure if we should clap. We don't.

I pat him on the leg, and he rises to his feet, holding a piece of paper. He's clearly nervous, but he's written such a good speech that it hardly matters.

He thanks me—James, his best friend since childhood. And then he pays tribute to the only family he has left—Rosie, his brilliant, supportive sister. She smiles, blushing slightly as a few eyes glance at her.

"There are times, at even the sharpest edge of worry, when you begin to rise above it," he says, bringing his speech to a close. "The sense of panic and fear lingers below. The memory of how you felt, the terror that you might revert, relapse, go back down again. You feel it in your chest. But as life goes on and things get better, that feeling diminishes. Like a perfect shadow of the plane you're on, following you eagerly, flickering and holding its form as it dances over the runway, then sweeps fields and hedgerows and rooftops, all the while shrinking. The shadow keeps shrinking.

"In no time at all the plane has banked and you've lost sight of it. Soon you're so high you couldn't find that shadow even if you wanted to. Eventually you simply enjoy the flight." Matthew pauses here, then gestures to me and Rosie, sitting on either side of him. "Thanks to these people, my family. Their support and sacrifice. I finally can. I can enjoy the flight." He folds the paper and accepts the applause, sitting down quickly. Rosie leans over and kisses his cheek. I tap a fist on his thigh and give him a smile.

But I already know what's going to happen. Matthew's going to say that he didn't mean it. He didn't mean what he said. He just said that stuff because he thought that's what we wanted to hear. He's not even on the plane. That's what he'll say.

He writes it somewhere.

I'm in our new house now. Standing in the empty living room.

I'm twenty-nine, and Rosie is thirty-one.

We've moved into a large property in Singers. The neighborhood is rough around the edges but, well, the house itself is pretty big for the price. This is because the previous owners were renovating, almost doubling the footprint of the ground floor. But then they ran out of money. So there's a half-finished kitchen tagged on the back of the building.

We can cover the cost of finishing the job with an extra loan and the last of our savings. Rosie said she's already found some really cool chessboard tiles. Red stools for the breakfast bar.

I'm swinging the new house keys around my finger as I stroll across the bare floor. Nice space for a TV, couch opposite. Coffee table in the middle. And then there's the window, which looks through to what will become the kitchen. *Maybe we should keep it*, I wonder. Keep the whole back wall.

My cell phone rings. It's Rosie.

"James," she says, her voice panicked. "I've tried calling Matthew this morning but there's no answer."

"He's probably lost his phone or some shit," I say, distracted by the peeling wallpaper as I consider ideal colors. I stroke my fingers over the doorframe.

"I thought that too, but I came to his apartment and he's not here. And it's locked."

"Maybe he's at work?" I check my watch; it's 9:30 a.m..

"Tried them. He isn't. What if he's run away again?"

"Did he say anything last night?" I ask.

"No. I just, I gave him the lasagna and he was fine. And now nothing. Silence. James, I'm really worried."

"Well, what do you want to do? Shall I . . ." Then I remember. "We've got a spare key for his apartment. I could come down there and we could check it out?"

"Please."

"OK, give me ten."

When I arrive at Matthew's place in the city, Rosie is outside, pacing the sidewalk, biting her thumbnail.

"Calm down," I say as I approach. "You're getting yourself worked up."

Up the stairs. Down the gloomy corridor. Around a bag of trash. One of his neighbors is cooking food. Warm air drifts between the apartments.

I push the spare key into the lock and the moment I've opened the door—just as I see the rug, his shoes, feel the temperature—I know. I already know.

I'm just certain.

Is this happening now? Or am I remembering? Is this *all* a memory?

"Matthew?" Rosie says. I follow her in and she checks the kitchen.

But I stop and stare at his bedroom door. I know what's waiting inside. I push it open with my fingers and—

"Oh fuck," I yell, spotting him.

He's lying on top of the covers, white and still, a syringe on the bedside table. The lamp still glowing. The curtains still closed. His burned-out candle, his burned black spoon—all the things I've seen before.

I'm screaming at Rosie to call 911 and checking his pulse and trying CPR and screaming at her to call them, call them. Pumping down, counting, counting, bouncing him on the bed springs and shouting.

Rosie's crying wild, panting tears and pacing, and he's cold. He's cold to the touch.

He's dead. He's dead. He's been dead for a long time.

While we wait for the paramedics, the police, all the usual suspects, we stand in his small kitchen and I hold Rosie's head still while she cries. I worry that this is going to destroy her. She's always been close to the edge.

And there on the fridge—behind a magnet shaped like a tree—I see a white envelope.

That's the note, I think. I know what it says. But that can't be possible. But I do. I know it by heart.

I move Rosie aside and reach out with my trembling, dreamy hand. Unfolding the flap, I lift it to my face to see a sheet of paper, printed words running down the center.

Rosie looks and realizes what it is, instantly turns and leaves the room.

I read it. I read it all.

"First, I'm sorry," Matthew wrote. "I'm sorry I couldn't get better. I'm sorry you all tried to help me and I still couldn't get better . . ."

This world.

"James?" Rosie is saying.

What's happening to me? I'm seeing things. It's like I've gone back in time. Or forward. Or . . . am I insane? Rosie, is this happening now?

She's nearby. "James."

We're not at Matthew's apartment. I'm somewhere else. Am I on the floor? No . . .

No, I'm at home. In Singers.

Matthew's been dead for five and a half years. Why do I keep thinking about his note?

"You're in shock," Rosie is saying.

And the choir at Matthew's funeral—I can hear their voices. I can hear the mighty sound above and beyond—it's echoing. Like angels. The organ. The church. I can hear it now. I'm the little boy.

Nell is dead. I remember what happened. Rosie is talking to me. I'm in shock, yes, I agree. That's why I'm not really here.

But Rosie strokes my cheek and tells me again that it's going to be OK.

"I don't think it is . . ." I whisper. "Rosie, something really bad is happening."

Chapter Thirty-One

We're back where we started. A dead body. It takes me a full hour to bring myself to look at her. And the moment I do, when I see the parts of Nell's head that are just gone, I lean over, put my hands on my knees, and puke on the floor.

I turn away, wipe my mouth with my sleeve, and go to the living room. Sit on the couch. Stare at the wall. Pull my knees up to my chest.

"Call him," Rosie says, dropping my phone onto the cushion next to me.

"Who?" I ask, glancing up at her, hugging my legs.

"Mr. Avery. They will be able to get rid of it."

"Oh, Rosie, no . . ."

"We have to do something."

"You want to ask the Carrillo cartel to help?"

"James, I'm eight months pregnant. You're in the middle of a breakdown. I don't think we can do this alone."

She's right. But we're just—"We're just swapping monsters," I say. "We'll just be in someone else's pocket."

"What choice do we have?" She holds her stomach, kneeling down in front of me.

Take care of Rosie. That's my only job.

"James." She's speaking softly, touching my shin. "You have blood on your face. We have to clean it all up." She nods me along to this conclusion.

I look down at my body—I have specks all over my shirt. Like I've been out in the rain. So I take my phone and make the call.

Mr. Avery agrees to help us dispose of Nell's body. I ask him how much it'll cost, but he seems surprised. "Good grief," he says. "For a friend like you, I wouldn't dare charge a penny for such a service."

The men who arrive at our house don't say a word to us. They only speak to each other. They're dressed like pest control—protective suits, gloves, and shoe covers. I watch them enter with all their equipment, their lights, their chemicals, their cold professionalism. Six men. They act as though we're not even here.

The main one looks around the entire ground floor before they begin. He squints up at corners, stroking his chin, making a plan. He even stands in the kitchen, framed by the broken window, and reconstructs the angle with the shotgun—having measured Nell's height, calculated where she must have been standing. And then they get to work.

Picking up the glass, wrapping Nell's body. Sweeping. Spraying, cleaning, scrubbing. One of them spends half an hour at the far end of the hallway around the front door, inspecting every inch of the walls for evidence. Pieces of bone. Rogue damage. They drill holes, fill the walls, repaint entire sections of the house like decorators.

Another one sits at the kitchen counter on a stool with a small metal surgeon's pot and a pair of tweezers. He counts every single pellet. Makes a note of everything.

I've seen this kind of work before—forensic officers combing over a scene. They're doing exactly the same thing. But in reverse. Undoing the story. I'm miles away as I watch them buzzing around, flicking fast from place to place, like a time-lapse video. Blurry. Ghostly streaks of white remember where they've been.

They go all night. Rosie and I leave them to it.

Staring at the ceiling in bed, I listen to vacuum cleaners, spray bottles, tools. In the morning when I go downstairs, they're still not finished.

It's almost midday before they're wrapping it all up.

"Will she be cremated?" I ask, rubbing my arm.

The main guy, the one in the kitchen, nods.

"Can I have the ashes?"

With his white hood and dust mask, I can only see his stern eyes. He shakes his head and returns to his notes.

They take Nell away. And it's as though it never even happened. I listen as their truck's engine starts outside and then they're gone. And there I am. It's me. Standing alone in the living room.

I have no idea what to do.

Now I realize I'm still repeating the note. I was trying to get to sleep and it's been going through my mind all night. How many times have I recited Matthew's words?

They boarded up our waving window. I stare at the new wood. Chipboard. Crudely screwed over where the glass used to be.

See? See the world. This world. I feel Rosie behind—her arm comes around my chest as she hugs me. She has to lean forward, over her bulge, to rest her head in the middle of my back.

"What have we done?" I say.

"Everything we had to do."

"Rosie, I think I'm going crazy. I keep seeing things. Seeing myself. And I can't think. Every time I close my eyes, I just repeat it. Matthew's suicide note. It keeps playing in my mind."

"You're just in shock," she says. "It'll pass."

It doesn't. But three days do. Four now. I haven't slept. It's getting worse. It's not just when I close my eyes. It's every waking moment. The note. The words. Again and again in my head.

Even when they ask about Nell. Where is she? When did I last see her? Her daughters are worried. Their questions wash over me. It's just playing and playing and I can't stop it and this must be what it feels like to be insane. Why won't it stop?

It's all like a dream, like a nightmare, like a dream. It's all here in my mind. Happening now.

Now. Now I know what to do. I should go upstairs and destroy it. I have to destroy the note. I'll burn the note and it'll go away.

It's 9 a.m.. A new day. Rosie is in the kitchen making breakfast. Pancakes.

I'm upstairs holding a small, metal trash can, opening the closet door to pull out the huge box of Matthew's things. I sit cross-legged and drag the box closer to myself. Fold the flaps down.

On top of the items, there's a folder containing all his paperwork. I move it aside and see the few possessions we kept. A T-shirt. He used to write slogans on T-shirts. His favorite cup. A baseball cap. The fucking medal they gave him when he finished his course at Pine Acre. We kept it. Why did we keep this? I fling it aside.

Underneath I find a bottle of oxy. A little white tub. An L&L label on the side. I pop it open with my thumb and tip one out onto my hand. I throw it straight in my mouth and swallow without water. I don't care. I just need some relief. Some sleep.

And his note. That note. The note I found on the fridge. I pull it out and hold it over the trash can. Then I flick open his lighter and spark up a flame.

Carefully I hover the corner of the white note above the fire until it turns black and smokes and then crinkles and catches. I tilt it upright to let the flames crawl higher. It burns and it keeps burning, and I let go only when it hurts my fingers.

It falls into the trash can like burning wreckage—the remains of a mid-air collision. The note is ash now. But it's still playing on repeat.

I'm not even on the plane.

Like a fucking song.

So the shadow metaphor makes no sense.

Louder now. It's mocking me. Laughing at my feeble attempt to destroy something that is not real. It's electricity, signals in my brain. Totally abstract. There's a paragraph all about this.

We're trapped, stuck in a chemical prison over which we have no control. And we're totally, in every conceivable sense, alone.

We're all alone.

But it's still there in my mind, on repeat. On shuffle now—words getting jumbled. I grab my hair and close my eyes and rock and groan and, God, fuck, *this world.*

Where is it coming from?

Take care of Rosie.

His laptop. His laptop. We kept his laptop.

Wiping my nose, I stand and grab the whole box of his stuff and carry it downstairs. It thuds heavy on the coffee table in the living room.

I think the drugs might be working, because the note is now a whisper and it's comforting. It's grounding me. Like when a religious person finds solace by looking to the sky and knowing there's a God. But there isn't. And I don't want to hear these words anymore. So I'm going to delete it.

I sit down on the couch, place his laptop on the wood in front of me. Lifting the lid, I turn it on. Nothing. Of course. I uncoil the power cable, lean down, and plug it in. Try again. And the screen lights up.

His laptop is slow—it takes five minutes to load Windows XP. And finally the screen flashes to his desktop. A snow scene background, a photograph of Treaston from when we were small.

I open the file. I'm going to read the letter one more time. Part of me hopes to find a discrepancy. As though if I'd slightly misremembered, that'd somehow make me less crazy. But no. Every word. I remembered every word perfectly. I even remembered the typo—where he spelled *because* without the *u*. I pronounce it "be case" when I recite it before I sleep.

It's working . . . I'm getting other thoughts breaking through, like sunlight cutting beams out of black, bulging, electric storm clouds.

Maybe I should have done this years ago. I need to move on. I can't keep thinking about him. Picturing him. Seeing him lying dead in that bed. Oh, that day. I'd actually tried to revive him. Ridiculous on reflection, as according to the autopsy report he died around 10 p.m. the previous evening. August 23.

When I get to the bottom, Matthew tells me to take care of Rosie—just like he's done every single night for the last five and a half years.

I am, I think. Rosie is in the kitchen right now cooking breakfast. She's safe. I'm feeling better already. Oh, wow, I can certainly see the appeal of these substances. *Goodbye, buddy*, I think as I close the window.

I place the mouse cursor over the note icon and I can hear the choir again—it's a grand moment. Catharsis, drama, total closure coming to me now, surging through my veins and granting me the peace I'd forgotten was even possible. It's the kind of bold symbolic gesture that'll change me for the better.

I'm dragging it to the recycling bin in the top left corner of the laptop screen. Here I am again, smiling, deleting files. I lift my finger and it falls inside. Then I open the recycling bin to get rid of it for good. Right-click.

Delete.

"Are you sure you wish to permanently delete this file?" the laptop asks.

I move the cursor to yes and—"Huh." Tells you the date the file was created and when he last modified it. *A long time ago*, I think. Years. He saved this at 7:45 a.m..

The idea unsettles me. The idea he wrote his suicide note early in the morning—somehow this thought adds a new layer of tragedy. He'd made up his mind. He spent the whole day alone in his apartment before finally sitting down on his bed with a spoon and a needle to—

Frowning, I look again at the date. "August 24."

Rubbing my eye, I take a moment to focus. That can't be right.

I sit up straight, quickly reaching into the box. I pull out a folder, rest it on my knees, flick through the files, the paperwork, his passport, his driver's—

Snatching up a document, I scan the report and leaf through to the death certificate. Where the fuck is the—

Here. I put the coroner's report flat on the coffee table, next to the laptop. He died around 10 p.m. on August 23. We found him the morning after. He was cold.

"What the . . . ?" I say, looking between the paper and the screen. The mouse cursor judders over the icon again. I right-click to be sure. Properties. A new window opens. Hand on my mouth, I wince and read and check . . .

And my hand falls gently onto the coffee table.

The file was created at 11 p.m. on August 23. And last edited at 7:45 a.m. the following day.

This final version was sent to Matthew's printer at 7:46 a.m. on August 24. More than nine hours after he died.

The clouds have gone completely and the singing has fallen to total deathly silence. Sudden, absolute, terrible clarity. I don't need to keep thinking about the suicide note Matthew wrote.

Because Matthew didn't write it.

Someone else did. Someone who was at the scene. Someone who'd visited him the night before. Someone violent. Someone dangerous. Someone like . . .

I turn slowly away from the laptop and look toward our kitchen. Rosie's inside. Making pancakes. But I can't see her, because our waving window has been boarded up and all that broken glass has been cleared away.

Chapter Thirty-Two

"Rosie," I say, stepping onto the chessboard tiles in our kitchen. It's still spotlessly clean in here.

She turns. The smell of pancakes cooking. Silent blue flames glowing on the stovetop. "Yes?" Her soft voice. She's wearing her polka-dot dress. Wooden spoon in her hand. She's radiant, lit up. So pretty. She looks just like one of those perfect wives from the posters. "Are you all right? You look . . . wasted."

"I took some oxycodone."

"Oh, James."

"No, it's fine. It doesn't matter."

"You need to go to sleep," she says. "I think it's time."

I blink. "Not yet. I have a question."

"OK?"

"Did you kill Matthew?" I ask, feeling my eyes droop slightly.

"What?"

"I was just wondering. Did you kill him?"

"Maybe you're right," she says. "Maybe you are going insane." She turns away, back to the kitchen counter, carries on cooking.

"Hey, Rosie," I say. She stands still. "Did you kill Matthew?"

Then she turns to me again. "What's wrong? Why are you saying this?"

I flex the muscles in my face. Surreal. Gentle feeling in my blood. I'm not sure it's the drugs though; it feels like something else? "Rosie," I try again, "did you kill Matthew?"

"James, Matthew killed himself." She nods at me slowly. The way you reassure an elderly person who's getting mixed up. "Remember?"

"Hmm." I think for a moment. Frown. "It's just . . . his suicide note was printed nine hours after he died, so I was just curious . . . Did you kill Matthew?"

"No."

"Don't fucking lie to me."

And now Rosie's brow comes down, her chin crinkled like she's about to cry. But she's not sad. Or scared. She's angry. I've seen this before. "You're yelling," she says. "Stop yelling."

"Answer the question."

"Stop it. Just stop."

We stand face to face in total silence.

I shrug and try one more time. "Rosie," I say, like I've just remembered something. "Did you kill Matthew?"

She lets out a strange sigh, drops the spoon on the kitchen worktop. "I mean . . . does it even matter?"

"Oh." I cover my face. "What did you do?" Sudden grief takes my breath away. God, I'd thought maybe, somehow, there might have been another explanation. It's all falling apart. I peep at her through my fingers. "Why would you do that?"

"James, come on, just go to sleep."

"Why would you kill him?"

"He was already . . . he was already killing himself."

"What does that mean? Please, just tell me the truth." I close my eyes. Bracing myself.

"The truth is, yeah, that night, I went to his apartment to drop off some food. I made him a lasagna and I had some cakes left over."

"And . . ."

She hesitates. "And he was on his bed. On the covers. He was so fucking high. He had a needle in his arm. Could hardly speak. He was too fucked up to even apologize."

"But he was alive?"

"We spent all our fucking savings on his rehab. Thousands of dollars. We spent *years* saving that. It's why we live in this shithole neighborhood." She points toward the front door. "It took him, what, a few months to relapse?" And she shakes her head. "All that money. And there he was, sticking a middle finger up at us. Throwing it all away."

"But, he, was, still, alive."

"Yes."

"You were angry, weren't you? It was a red day."

"I was extremely angry."

"So what did you do, Rosie? Hmm? What did you do?"

"Matthew wanted to take heroin." She holds up a hand and shrugs. "So I gave him some heroin. And then I gave him some more." She pouts, but not like she's upset. More like she's, I don't even know, appreciating a new paint job on a car. It's all wrong. "And some more."

I push a fist into my eye socket. "Oh . . ."

"Why are you so surprised? We're playing the same game, James."

"No, no, no, no we are not. He was your brother. Your *brother*. You wrote . . ." This is the bit that hurts most. "You wrote his suicide note?"

She hesitates again, maybe even exhibits a shred of shame. But only for my benefit, only for show. "It had to look real."

"Why was it so long—and so detailed? Why . . ." My voice cracks slightly. "Why did you mention *me* so many times?"

"I . . ." Rosie exhales, waves a hand. "Just, I don't know. It worked, didn't it?" She says this like I should give her some credit.

I stare at her for a few seconds. "Oh, Jesus, you're such a crazy fucking bitch." Fingers on my temples, disbelief fading. "That note changed me. I think about it every day, Rosie. Every single fucking day of my life," I shout. And breathe. "Everything you wrote," I speak quieter. "He said sorry. He said he was selfish." Shaking my head, eyes wide and on the floor. I laugh. "He told me to take care of you." I look up at her. "Take care of Rosie."

"That's exactly the kind of thing he would say."

I nod. "Yeah."

"Listen, I loved Matthew. I loved him. But he was a drain. We'd had setback after setback."

"Oh no, no . . . no . . ."

"It's your favorite fucking line, James—everything I've done, I've done for *us*. For our future. For this baby. For our family."

"*Family?*"

"Me and you. No matter what. We promised."

Glancing at the tiles, I realize I'm standing right where Frank's body was—in the center of that imaginary chalk figure.

"The last eight months. All this violence. Death. How *exactly* did killing your boss help us?"

"What did she say?" Rosie spreads her arms to show off her bulging stomach. "What did the fertility doctor say? We were both healthy. Why couldn't we conceive? Go on. What did she say?"

"It could be stress."

"Stress. *Stress* from a fucking piece of shit boss who didn't let me rest for even a moment. Look, I tried, OK. I tried to act like a normal person with a normal job. I tried to take it all on the chin. I kept my head down at work for years. I have no idea how people do it."

"That's it, isn't it? It wasn't Frank, it was you. You've never taken shit from anyone. You were just holding it all in. Just acting. That's why you were stressed."

"Finally you're paying attention, James. Those red days, as you call them . . . that's the real Rosie. The rest of the time, I'm just pretending. I'm always pretending."

"You're a fucking psycho."

I can tell she's getting really angry. Her lip twitches. The spite and venom circling on her tongue, behind the teeth she's exposing more and more with each passing second.

"You know what?" She stares, lowering her head. "You know what Frank said to me that night?" Rosie strides toward me. Comes real close. Eyes wide. "His final words before I punctured his windpipe? Guess." She squints now. "*Guess* what tipped me over?"

"Who fucking knows."

"He said the sponge in my cupcakes was," she whispers, "dry."

"Fucking hell."

"Nell was going to talk, you heard her. We had no choice. Matthew was going to take our money and energy and sap the soul from us for the rest of our lives. He had plenty of chances. But he was weak. And Frank? Frank was a bully. Fuck that prick. James, to be honest, I kind of feel you're making this a bigger deal than it is."

A big, slow breath before I respond. "I respectfully disagree with that."

"It's about sacrifice. And let's face it, you're not exactly a saint yourself. Do you want to talk about the bad things you've done?"

"No."

"Thought not." She smiles like she pities how naive I am. "Best keep that box closed, hey? Too dangerous to unpack all that. Mary would have died anyway."

"Don't."

"Matthew would have gone off the rails, even if his best friend hadn't been trying to fuck his sister every minute of the—"

"Shut up, shut the fuck up."

"You went all in on me," she says. "Loyal to a fault."

"No, that's not . . ."

"It's just deflection and repression with you, James. It's astonishing. So blind. You really want to stand here and play this game?"

"Rosie, just—"

"Because one day you'll be all by yourself and you'll have run out of people to blame. And then what?"

"Stop—"

"You have absolutely no footing on the moral high ground. And you fucking know it."

"Stop trying to turn this around."

"Your shock says far more about *you* than it does about me."

Again, I put my face in my palms. "Where do we go from here? What now?"

"What do you mean? I'm making pancakes with shitloads of bacon and syrup, and we're going to sit down at the breakfast bar and enjoy it together. Maybe you could make some coffee?"

"Rosie." Hand out, I splay my fingers, make a fist. "I think maybe we should . . . I don't know, get a divorce?"

"Oh, James, we can't get a divorce—I'm having a baby in a couple of weeks."

"I need to go outside for a while." I walk backward, backing away, getting away from her.

She just stands in the kitchen doorway, watching me. "James."

Her polka-dot dress, her hair pinned up. It's all so normal. A dream too real to question.

I back away more and then turn to leave. Leave the house. Run. I run down the hill. Toward the city. Oh my God. Crossing streets, sprinting downtown, my reflection blurred and fast in every store window, past the homeless man—he drums and drums and drums—I keep running and running until I'm panting so hard I can't think and it's not real. None of it's real.

I'm not even here. This isn't even now.

I just run. For hours. As though I'm chasing something I can't even see. I stop. I rest. But then I'm running again. Pounding my feet into the earth until they burn and bleed. And I keep going until finally I stumble and fall. Hands slapping onto the ground, I pant, arch my spine, breathing and thinking.

What do I do now? What do I do?

In the bright afternoon sunshine, on my hands and knees, I look up along the sidewalk. At the tents under the overpass. The junkies. The shopping carts. The city's squalor. An overweight woman trundles past on a scooter, its suspension pushed to the limit.

We're dying. But there's no famine, no disease. We have no predators. We're killing ourselves. We're eating too much. Taking too many drugs. Filling empty holes because something is missing. Have we lost it? Was it ever even real?

And I'm one of them. The lunatic on the street, searching for the same fucking thing as everyone else. Whatever it is. Whatever we're all out here chasing, I know now that I'm never going to find it. Like the mansion, the helicopter, any one of a thousand dreams that come flooding into our minds from a pipe, from the TV screen, from the perfect smiles of pretty women in commercials that sell us lies.

I've yearned and earned; I've killed and tried. So, I ask myself again, what do I do now?

And the answer comes to me. But not like I've thought it up myself. More like it's fate. As though I've done it before. As though I'm on rails, in a ghost train on tracks, just a witness to these next few moves.

I'm going to do what I've always done. All that anyone ever can. I'm going to do the right thing.

Now I stand up, turn around, and set off walking home. My feet are stinging, blistered, and damp as I stumble and sway up the Singers hill, up the drive. It's 7 p.m.. I've been gone all day. Through the front door and inside; I find Rosie in the kitchen.

"Where were you, James?" she says. "I was worried."

"I feel better now."

"Good. Does that mean you'll go to sleep?"

Go to sleep. She's said that to me before. "Maybe. But not yet. I have to do one more thing."

"What?"

"I've decided . . . I'm going to turn myself in."

"No, James, you're not."

"I'm sorry. Everything I did, it's true, I did it all for you." I'm amazed I'm even saying something this cliché. "I did it for love."

"Then keep doing it."

"What do they say about the road to hell?"

"Paved with good intentions," she says. "I wonder where bad ones take us?"

Stepping closer, I remove my gun from its holster, placing it carefully on the breakfast bar. Rosie looks at it, confused, then back up to me.

"I'm taking everything over to the new house," I explain. "All the money. The evidence. I'm going to spend the night there. I'll record a detailed confession."

"James, I can't let you do that." We both seem to be aware of the loaded pistol.

This is what Foster did—forced me into a corner. Gave me an ultimatum.

Now the ball is in her court. Rosie can stop me if she wants. But there's only one way. And I know, *I know*, that she won't be able to do it. "Why are you even telling me?" she asks.

"I want you to come and confess. Serve time. Maybe get yourself committed? I mean, with all due respect, you are a fucking nutcase."

"I'm not having a baby in cuffs. I'm not giving her away." Prolonged eye contact. "That is not happening."

"I'm afraid it is." A tear drips from my eyelashes.

Rosie looks devastated. "You want her to grow up like we did, without a family?"

"You'll get visits. Updates. And honestly I think she's better off without us."

"I'll say it was all you." She's speaking quietly. Desperate last-ditch attempts to sway my decision. "Little Rosie Casper, terrified of her husband. Her criminal husband. A mastermind. A crooked DEA agent."

"Sure," I say. "You could go down that road. Maybe it'll work. We'll play it all out in court. I don't mind. I'm doing this for myself. But you should know that I'm not telling any more lies."

"OK. Now I am warning you. Do not do this."

"You are a monster, Rosie," I think out loud. "But you'd never hurt me."

"Really, James, you have no idea what I'm capable of."

I smile. "Hollow threats."

"So that's it. Nell was right, you really have betrayed *everyone*. Is that who you are? Corrupt to your fucking bones? All alone in the world. I mean it. If you walk out that door."

"You'll what? What will you do?"

She can't bring herself to say it. Because she knows it's true too. She wouldn't hurt me. Those are the rules.

"I'll give you until 10 a.m. tomorrow morning to come and join me," I add. "Come and do the right thing."

I tap my knuckle on the breakfast bar, then go upstairs and grab the heavy bags of cash. A million bucks in each. One by one I load them into the trunk of my car. Back inside I pick up the huge box of Matthew's things from the coffee table. It's all evidence now.

My pistol, still at Rosie's side when I step into the kitchen, is the final item to collect. She looks like she's about to cry as I stand in front of her, offering one last chance to stop me. A test I know she'll pass. *Flying colors*, I think, when I hold out my hand and she passes it over—hesitating only once.

And then, for the final time in my life, I turn and walk toward the front door.

"I thought . . ." she says. "I thought it was a love story?"

I stop. But I don't look back. "It is."

Chapter Thirty-Three

At the new house I set everything out on the kitchen table. All the evidence, all the money and mementos. I hold my voice recorder like a microphone as I pace around the place and confess my crimes. My long list of sins.

Recounting the past eight months is a cathartic, strangely comforting experience. But I go back further—I tell the whole story from the top. The truth. Every detail, every call I made, every call I didn't.

All those perfect memories. Blended hybrids. Milestones contaminated by time, by hindsight's endlessly artistic license. I read somewhere that when you're old, all you have is your memories—these stories you tell yourself.

As I go, as I talk, I can't help but tally up my charges. When I'm gray and reminiscing, I'll still be in a cell. But that's fine. I'll be the happiest grandpa in prison. Old man James, they'll ask, why are you always smiling like that? Did you find it out there? Did you see true love in the wild?

And that's why this confession lacks remorse. When I'm judged—by this world and whoever's waiting after—I won't be able to repent.

Because it was real. It was all real. I proved that. I gave Rosie every chance to stop me and she couldn't do it.

That fact alone makes it all worthwhile. That is how powerful our love was—she'd kill her own flesh and blood; she'd burn the whole world to the ground. But me? I was different.

When it's dark I lie on the bed but don't sleep. Instead I spend the night talking to myself. The window wide open, the midnight bugs hissing and rustling beneath the moon.

Early in the morning, I rise and go for a walk. A gentle stroll along the lake's edge. Dawn blue, no shoes. The grass cold on my feet, the fog soft on my shins.

Crouching down, I put a hand in the numb water, stroke some of the silt and sand to see it swirl. And I look up at the clouds, fingers dripping. The new day's sun absorbing the last few stars. The bright ones holding on—white holes in a purple canvas. Shame. I should have learned their names.

Taking deep, swelling breaths of fresh air and freedom, I close my eyes and soak it all in. Morning songbirds. Moving green. Five minutes and then I look again. Across the water. It's time to go.

With a sigh I put my hand on my knee and push myself upright. Back up to the house. The glass doors slide aside when I thumb the switch on the wooden wall. Smooth, quiet, expensive. I leave them open, letting nature join me as I check the time.

It's 7 a.m.. Rosie has three more hours before I hit send on this confession. I'm going to forward a copy to Rob Sanders. To the city police. Detective Cohen. Maybe even some newspapers. Then I'll post it all online. Just so there's no way out. Not that retreating has ever really been an option.

First, though, I cook up a nice breakfast. A final meal. Crispy bacon, steaming coffee, ice-cold orange juice. Ticking off every sense—enjoying the kind of things I'm going to miss. I sit and eat it slowly. Alone with a knife and fork, savoring every mouthful. When this is done, it's 8 a.m.. OK. With another sigh, I wipe my mouth and stand, step over to the mountain of physical evidence I've amassed on the kitchen table.

It's like a ceremony. I slip every object into a series of transparent plastic bags. Sealed with my finger and thumb. All official. By the book. Bagged and tagged. This very building can and will be used against me in a court of law. I smile as I read myself these rights.

The last thing I do is count the cash. I've left this until the end on purpose. I don't want anyone to think I was motivated by money. As I told my beautiful wife just yesterday, this is a love story.

"Edward paid me well," I say into the recorder. "Think maybe he was showing off. Trying to impress me. I don't know. It doesn't matter . . . I have five bags left. Should be a million in each."

I pause the device, crouch and tug the zipper across the top of the first bag. Reaching inside, I lift it all out and stack it into neat cubes at the edge of the table. And then I count.

"First one," I say, speaking into the microphone again, "contains exactly one million dollars."

Next I heave the second black gym bag onto the table and shake tumbling wads out, dragging it all closer. "Bag two," I complete another perfect pile, "the same."

Counting faster now I know the size, bags three and four take half as long. And then I reach down for bag five, placing it on the chair, as the table's nearly full.

Halfway through counting, the last few bricks slotted onto the final tower of money, I sense it's coming in smaller than the others. I've got a really strange feeling.

"Bag five is less," I say, jotting down a quick note. "It contains"—I thumb out the last few loose-leaf bills and drop them on top—"$666,667." And I stop. "It's short by—"

It's short by exactly $333,333. I freeze.

Oh, shit. I left her at the house. Rosie was with the money all day. She had his burner phone. My eyes dart, my heart picks up. I'd told her it was over—said her threats were hollow. And she'd already booked it. She'd already paid.

The final test I thought she'd pass.

Standing straight, I take a step back from the table. Breathing more and more, the sensation coming in strong. And then I realize.

I know what this feeling is.

I'm not alone. Someone is here with me. I can feel him.

And then I hear something—movement behind. Biting down, my eyes fall closed.

Fuck.

"I thought," I say, looking again, staring at the table. "I thought I wasn't meant to see you."

There's a long silence before he replies. "You won't." The Carpenter's voice is unmistakable.

Without moving a muscle, I start to search the clutter. My pistol is here somewhere—amid these evidence bags. Behind these piles of money. And then I spot it. Right there in the middle. The barrel resting on the edge of a bright-green, fluorescent frisbee.

How the fuck did that get here?

Jesus Christ. It's *all* here. There's the drawing of a tiger. And that framed portrait of me as a little boy. Didn't I throw it in the sea? There's the cigarette butt from the first time we smoked. The red phone I never picked up. Clean bullet holes in the snow painting—I can see right through. Right into that first kiss furnace, where I've bagged the crowbar and even retrieved the screwed-up ball of cupcake paper. Wow. Look at her go. She's dancing in the snow—the gentle hissing from a Sony Walkman still playing that song. What the fuck is going on?

"Can we . . ." I whisper, trying to buy some time. "Can we do this outside?"

I'm going to dive for my gun.

"Of course," he says. "Though in my experience these things are significantly less traumatic if there is no anticipation."

"I appreciate that. But I just want to see the sky one more time. I want to—"

Two drumbeats. A quick *thud-thud.* It's a sound.

Did I get him? Did I even make my move?

I'm not entirely sure what happened. I can see the ceiling. A feeling. Almost pain but not quite. But then, steadily, it begins to make sense. I was wrong. All those nameless stars disappeared a long time ago.

"James?" Rosie whispers from somewhere in these pictures. "Is it working?"

"Yeah," I reply, wide-eyed. "It's just like you said. A whole new light."

You really do get a different perspective when you're lying on the floor.

ACKNOWLEDGMENTS

Thanks go to editors Jack Butler and Jane Snelgrove for their enthusiasm and surgical wisdom. To the all-important American eyes of Augustin Kendall and colleagues for their copy-editing. And to everyone else working behind the scenes at Thomas & Mercer. I'm indebted to my agent Clare Wallace for her endless guidance, expertise and instant access to all the bright minds at the Darley Anderson Agency.

Books are more a team effort than many people realise and the members of this one are surely among the best in the business.

ABOUT THE AUTHOR

Photo © Kayt Webster-Brown

Martyn Ford is a journalist and author from the UK. His debut middle-grade children's book, *The Imagination Box*, was published by Faber & Faber in 2015 to critical acclaim and went on to become a trilogy. This was followed by 2019's standalone title, *Chester Parsons is Not a Gorilla*. *Every Missing Thing* was his first novel for adult readers, published in 2020, and *All Our Darkest Secrets* is his second.